THE GREEN
KNIGHT'S SQUIRE

Books by John C. Wright

THE GREEN
KNIGHT'S SQUIRE

Moth & Cobweb Books 1-3

JOHN C. WRIGHT

CASTALIA HOUSE

The Green Knight's Squire

John C. Wright

Published by Castalia House
Kouvola, Finland
www.castaliahouse.com

Editor: Vox Day
Cover Art: Scott Vigil

CONTENTS

SWAN KNIGHT'S SON

FEAST OF THE ELFS

SWAN KNIGHT'S SWORD

SWAN KNIGHT'S SON

FOR *knighthood is not in the feats of warre*
As for to fight in quarrel right or wrong,
But in a cause which truth can not defarre:
He ought himself for to make sure and strong,
Justice to keep mixt with mercy among:
And no quarrell a knight ought to take
But for a truth, or for the common's sake.

Stephen Hawes (1523)

Chapter 1

The Thirteenth Hour

1. The Midnight Walkers

Gilberec Parzival Moth woke up, startled, when a large black raven landed on his chest at midnight. It was the night of the day before his sixteenth birthday. He was a tall boy, strong for his age, and his hair was an unusual shade of silver-white that he had never seen on anyone else. He usually kept it hidden, tucked into a Gamecocks ball cap he wore. His shirt and dungarees were simple, sturdy, worn, and patched.

He sat up. The raven squawked and flapped in a flurry of black wings to the back of the park bench. It was dark out, and the moon was high and full, a warm evening in April. He could not see the clock tower overlooking the town square from where he was, sitting in the little bus shelter, but from the smell of the air, the cool of the breeze, and the positions of the stars, he knew it was the middle of the night. "What are you doing up at this hour, big guy?" he said to the raven. Ravens, as he well knew, were not nocturnal birds.

Gil also had a black eye, a swollen lip, some small cuts on his face, and an ache in his ribs. He said, "Look like a mess, don't I? Well, you should see the other guy. I didn't mean to nod off. Mom must be worried sick. Don't suppose you could go tell her I am all right?"

But the raven merely hunched its shoulders, spread its wings, and flew up into the night sky, vanishing against the stars.

Gil started to lay himself back down. "Darn ravens. Never do what you ask."

That was when he noticed how bright the stars were. Bright as when he camped in the wilderness. They should have been dimmer, washed out. He looked left and right. The streetlamp near him was not lit.

He stood. He stepped out into the street. The small town of Blowing Rock, North Carolina, lay sleeping around him. No streetlamps anywhere were lit. No porch lights on any houses. No neon signs on any small shops. Even the traffic lights were dark.

Just then, the bell in the clocktower above the town hall started ringing. Gil turned. Usually the clock face was lit. Now, it was dark. Gil had sharp eyes and excellent night vision, but he could see only a pale circular shadow in the darker oblong shadow of the tower. He counted the strokes of the bell. Ten… eleven… twelve… thirteen….

Gil felt a cold sensation trickle down his spine. "Maybe it is just a mistake. A mechanical failure…"

His voice sounded so unconvincing to his own ears that he snapped his teeth shut and told himself not to say anything more.

That was when he saw a group of people. They were a block or two away, in the center of the lane, walking. Their pace was not quick, but slow and reluctant. No one carried any lights. They were walking toward him.

Some instinct told Gil to move away slowly and to make no startling moves. He turned and walked across the square of greenery that formed the little park at the center of town. He passed underneath the tall pine which, in winter, was decorated with Christmas lights, but which now was dark.

Opposite the town hall was an old abandoned church, built in the colonial days, built of gray brick, with narrow windows of leaded glass. A belltower was perched atop and faced the town hall clocktower from the opposite side of the town square park.

Gil looked back. He saw men and women, young and old, walking in utter silence. Most were carrying burdens on their backs or in their arms. It was a strange collection: Gil saw a china doll, a gold clock under glass, an embroidered pillow, a jeweled necklace, a set of gilt-edged old books, a tray of silverware, a decanter of wine, a box of cigars. Many of the women had shining fabrics folded over their arms, silks and satins of expensive dresses. Several people were carrying portraits in frames. It was hard to see in the dark, at a distance, but everything he saw was finely-crafted or antique.

2. The Forsaken House

The door of the abandoned church behind Gil now swung open a crack. Gil was almost positive that the door had been nailed shut. Gil looked up at the moon. It was full.

A soft voice from the darkness in the door crack said, "Enter."

Gil looked doubtfully at the dark church door and looked again back the way he had come. Gil saw the stream of silent walking people was being met by a second crowd of people, shambling with hesitant steps in from a side street. It mingled with the first group. Both were headed for the town hall.

Gil now saw that all three of the big main doors leading into the town hall were open. He had never seen all three open before. There was a dim set of floating lights inside the town hall, like candlelights, or fireflies, or captive stars, moving and swaying, as if to music no one could hear.

"Sanctuary is here," said the voice from the church, very quietly.

That was when Gil realized something was missing. He heard no insistent noises. Where was the chirruping that went on all night this time of year? Usually, it was as loud as a brass band. But now the air was utterly silent.

Gil hurried up the gray stone stairs to the door and slipped inside. An unseen hand closed the door behind him. It was utterly dark in here, except for the tall, thin windows, high above his head, where the bright, clear stars could be seen.

3. All Men Are Welcome

A figure stepped in front of the window, so Gil could see the silhouette of a tall shape with a peaked hood outlined against the stars.

Gil said, "I thought this door was nailed shut. Isn't this church abandoned?"

The hood nodded. "My task is to rebuild the old church. All men are welcome to enter by the door."

Gil said, "That's kind of funny. There is a door in my place that sometimes opens on the full moon. Other times I cannot find it. Do you know about doors like that? I see strange things some times. Hear them, too."

"What things have you seen?"

"So can you open the door I keep seeing in my house?"

"Not I. What things have you seen?"

"About a week ago. Me and some boys from school were playing by the banks of the river. I looked, and I saw a barge on the water. It had black cloth draped over the bow and stern, and a black flag. There were girls in veils and black cloaks poling the barge, and they yelled and wailed and wept as they went. I pointed, but the other boys did not see anything. They saw mist on the water and heard birds screaming. One of them called me a liar, so I had to punch him."

Gil drew a breath, and his bruised ribs twinged, so he winced.

The voice said, "You have been fighting again today." There was a sad note in the voice.

Gil said, "Yes, sir. That happens to me a lot."

The hooded figure took a step. From the sound of the footfall on the stone floor, he knew the man was barefoot. The starlight glinted on the crucifix hanging at his neck as well as the pale length of rope which belted his robe. Gil felt a sensation of relief and laughed.

"You are a monk, aren't you, sir? In that hood, I thought you were a ghost."

"Everyone is a ghost, my son. The ones who tarry on earth, like you, are still inside the body of clay their mothers bestowed."

At that moment, there came a scratching at the door. It reminded Gil of the sound his dog made when he scratched to be let in, but it sounded larger than a dog.

A voice from outside said, "Open to me! All sons of Adam must bring their tribute forth!"

The monk laid a warning hand on Gil's arm. "Do not answer."

Gil whispered, "You said all men are welcome to enter by the door."

The monk said, "It is not a man."

The scratching came again, louder. "Open, open! Who walks abroad? It is the witching hour of the elf's eve, and the goddess in the moon draws nigh the earth to spread her pallid madness and contagion! Who dares wake and walk? Who are you? Who is your father?"

But the monk said to Gil, "Answer not a word."

The voice outside the door grew louder: "I smell sweat and living blood! Warm air passes out of living nostrils! I hear the thudding of a frightened heart! Open, I say, in the name of the Lord of Air and Darkness!"

Gil whispered, "You said you were rebuilding this building. Where are the tools? Do you have a hammer or something I could use to bash in his skull? I think he just called me a coward."

The monk said softly back, "Peace! Your strength is a gift. Use it wisely, and do not shame the giver. Stay here. You will sleep until dawn, and I will keep the Winged Nightmare away. Do not fear. You will not walk in your sleep like the others. I will go and speak with the shadow."

The door opened a crack, and the tall figure stepped through. The line of moonlight narrowed, and the door slammed shut again. Gil said, "Wait! I can't let you face that guy alone! Hold on!"

But in the dark he could find no handle nor knob. His fingers felt a cold, hard knot in the wood, and he realized this was the head of a large spike that had been pounded through what felt like a bar across the door. He felt around and found other spikes. The door was nailed shut.

"It's impossible," whispered Gil to himself. He sat down with his back to the door and yawned. A sudden fatigue washed over him, and he fought to keep his eyes open.

4. The Yellow Wren

Gil woke. Rays of dusty sunlight slanted in through the leaden windows. Gil now saw that the entire interior of the church was bare. There was a pale and cross-shaped patch on the far wall where the bricks were bright and unworn, and the dust there was less. A large rectangular hole had been dug through the stones where the altar had been torn out.

He soon found he was trapped. The main doors and the smaller door in the chamber behind the altar leading into the vestry were both nailed shut. The windows were too high to reach and too narrow to squeeze through.

Gil sat down heavily on the floor, sighing. The air in here was musty. He sat in the beam of sunlight from the window, and it struck his hair when he doffed his cap to mop his brow. His hair, though white, was not like an old man's hair. It was a shining blend of silver and pewter and snowy hues, rich and lustrous, almost luminous. His eyebrows were dark and his eyes gray like a storm at sea. There were streaks of red in his snow-bright hair from where his scalp had been cut.

A shadow flicked across his chest. There came a tap-tapping on the window. He looked up and saw the yellow shape of a little bird smaller than his hand. A wren was tapping on the window with her bill.

The little wren pecked at a spot in the old, mottled glass, perhaps thinking it was a bug.

Gil smiled. He lifted the baseball cap from his knee and spun it on his finger. "Look at that! Here is a strand of hair caught in my cap. I can give it to you if you get me out of here. I assume you want it for your nest."

He lifted a tiny, nearly invisible strand of hair. In the dusty beam, it almost seemed to glow like starlight.

The little wren twitched her head to the left and stared at him from one eye. The bird yanked back, and dropped out of sight.

Gil stared up at the empty window, wondering what he should do next. But then he heard a noise overhead, the fluttering of little wings. Down from the rafters flew the little yellow wren and landed on his finger.

Gil said, "Wren? You get me in a lot of trouble, you know. Whenever people find out I know things I shouldn't know, and I tell them *a little bird told me*, guess what? They don't believe me! I get called a liar, and then… Well, I cannot let them call me that!" He looked at his skinned knuckles and rubbed his bruises wryly.

The wren groomed herself and looked nonchalant. She hopped to his other finger, the one holding the silver hair.

Gil said, "Wait up! You need to help me get out of here first!"

The bird cocked her head to one side, flew off his finger, and landed on a spot a few yards away. Gil rose and followed. The little bird hopped over into an alcove and rapped on the wood with her bill. Gil stepped after and saw a narrow door he had overlooked before.

He pushed open the warped dark wood on creaking hinges and sneezed at the dust stirred up.

"Bless you," the wren said.

"Thanks," he replied automatically. Inside was a spiral staircase steep as a ladder.

The wren said, "This leads up to the belfry where the churchbell once hung. From there, it is a short drop to the slate roof. It you don't slip and plunge to your death, you can cross the gable to the rear, where a very large and friendly elm tree has branches waiting for you haply to climb down."

"Fair is fair. Here is your fee." And he proffered the silver strand of hair.

"However, you already missed the morning bus. You will have to walk home."

Gil groaned. It was a two-hour walk from here.

The wren nodded sagely, "Things would be much merrier for you if you only had wings. Some other members of your family do, you know."

Gil straightened up. "What? What do you know about my family? Who has wings?"

But the wren was already high in the rafters, the silver strand dangling from her beak. "Of her we never speak!" the little bird called back. And then she was gone, out of his sight.

Gil climbed his way up the spiral staircase up to the empty belfry where no bells hung. He glanced through the hole in the floor through which no bellrope passed.

But the view from here was fine and fair. He could see the school from which he had been expelled, and, across the street from it, the gas station in whose back lot he had faced and fought the most popular kid in school.

Chapter 2

The Wandering Moths

1. Ruff

After three hours, Gil arrived home. It should have taken two hours, but he stopped and bathed in Pell Lake during the hottest part of the morning, then cut through the woods, and stopped again at Tom's Creek Primitive Baptist Church. He asked the pastor there if there was anyone refurbishing the old Anglican Church that fronted the town square, but the little old man knew nothing. Then he tramped up Church Road through the woods to the auto repair shop.

He and his mom lived in the second story above the garage, in a cramped apartment of rooms reached by some rickety wooden steps in the back, half overgrown with kudzu vines. The boards were warped with age and scruffy with fading paint, all but the top last four, which smelled of newly-sanded wood and gleamed with fresh green paint. Some weeks ago, when his mother had received a healthy tip and things were looking up, Gil had bought a board, sawed it into four parts, and sought to replace the bad stairs, starting at the top. Without money for lumber and nails, the work was slow. Sometimes Gil wondered if the kudzu was the only thing holding up the staircase.

There was a crooked old Cornelian Cherry tree that grew right next to the old garage. Its roots over the years had been slowly tearing up the sidewalk, so that the slabs of concrete staggered drunkenly, with grass and weeds growing between them. With every storm it threatened to drop a branch on the roof.

The tree grew a bitter red berry the size of a cherry tomato called a cornel. Last night the tree had dropped a load of these cornel berries again, making little red bloodlike stains all over the stairs and door and the two windows on this side of the house. His mother liked the house kept as neat as possible, so Gil would have to get the ladder and scrub brushes to remove the stubborn stains.

As he reached the top step, he realized two things. First, his latchkey was in his jacket pocket, but his jacket was in his school locker four miles away. Second, he did not remember what his mother's hours were today. She worked a different shift on different days. She might be home an hour from now, or four hours, or even eight.

He sat down on the tiny wooden landing before the door. There was a happy barking, and a dog that was half Border Collie and half who-knew-what came bounding up the stairs. He had a white muzzle and chest, black ears, black flanks, white stockings, and bright eyes with a black mask around them. However, he lacked any collar, dog tags, or fixed place of residence. He was Gil's dog in every way but legally. Gil did not know where he went during the day or where he slept, and he thought it too nosy to ask.

Gil rubbed the dog affectionately under the chin and behind both ears. "How you doing, Ruff? How is my boy? You are a good dog!"

The dog jumped and slobbered and barked happily. He licked Gil's face but then drew back, his eyes liquid and dark. The dog said sadly, "Eh! Eh! You were wounded in battle."

Gil scowled. "You know that by tasting my face?"

"Yup! Yup! And there is also the fact that there are a big bandage around your head, skinned knuckles on your forepaws, and contusions all over your hide. You were expelled this time, weren't you? Not just suspended?"

"How did you know?"

Ruff cocked his head to one side and made a chuffing noise through his nose, half snort and half sneeze. "Ha! I can smell defeat. And there is also the fact that you are here too soon in the day. You want I should lick your wounds?"

"I'd get dog germs."

"Ha! Ha! That's a myth. Dog spit is the best thing for abrasions, contusions, lacerations, and scrapes. A dog's mouth is a wonder of all-natural medicinal drool!"

So, when Gil shrugged, Ruff licked his knuckles assiduously. Gil said,

"That *does* make them feel a little better, now that you mention it. Good grief, it is hot today. There is a pitcher of sweet tea there in the kitchen window, just sitting on the sill. You know any way I could get in and get it?"

"Ah! Ha! You mean like a secret doggy path we can find beneath the mountains to the buried kingdoms of the hidden folk? Uh! Oh! No, there is nothing like that here. There is a puddle in the culvert outside town I can show you. And I found a raccoon who'd been killed by a car! I can bark and scare off the crows. Some of his guts had fluid in them, or his heart maybe. That will quell any thirst! What about these dogwood fruits?"

"That is called a Cornelian Cherry. It is not a dogwood."

"Ha! Ha! Don't argue. I know trees. Here, lie down, and I will lick your head. Make you feel better!"

Gil, eyes closed and covered with sweat, was supine on the landing with his feet dangling down the steps. His shirt was unbuttoned in the hope that a breeze might wander by, exposing the ruddy, purple, blue and sooty hues of the bruises covering him. And a black and white dog was busily licking his silvery hair with its leaking red stains.

Ruff said, "Oh, you gotta tell me. I am naturally curious. I am a naturally curious dog."

"Anything, Ruff," said Gil lazily.

"Why do you get in fights so much? Why not just, you know, flop on your back and expose your throat? It is what I do when I am outmatched. Saves on stress."

2. The Once and Future King

"Let me tell you the story. Once upon a time–"

"Good! Good! I love stories. Especially the once-upon-a-time kind. Those stories are true!"

"Actually, it was six years ago to the day on my tenth birthday. I came home sporting a black eye and bawling like a baby. I started a fight, but I could not finish it. Well, my mom quizzed me, and I handed her half-truths and lame excuses. She was too wise to believe me but too softhearted to punish me, not on a day when she had baked me a cake. That cake was shaped like an Eskimo hut, complete with an Eskimo made of icing crawling out the door, and coconut shavings were the snow.

"And I got a present, a telescope with a tripod, from my cousin Tom. We had a flat roof because we lived in California in those days, and it never rained or snowed, and from the first time I saw it when we moved there, I wanted to camp out on that roof. That night I got my wish. I slept on the roof in a sleeping bag under the stars and was allowed that night to stay up as late as I liked, looking at the beautiful stars through my new telescope. It was an 80-millimeter refractor on a two-axis mount. I had duct-taped red plastic over my flashlight. I saw the Orion Nebula and the three stars of Polaris. Along the arch of the Milky Way, I saw a white swan flying at night, something I have never seen since.

"It should have been the best night of my life. It was the worst.

"It was the worst night of my life," he continued. "I was a total crybaby, and a total liar, and a total coward, and my mom just… coddled me. I needed a dad. Someone to beat some sense into me."

Gil raised his hand and wiped his eyes.

Ruff said, "You weeping? Dogs don't weep."

Gil said, "Must be dog slobber in my eyes."

Ruff said, "Must have come from some other dog then because I have been extra careful. Dogs are careful, careful creatures. What happened next? In your story?"

"So I picked one."

"One what?"

"A Dad! I picked a dad for me."

"Can you do that?"

"I did. I picked a Dad whose son was the worst son in history, a son named Mordred. He ended up killing his Dad, or almost. I promised to live up to the ideals of this great king even if he never knew. Some say he never lived, but I say he never died. Do you know who I mean?"

"Um. I am not good at riddle games. Foxes are good with riddles."

"I read a book about him. It was called *The Once and Future King*. He said, 'I don't think things ought to be done because you are *able* to do them. I think they should be done because you *ought* to do them. Not *might makes right*, but *might for right*. After all, a penny is a penny in any case, however much might is exerted on either side, to prove that it is or is not.' He said that as a kid, and he grew up and lived it. The forces of evil destroyed him for that."

"Darn those forces of evil! I'd bite them. I'd bite them hard!"

"Good dog."

"Where is he now? This guy?"

"Buried under a mountain in England, but some say three fair queens carried him to Avalon to be healed of his great wound."

"Hmm. No. England is your better bet. Avalon? Nope. No one there."

"So, anyway, that became my lesson. But you see the problem. I had to know what I ought to do! I had to pick my own *oughts*. I needed *oughts* that would make him proud."

The dog stopped licking. Gil looked at the reddish glow of sunlight seen through closed lids. The warmth made him feel drowsy.

"Aha! So now you are curious, aren't you? I made myself a promise then. A solemn and sacred vow. This is what I swore: *Never curse and never cry! Never cower and never lie! Do what's right and never shirk! Be polite and not a jerk!*

"And after that, I added another line, to bring my number of commandments up to ten. *No blaming another and no shaming your mother!* Okay, it is not Shakespeare, but I was a little kid, and the rhyme was good enough. I never forget those vows."

Gil lay in comfort, exhausted and aching and half-asleep, lulled by the heat, lounging on the stairs. He was beginning to realize how wonderful it would be not to have to deal with the gangs of kids at school, or the maddening teachers, or the cowardly principal any more.

But he sighed, "I just hope Mom does not get shamed by this! Maybe I should just not tell her."

That was when he heard his mother's voice.

"Those had better be berry stains and not bloodstains, young man," she said. She was standing over him. How she had come up the rickety stairs without any noise of footfall, he did not know.

He opened his eyes, hoping to see anger in her face. He did not. There was nothing but a deep and abiding sorrow there, and beneath that, fear.

3. Ygraine

Mrs. Moth had one of those unwrinkled and tranquil faces which betrays no sign of age. She might have been anywhere between fourteen and forty. Gil's craggy and hawklike features must have come from his father, for her face was oval, smooth, strong, and sharp-chinned. But his gray eyes, long and narrow, and touched with hints of green, he had from her.

She was in her dull beige uniform of the coffee house and winebar. Her silver hair was carefully hidden in a long scarf that trailed down her back, and the lacy waitress cap was pinned atop it. The tag on her chest said IRENE since no one in this town could pronounce her real name.

Ruff said, "Hi! Hi! Hello there, Ma'am! Hi, Gil's Mom! Gil was expelled yesterday! Kicked out of school for good! You smell nice!"

She said, "What did he just say?"

Gil sighed and winced in pain. "He said hi. That I am expelled."

She took out her latchkey and unlocked the door. "The stray dog must stay outside our home. He is most likely a spy for the elfs."

"He also said you smell nice."

She smiled sadly. "He still may not cross the threshold, but for his flattery, you may give him the rib bone I saved from the restaurant garbage. Say your farewells to him swiftly, clean yourself up, and go to your room to pack. Whatever we cannot carry, you must burn, and leave no trace."

"Mom! We're not moving again! Please!"

Her smile did not waver, nor did the sorrow in her eyes grow less. "I will decide this once I have heard the details of your adventures yesterday."

"Can we take Ruff?" he said in a very small voice.

But she had turned away and stepped inside.

4. Questioning

Gil took as long as he dared showering and cleaning himself. He rubbed the condensation from the bathroom mirror and put his hands to his head to part the hair. It did not look like he would need stitches. Some of the bruises had already faded. Maybe the dog spit had helped. He looked doubtfully at the slight shadow of fuzz on his jawline. He had never yet needed a razor, and he wondered who could teach him how to shave.

He dressed and came shuffling out into the corridor. His bedroom door was to the right. There were two doors to the left, one leading to his mother's room, and one to the bathroom. His fingers touched the blank patch of wall between the two. As he always did, he rapped the panel there to see if it were hollow, containing a secret passage. The wall felt solid. There was an empty light socket near the ceiling above where he rapped. As he always did, he took a moment to pull, twist, and push on the light socket to see if there were a switch or latch hidden there. As ever, there was not.

He walked slowly to the front room. The kitchen counter and sink were to one side. The swaybacked couch where his mother sat was to the other. The card table on which they ate their meals was folded carefully into the corner. There was no television set. A tall radio box whose front was carved with grinning cherub faces stood in the corner, a lace doily on its head. He took one of the folding metal chairs from the wall and sat down. He stared diligently at his bare feet.

His mother had unbraided her long hair. Had she been standing, it would have fallen past her hips. Seated, the long, shimmering, shining locks hung over one shoulder down past her knees. It looked like a waterfall of bright moonlight. She had drawn the window blinds as she always did when she combed her hair, so the light was dim. In the gloom, Gil thought he saw little sparks like fireflies following her comb as she stroked.

He said nothing but simply sat there for a very long time, staring at his feet. Finally, he raised his eyes. "You could yell at me, you know."

She said, "What have you done wrong?"

He pursed his lips. "Nothing. I was in the right. I fought bravely, I stopped some kids from committing a crime. Heck, I even put two of them into the emergency room! Four against one!"

"Did you win?"

"Not really."

"Tell me the tale from start to finish."

"The PA system is broken, so every day after homeroom we all go to the cafeteria to hear whatever the principal wants to say. Announcements and stuff. I went to the other building to my locker to put my jacket away because it was hot. As I was cutting back between the two buildings to get to morning assembly, a little wren popped out of the bushes and told me a gang of boys were breaking into the locker in the principal's office where they keep the phones and stuff kids aren't supposed to bring to school. But yesterday one of the teachers found a stash of drugs. I don't know what kind."

She said, "They kept it overnight at the school rather than turning it over to the County Police?"

Gil shrugged. "I guess. Anyway, it was like the wren said. The kids were in the principal's office, working the combination lock. I climbed in the window, surprised them, and told them to kneel and surrender."

"You were polite?"

"Yes."

"The window was open?"

"No. I smashed it with my bookbag and worked the latch. It was on the first floor. I held the bag by the straps and used my Algebra book like a hammer throw."

"What was the species of wren?"

He said, "*Sylvia ludoviciana.*"

"Male or female?"

"Female. The males will sing about their territory, but the females only give warning cries. This was a warning cry."

"Tell me the rest."

5. After

She had many more questions. He spoke for a long time. After he was done speaking, she said nothing, but continued to comb her hair. She braided it, wrapped it in a scarf, and only then opened the blinds. The sunlight was shockingly bright. Gil was surprised that it was not sunset yet. It had seemed like many slow and grinding hours had gone by, but from the position of the sun, he saw that it had been less than one.

Ygraine said, "Who knows, or knows enough to guess, that you can understand the speech of birds and beasts?"

"I told Jeery."

"Did he believe you?"

"He punched me in the face. I got ten dollars in quarters from him. He was using a roll of quarters as brass knuckles."

"Did you take it, or did he yield it as a forfeit?"

"I took it."

"You must return it to him and apologize for this fault."

"A– *agh*– apologize! To *him*?"

"For the wrongs he did you. Did you not beat him? But he cannot beat you for this wrong you did him. He lacks the strength. Is justice due only to the strong or to all?"

"To all." Gil looked at his bare feet again. He heaved yet another sigh. "If I—if he accepts my apology—can we stay?"

She stood. "I will go with you to his house, and see his eyes, and guess at his heart. If he suspects nothing, we can stay."

He said, "But I told the truth. I did hear it from a little bird. You do not want me to lie, do you?"

"No, but telling the truth is expensive," she said in a soft, distant voice. "And no man builds a tower without he first counts out the price, lest haply he must cease work halfway and be a laughingstock. What worth is a tower half-built and without height? And if it rest on a hilltop, who can hide it?"

Gil looked at his mother's kind and serene face. "What do we do if they set the police on us? Mr. Wartworth said he was sending the deputies to search my locker."

She said, "He will make no complaint to the police."

Gil said, "Why not?"

Ygraine said, "Mr. Wartworth was the one behind the crime. He hoped to sell the package of drugs to his profit."

Gil did not know how she had come to that conclusion, but he had never known her to be wrong before.

She peered at him closely. "What else have you seen?"

Gil had a strange, strong intuition. He said, "I saw a dark boat on the river. Like a week ago."

She said, "Was there music of fife, with veiled maidens mourning and lamenting?"

"Yes to the lamenting, no to the fife. Who was on that boat?"

"The mementos of someone taken. A lord or lady of this area was slain. It portends that there will be a battle here over the measures and times and seasons. It means you and I must be apart for a time."

She said, "Come! We have a long way. It is an hour's walk to the bus stop, and from the Food Lion to Mr. Wartworth's house is another mile. You will not return with me on the bus."

"What? What will I do?"

"If your schooling days are done, as it seems they are, then you must find work."

"Where? How?"

"Start searching the shops in town until you find a job. I do not mean mere chores or yardwork, but a steady and honest trade. You will not be welcome here over my threshold until then."

"You're kicking me out?"

She shook her head. Her voice was serene. "No. I am showing my faith in you."

"What if I don't find a job in one day? The sun will be setting by the time we even get there. Where will I sleep?"

"You may ask the sheriff to put you in a cell overnight. He seems a kindly man."

6. Embering

Gil packed a knapsack, into which he put two changes of clothing, his knife and flashlight and a few other things he thought he might need, such as a ball of string, a roll of tinfoil, a shaker of salt, and a bar of soap.

He went into the kitchen to get a few cans of beans or a loaf of bread and maybe an empty bottle to fill with water, when he came across his birthday cake. It was coated with blue frosting sculpted into waves and decorated with images of the *Monitor* and the *Merrimack*, with cannonballs made of sugar-paste. He wondered how old the sailors had been aboard those two Civil War riverboats. A weird twinge of pride ran through him then, and he decided not to eat any of his mother's food, not even a morsel, until he had earned his own bread himself. He left the cake untouched, the candles unlit, and no wishes made.

Gil did not speak again until they were out of the house and had been trudging down the hot road for a long while. Gil squinted up at the sun and pulled his baseball cap low over his head.

"Why do we keep moving all the time?"

She said, "We may not be moving again, not now. When I was young, hitchhiking was safe, and many a car would stop to pick up a penniless traveler. In those days, no one locked his door or failed to open his hand to the poor. These days it is far different. Each time we move, I find a place where the old ways linger. Even as late as fifteen years ago, there were still places where a young mother with a babe in her arms could find sanctuary. But the pools of light are drying up and dying, and the places are fewer and farther between. And a youth of your size should not take the bread away from whatever babe's mothers younger than I now beg for."

"You did not answer me."

"No, that is true; I did not. The answer would crush your bones beneath its weight. Leave the matter alone."

He was silent for a moment, then said, "Last night I was locked in a church. I think a ghost locked me in there."

"That's unusual. Ghosts tend to avoid hallowed ground."

"Everyone in town was out last night, walking in the dark, carrying stuff. What was that?"

She didn't look surprised. "The black spell."

"What? What is that?"

"It is the source of all the woes man does not bring upon himself by his own devising. This is the first year you have ever remained awake when it fell. It is sad, but not unexpected."

"Sad? Why?"

"Sad because it means you cannot blend in easily with ordinary people, not if you are seen awake among the hosts of sleepwalkers. The next time it happens, you must remain out of sight, and tell no one what you saw."

He said, "Mother, tell me what is going on! What is the black spell? Who casts it?"

She shook her head and would not reply.

He tramped down the road, frowning. A short while later, he spoke again.

"Can I sleep in the extra room? The attic?"

"There is no attic in which to sleep, my son."

"There is an attic! There is a door that appears and disappears. Sometimes it is there; sometimes it is not. It is always when the moon is full, but some months it does not come at all. It has a glass doorknob and a big old-fashioned lock you can see through. The top of the door is curved, not straight. When the moon is bright, through the keyhole, you can see the stairs leading up to an attic. In this place, it shows up between your door and the bathroom door. But in that place we lived in Utah, it showed up at the end of the hall next to the broken window. Before that, in California, it appeared in the back of the closet door in my room, but only when I was alone. I have asked you about this before. You never answered. Well? If I am old enough to work, I am old enough to know. Don't I get a birthday present?"

She smiled sweetly. "It is a poor gift, for I know nothing of the glass-knobbed door and can guess only a trifle. But I grant it."

He said, "Sometimes I put my ear to the keyhole and listen. Once or twice, I have heard the dim noise of trumpets blowing in the distance. Whose trumpets are those?"

"It is an echo from another world."

"What is that door? Who made it?"

"I know not."

"Why did you never talk about it or answer me?"

She said, "I would hide the door if I could, but I have not the art, nor can I open it. To speak of such doors is unwise. Sometimes they hear, and they come." She shivered. "I thought we had left it behind in Ophir."

"The door is following us, isn't it?"

Ygraine pursed her lips, "Not quite. We bring it with us, unknowing."

"Is it magic?"

"An odd question! The art of weaving the unseen is not of man's world, but it has it own rules to keep. This glass-knobbed door is not diabolical if that is what you mean. Nor is it of Heaven. The door-maker did not mean for his door to do the harm it one day must."

"What harm?"

She merely shook her head. "Think on today's evils and leave the morrows' be. The closed door is like a buried memory; it is kept from us. No need to unearth what is best forgotten."

"Why does it appear and disappear?"

"There are days of the year when the mists are thin, and such hidden doors open. But even then, the door is unseen and unopened if the full moon shines not."

"What days?"

"Ember days, quarter days, and cross-quarter days."

"When is that?"

She gave him a sidelong look. "Your schoolmasters never taught you the calendar?" Then she chanted:

Fasting days and Emberings be
Lent, Whitsun, Holyrood, and Lucie

He said, "What calendar is that?"

She seemed bewildered. "Our calendar. Everyone's calendar."

"The Gregorian calendar?"

"The Men of the East spell time differently, by the moon, but the Sons of Europa count by the sun. The Wednesday, Friday, and Saturday after the Feast of Saint Lucy are the Embertide; and again, after Whitsunday; after the Exultation of the Cross; and again in Lent. The cross quarter days are Candlemas, May Day, Lammas, and All Hallows. The quarter days are Lady Day, Midsummer Day, Michaelmas, Christmas."

"The school does not mention any of these."

She suddenly looked frightened. "Have men truly forgotten how to keep time?"

"Except Christmas. But they call it *Winter Holiday* now. And you have to mention *Chanukah* and *Kwanzaa* whenever you talk about it."

She said, "This is an ill omen. Some great lord or lady has been tithed or a fair king slain, and the days and seasons have lost their true names."

"What does that mean?"

"It means the darkness gathers." She swallowed, and her eyes were bright with unshed tears. "It means I cannot protect my son."

He put his arms around her. "Mom! It is time for me to protect you."

She put her face in the hollow of his shoulder, for he overtopped her now.

Gingerly, he patted her on the shoulder. He said, "Don't be sad! It is just the school calendar! It does not mean anything. And there are plenty of other holidays, like Earth Day, and, uh, Recycling Day."

She murmured something softly, but he could not hear her words.

"What are you afraid of? What is following us?"

She did not reply, but instead broke down and wept, trembling in his arms, and his heart was filled with pain. He whispered, "I *will* protect you, Mother! I *will*!"

She wiped her eyes and drew back. "You are too tender yet."

"I promise!"

She shook her head. "You know not what you vow."

He said, "I have vowed it all the same, and I cannot take back my word!"

She shook her head again, grieving, saying nothing.

"Mom. I know we are hiding from someone. Who is it? Why can't we face them instead?"

"The sea rises higher and higher. What sword can frighten back the tide? The storm is come. Who can outrun it? The Old Night rises. Darkness gathers."

"What does that mean?"

"Who can escape a darkness without end? What cup can bring a light long-dead to life again?"

"Not your riddles, Mom!" Gil groaned in exasperation. "Not riddles again! I never know the answers."

"We cannot face the sea, the storm, the night, the dark, for these have no faces."

He said, "Who are you hiding from?"

She answered softly, "It is not myself I hide." And she said no more, but turned from him and trudged down the road in the bitter, merciless heat.

Chapter 3

Town and Wood

1. Job Hunting

As it turned out, even after Gil apologized, Jeery was afraid to step close enough to Gil to take the roll of quarters back. And ten dollars was enough to buy a membership, for someone his age, at the local YMCA. He had a cot for the next seven days and use of the gym, tennis court, and swimming pool.

He stayed the night and woke hungry before dawn the next day. He had no money for food.

At dawn, Gil waited next to the newspaper box at the bus stop corner and politely asked the first man who bought a newspaper if he could have the want ads. Then, he walked to the north side of the town of Blowing Rock and began working his way, street by street, past every shop and each address listing anything he thought he could do.

Now, many hours later, he sat on the curb with the paper at the south side of town. All the buildings were behind him. The lonely highway wound down the slope into the forest before him. There was not a car in sight.

Ruff came trotting up, with a dead squirrel in his mouth. The dog laid the squirrel carefully in the gutter at Gil's feet and sat back, bright-eyed and wagging his tail, and he barked, "Look! Look! I brought a squirrel! A squirrel!"

Gil folded the newspaper and threw it down into the gutter.

Ruff said, "Hi! Hi! You can eat it. I brought a squirrel you can eat!"

"Thanks, Ruff. You are a pal. Good dog. You are a good dog!" And he scratched the dog behind the ears.

Ruff sniffed the newspaper, and his ears drooped. The tail stopped wagging. Ruff looked up with a mournful expression into Gil's face. "Oh, no! Oh, no! It is a day of failure. You failed. Didn't find what you were hunting, did you?"

"How did you know?"

"I can smell failure."

Gil looked up. "Really?"

"Yup! Yup! Well, and there is also the fact that you are sitting in the gutter looking glum rather than flipping burgers or changing tires."

"There was one guy who wanted to hire me for carpentry. I showed him I knew how to pound a nail and hang a door. Another guy at the shooting range needed someone to clean the guns, mind the customers, and lock up at night. Even the car wash needed someone. But not me. I am not in the union, not old enough, don't have a birth certificate. Cannot prove I am allowed to work. The old lady who runs the flower shop wanted someone just to sweep up the place, pick up dead petals and leaves, and take out the trash, but she said she could not pay me ten bucks an hour. I said I would work for half of that. She said she was not allowed to pay me so little. Not allowed! In her own store! Who has the right to tell her she can't hire me?"

Ruff jumped up, his ears high, "Oh! Oh! I think you should sneak into her shop at night and do all the work she wants without telling anyone! Then, if she likes the work, she will leave a bowl of cream out on her back doorstep for you. And on All Hallows, she has to sew you a new suit of clothing. And then you vanish and never come again."

Gil said, "What?"

Ruff's ears drooped again. "Oh, no! I thought that is how things like this were done."

"Maybe in Dog Land. The way they are done in Burke County is less exciting. If you stand on the corner at the library, sometimes landscapers will come by to pick you up for a day's work with a shovel or a rake. But Mom said honest labor. Does honest labor mean I have to obey laws about carrying paperwork and being old and whatever else? Because that I am not allowed. Or does it just mean your full effort for a full day with no slacking and no backtalk? That I can do."

Ruff said, "Hey! I have an idea! Why not go to Dog Land?"

Gil looked at the mutt in surprise. "Is there really such a place?"

Ruff cocked his head to one side, so one ear was up and the other down. "Um! Um! You just said. You said how they do things in Dog Land. I thought it sounded like a swell place. Swell! Because of the dogs."

Gil scowled at the road. "I asked some of the birds to tell me what my mother was up to, but they would not tell me."

Ruff cocked one ear.

Gil said, "Don't you think it strange that she wants me out of our place, not even to sleep there?"

Ruff said, "I saw her walking around the place counterclockwise, three times. Maybe she is trying to summon the Greater Tree."

Gil said, "What is that?"

"Well, you know the World Tree?"

"Nope."

"This is greater. Greater than the world."

"What is it? What does it do?"

"Beats me. But if she is doing something that might draw attention to herself, she wants you out of the way."

Gil said, "So the whole getting a job thing is a trick? We should go back and protect her."

Ruff shook his head. "Maybe. Or maybe you should listen to your mother. I always listened to mine. Except when I didn't. Then, it did not go so good. Besides, you need to work to eat, right?"

Just then a jeep came barreling down the street, pulled out onto the empty highway, and took the turn to head toward Knob Hill, where the State Park was. Behind the wheel was a boy about Gil's age.

There was a six-pack on the seat behind him, some fishing rods, a knapsack of camping gear, and a strawberry-haired girl with a big smile and freckled cheeks sitting next to him, chatting. They both had their cellphones in their hands and their earphones in their ears, so it was not clear if they were talking to each other or to someone else. It was also not clear how the driver planned to survive the trip since he was looking at his gizmo and not at the road.

The girl pitched a paper bag decorated with clowns out the back of the jeep. It fell near an oil stain in the middle of the road not far away. "Hey! Hey!" barked Ruff, trotting quickly over to the bag and sniffing it.

Gil stared glumly after the retreating jeep, wondering silently why kids no different than he had gas to burn and camping trips to go on.

Ruff said, "Wow! Wow! There is half a burger in here!"

"You know," said Gil, "I have never eaten junk food."

"Wow! Are you missing out! Junk food is great. There are some fries left too, but I don't like fries."

"I guess that guy's dad bought him stuff. Taught him how to fish. You know."

"I know! I know! They are made of potato. It is like boiled potato. Boiled in oil, and salted. I like the salt."

Ruff lifted his nose out of the dropped bag. There was catsup on his nose. "I'll lick the fries, and then you can eat them. I'll lick the salt! You want some?"

"Let me cook the squirrel first, and I'll see how I feel about eating someone else's trash that a dog licked. But I'll share the half a burger with you."

The dog picked up the bag in his mouth and trotted back over.

2. Job Tracking

It was about an hour later, and the two were in the woods, out of the heat. The sun was low in the sky, and it was an hour before sunset. Gil had made a fire with his magnifying glass, using pages ripped out of his Algebra book for tinder, and skinned and eviscerated the squirrel with his knife. Ruff got the head and entrails. Gil sharpened a green stick, and held the rodent over the fire, smelling the savory smell of meat and watching the blood and fat drip. The flames were almost invisible in the shaft of sunlight that fell through the leafy branches.

Gil said suddenly, "I wonder if that was his sister or his girlfriend?"

"Who?"

"The couple in the jeep."

"Yup! Girlfriend."

He looked at the dog. "Don't tell me you can smell the difference between a girlfriend and a sister?"

Ruff shrugged. "Eh? There are smells in the air when humans want to mate."

"And you smelled–? In a passing car? That those two were thinking about–?"

"No, that is Erica Lee. She is editor-in-chief of the yearbook at the high school you just got kicked out of. She was a varsity cheerleader for two years. Jack Merritt is their star quarterback. They are an item. Prom King and Prom Queen this year. Say! Say! How come you are not moving away?"

Gil said, "I'm not sure. Mom spoke to the principal privately in his house, and there were no birds in the bushes or anything I could ask to eavesdrop. But you know how his face is red as a beet? It was white like ashes when she was done. Wonder what she said. Anyway, she told me we could stay."

"I'm glad! I'm glad! Your mom threatened him."

"Not likely," said Gil.

"She had her teeth in his throat. Otherwise, he would have filed a police report, and you would have been named in the papers."

"What papers?"

"Papers! Papers! Humans always have tons of papers around."

"Records? Police records?"

"Humans write things down so you don't forget. You have terrible memories."

The thought of his mom with her serene face and gentle voice threatening the principal warmed him. He knew what it was like to be on her bad side. Gil almost felt sorry for Mr. Wartworth.

Gil gnawed on his rodent dinner. With a little salt, it did not taste bad at all.

He tossed a scrap to the dog and then peered at Ruff closely. "If you animals are so smart, how come you don't have any civilization?"

Ruff said, "I'm different."

"Because you are a spy for the elfs?"

Ruff said, "Something like that."

"Tell me about elfs."

Ruff looked wary, and he put his head down. "You know! You know! Not really wise to talk about them. Not really safe. Enslave you at night, make you do work, take your stuff, and then put mist in your eyes so that you all think it is because your taxes are high. It is not. Just the thieving elfs at their games. More than half of human toil goes to them, and you blame each other, or the economy, or the weather. But they walk unseen and can dwindle to hide in a cowslip or ride a bumblebee. So they might be listening. Shh! Shh!"

Gil saw this made Ruff nervous. So he said, "Fine, you are special. But back to my other question. Other animals talk. At least to me. Normal people should be able to see you all animals are smart even if they cannot talk to you, shouldn't they?"

"Nope! Nope! That is not how it works. Beasts live for the day and don't fret about the morrow. You lost that when you left Eden."

"Foresight, you mean? Sounds like a gain, not a loss."

"Trust. You lost trust. You think tomorrow is not trustworthy, that the story of the world is not in good hands. Nope. Nope. You lost a lot."

"We're civilized."

"You don't have good noses, though."

"I still don't get why if animals can talk to me, you are not smart enough for humans to notice."

"Beasts are smart only when humans love us. That makes us smarter. It improves our nature but does not change our nature. So we are not going to start thinking about tomorrow and building forts and factories and stuff."

"How can human love change animals?"

"It's their authority."

"Normal people love dogs, but cannot talk like you and I do."

"You must have more authority or something. Besides, normal people have their eyes held. They cannot see their world."

"Their eyes held? What does that mean?"

"Mist. Mist in their eyes. In their brains. Darkness in their brains. Makes them stupid. Not see things. Forget things. Forget what is important. Men are fools. How you guys ended up in charge, who knows?"

Gil sighed impatiently. "Only got six more days at the YMCA. I cannot even grab a bus to get to a bigger town that might have more work."

Ruff said, "Hey! Hey! I have an idea! I know a job you'd be good at. Great at! Great!"

Gil stared in surprise. Ruff was bristling with excitement, hopping on all fours, wagging his tail, practically dancing.

Gil said, "Well, you knew who the prom queen was dating, so maybe you know everything. Where is there a job for me? What job?"

"Be a knight!"

"You mean, enlist in the Army? Hmm. That's not a bad idea. I hear they pay for college. And they would certainly be more my kind of people than—"

"No! No! Didn't you hear me? A knight! A *knight*!"

"I am not sure there is that much money in knighthood, these days. And who is hiring?"

"Plenty of money!"

"There is something in the Constitution that says the government cannot grant titles of nobility or something."

"Come on! Come on! If Ringo Starr the Beatle can be knighted, Gilberec the Moth can, too! We need to find someone to train you, though. Before your six days are up. Boy!" Ruff jumped up and put his muddy paws against Gil's chest. "What a good idea! What a doozy of an idea! Great! Great!"

Gil said, "Ruff! Nice dog! Down, boy!" He stood up, lest Ruff knock him over. "I don't think there is much call for knights. I do not think it is possible."

"You are a kid who talks to dogs and busts up drug rings, and you are going to tell me what is and is not possible? You're impossible! And I don't mean that in a good way!"

Gil chewed on his cooked squirrel thoughtfully. "Who could train me? Where would I find a horse and lance and stuff?"

"Beat someone up and take his horse! Ha! Ha! Dogs get along with horses. I like horses! But— let me see. Training, eh? You don't have a father."

Gil let the last morsel of cooked squirrel drop to the ground. "Thanks. I noticed."

"Yup! No dad. No dad for you! Because you are a bastard." Ruff sniffed the dropped morsel and then snatched it up happily in his jaws.

"Thanks. I know." His tone was flat.

"What about a grandfather? Your mother's dad?"

"I don't know his name. Mom never talks about her family, except to say that it is really, really big."

Ruff said, "Yeah! I heard that, too. The Moths are everywhere. The Moths get into everything."

Gil brightened. "Wait! Really? You know about my family? What have you heard?"

"Ah. That the Moths are everywhere. Like I just said. Just now."

Gil's smile faded. "Anything else?"

"Sure! Sure! *The Moths get into everything.* Anyhow, I thought of someone."

"Someone who?"

"To train you how to fight!" Ruff jumped excitedly back and forth. "Come on! Come on! You coming? I am going, so you had better be coming!"

"Who? Tell me his name."

"He does not have a name. You get to pick a name! You coming?"

"Yeah. I am coming. Give me a moment."

He threw the useless newspaper on the campfire and then began piling dirt to smother the flames.

3. Rabbit

Gil had fashioned himself a hiking stick by finding a likely length of wood and trimming off the twigs. As they hiked, Gil said, "Are you sure there is a need for knights?"

Ruff said, "Sure! Sure! Anyone can tell you. Ask anyone!"

Gil thought it actually might be a good idea to ask around. Gil looked at the long grass in the meadow, saw a rustle, and perceived it was a rabbit. He called the rabbit over, telling Ruff to stand a bit away.

The rabbit sat up on its hindquarters. "What can I do for you, my good sir?"

"Um. I am looking for a job."

"Everyone is welcome in the warren! How are you at digging holes? Plenty of clover this time of year, the does are in heat, and no need to worry about the wolf. You see, you don't need to outrun the wolf; you only need to outrun your brother." The rabbit wore a smug look. "That is a saying we have! When danger comes, abandon your loved ones! So, will you join? The more among us, the merrier! The more targets for the hungry wolf, the better our chances to stay alive!"

"No, not a job as a bunny. I was thinking of being a knight. Have you heard that they have any openings? Um– within walking distance of Blowing Rock, North Carolina?"

The rabbit scratched his ear with his hind leg thoughtfully. "I heard something about knights over around Pisgah National Forest. Something in the wind. Winter knights and Summer knights getting ready for Michaelmas. But I think they were elfs. You know, the hidden people, the Night Folk."

"Elfs? What can you tell me about them?"

The rabbit shivered. "Nothing. I mean, they steal human beings from the daylight world. Put the come-hither on them. Take you down into their warrens. More targets for the hungry mouths, so more chances to stay alive if you get me. A lot like rabbits, elfs. The more, the merrier." The rabbit shivered again. "Say nothing! They have sharp ears and many spies."

"Yeah, I think I met one."

"They don't like people talking about them. It is better to call them 'the Good People' or 'the Kindly Folk' or 'The Rich Ones' or something like that."

Gil said, "Are they real? Where do they come from?"

The rabbit said, "*Kindly* and *good* and *rich*. Like I said. Don't talk about them. As for knighthood, stupid idea. Knights wear metal for their fur, and they fight. Outmoded, outdated, old-fashioned idea. The latest and best way is to study how to run away!"

Another rabbit, this one smaller and with a nose that never stopped twitching, emerged from the grass just then. "Sir, I could not help but overhear the conversation. Knighthood is one of those theories whose days are past! Rabbits are forward-looking! It is not for nothing that we have such ears, to hear of all the latest trends in the newest thought! Running away is the new fashion!"

Other rabbit voices now came from the grasses. "Quite so! Everyone agrees," said one, and another said, "Always listen to rabbits! We have the more recent and most profound ideas on all matters!" and a third, "A consensus has been reached! The debate is over!"

Gil said, "But rabbits always run away. Always have. Isn't that like your thing you are famous for? How is that new?"

But then the two rabbits he could see froze, ears high, motionless as statues. In the near distance was a thrumming noise of a rabbit rapping his hindleg against the ground, their warning signal. The two visible rabbits bounded away with astonishing speed and were gone, and no rustle was heard from the grass.

4. Wolf

Gil looked up and saw a wolf across the meadow, grinning. Gil beckoned him over. The wolf, tongue lolling, came trotting closer but slowed warily and stopped several yards away. The wolf sat down on his haunches.

"Well, you have a strange smell about you," said the wolf, "A scent not of this world. You look like a Son of Adam, but I think you are a Son of someone else."

"Who?" asked Gil. "Whose son am I?"

"Cut off all your fine silver hair, and give it to me, and perhaps I will tell."

Gil said curtly, "No."

The wolf stood up, and his ears flattened. "You do not know where my pack is or how you are surrounded, do you?"

Gil said, "Pardon my manners, Brother Wolf. Your request took me by surprise. I am not able to cut off all my hair at this time to present to you, for I promised some to my friend, a wren who is using it to line her nest. Please tell me why you want it."

The wolf sat on his haunches again, green eyes glinting like flames. "You are well spoken, Brother Man-cub. But it would be rude of me to tell you the secret of your own hair that grows on your own head."

Gil said, "What if I cut a handful of it and present it to you as a gift?"

The glitter in the wolf's eyes changed, growing less dangerous but more greedy. "That would be noble courtesy indeed, Brother Man-cub."

Gil drew his knife and cut off a tail of hair from behind his ear. He opened his fingers, and the strands floated down to the grass just before him. The wolf stood up and started to step forward but then paused, as if measuring the distance between the knife still in Gil's hand and himself. He looked then at the silver hair on the grass, then at Gil's eyes, and then back at the knife.

Gil said, "What, pray tell, is the matter, Brother Wolf?"

"You still have your knife in your hand, Brother Man-cub."

"So? It would be discourteous not to offer my hair to your pack mates as well. Have them come out of hiding and show themselves, and we will exchange gifts and secrets of noble worth."

The wolf said, "No, not so, my packmates—which are many in number, and ferocious fighters—would deem it untoward to impose on a generous heart like yours."

Gil said, "Come, Brother Wolf. Please take these strands of hair as a gift."

The wolf stepped slowly and warily toward the spot at Gil's feet where the hair lay gleaming. Very gingerly, watching Gil and Gil's knifehand with both eyes, the wolf lowered his head and gently took the hairs between his teeth.

Gil tightened his grip on his knife. It was a tiny, almost invisible motion, but the wolf froze. His head was still down, and he was very close to Gil, but not in any position to spring.

"True courtesy," said Gil softly, "would be truly satisfied if we both performed as we said. Have you no gift to offer in return?"

The wolf's eyes were locked on the knife, whose blade gleamed brightly.

The wolf spoke in a husky whisper, moving his lips but not his teeth. "Ask me three questions if you please. That will be my gift."

"Thank you," said Gil.

"You are most welcome."

"Whose son am I?"

"I know not."

"But you said–"

"The scent of death is upon you, which marks you as a Son of Eve and Adam. Yet also the scent of the mists of otherworld around you, which follows the Sons of Titania and Oberon. Yet you are not of one nor of the other, neither of the Day-born nor the Night-kin. You are one of the Twilight Folk. You are a son of Moth. Your family is called Moth."

"That does not tell me much, Brother Wolf."

"You did not give me much hair, Brother Man."

"What makes my hair precious?"

"Long ago, were men who were my brothers, wolves who walked on two legs and who walked through the wood as warily and swiftly as do I. They worshiped many spirits, including the great wolf spirit. They danced the Ghost Dance, to turn the bullets of the white men away. Those who had hair like yours to weave into their ghost shirts had charmed lives, and the weapon they most feared, the weapon with no dreams, would not bite them. So it is for you: you will not die by firearms."

"What? Am I bulletproof?"

"Ask your third question, kindly and gracious brother, for I must be away!"

"Uh, sure, uh. What about knighthood as a career? Are there any jobs open?"

"For that profession?" and now the wolf made a low and ugly chuckle in its throat. Then, the wolf recited:

> And ever and anon the wolf would steal
> The children and devour, but now and then,
> Her own brood lost or dead, lent her fierce teat
> To human sucklings; and the children, housed
> In her foul den, there at their meat would growl,
> And mock their foster-mother on four feet,
> Till, straightened, they grew up to wolf-like men,
> Worse than the wolves.

"What does that mean?" asked Gil. "Uh, if you please?"

And the wolf answered, "If you please, dear brother, it means that in the land of wolves, there is always a need for wolfhounds. In the land of darkness, there is always a need for lanterns of light. The pay is poor, however. Glory is the payment, glory and death. Farewell, young knight. You have been courteous to me, an enemy of your race, and given me a boon beyond your reckoning. I will tell others of my kind of your gracious spirit if you will tell me your name, and I will glorify it."

"Tell me your name first."

"Beasts have no names. You may call me Krasny Volk Odinokyy, the Lone Red Wolf."

"Lone? So there is no pack surrounding me?"

The green-eyed wolf grinned. "I am ecumenical and cosmopolitan. I consider all wolves wherever in the world to be my pack. Think about it. From any spot on the globe, if you look in any quarter, north or south or east or west, and if you are willing to look far enough, eventually you will find a wolf! In a figurative sense, I think of all men as surrounded! A striking image, is it not?"

"Poetry worthy of a nightingale, dear brother."

"Thank you, good brother. Will you honor me in turn with your name?"

"I am Gilberec Parzival Moth."

The wolf looked startled and almost dropped the hairs. "The son of Ygraine of the Riddles? How can this be? How? They said you were dead! They said your mother was flown away, far away, on swan-wings to the place in the Summer Stars!" He twitched his ears and turned his frightened eyes left and right. "I take my leave of you, good sir."

"Wait a minute! Who? Who said that?"

But the gray wolf had slunk away swiftly into the dark wood and was gone.

"*Who said I was dead?*" Gil shouted toward the trees.

There was no answer.

5. Thrush

Even as he stood looking after the wolf, wondering, a thrush flew down from the branches overhead and landed on Gil's shoulder. "I could not help but overhear. Are you indeed Gilberec Moth?" piped the bird.

"Sure, that's me. I am looking for a job. You heard anything?"

The thrush said, "I have heard."

Gil brightened. "About a job?"

"No. I heard the voice of your cousin under the river water."

Gil frowned, wondering if this were some bird joke. "Drowned? Or swimming?"

"Both."

"How did you know it was my cousin?"

"You are the son of Ygraine Moth, Ygraine Silverlocks of the Many Riddles, Ygraine of the Wise Reeds, Ygraine of the Celestial Cloak. All birds know her, but of her we never speak."

"Where is she from? Who did she marry? What is she?"

"Of her we never speak."

"But you just– argh!– okay, whatever. What about my drowned cousin? You heard what? Yells for help?"

"I heard the song that was sung. Know you the waterfall called Linville Falls?" the thrush asked.

"Sure. It's in the national forest. At the head of the gorge."

"The Cherokee would slay their prisoners cruelly by throwing them over these falls. Only one man ever survived a plunge over it. The ghosts of the dead are thick in the gorge beneath. The door to the other world can open there. Your cousin entered through the opening, having heard that there are lights on Brown Mountain at night, not lit by human hands. One of the best vantage points to spy these lights, Wiseman's View, is one league from the falls as the thrush flies. So said the song that was sung."

"Well– wait a minute! There is a door in my house I want to open. He knows how to do it? What is his name?"

The bird said, "Whose name?"

"My cousin!"

"Moth." And with this, the thrush flew up and away.

6. Wise Reeds

Gil beckoned Ruff, who came trotting over. Ruff said, "So, you talked to the rabbits. What did they say about my idea of you being a knight? Said it was great! Said it was great! I am sure! Everyone agrees!"

"The rabbits said knighthood was a terrible idea."

"Bah! Nah! Don't listen to rabbits. They never know what they are talking about."

"The rabbits also told me not to talk about elfs."

"Yup! You should listen. Rabbits are wise. Also, I saw you talking to a wolf. Never trust them. They only speak lies."

"The wolf said being a knight was always something that is needed, a lamp in a dark land, but that the wages were glory and death."

Ruff nodded. "Very wise. Always listen to wolves. They know what is what!"

"And you heard what the thrush said? Cousins and ghosts and lights on Brown Mountain and never talking about my mother. And the rabbit said something about the winter and summer knights at the national park. It sounds like something is up. What was that all about?"

Ruff said, "Yeah! Yeah! I know!"

"What do you know?"

"I know something is up. Something must be up!"

"What? What is up?"

Ruff sat and scratched and bit a flea on his hindquarters. "Dunno. Dunno. But something!"

"Wow. Brilliant."

"Hey! Hey! I am a dog. You want brilliance, talk to a fox. They will swap riddles with you like a sphinx. You want to hunt the fox, talk to me. Who is more brilliant in the long run then? The dog or the fox?"

Gil just scratched the dog's head. "Dog!" he said. "Best animal ever."

Ruff looked proud.

Chapter 4

Tough Training

1. Bruno

They hiked and rested and hiked some more. The heat of noon had passed, and the sun was in the west, high in a cloudless blue sky, when Ruff led the way down the rocks of a gorge. As Gil descended from rock to rock, sometimes walking, sometimes going on all fours, he could see a slender waterfall, endlessly roaring. It fell in a series of three great steps from shelf to woody shelf into a deep pool it had carved out over the centuries. One rock, taller than the others, stood up in the middle of the water.

Around the pool was a fringe of rushes and cattails, brilliant in the sunlight with insects and the scent of mud. Beyond was a circle of waist-high grass and man-high rocks that had fallen in ages past from the surrounding green cliffs.

A stream meandered from the pool into the surrounding wood. The trees to either side of the stream met overhead, forming a living colonnade with a leafy roof, as shadowy and solemn as the nave of a cathedral. Brilliant glints from slanting sunbeams that pierced that canopy danced on the moving carpet of the waters like flakes of fire.

Gil walked toward the pool until his feet started making sloppy, wet noises in the grass. He looked down at Ruff. The dog was almost invisible in the tall grass but had his nose sticking up like the periscope of a submarine.

"There! There!" said Ruff.

Ahead, Gil could see nothing but a brown lumpish rock looming up between the reeds near the shore of the pond. It had an odd texture. It seemed to be coated with moss that looked brown, as if it had dried up in the sun. But the moss was quite bristly.

"I don't see anyone. Is he here? Whoever we are looking for?"

"Right there!" said Ruff.

Gil stepped closer, wading through the waist-high grass, his footsteps sinking a bit into the muddy soil. There was something odd about the rock. It was rounded in its main mass, with a smaller hump above that and two lumps to either side that almost looked like shoulders. In fact, the whole mass looked almost like...

Then it moved.

The lump was a bear, who was facing away from Gil. The beast straightened up and turned and looked over his shoulder. Instead of a right eye, there was only a mass of scar tissue about an empty socket. In the bear's muzzle was a live fish, still twitching and dripping pond water.

The one-eyed bear turned massively and padded forward. Gil backed up step by step but took his hiking staff in both hands. The bear stopped, lowered his head, dropped the fish, and put his paw on it. Gil could not see the fish under the tall grass, but he saw the grassblades shaking as the fish flopped.

"I was about to eat my lunch," said the bear. "But here you are, stomping and tramping up like a blind thing. Ready to step on me, eh? You've riled up my food."

Gil bowed his head without taking his eyes from the bear. "I beg your pardon, Master Bear."

The one-eyed bear stared at him without speaking for a while. Then, its small ears twitched. "I was not riled up. I heard your racket coming down the cliffs. You should apologize to the fish."

Gil said, "I am not apologizing to your lunch."

"Really? What if I say *you must*?"

Gil drew a breath and set his feet and tightened his grip on his hiking staff. "Who knows? Try it and see. But ask yourself if the answer is worth it. Curiosity gets men into trouble all the time. Bears can be wiser."

"A good answer, but I can smell your fear."

Gil nodded warily. "I can smell it, too. But you cannot see my back because I am not running."

The bear grunted. "Also a good answer. So. You think you can take me?"

"No, sir. That thought honestly never entered my mind. But I think I can hurt you, maybe poke out your other eye before you kill me, and I was thinking what a shame that would be."

"Why is that a shame? If that happens, I win."

"Yes, sir. But at what cost? Is it worth it? I have heard that no man builds a tower without he first counts out the cost, lest he leave off with the tower half-built and be a laughingstock!"

"Bears don't build towers. What does it mean?"

"I am not sure, but I know it is wise."

"Hmm. What are you doing in my part of the woods? Man and bear eat much the same stuffs, and I don't need the competition."

"I was following my dog."

"Where is he?"

Ruff came crawling forward on his belly, head down, through the tall grass toward the bear, whining and letting his ears droop. "Sir! Sir! We need someone to train my boy here, see? What do you think? What do you think? To be a knight!"

The bear sat down heavily on his haunches, still keeping a forepaw on the flopping fish. "Me? I don't know about stuff like that. Why should I? He smells like an elf, a little bit. What is he? A mongrel? Half an elf? I don't like elfs. Thieving little pests, elfs."

Ruff whined piteously, rolling his eyes, and belly-crawled another foot forward, "Yes! Yes! But what if he beats up some for you? What then? What about that?"

The bear twisted his head to bring his one good eye around to glare at the crawling, sniveling dog. "You've eaten elf food, Son of Old Hemp."

"I was hungry! I was hungry!"

The bear brought his head back up to stare coldly at Gil. "You are the boy who talks to beasts, aren't you? I heard the rabbits yammering about you."

"News travels fast," said Gil. "What is your name?"

"Beasts do not have names until a Son of Adam names us," said the bear. "But, yes, I am the one you were looking for."

"What did the rabbits say about me?"

"Great ones for gossip, rabbits," continued the one-eyed bear, with no change of expression in his cold eye. "You can step into a meadow with rabbits, and they will ignore you and just go on chewing clover. Even come right up and talk to you if there are a bunch of them, to swap rumors and such. Only come up in pairs, though. Each one thinks you'll eat his brother first, see. No sense of loyalty. Which is the rabbit you can trust?"

Gil sighed. "My mom always asks me riddles like this. I would say *none*."

"Good answer. Why?"

The bear had not relaxed his gaze. Gil, however, put the heel of his hiking staff to the marshy ground and leaned on it, for he supposed the bear would not attack while waiting for an answer. Gil said, "Rabbits will always say what other rabbits say because they are afraid to disagree, but they will never check to see if what they are repeating is truth."

"And bears?"

"Sir, I expect bears to tell the truth."

"And why would that be?"

"Because I expect no bear fears a disagreement."

The bear nodded. "Good answer. I like you."

Gil breathed out a pent-up breath he had not realized he was holding.

"Not sure I can help you, though. The rabbits said you are looking to be taught how to fight?"

"To be trained as a knight."

The bear shook his head. "Knighthood is something men did not learn from any beast of the earth or spirit from below, so I cannot train you in its mysteries. Not me. I can show you a few moves, maybe some basic physical training, but chivalry is really not my field. Let me chow down and think this over. If I agree, what name will you call me?"

"Um. You are brown. How about Bruno?"

"I was hoping for something more like bee-wolf."

"Master Bear, I can call you Bee-wolf if you like."

The bear gave him a cold look. "That is not how it works. To fight, you have to think like a beast, think about what is before your nose here and now, not looking over your shoulder. No regrets, no hopes, no fretting about tomorrow. You named me my name, and you cannot take it back. If you land a blow and break a bone, you cannot take it back. See?"

"Yes, I see."

"And Bruno is a good name. Sounds solid. Not like Moth. That is a name that is neither here nor there. Always flitting, moths. Hmph."

"How did you know my name, ah, Bruno?"

The bear was not listening and did not answer. Instead, Bruno spoke, as if musing aloud, "A good name giver means you have a good eye. So you might make a good fighter. I don't know. Lots to think over. I'll be back again after lunch if you are still here." And he bowed his head, picked up his fish, and moved away heavily but silently through the tall grass to a point near the cliff where the westerly sun was already casting a narrow slip of dark shade.

2. The Basics

Lesson One was in how to awe and terrify. Bruno showed Gil how to rear up and raise his arms overhead and roar at the top of his lungs.

"This part is important," said the bear. "Critters get stupid when they fight. If you hold your forepaws up like that, you look like you are ten-feet-tall. Also, make as much racket as you can. That shows you are not scared. Do you have any pots and pans to bang together? Works wonders."

While Gil was practicing waving his arms overhead and uttering shouts loud enough to echo off the canyon walls, he heard a lilt of girlish laughter in the distance.

Gil looked.

Kneeling on the rock in the middle of the pool was a shapely young woman in a skintight black wetsuit.

She had long hair as dark as her suit which she lay over her shoulder. Even from a distance, Gil recognized from her arm motions that she was combing her locks. Her face and hands, by contrast, seemed very white, white as a lily petal. Her feet were bare.

And she was giggling at him.

Without warning, the bear cuffed Gil smartly, knocking him from his feet. "Not paying attention, is it? Look sharp! Keep up with the practice. Roar!"

The length and thickness of the grass and the softness of the muddy, marshy soil beneath saved Gil from any broken bones, but the blow had dazed him. "But there is someone watching us!"

The bear growled, "Let 'em!"

So Gil continued to roar and shout and wave his arms, painfully aware of his audience. Time went by, but whenever Gil stole a glance toward the girl, she was still combing. He wondered how long it took this girl to do her hair. His mother had hair twice as long, and she did not spend hour after hour combing it.

The bear said, "Now for Lesson Two. Fleeing. Run up a slope if you want to get out of reach, but down slope if you want to wear them out. Bears and horses aren't built for running down sharp slopes. Bears can climb trees, but knights on horses can't. Ready to run?"

Lesson Two lasted a long time. The girl combing her hair on the rock watched as Gil was chased by the galloping bear round and round the pool, splashing through mud and water, trying to lift his heavy legs out of clinging and sticky soil, being lashed in the face by stubborn reeds and grass.

This running took Gil nearer the pond, and he got a better look at the girl. She wore a pair of round mirrored glasses that hid her eyes, but, strangely enough, they seemed to be sunglasses, not swimming goggles.

There was a flash of brightness in her hand as she stroked her hair, and Gil realized her comb was a comb of gold.

She pushed her glasses to the top of her head, revealing eyes that were large, dark, and with very thick lashes. She waved cheerfully when she saw Gil turn his head her way.

Then, she hid her mouth behind her slender white hand when the bear slapped Gil off his feet, and the peals of her silvery laughter echoed from across the water and mingled with the music of the falls.

"Look sharp!" bellowed the bear.

Lesson Three was in how to play dead. Gil, now coated in sweat and mud and bruised from where the bear had cuffed him, was taught how to back up while avoiding eye contact and then throw himself supine.

"Don't resist if a bear flips you over," said Bruno. "And keep in mind, playing dead only works on my folk. We don't eat dead meat."

Gil said, "What if I fight someone who does eat dead meat?"

"Play live." And the bear smote him again, for talking while he was pretending to be dead.

"But how do I actually fight?" asked Gil.

"Fight? A man fight a bear?"

"Yeah."

"You got a cannon? A big gun of some sort? All the humans I meet carry guns."

"Nope," said Gil. "Nothing like that."

"A sword? Knights have things called swords. Like a knife, but bigger."

"I got a stick," said Gil.

So Lesson Four was staff fighting. The sun, by this time, had traveled beyond the cliffs, the whole gorge was in shadow, and the air was cooler.

Bruno said, "Beasts like me get confused when you humans hit us with something at a distance. Best to use a stick. It is like magic to us. Hold it like I told you. Remember, the hand and leg should agree, which means whichever leg is forward, the same hand should be forward on the staff. No, you are holding it wrong...."

There followed another long, long period of the bear effortlessly blocking Gil's best blows and slapping Gil easily to the grass. The bear spoke while Gil struck again and again with his hiking staff.

"The key is to hit the head, the eyes, the snout, and the chest. Those are the weak spots. A swift kick or hard blow to the foe's left hind leg is good. Or aim for the top of the neck, just below the jawline. That could stun 'em. Then run away because anyone you knock down like that is not going to be too happy when he gets back up."

Gil glanced over at the rock, but the shapely raven-haired maiden was gone. He felt a moment of strange emptiness, but then he saw that she had merely moved to a smaller, flatter rock nearer to the shore. But then the bear swatted Gil again and sent him flying into the wet grass. "Look sharp!" bellowed the bear.

When the staff broke, it was time for Lesson Five: grappling. "This is a simple move, and it always works. Rear up on your hind legs, get your forepaws around the prey, and hug him. This will crush his lungs and break his ribs. And rip off his face with your teeth while you are doing it; that always demoralizes him."

Gil and the bear wrestled, or, rather, the bear crushed Gil helplessly while Gil struggled pathetically. Because the bear could not sheathe his claws, despite his attempts to be careful, Gil ended up with many long, shallow, and very painful lacerations on his back. And each time he climbed up out of the muddy grass, coated with blood and black with contusions, the next bear hug was even stronger, lasted longer, and drove him nearer to blacking out. The final time he did not even remember as the crushing grip was so powerful and so painful.

But he did remember that he heard the girl laughing a merry peal of laughter as he flopped once more to the soggy, trampled grass and mud. Then, he passed out.

3. Chow

When Gil regained consciousness, he leaned forward and shrugged out of the remnants of his torn shirt. Ruff came out of the grass and licked the claw wounds on Gil's back. Bruno said, "We're almost done for the day. Come back every day here before dawn, and we do this until the first snow falls, and you might start to get the hang of fighting."

The bear was talking about a period of time between ten and fourteen weeks. Gil sighed a long, sad sigh. "I would love nothing better, Master Bear. But my mom says I have to find honest work. How do I make money?"

The bear said, "Money? What is that?"

"You use it to get food."

The bear said, "Oh! Come on. I'll show you."

They waded through the reeds into the water of the pool itself, about chest deep on the boy, waist deep on the bear, who was a foot or two taller. "It is a little early in the season, but there are fish here. They are easy to catch, and this is good training for your speed and hand-eye coordination. Don't try slapping the fish out of the water onto shore. That is a showoff mistake. The fish, even if it is dead, could fall in the water and be carried away by the current. The important part is to snag the fish with the front of your muzzle when you strike, and then hold the fish against the crook of your elbow. This lets you grip the body securely with your molars and carry the fish to the shore."

They were closer to the brunette on the rock than they had been all day. The girl, by this time, had finished combing and was starting to braid her hair. She looked quite pretty kneeling on the rock with her elbows above her head as she braided a French braid on herself.

When she saw Gil once again looking at her, she put her nose in the air and turned partly away from him. Once, he caught her glancing sidelong over her shoulder curiously at him, as if she wanted to see whether he had noticed he was being ignored.

And then Bruno hit him in the face with a fish. "Look sharp!" bellowed the bear.

Gil splashed and lunged and slipped and slid and grabbed. Again and again he plunged into the water with his hands or threw himself into the mud, pursuing some elusive shape.

He looked down and saw, there beneath the waters, her pretty eyes hidden behind the round lenses of her sunglasses, the face of the girl. She stood up, and water sluiced from her head, shoulders, and arms. She had her hair up in a jeweled snood or hair-net so that a bun of twined hair, about the size of her two fists, was held at the back of her neck in a shape like a lobster's tail. The interstices of the snood were set with pearls and opals, and little scales or flakes of gold and lapis lazuli hung at her temples and ears and between her dark eyebrows.

The mirrored sunglasses hid her expression. In her hand was a living fish, writhing and gasping. She tossed it lightly to Gil, who, surprised, slapped the slender silvery fish in midair, let it slip out of his grasp, and watched it fall into the water.

He jerked up his knees in a convulsive motion, lunging through the mass of stubborn water, and threw himself after the fish. He slapped at the darting shape with his hands and managed to yank it toward his mouth. The only way to retain his grip was to clutch the fish with both hands and bite into it with his teeth. The frantic tailfin slapped him in the left cheek and eye as he splashed toward shore.

Ruff hopped up and down in the tall reeds of the shore, barking, "Toss it! Toss it! I'm open!"

Against his better judgment, Gil threw the twitching fish with both hands. Ruff leaped up into the air with an athletic bound, snapped his jaws shut on the fish, landed, and jerked his neck back and forth to worry it. The fish slipped out of his jaws and flopped energetically, but Ruff pinned it with both forepaws and bit off the head.

Gil threw both arms overhead and uttered a war-whoop of victory, raising little waves around his knees as he jumped. He turned, hoping to see the swimming girl's expression. But there was no expression because there was no girl.

She was gone.

Chapter 5

Daughter of the Deep

1. Being Schooled

The next day, to get to the gorge before dawn, he woke at 2:30 in the morning, took up the cot he was renting, slung it over his sore and aching back, and set out with Ruff. The pair hiked for four hours through wood and meadow, thicket and grass, following the deer trails. Once or twice when Ruff lost the way, Gil asked a morose crow or hectic squirrel for directions. Linville Gorge itself was on the lands of the National Forest, but Gil saw no sign of campers, park rangers, or any other soul. He wondered if he would be seeing the skin-diving girl again.

Gil found a narrow cave mouth in the gorge wall that led down a steep and crooked passage to a wide and sandy floor. He managed to wrestle the cot in through the cramped opening. Gil was not sure if training with a bear counted as having an honest job. The only payment he could see coming out of this would be lacerations, bruises, and sprains, frequent plunges into mud, reeds, cattails, and murk, and a fish dinner when he could catch it.

Gil looked around the cave with satisfaction. There on that rock he could start a campfire with a friction bow, which was something he had learned in the Boy Scouts. He had been a member of Troop Two when they lived in Tillamook, Oregon. Perhaps he could cut a likely treebranch into a trident to help catch fish. Ruff helpfully urinated outside the cave mouth to show that the cave was theirs.

The birds were twittering in the pre-dawn gloom, praising the coming light, and talking about their territorial claims or boasting about their mates. Gil could smell the freshness in the air. He stepped out of the cave, ready to start his first day of work.

That day, the girl reappeared on the rock at about noon. This time, he saw her appear. She swam up out of the deep part of the pool beneath the waterfall and climbed the rock nimbly. She took off the jeweled net or snood holding her hair bun at her neck and then undid her hair and shook it free with a toss of her head so that flying droplets caught the sunlight like jewels. She arranged her combs and long gold hairpins, her small silver mirror, and other toiletries on the rock before her.

She stayed and watched all afternoon while Gil practiced roaring, fleeing, playing dead, fighting with a stick, wrestling, and fishing. She sat watching him and his exercises and antics in the hot or blistering sun and in the wet or suffocating mud.

Unlike before, when she had watched and laughed, now she merely slept on the rock most of the day, coiled on the sunny stone surface like a graceful cat, her cheek upon her elbow. After her nap, she sang to accompany the sound of the waterfall, but Gil heard only a faint echo and could not make out the tune.

She only became interested after the day's practice was done, and Gil once again attempted to catch a fish with his hand. She crept to a closer rock and peered around the side impishly, showing only her eyes above the waterline. She had pushed her mirrored sunglasses back on her brow, or so Gil assumed, so he could see her roll her eyes.

That day, Gil caught nothing except a sea lamprey, which bit him. The girl laughed until her cheeks turned pink.

Gil asked Ruff to swim across the pool and find out who she was, but the dog gave him an odd look and pretended not to have heard him.

On Thursday she was not there at all.

On Friday she returned.

2. Water Sports

She watched carefully that day, applauding whenever the bear smote Gil to the ground, clapping her hands prettily.

After playing dead practice and before stick fighting practice, Gil begged the bear for a lunch break, so he could go talk to the girl. "At least I want to find out her name!"

The bear said, "Fine. I am going to go mug some bees and eat their honey. You have until I get back."

So at noon, Gil took off his one remaining shirt and swam out to the cluster of rocks near the middle of the pool. The wind was blowing across the top of the gorge, so a little fine spray from the waterfall was raining down onto the rocks every now and then. However, when he got to the big rock in the middle and climbed up to the top, he found it empty. She was gone.

Ruff, from the shore, said, "Hey! Hey! She's behind you! Look!"

Gil turned. There she was, seated on a second rock a little ways across the water behind him, tucking her hair into her jeweled cap, facing the other direction, paying him no attention. He called out to her, but either the noise of the waterfall drowned his voice, or, more likely, she was ignoring him.

He ran across the flat upper surface of the tall rock and dove like an arrow, hitting the water cleanly with little splash, and swam rapidly toward this second rock with his best overarm stroke. His head broke the water, and he clung to this second rock and shook the drops from his eyes.

He looked up. No one was here. This rock was now empty.

Ruff was barking. Gil looked back at the first rock. There she was, draped across the high, stony surface, resting on one elbow, holding up a mirror in her hand, the two smaller mirrors of her sunglasses hiding her eyes. Over the sound of the fall, he could hear her humming to herself, a serene, strange, tuneless melody of trills and drifting, dreamlike notes.

Gil wondered if there were a trick involved. How had she gotten over there so quickly?

So he dove and tried again. This time, when he reached where she had been lounging, he looked up and found her standing among the reeds of the shore, doing what looked like ballerina practice. She held her arms in the air, stood on one toe on the marshy ground, and lifted one leg so high her naked foot was over her head. It was incredibly graceful, but with her eyes hidden and expressionless, Gil could not tell if she were mocking him or fleeing because she was shy or simply crazy or what.

So he swam toward shore. This time, he saw her move. She made an astonishing leap, like something an Olympic athlete would make, from the shore into the pool, and then he saw her legs kick high above the surface as she dove under.

So with his best breaststroke he splashed toward that spot, only to find she was below him, swimming upside down, paralleling his course, peering up at him curiously. Gil wondered how she kept her glasses on her face when she dove and swam.

He drew a deep breath, kicked his legs in the air, and dove down toward her. Her face was expressionless as she drifted in a leisurely fashion into the deeper part of the pool, near the column of the waterfall. Gil could hear a throbbing in his ears. He did not know whether it was his heartbeat or the falling water.

The water grew darker as the two sank away from the sun. Gil was swimming forward with the whole of his considerable strength, and the girl was always just a little ways out of reach below him. She swam backward, waving her arms slowly in the water with her stroke, almost as if beckoning him. She could swim backward using only gentle, casual motions of her hands faster that he could swim forward with all four limbs and furious effort.

Then, she drew out her small silver mirror and looked at herself critically, pouting and pushing a hair strand neatly back into her gem-studded snood. And, somehow, she could still swim faster than he could, and deeper, using only her bare feet.

Gil was surprised at how deep the pool was in this spot. In the gloom, he could see a wall of rock to his left and his right. He saw the columns and pyramids of stone that rose to form the rocks of the surface. But he saw no bottom.

His lungs were aching, and his vision pulsing with a creeping darkness around the edge. So he turned, and, clawing with his hands and feet, he made for the surface. A streamlined shape darted up from underfoot, swift as a dolphin, and torpedoed past him. It was the girl, of course. He saw her silhouette above him, outlined against the wavering and wobbling image of the sun seen through the rippling water. She looked over her shoulder, her eyes hidden in her glasses, but she wiggled her fingers at him in a playful salute, kicked her legs once, and was gone in a spray of bubbles.

He broke the surface and stroked wearily toward shallower water. He heard Ruff bark. "There! There! There he is! Say, Gil, I was sure you were drowned!"

Gil's feet found the muddy bottom, and he raised his head. The girl was nowhere in sight. The one-eyed bear was waiting in the reeds, honey stains on his chest, but a grumpy look on his muzzle. "Are you going to play all day like an otter, or are you going to get to work? Look sharp!"

3. Tool-Using Creature

On Saturday Gil found himself unable to rise from his cot, overcome by the wounds and sprains of his rough training at the hands, or, rather, paws, of Bruno the Bear. For his lunch, he relied on what Ruff brought him. They ate a rabbit. Gil said, "I hope this is not the one I talked to. Maybe I should become a vegetarian."

Ruff shivered from nose to tail. "Brr! Don't joke like that. You give me the creeps. Besides, if we don't eat the lunchmeat animals, soon there will be too many of them. You should see what happened in Australia."

Gil spent the time writing a letter to his mother. Ruff wagged his tail and eagerly agreed to make the long trek back to deliver it. Gil wrapped the letter in some tinfoil he carried in his knapsack so that the dog could carry it in his mouth without wetting it.

The one-eyed bear looked him over and sniffed his various wounds. "I have some business to see to today anyway. Rest up. In the afternoon, do a hundred laps around the pond, alternating walking and running, forty push-ups, twenty squat-thrusts, twenty battlecries, and twenty play-deads. Your claws are too small. See what you can do about growing them bigger."

Gil stared at his fingernails doubtfully. "Men use knives. Speaking of which, may I today use that fishspear I made?" For, earlier this week, Bruno had strictly forbidden him to use it on the theory that barehanded fishing was good for developing his hand-eye coordination.

The bear said, "You Sons of Adam with your tricks and tools do not understand that strong tools make you weak."

"We need tools to conquer nature."

"Nature would have served you unconquered had your fathers not rebelled and eaten the food of angels before it was ripe, inviting death into the world before they were granted the authority to banish it. The mother of your race sought a crown above her station in the Night World, and the Night Lords answered and came. Too late now! Men have misplaced their names and do not know whose sons they are!"

Gil said, "Whose son am I?"

The one-eyed bear said, "You are not a bear cub, so how should I know? You must have the iron claw and iron hide called sword and hauberk to be attired as a knight. What I can teach is not fit for you. Another teacher would be better."

"I am not a quitter, Master Bear!"

"You cannot get the honey if you are too thin-skinned and bee-fearing to pry open the hive, but if it is a wasp's nest, there is no honey to get. I will tell you my verdict when I return after I talk with a wiser heart than mine. So, in the meanwhile, use your fish spear, Son of Adam!"

The one-eyed bear climbed out of the cave, turned, and thrust his head back in the cave mouth. "There is watercress downstream and honey in the hive by the old oak stump. Mind the bees. Try to grow your fur thicker to fend them off. That little bit you have on your head and chest is pathetic."

Bruno lumbered off.

4. The Mermaid

Later that afternoon, Gil was sitting on the one comfortable spot on the shore that was free of reeds and pebbles. A small stretch of golden sand, less than two yards across, formed a comfortable place to sit or nap, and he could put his elbows on the shore and lower his bruised body in the water and let the cool sensations soothe his many aches and sprains.

He took off his shirt, folded his arms behind his head as a pillow, closed his eyes, and rested.

When he opened his eyes again, the sun was in the western half of the sky so that the shadow of the cliff cut the vale neatly in half. The part of the pool near him was in shadow and looked as opaque as a gray mirror, in which the high blue sky was caught, and the far side of the pool was in sunlight and shined and moved like a restless living thing. Concentric ripples washed endlessly out from the pillar of the waterfall, going both into the light and shadow.

He saw the girl in the black wetsuit under the water a few yards away, looking up at him with her mirrored spectacles. She hung motionless in a deep part of the pool, almost touching the sand of the lakebed. Gil wondered why her body did not bob to the surface because she was not making any motion with her hands or feet to counteract her buoyancy. As he watched, and a minute went by, and then five, and then ten, he wondered how long she could hold her breath.

He knew it was good manners to stand up when a lady entered the room but did not know what the rule was when she entered a pool. He decided that a polite wave of the hand would have to do.

She must have taken his hand-wave as an invitation, for she darted with the grace of a seal to the shallower depth and stood up, the water sluicing from her black outfit. She wore her jeweled hairnet with its glinting scales of gold and pearl.

She pushed her glasses up onto the top of her head. Her eyes were very pretty, but he was not sure he liked the mirth he saw there. Was she laughing at him?

She said nothing, just looked at him a moment. He continued to sit with his body in the water and his head propped up on the sand of the beach, his brawny arms folded behind him, his silver hair shining.

He said, "I would offer you welcome, miss, but I think you were here before me."

She shook her head, bit her lip, and looked uncertain. "Where is the pooka?"

Gil raised a puzzled eyebrow. "Pardon me, miss, but did you just ask me where the poker is? I don't play cards. But, um, I can show you how to play mumbly-peg."

She scanned the shore, as if seeking something. Then, she turned back toward him and said, "I have an ointment."

Gil said, "Yes? I am sure it is nice to have an ointment." He suddenly found himself flummoxed. He had no idea what to say or how to say it without sounding like an idiot.

She took a few steps toward him so that the water was at her thighs, then her calves, and then her ankles. She wore a flat and narrow purse of folded leather on her leg, held in place by straps circling her upper thigh and knee. This was no doubt where she carried her mirror of silver and combs of gold and her other dainty gear. She was undoing the mother-of-pearl buckles as she walked toward him.

Her head for a moment blocked out the sun. Then, she stepped over him and knelt behind him on the sand. Gil was startled by this, wondering why she was getting so close, and he did not like having her behind him where he could not see. He sat up and would have stood up, except she put her hand on his shoulder.

"Sit!" she said, "This will mend your wounds, and it will not sting." In her hand was what looked like a silver clamshell about the size of a lady's compact.

Gil was not sure he trusted the look he saw in her eyes. She seemed to be having rather too much fun. "Is this medicine?"

She said, "I am the daughter of Glaucon and Narissa. Of course it is medicine, most virtuous and potent."

Gil turned around and showed her his back. "Go ahead. If you say it won't sting, then I– *YEEOOOW!*" He gritted his teeth and splashed water on his face to hide the tears of pain gathering in his eyes. It felt like someone had taken a lit match and run it down the scratches and lacerations on his back. "I thought you said it would not sting!"

She said, "What you feel is a bracing tingle. I have admixtures more potent that cause convulsions, hairloss, vomiting, and paroxysms. *They* sting. This is nothing. Hold still and stop whimpering. Let me spread this."

He could feel her fingers and palms running up and down the wounds on his back, and the painful sensation of heat spread and grew calm and sank into his skin. Her hands were incredibly soft.

While she spread the gel over his back, she began to sing. It was a strange, wordless song, lilting and warbling, with loon-like moans and high arpeggios. It did not seem to be on a diatonic scale but sounded more like something from ancient Japan, or perhaps from India.

The warmth and the calm were very relaxing, even mesmeric, but he resisted the temptation to fall asleep. He said, "Miss, we have not been introduced."

She said, "I have, but not you."

That strange sensation he often had of neither understanding nor being understood, as if ordinary words had gone on strike, now overcame him again. "You have what?"

"Have been introduced. I did it myself. Were you not paying attention? I have seen the bear many a time smite you for this fault, and it makes me laugh. Your eyes bug out wonderfully when you fall on your face or on your behind, and your arms and legs jerk this way and that!"

"Who are you?"

"I am the daughter of Narissa, who is the daughter of Nausithöe, and she in turn is the sister of Danae of Arcadia, who married Pelenore of Listenoise and bore him Dandrenor the Grail Maiden; and she is the sister of Elyezer of the Broken Sword and also of Elaine of the Sea (who married Garis le Gros son of Nichodemas the Fisher King), and, of course, Dandrenor is also the sister of...."

This all came out in one long, happy rush of unknown names and strange titles. "Miss, hold up. You did not actually introduce yourself."

Her voice was suddenly flat. "Ha! Well, I like that! You interrupted!"

"Do you have a name?" said Gil. "Or should I just call you Chatterbox?"

"I am of the Vespertine. You can call me Nerea."

"Nerea." He rather liked her name. "Nerea, if I may ask—"

"What is it?"

"—are you human?"

"Well!" she replied. He could practically hear her rolling her eyes. "What kind of question is that?"

"It is just that, well, you cannot be a camper, and you can hold your breath for so long, and there are no parents driving you here in a station wagon or anything, but you have jewelry and gold that most girls from North Carolina don't have. So I thought you weren't human."

"I cannot hold my breath very long."

"When you were swimming, you did not surface for fifteen minutes. Even a pearl diver cannot do that."

Nerea said, "I don't see how– eh?– well, now you've confounded me! What makes you think I was holding my breath while I was under water? I was breathing just fine. There! All done!" And she slapped him on the back.

There was no pain at all. He stood, craning his neck to try to see his own back. He reached around behind him with his arm and felt with his fingers. There were no tender spots nor bruises, and the long savage cuts had vanished. He felt no scars either.

He looked down at where she knelt. She had placed her purse on the stone and unfolded it into a larger shape and was tucking the little clamshell away. He wondered if his eyes were deceiving him because the folds of the purse fit into a smaller space than should have been possible.

"What kind of ointment is that?" he asked.

"It is made from the glands of a kraken who dies on Christmas Day and from the venom in the tooth of a sea serpent, mingled with mephitic and chthonic fumes that leak from the sub-sea volcanoes standing over the ruins of Atlantis, whose walls and fanes of gold and orichalchum the sea cannot corrupt. My father mingles it."

"You're a mermaid!"

She looked up and squinted. "You are a strange one! What strange things you say!"

He said, "My name is Gilberec Moth."

She nodded, but her eyes were not on him. She took out of her purse some phials made of ruby in which glowworms writhed, and other small glittering objects he did not recognize, such as an orb of luminous crystal and a gold instrument smaller than a pocketwatch. Then, she put them back in again and folded the purse flaps once more, as if trying to get her gear to nestle properly.

"I know who you are," she said absentmindedly. "I was looking for you."

"Looking for m– why?"

"We are cousins. No one in the family knows you are alive, but me." She took up the purse and its belt and buckled it around her waist and thigh once more.

"What family?"

She looked up, a look of surprise on her features. "If your mother did not tell you, I am not sure if I should say anything. She is known to be wise, so she must have a reason."

"Do you know who my father is?"

Nerea shook her head. "No one knows that."

"What about my grandfather?"

Nerea cocked her head to one side, a gesture oddly similar to Ruff's. "I did not forget him. Pelenore of Listenoise."

"What?"

"Pelenore Moth. He is the father of Dandrenor the Grail Maiden. Didn't you hear me? And Pelenore is the father of Elyezer, Elaine, and Ygraine. It is important whenever you meet another cousin, always to give your lineage, to see how close you are. We share a great-grandfather, which makes us second cousins."

"Then you are a member of the Moth family."

She squinted, which made her eyes glitter like amber. "You– it is very creepy that you did not know that. Your mother told you nothing? I had better not say anything either. She might—who knows?—hit me over the head with a riddle or something."

If Gil had entertained a doubt that this mermaid girl knew his mom, the doubt evaporated at that moment. "At least tell me what I am! Who I am? Who are the Moths? And don't just tell me that we are everywhere and get into everything. I already heard that!"

She seemed frightened by his intensity, but there was also pity in her eye. Nervously, she looked over her shoulders to the left and right, as if she feared eavesdroppers, but then she shrugged. "I suppose I could tell you that. Very well! The Moth Clan is the largest in the world, the largest of all time. You have relatives in all the worlds. Fairies and Phantoms, Elfs and Efts, Woodwoses and Wolfensarks, Verminlings and Vampires, Lamia and Lilim, Mermaids and Monsters of the Sea, all roam the world unseen of Men. And there are branches of the family who married all of them."

Gil was confused. "What does that all mean?"

"It means the family always takes care of its own," said she, and there was a prim but solemn note in her voice. "No one else will help us. The humans fear us for our elfin blood, and the elfs mock us for our mortal blood. We do not take part in feuds between the other talking races that escaped when Atlantis sank, because we have blood kin on every side of their quarrels. So we belong truly to no world. But we have kin in all."

"You mean worlds like in outer space? Mars and Venus and so on?"

"No. My cousin Mathonwy Moth, who is the greatest sorcerer of our generation, says no one lives on those frozen or boiling orbs except the ghosts of long-dead and monstrous civilizations, utterly given over to evil, whose graves and prisons must never be disturbed. My cousin Tomorrow Moth—everyone calls him Tom—flew once to the dark side of the moon, to the haunted ruins, in his father's aether-ship made of Cavor alloy mined from Laputa, greatest of the sky islands. Tom returned, but possessed by a morbid phantasm from outer space, and strange voices spoke from his mouth. He had to be saved by my gentle cousin Matthias, who is learning the art of quelling ghosts from a Holy Father."

Gil scowled. "So I have cousins who are mermaids and sorcerers, space pilots and ghostbusters, and I get to live in a cave, unemployed, in North Carolina?"

Nerea shook her head energetically. "Tom stole the aether ship! He is a very naughty lad! To venture into the upper void is forbidden. No Moths live there. When I speak of other worlds where we sojourn, I mean worlds like in the other hemisphere beyond the human two or the deeper levels of the mist. Lands of dream or death, or elflands or ogrelands. Places like that. Undersea. The Night World. You have the second sight, so you can see things that are not fully in the world of Daylight, the World of Men. Do you understand?"

"Not really," said Gil, perhaps a little crossly.

"We have the best family ever and the biggest. We get into everywhere."

"Why don't you have a fish's tail if you are a mermaid?"

She said, "I have a fake tail I can wear like a skirt on formal occasions."

"Why do you need a fake tail?"

"Like you, I am half and half. That is why I have to wear spectacles. I cannot see in the darkness far below the waves as well as my sisters. I also need my mermaid cap to breathe water."

"What keeps your glasses on your face when you dive or swim?"

"That is a dumb question."

"I am a dumb kid, and likely to stay dumb if no one answers my questions. What keeps them on your face?"

"Magic."

"What kind of magic?"

"Sea magic."

"What kind is that?"

"The kind that asks the elements of the world pretty please not to knock my glasses off my nose when I dive or swim."

"Why do the elements listen to the charm?"

"Because it's magic! I don't know. Why do animals listen to you?"

"I don't know." But then he frowned. Hadn't Ruff said something to him earlier this week about that? "Something to do with love."

She smiled a smug smile and nodded. "All good magic ultimately boils down to love. My cousin Mathonwy told me that! He is a magician."

"Do you know any magic?"

She shook her head. "I know it is dangerous. If you traffic or talk with dark powers, they come to live with you, in your house, whether you know it or not. And even the good magic is unlawful for true humans. There are some things people like us are allowed to do if we are discreet, but there is always a price. Even something as simple as never losing your glasses."

"People like us?"

"The Twilight Folk. We are neither of Dark nor Day. The Moths are the most numerous, and we are attracted to the light; the Cobwebs to the darkness. There are two other great families, the Peaseblossoms and the Mustardseeds, and several lesser ones, such as the Smithwicks. Twilights can interbreed with Daylights, and their children possess the second sight or selkie blood."

"Daylights are normal humans?"

"Yes. In times of old, certain noble families or doomed heroes were children of Melusine or serpent queens or pagan gods. Some of their descendants are also counted as Twilightish. The purebred selkie or elfs look down on us. Even the sad pagan gods look down, what few are left. In their worlds, we can only be servants and menials. But in a way, we have the best of both worlds because we can travel, explore, and invent like men of the Day world do and also work some magic like elfs of the Night world and behold their unearthly splendors and get away with it."

"There is a door in my house I want to open. It follows my mom and me around when we move. It leads to an attic that is not there. Can you open it?"

Nerea shook her head and shrugged. "I don't know anything about such doors. I mean, I know they exist, but that is an elf magic. They open and close according to the times and seasons and the stars, into places that were left over after the first garden was destroyed."

"Left over?"

"The cosmos is a made thing." She raised one arm and pointed at the mountains, trees, grass underfoot, great blue dome of the sky overhead. "All of it. All this. An artifact, built like a house is built. The Sons of Israel were told the name of the builder, but they never wrote it down. When all the paths to the first garden were blocked and the mountain on which it stood was thrown into the sea and lost, the whole world was jarred off its axis, and many things originally meant for joy turned into pests and plagues. The world started to age and fall apart. There were passages like servants' corridors hidden in a house where those dread powers tasked with the construction (and, now that it was marred, the repair) of the many chambers and mansions of the house were allowed to walk. These corridors were hidden behind secret doors or unsolid walls. The stars turn and keep the time, and the doors open and close."

"A bird told me you knew how to open a door like this."

"Not like this."

"How is it unlike?"

"The door you describe is controlled by the stars. We of Undersea know little about the stars. Our magic is of the whalesong and raging waves, of far horizons and of the deep where winds do not blow and sunbeams not reach. The Sea Fairies have different doors and different paths we swim. The star magic is not for us. The elfs have no charms against drowning in the waters, and only thus are we free from their wicked meddling."

"But you can open your door?"

"It is controlled by the tides. Yes. There is a passage leading from certain unhallowed ground nearby to a river in the dreamworld, which leads past gates of horn and ivory into the Witch City of Ys, and from there into Cantriff Gwylodd and Aegai and the lands beneath the sea. But the passwords I have for the one door I know will not work on any others. And I cannot make the doors move from here to there, as yours can do. That sounds like magic of the highest and most ancient blood to me. So, I answered your questions, you admit, cousin Gilberec?"

"Yes," he agreed. "But I have more. Lots more."

She held up a slender finger and gave him a look of mock sternness. "Fair is fair!"

"What is your question?"

Nerea Moth pointed at something Gil could not see. Then, he realized she was gesturing toward his cave.

"I am going to have to bring that cot back tomorrow," he said.

She said, "That is not my question. What is all this? What are you doing? Why are you living in the woods? With a bear? And letting him pummel you?"

"He is teaching me how to be a knight." He peered at her. "You are not laughing. You do not think being a knight is ridiculous?"

She shrugged her shoulders. "I do not know how surface dwellers do things, but being squire to a bear seems perfectly reasonable to me. You can never be a squire to an elf because you are a Moth and thus of mixed and impure blood. Although I had heard that in cases like this, the teacher is never seen, and the prentice is supposed to give him a bowl of cream on the doorstep every night. And make him a new suit of clothing before Michaelmas."

"You know when Michaelmas is?"

"Of course. Didn't anyone ever teach you the calendar?"

"Apparently not."

"How did you squire yourself to a bear?"

"I was looking for a job. A trade. You know, when you do work for money...."

She nodded. "I know. We have toil and trade in Undersea. My father ran an apothecary shop before he became the court physician to Queen Amphitrite."

"Sorry. I am used to talking to animals."

"But being squired to a bear is not a trade."

"I am not his squire. In fact, I think he is having second thoughts about training me."

"Well, of course. The squire owes fealty to his knight and liege, and it is a lifelong bond. Your bear probably cannot carry out his side of the bargain. I guess he is having trouble finding you arms and armor and a horse and such."

"You seem to know a lot about knights," he said.

The comment clearly pleased her because she looked down and smiled and said, "Oh, no, not really."

"Is knighthood still around in your world? Can I go there?"

She shook her head. "There are indeed knights in Undersea, and they are terrifying to behold because their weapons are typhoons. Our knights ride in coracles of shell, in chariots drawn by the hippocampus, or go upon the backs of war-trained whales in barding and plate like unto an ironclad, or in towers built upon the spine or brow of the mighty sea-serpent. You cannot go, not unless you learn to breathe water. And if I may ask…"

"Go ahead. Fair is fair."

"Why do you want to be a knight?"

Gil did not need to pause to find words. "Because my mom and I have lived in some pretty poor places, and in some pretty bad neighborhoods, but I never saw one which would not have been better if the people had helped each other out more. Usually, poor people do that, and a lot more than the fatter and happier people I've seen. But if they cannot trust each other, they stop. Stop helping each other, I mean. And if they prey on each other like wolves eating rabbits, they cannot trust each other. Every place I've lived, from California to Utah to here, if there were only someone to beat up the strong and protect the weak, then the neighborhoods would not be so bad, and the poor would not be so poor. It is as simple as that."

She said, "Why don't you go to where the knights are? They will scorn you because of your mixed blood, but if you watch them unseen, from a hidden covert, perhaps you can learn their arts. This can tell you more of their mysteries than any bear."

Gil said, "Real knights? In this world?"

"Somewhat."

"Do you know where they are found?"

Nerea Moth nodded eagerly. "The summer knights and winter knights shall meet in tourney over by Brown Mountain on Lammas Day. I know not the causes of the dispute, but the Summer King and Winter King both fear a general war would shatter the world, and so have agreed to allow Heaven to judge the outcome of their quarrel by the omen of the tournament. However, if you come, you must be very stealthy and subtle of foot! The Night Folk are not to be trifled with!"

But then she straightened up and pulled her glasses over her eyes. There was a click of noise from the lenses, and they both rotated and changed from silver-white to rose red. Then, the lenses clicked again and became a vibrant blue.

"The pooka returns; I see his heat patterns. Do not tell him we talked, please! I might get in trouble."

The warm sensation from his back now seemed to enter into his heart. "Miss, if you are in trouble, I will protect you."

She touched him shyly on the cheek with her hand. "That is sweet, but this is something that needs your silence to protect me, not your strength. Can you offer me that?"

"But you said the Moths always looked out for each other. I can be silent. I promise."

"Then don't tell the pooka that we spoke or where we are going. I will return when the day is right and not before. Don't bring the pooka with us! He is of them! More than a moon must pass before we meet again."

Gil said, "More than a month!"

She smiled archly.

Gil was not sure why she was so pleased.

"I return Lammas Eve," she said. "On the night of the Feast of Saint Calimerius, who protects against droughts, and so he is beloved, along with Nicholas, of the sea people. Look for me then!" She waded from the shore into the deeper water, dove, and vanished.

"Wait!" Gil called after her. "What date is that on the real calendar?"

5. The Pooka

A few moments later, Ruff came bounding through the reeds and tall grass to the little patch of beach. "Hi! Hi! Your mom says you have to come with her to church tomorrow because it is Sunday. Sunday is tomorrow. And she is glad you are not dead. Also, remember to eat vegetables and not just fish. And change your underwear every day. I think that is it. Oh! Oh! There is one more. She loves you. I told her you found a job wrestling bears and had your own place to stay. I don't think she understood what I said, so I kind of had to act it out with pantomime. She said you have to dig a proper latrine and smother your campfires completely. Uh! Uh! I think that is it."

Gil said, "Ruff? What is a Pooka? I have never heard the word before."

Ruff said, "An animal spirit. Ireland is mostly where we come from."

"We?"

Gil's heart sank. He had not realized that he had promised Nerea not to tell Ruff.

"Sure! Sure! I have relatives in Brittany and Aragon and Basque lands, and some in Germany, and I have heard of a tribe of us around the shores of the Caspian Sea. Why do you ask?"

Gil sighed, "Because I just think I did a really unwise thing, and I made a promise, but I don't want it to come between us."

Ruff sat down and let his tongue loll out. "Sure! Sure! Nothing can come between us! We're best friends! No secrets between friends! Share and share alike!"

Gil petted the dog, but a gloom was in his heart, and his face was sad. "Maybe everything will turn out okay," he said softly.

"Anything happen while I was gone?" asked Ruff brightly.

Gil wondered when keeping silence was the same as lying. It certainly felt as rotten in his stomach as a lie would feel. But he did not know how breaking a promise to the girl would feel either. "Do you know when Lammas is?"

"Sure. Feast day of Saint Peter in Chains. The Feast of the First Fruits. The Blessing of the Loaves. Everyone knows that! I am a smart dog! I know things like that!"

"When is it?"

"First of August."

"Well, I got a place I have to go when that date rolls around. You can't come."

The dog's ears drooped. "If it is dangerous, I can bite them. I can. Is that why?"

"No. That is not why."

"Then why?"

Gil only shook his head and sat down with a sad sigh and put his arm around the mutt. "I made a foolish promise. I cannot break a promise."

Immediately, the dog brightened up, and his ears stood up like little flying flags. "Oh! It's one of those honor things! I got it. Dogs know all about honor. Don't worry! You didn't hurt my feelings!"

And to prove it, he licked Gil's face.

Chapter 6

The Lights of the Haunted Mountain

1. Lady Day to Lammas

Weeks turned into months, and the days grew hotter, then scalding, and then hellish.

He saw the mermaid girl, Nerea, only once more as June turned into July, and then only at a distance because she fled when Ruff barked at her.

Gil outgrew his shirts because his biceps were bigger as summer passed away. He was not handy with a needle and thread, so he merely ripped the sleeves off. The exercises grew easier, almost as if the distances he ran and the weights he lifted grew smaller.

The bear he wrestled every day seemed never to grow any weaker, however.

The only count of time he kept was his Sundays, when he would trek back to church to meet his mother there before services. She did not let him spend even one night under her roof, which convinced him that she was up to something.

She rarely had much to say and answered obliquely when he asked about mermaids and exorcists and cousins flying to the moon. She did, however, buy him a thick leather jacket to wear to protect him from bear claws.

He did not tell her about his date with Nerea. He began marking off the days with a bit of chalk on the walls of his cave.

Gil wondered how to keep Ruff from simply following him.

2. Lammas Eve

Finally, the night came. Ruff was curled on his cot next to him, snoring.
Gil slipped away, taking his clothing in a bundle, and then only making
the noise and motion of getting dressed once he was out of the cave in
the cool night air.

He went to the waterfall. The moon rose and painted the cloudy sky
silver, and Gil saw the girl's slim silhouette rise from the waters of the pool.
In the dark, her mirrored lenses shined like the eyes of a frog.

She waded toward shore, saying, "Well met, cousin. This is for you."
She drew a pin from her hair and proffered it to him.

He looked at it in the moonlight. It was a nine-inch-long needle of
solid gold, topped with a pearl.

"What is this for?" he asked.

She smiled, "We Moths always look out for each other. Sell it for rent
money or groceries."

He proffered it back. "I cannot take a gift from you."

She would not take it. "Wages then. As my protector. We go into
danger."

Gil folded the pin into his handkerchief and put it in his coat pocket.
"Which way?"

She said, "I have brought an herb from the bottom of the sea that will
enable you to breathe water until the stroke of midnight. You must be out
of the water by then and not a moment after! All charms end at midnight!
We have many miles to go, and it is upstream the whole way."

Gil said, "What? We are swimming? Why not hike?"

"The watchful Night Folk walk the air unseen after dusk and have allies
among the insects, especially those that eat their mates or mothers. The
oak, the ashtree, and the willow, and any tree to whose ancestors in ages
past human blood was spilled in grisly sacrifice is theirs. They would not
wish their melee seen by common eyes. They are a proud folk and proud
of their noble blood, pure and fine. Take and eat this herb. It is bitter on
the tongue but sweet in the stomach."

The two of them climbed the rocks beside the falls. Gil started below
the girl, scampered up the rock to pass her, and at the top held out his
hand to help her up.

She said shyly, "That is not really necessary...."

He picked her up and put her on firm footing. "Consider it part of the services you paid for. Protecting you from falling." The moon was visible here now that they were above the shadow of the gorge, and it was full and bright, touching the trees and waters with silver light and blue shadows. He could see her face and saw her twining a strand of hair nervously about one finger.

He said, "Don't be embarrassed! You are stronger and faster at rock climbing than any of the girls at my school. My former school. None of them could get to the top of the peg board."

She giggled. "Were we competing? I would have picked a different contest. Do the girls of the surface world think there is shame if a tall boy made mostly of muscles has more strength in his arms than they do? I would be more ashamed if my fine and pretty arms were all thick and hairy like yours." Nerea held up her black-clad arms, one overhead, the other flung out at shoulder height, in what looked like a ballet pose. "Are my arms prettier than those of your girlfriend?"

They were interrupted. In the moonlight, they saw a large bulk emerging from the brush near the lip the cliff. It was the one-eyed bear.

3. The Parting

"Farewell!" said the bear solemnly.

Gil said, "Wait. What are you saying?"

"I spoke with Francis, and he told me you would go to look at the elfs. He said that once that happens, the training is done. You should return to the house of your mother after this."

Gil felt a stab of unexpected sorrow in his heart. The bear was better company than most people he knew. "Why? What have I done wrong?"

"Nothing wrong. You are not meant to be an apprentice to a bear. But tell your mother you put in a good, solid summer of work, the labor was hard and honest, and that your master was satisfied. You will find your wages on your doorstep when you return."

"Who is Francis?"

"He is a man who rebuilds old and broken churches. He was born a

Son of Adam but now has a better father. The beasts of the wild are in his charge. He and I are old friends. Anyway, it is time to part. My heart tells me we will not meet again, Gilberec Moth.

"Remember your lessons and learn to look sharp. You are too easily distracted."

4. The Upstream Way

Gil had a thousand questions to ask Nerea, but even though the herb allowed him to breathe under water, it did not allow him to talk. It tasted truly terrible, like a combination of lemon juice and Tabasco sauce. It also did not prevent him from suffering a terrible, nightmarish choking sensation when the water first entered his lungs.

For hours and hours he swam against the stream, watching the girl dart ahead of him and then fall behind. She rarely used her arms and kicked with both legs together. When he paused for a break, as he did every half hour, she would swim in a circle around him, tickling fish and doing loops.

On land her playful demeanor vanished; ashore, she was frightened and crouched, sneaking from shadow to shadow to go from one branch of the river to another, trying to stay out of the moonlight. But she shushed him when he tried to talk.

They stopped halfway in their journey to eat. Nerea had disappeared ahead of him, and when he came around a bend in the stream, he saw she had spread a white cloth on the sand of the streambed and had two fish, one in either hand. He was surprised to see that she cooked her fish. She took a small crystal stone out of her pouch and thrust it into the fish's mouth. The stone grew red-hot: the light of it could be seen shining through the flesh of the fish, and steam bubbled from its mouth. She took out something that looked like a cross between a switchblade and a two-pronged fork. It had two parallel blades, and she used one of them to skin and gut the cooked fish, which she proffered to Gil.

It was weird eating under water, but the fish had a sharper and more delicious taste here. Obviously, there was nothing to drink.

Then came more swimming.

Eventually, they reached a place where the stream was narrow, shallow, and swift. He put his eyes above the water but kept his mouth and nose under the surface. He saw her head next to his, the jeweled net in her hair glittering, her eyes invisible behind the round silver disks of her glasses. Silently, she raised her wet and black-glistening arm from the water and pointed.

There, huge in the moonlight, was the mountain peak. At the side of the stream were tall and silent trees. Between the trees, not far above them on the slope, were strange lights shining like a line of red-colored lanterns.

Gil heard trumpets blowing.

5. The Portcullis

Gil had excellent night vision, and the moonlight was bright enough to show him where not to put his feet, so he was able to rush up the slope without stepping on twigs or rustling leaves.

His heart pounded in his chest; his breath was short, but this was more from excitement than exercise. The exertion helped warm his body, which was cold in the dank, dripping clothes he wore.

On he ran, seeking the source of the silvery horn calls and the strange lights. He glanced over his shoulder. He could see the barefoot mermaid in her black wetsuit loping after him. The lenses of her spectacles were dark, perhaps turned to the setting she used in unlit sea-trenches, for she lithely avoided thorns and brush in the night under the trees.

She hissed a warning. He looked back. She was frantically gesturing to him to get down, to hide, and she jumped and rolled beneath a likely bush herself. He crouched down, wondering what had startled her.

The ground was trembling. He could feel it in his fingers beneath the grass. It was like a small but continuous earthquake, or the murmur of vast subterranean machinery.

Then he saw a huge slab of the ground, bearing trees, rocks, underbrush, and all, tilt down into the ground and form a ramp. Starting from the top, a sunken wall of rock was revealed. The rock was rich with geodes and crystals. In the midst of this rock wall, a vast open gateway was dug, leading into an underground corridor of polished onyx through which veins of cobalt and silver ran. From somewhere deep in the corridor came a golden light that rippled and swam. It was not firelight nor electric light, nor anything Gil knew.

When the lip of the tilting slab touched the bottom of the sunken gateway, there came another blast of silver trumpets, and up the ramp of grassy ground came floating lamps carved of titanic emeralds held in golden frames, as weightless as balloons, serene as fireflies, lifting themselves up into the night air, shedding light on the leafy trees.

Gil crept closer, straining for a view, ignoring the frantic whispers of Nerea telling him to stay back. He heard the tramp and stamp of marching men and the hoofbeats of cavalry.

A she-lion, gold of eye and gold of coat, came into view, and on her back was a naked child wearing a crown of white roses. In the child's hand was a banner of green. On the green field was the image of a lioness rearing up to claw a golden disk of rays.

Four warlords of the hidden world next emerged, their silver helms gleaming, plumes nodding, and their habergeons of white metal were set with emeralds and opals, crusted with diamond dust, and their spears of solid moonlight and silvery fire were inset with chalcedony, smargads, crysoberyls, and malachite green as blown glass. Their steeds were of some slim and lightfooted breed with tails and manes of white and tawny coats like creamy gold. At the feet of their prancing steeds sported swift and slender hunting dogs with silver collars and red ears.

The steeds moved in step. Bells on the harnesses rang with a strange hypnotic chime that sounded as if it were coming from beyond the horizon countless miles away, but also from a point inside Gil's head beneath his ear, both at once.

The steeds wore barding of silver mail and breastplates set with diamond-hued sparks of light. They wore helms fitted to their equine skulls, with crests and plumes to match those of their riders, and each was caparisoned and adorned in the colors, patterns, and images of the riders, shields, and surcoats: the first was a knight of roses, with images of the red rose on his shield and breast, and a coronet of sharpened steel blooms, set with thorns, was on the crest of his helm; the second was of lilies, adorned in purple and white; the third was the forget-me-not in blue; the fourth was the brilliant sunflower in yellow and black.

Behind were four more knights, adorned with the heraldry of hawk and hippogriff, falcon and martin-bird. But their mounts were some strange and graceful creature with the body of a horse, the tail of a lion, and the head of a stag. These steeds had split hooves like the hooves of a deer.

Behind them were four more, and on their shields and coats were images of apple, pomegranate, olive, and clustered grape with vine leaves; but these four were riding what seemed horses with the heads of rams. And the next four rode ibexes and were adorned with images of stars and crescent moons; and knights even more fantastically caparisoned on beasts even stranger came behind.

Gil saw windows cut into the sides of the underground corridor set with grilles of silver wrought into intricate floral shapes. From these windows leaned maidens of unearthly beauty in robes of woven moonlight. They showered flower petals onto the parade of knights.

There came a shout, and the elfin knights began to sing. Their voices were deep, beautiful, and sad, and Gil could not understand the words.

Now came a figure adorned in green and gold, and on his helm was bolted a kingly crown of golden tines set with emeralds, and on his shield was the image of a she-lion rearing, a golden sun caught in her claws. His horse was a massive black Clydesdale with a black mane and socks of white. He wore a face of gold with a beard of silver as the faceplate of his helm.

On four sides of this figure rode knights in black and gold mounted on leopards, each holding up a wand, and between the wands a canopy adorned with figures of stars and constellations hung over the head of the crowned horseman. Before them came a black chariot with diamond wheels pulled by a yellow lion in whose car rode a herald with a silver trumpet as long as his arm. Behind the crowned horseman came two massive and silent creatures that looked like walking trees of black bark and silvery leaves, with the faces of wrinkled old men solemn with beards of leafy twigs peering from the bark, and lanterns hung in their branches. Incense was mingled with the lamp-oil, and a savory fume in lines of blue smoke ascended from the tree-creatures.

The cavalcade moved down the slope of mountain, and Nerea and Gil followed at a distance, creeping from tree to tree.

6. The Tourney

Nerea said in fear, "I was not expecting to come across the portcullis to the underkingdom! We are too near…."

Gil said, "Not near enough, you mean! But now that I know where it is, I am coming back here…."

"It is never in the same place twice."

"How can it move?" asked Gil.

"How can the stars move? Keep your voice down! You must take care not to be seen! Be less reckless!"

Gil's voice trembled with awe and wonder. "Why is there a host of supernatural beings living underground in the national park? How can these things be? Why does no one know about them?"

Nerea said, "Because they enchant or slay those who glimpse them! At least cover up your hair! It shines in the moonlight!"

Gil had crammed his Gamecocks hat in his back pocket during the long swim, so now he stuck it on his head, wet and sopping. Gil took Nerea by the wrist and pulled her along after him, and she was unwilling to speak any complaint. Perhaps her eyes were flashing with anger at him, but behind the opaque black disks of her lenses, Gil did not see.

The two of them followed the marching cavalcade and floating lanterns.

They came to a meadow beyond which the wooded slope rose to a dark crest where a stand of conifers grew. A wide circle of the hills and gorges was visible over the shoulders of this crest, and unwooded peaks hung above them like clouds, gleaming in the moon, for the meadow was halfway up the slope of Brown Mountain, which was a very great mountain.

Between the trees were a line of red lanterns of black metal, floating motionlessly. They were the lights in the distance Gil had seen during the trip upriver.

A blare of trumpets, harsh and brassy, and the sound of gongs and drums answered the silvery shrill horns of the knights who followed the banner of the lioness.

From the pine trees now emerged a line of knights in silver and black, following the banner of a white wolf on a black field. In the cloaks and caparisons of the cavalry the winter constellations shone like bright diamonds on sable fabric. On their shields and helms were images and

crests of pinecone, spruce bough, and mistletoe leaf. Many of the knights
following the banner of the white wolf were mounted on horses, but some
rode wolves or reindeer or polar bears. One was seated on the back of a
monstrous snowy owl larger than a barrel.

Forth from the pine trees now came a woolly mammoth white as snow,
and on his back was a tower where a throne of white glass was erected.
On the throne was a figure in a dark mantle. His mask was a featureless
visor of white metal, and his crown was a rack of antlers.

All about his person strange lights like St. Elmo's Fire or Will-o'-Wisps
were seen. He raised his black scepter, and, at that motion, a chariot
pulled by a polar bear and carrying the banner of the white wolf rolled
forth into the empty field between the two armies.

The king in gold and green raised his hand, and the chariot pulled by
the lioness and carrying the banner of the lioness likewise came forth.

A youth in white standing in the chariot of the bear winded a semicir-
cular trumpet of brass and called out in a clear voice, "The High King
of Winter, Imperator of Elfinkind, Erlkoenig of Evergreen, hath decreed
that the cold and dark shall descend upon the cities of men before its
season this year, the first snow to fall on the Feast of Martin, and the
crops be poor so that the wealthy nations of the earth wax fat and proud
while the poor quarters starve in despair and misery, given over to envy.
Such is his decree!"

The herald in the lioness chariot winded his trumpet and called, "The
King of the Summer Country, Alberec of the Leaves, calls rogation and
defiance and says the winter snow shall not fall until Candlemas, that the
warmth of the world shall grow and the cities of men suffer floodwaters.
All plagues and bugs and pests that thrive in the overwarmth shall be
unleashed on mankind, much to their hurt, that they may blame their
benefactors, that ire and hate, riot and tyranny, descend upon the fools."

The youth in white called out, "Then His Imperial Majesty Erlkoenig
of Evergreen, the High King, calls insubordination, breach of peace and
insolence upon His Majesty, Alberec the King, and will prove the same
by force of arms; no untoward nor uncouth practice shall be permitted
here, nor chanted spell, nor sleight, nor miracle of the dark arts, but feats
of arms alone! Let he who cannot hold the field yield him gracefully and
without reserve!"

"So be it! Summertide accepts the terms!"

"The wood and wind, running stream and starry welkin are the witnesses! Look to yourself, thou wicked and stubborn-hearted King!"

The horses neighed, and lions roared, and bears growled, and all the chivalry of the gathered elfs sang and chanted a paean of war.

The two lines of knights readied themselves, and, at the signal given, charged. The lines met. Horses reared. Spears broke, showering sparks of moonlight. Riders were thrown headlong. The warriors drew their great swords, maces with heads like comets, or slender axes with long necks, and lashed with grace and fury. Blood and ichor flowed from steed and cavalier, and all was uproar.

Gil climbed a tree to get a closer look. Nerea crouched near the bottom of the tree and called up in a soft voice, "Now you have seen the knights of the seelie court and the unseelie. Come away now! I had not known the kings would be here!"

Gil was staring avidly, astonished at the spectacle. The bear-riders had broken through the line of chivalry at one point, and swift riders with crests of holly whose spearpoints shined with moonlight rushed in the gap, turning left and right to take the knights crowned in the flowers and feathers of summer in the flanks.

The chance of battle pushed the melee to one side of the field, and now it was practically under Gil's feet. Had he dared, he could have leaned down and touched the brilliant plumes of the struggling warriors.

Nerea climbed quickly up the branches and clung to the far side of the bole, not daring to look out, as the shouts and screams, beast-roars and clash of metal sounded just below her naked feet, and the dreadful, clear-voiced singing of the elvish knights, who chanted paeans and poems as they slew.

7. The Knights of Rose and Mistletoe

One stalwart knight, he who had been in the front rank and bore the heraldry of the red rose, came charging in, but had his horse slain under him. A knight adorned from head to spurs in gold and bearing the crest of the she-lion in his helm, came to the aid of the rose-red knight and levered him free from his horse, all the while striking left and right with a mighty sword, and no knight in the pale and sable of the Winterking dared approach. The rose-red knight came to his feet and fought on foot and rushed against one of the bear-riders.

They were close enough to where Gil hid that he heard their words. The rider on the bear had a mistletoe on his shield and an ermine studded with white diamonds rearing from the peak of his helm. He called out to the rose-red knight, "Withdraw! There is no shame for an unhorsed rider to stand away from battle!"

The rose-red knight called back, "I defy you! Face my blade, which is named Perledor!"

The first called, "That name is known to me: a valiant blade. And yet with ease might I charge and trample thee, Knight of the Roses."

"Who treads the rose shall feel its thorns, Knight of the Mistletoe!"

The Knight of the Mistletoe laughed and dismounted and lightly tossed his spear aside, instead drawing his own sword, which was made of black metal, in which silver runes curiously wrought caught the lantern-light and shined. "You are brave, sir! Then let us meet blade to blade, equally, that if you fall none will demean my name."

"Well spoken, sir!" said the Knight of the Roses and saluted his foe with his sword.

The two clashed, their blades ringing like bells, and the moonlight reflected from their silver armor grew brighter. Their shields were soon marred and dented, coats slashed, mail shirts torn, and copious ichor, brighter than mortal blood, steaming with heat, flowed from many wounds.

The Knight of the Roses dealt a ferocious blow to the helm of the other. The Knight of the Mistletoe staggered and fell to one knee.

"Gentle right!" called the kneeling Mistletoe Knight. "Will you grant me the gentle right?"

The Knight of the Roses was blowing and panting and did not answer but staggered with weariness. Another of the Winter Knights, crowned in a wreath of holly, seeing all this, galloped forward on a doe, lance ready, singing a death hymn, but the Knight of the Mistletoe called out, "Avoid! Avoid! This fight is mine!"

The Holly Knight reigned back his steed so sharply that she reared on her hind legs. The Holly Knight called, "Are you mad? He will defeat you! You are fallen! Forbid me not!"

"Back!" called the bleeding, kneeling knight.

"Proud folly!" shouted the Holly Knight. "The shadows will claim you this night!"

The Rose Knight called to the Mistletoe, "What is your name, Sir Knight?"

"I am Balin of Darkmere, youngest son of Bolverk. This sword is Woebrand, and it was forged by Weyland in Ultima Thule."

"I am Callidore son of Coll. You are of gentle blood. Rise. I will not strike until you have found your feet."

The Mistletoe Knight stood, pale ichor dripping from his arms and legs, leaning on his black sword.

Sir Callidore called, "Look to yourself!"

Sir Balin called, "I am ready!" and with a great groan lifted the black sword on high. But Sir Callidore of the Roses smote so fiercely the blade was dashed from his hands, and, falling, smote a stone, and broke in two pieces.

"I shall not yield!" called Sir Balin.

"Folly!" shouted the Holly Knight.

But Sir Callidore put his own blade, pale and shining Perledor, across his forearm and proffered it hilt first to his foe. "Sir, if you will not yield, nor will I disgrace you by granting you an unasked mercy. Take my blade, and we shall continue."

The Holly Knight said, "Ask for quarter, Son of Bolverk! Yield yourself, Sir Knight, for his might is greater than your own, as is his prowess!"

But instead Sir Balin of the Mistletoe took up the white sword. "I vowed to my father neither to retreat nor beg quarter this night. I cannot take back my word. Yet will you battle with nothing but a misericorde in your gauntlet, Sir Callidore?"

Gil saw that Sir Callidore had drawn a long knife from his belt and was prepared to do battle with it.

At this, the Holly Knight dismounted from the deer he rode, and came, and knelt, and proffered his sword to Sir Callidore. "I see you are a true knight of noble blood! Let it not be said that a Knight of Erlkoenig fought a man armed only with a dirk. This blade has no name, but after this night, poets shall call him Deathgift." The sword was adorned with holly leaves about the hilts and rubies shaped like holly berries in the pommel.

So the fight continued. Other knights looked on, but none interfered. By strange mischance, it was Callidore who fell, struck through the heart. He called out, "I am undone! Mine own blade takes my life which so long defended it! Sir Knight! To you I yield my steed and sword and armor, as is yours by right of victory. Other goods and lands, have I none. Sir Knight, see to my widow, Pastorella. I leave her in penury."

Sir Balin knelt and cradled the dying man's helm in his lap. "Let the stars witness mine oath unbreakable! Never shall I feast when she is in want nor call two coins mine own save one is in her hand. So swears Balin of the blood of Bolverk! And may all shame until the end of time be mine and my blood if I am forsworn!"

And he doffed his helm, and removed that of the dying man, his enemy, and kissed him on the cheek a peaceful kiss. Callidore breathed no more. And Balin sobbed.

Knights now came forward, awed and silent, and laid the corpse upon their spears, knights in green and gold upholding the right side, and knights in silver and sable upholding the left, deadliest foes putting aside their quarrel to honor the fallen.

And slowly they walked from the battlefield, bearing the dead knight gently aloft, and the floating lamps of gold or black, gleaming ruby or emerald, followed after.

8. The Discovery

Where the procession passed, battle was halted, clang of sword and battlecry fell silent. Friend or foe alike solemnly flourished lance or sword before his eyes to salute the dead, or lifted his visor on the backs of his fingers, or doffed his plumed helm entirely.

The lanterns that descended to follow the procession were now low enough to cast light into these open helmets.

For the first time Gil saw the elfin features. Their faces were those of youths, but fairer and nobler, unblemished and without spot or mole, with eyes shining with cruel wisdom. A strange and wild spirit hung about them like an inaudible music. Some were fair-haired, or dark, or had hair of blue or green, hues not found among men. Many were sharp-featured, with high cheeks and pointed chins and ears.

Not all had human faces. Gil was puzzled to see the face of a red-whiskered fox with a pointed muzzle and white teeth peering from the helm of one knight; another had the brutal features and blue cheeks of a baboon. Some who removed their helms had horns or antlers Gil had thought were part of their helmet crest.

Unfortunately, as the lanterns floated down to stream through the air after the procession, they passed near the tree where Gil sat, and the fighting in that quarter of the battlefield had ceased and was silent. So it was that when one sharp-eyed knight pointed at the tree and gave a cry, it was loud in the silence, and many eyes turned toward Gil, and the beams of the lamps of green and scarlet turned toward him, too. He was transfixed, as if with a dozen spotlights.

"Whoops," he whispered.

Nerea slid from the tree to the ground with acrobatic grace and began running with lithe, swift steps downslope toward a nearby stream. Gil came down from the branches more clumsily but just as swiftly when the tree branch to which he clung suddenly sagged and gave way. The branch broke, and he dropped.

There came a harsh cry from behind him. He saw one of the Winter Knights, a shape in silver armor mounted on a polar bear, bearing down on him, deadly lance-head pointing toward Gil's chest, with all the speed and weight of the charging beast behind it. Gil still had the branch in his hand, a long and stout length of wood. He parried the lance head, knocking it aside just enough so that it passed to one side of his body without piercing him.

Then, remembering his lessons, he played dead and flung himself on the ground. The rider, startled, reined up short.

Gil leaped to his feet, waved his treebranch overhead, and shouted an earsplitting shout. The bear steed reared up, shocked. With the branch, Gil smote the bear at the tender part of the neck just below the jaw, with all the force of his body, shoulders, and arms, just like a batter's best homerun swing. The bear-steed stumbled and threw the rider, who fell over the bear's head into a thornbush, and yowled.

Gil knew it would be wiser at this moment to run, perhaps to outdistance the bear on the steep downward slope leading toward the stream (for they were no longer in the flat meadow where the battle had been), but he did not run.

Instead, he tightened his grip on the stout branch in his hand and stood his ground.

The bear was rearing up on its hand legs and roaring. The elfin knight called on the thornbush to release him, and the branches moved and thrust the knight upright.

He faced Gil. In one hand was a shield painted with the image of a leafless tree, and in the other a pale sword. In the moonlit gloom, the eyeholes of the helm seemed as empty as the eyes of a skull.

Of a sudden three more knights crashed through the brush toward them. One was mounted on a horse; the second rode the strange deer-headed steeds of the elfs; the third, a ram. The steeds and men wore matching livery of silver and azure with the image of a winged gold cup. But each shield bore a different charge along the upper border: the first a crenellated label, the second a crescent, the third a star.

The first spoke, "My brother Sir Lamorak! My brother Sir Dornar! Behold a wonder: Sir Grimnir of the Dry Tree honors this ruck of common clay by dismounting to fight him afoot. The noble courtesy of Sir Bolverk so recently displayed has inspired this clownish mock!"

The second said, "Well spoken, Sir Aglovale: for I see the son of dirt repays the courtesy by assisting him dismount!"

But the third spoke in a bitter tone, "Jest not. This wretch and villain must be enchanted now or slain, for he uncouthly and knavishly smites the mount, not the man."

Gil shouted at the third rider, "Who calls me knave I call a base liar! I struck that bear fair and square! He was part of the attack!"

The third rider said, "Dare you address me thus, baseborn son of a whore?"

Gil stepped forward and struck the ram-faced steed in the skull right between the horns like an axman who cleaves a log in two with one stroke. Despite the armor protecting its head, the animal staggered and reared. The third rider wrestled with his reins, trying to bring his nervous, dazed steed under control.

The third rider shouted something, but Gil shouted louder, "Sir! Dare not to speak ill of my mother, who is the finest and noblest woman of the earth, lest you be made to pay for your foul tongue with your heart's blood!"

But the second rider said, "Who is this boy? He speaks not like a mortal man."

The first rider said, "What boots it, Sir Lamorak? By chanted spells let him be cast into sleep, and locked in the heart of an oak to grow up around him, and slumber until the day when all the seas cast forth their dead to judgment."

The third rider, who had regained control of his steed, shouted, "Thine is too mild a punishment for mortal insolence, Sir Aglovale! Let darker songs be sung, his limbs to shrivel to palsy, his hands and feet to swell, the pest and worm to torment his innards!"

Gil raised the tree branch again and called, "Who is this who uses tricks and spells to undo his foe? Knights trust in their arms and might, their courage and force! Are there no true knights among the hosts of Alberec and Erlkoenig?" For he had heard the heralds say these names not long before.

The Winter Knight, Sir Grimnir of the Dry Tree, chose that moment to sling his lance aside, draw his sword, and attack. He ran toward Gil, his shield high before him, and elbow high and sword behind his back, ready for the stroke.

But Gil recalled what the bear had taught him, so he struck the shield midmost with the butt of his tree branch and brought the branch over-head to block the downward stroke of the blade. The knight was strong, and the blade bit into the wood.

In one motion, Gil twisted, yanked, and struck. The blade was caught between two branches and forced out of the knight's surprised grip just as the branch came down and struck the knight on the side of the helm with such force that the Winter Knight staggered, his proud plumes broken.

The bear steed now roared and lunged, but Gil was quicker. He dropped the branch, knocked the shield aside, and stepped breast-to-breast to the dazed knight. Gil pinned the other man's arms in a vast hug, just as he had been taught. Then, Gil swung the other man's whole body toward the oncoming bear's jaws. The bear reared, confused, and raised its forepaws but could not strike for fear of striking its master.

The Winter Knight writhed in the hug, kicking his legs, and sought to draw his dirk from his belt, but Gil tightened his grip until the rings of the mail groaned and shattered. The elfin knight was as helpless in his handgrasp as a child.

The third rider, the one who bore a star above the winged cup on his shield, now lowered his lance, but Gil put his back against a nearby tree. The knight charged nonetheless, perhaps hoping to run his spear through Sir Grimnir and through Gil as well, but the bear-steed reared up to protect its master, roaring, and the ram-horned steed shied aside.

A cloud of black mist now came suddenly with a great noise of wind from the open meadow into the thicket of trees and parted Gil from the three knights. The mist turned white and then transparent, and here on a huge black horse sat a kingly figure in green and gold. His shield was adorned with the image of the lioness. In his other hand, a truncheon of gold set with pearls. "Halt this strife! Who mars the melee of the elfin kind with the gaze of mortal eyes?"

The third rider pointed toward Gil and said, "Sire, 'tis he! Stinking and swaggering, this son of a dirt pile, exiled of Eden, accursed, baseborn, and low, has the effrontery to intrude into our solemn tourney! How shall the oracle of victory be read if the fight was meddled with?"

The Elf-King Alberec turned his helm toward Gil. His faceplate was carven into a solemn mask of a hawk-nosed and bearded youth of craggy features; perhaps this was a true image of the face beneath, or perhaps not. There was no eyehole on the right. The eye within the lefthand eyehole was as green as the sea. "Unhand that knight!"

Gil tightened his grip until the silver-clad knight groaned and fainted. Gil opened his arms, and the body fell into the underbrush with a great clash of armor and did not rise.

Gil said boldly, "Your Majesty, with all due respect, your knight called my mother a name too vile to repeat, and I demand he stand against me for it and satisfy my honor!"

The Elfking Alberec turned his head and said to the bear steed, "What is he?"

The bear was still crouching tensely, his nose pointed at Gil. It said, "I don't know. He smells a bit like a human and a bit like something else—but a bear taught him to fight, and that is not normal."

The Elfking Alberec turned back to Gil and said, "Sir Dornar of Corbenec is the son of Alain le Gros, who is the son of Garis. In his veins runs the blood of the Fisher King. Why can he not call a man of no birth whatever hard names he will? Of what birth can you boast? Whose son are you?"

Gil said, "Sir, I cannot say." But he now picked up the dropped sword and shield of Sir Grimnir.

The second rider, who bore a crescent above the cup on his shield said, "What discourtesy is this? Why does this mortal son of the dirt befoul the celestially tempered weapons of elfland, rune-begirt and gem-beset, with the touch of his hand of clay?"

Gil said, "Pardon my impatience. I could wait until Sir Grimnir wakes and faces the choice either to yield them to me or to forfeit his very life, but I fear traitorous and unvaliant attack might come at any moment from your discourteous and rash brothers, Sir Knight."

The second rider said, "Discourteous, indeed?"

"Your brother Sir Dornar sought to spear me. There was no call, no challenge given, no defiance, no equality of weapons; I was merely set upon as a farmer might set his dogs upon a chicken thief. I would be imprudent to speak with rogues and highwaymen without a weapon in hand since there are no knights here to defend the innocent."

The first rider, with a growl of anger, now lowered his lance. "Is Sir Aglovale of Corbenec a rogue? The slander is not to be borne!" Gil, his face frowning but unafraid, held up the shield and gripped the sword as he had seen Sir Grimnir do, holding the blade back behind his spine. He set his feet so that his shoulders were pointed in a line toward his enemy.

"Halt!" cried Alberec, and with his knees urged his huge black horse to step between Gil and Aglovale. Gil now stood with sword and shield in hand, a tree bole at his back, and a dazed knight at his feet, and the great black horse before him. The gold-trimmed green cloak of the king fell across the steed's flanks like a tent. The three knights, Aglovale, Lamorak, and Dornar, were on the far side of the horse, and Gil could only see their plumes and spears.

Turning his golden mask toward Gil, the Elfking said, "Why comes this mortal here, who dares to trespass where the feet of the Sons of Adam are unwelcome and the eyes are blind?"

"Majesty! I climbed yonder tree to behold the splendor and courtesy of your knights, harming none and willing ill to none, and was suddenly beset by your loyal minion, who no doubt mistook me for an interloper."

"You say you came to gaze upon our splendor and courtesy. How is this not a trespass?"

"Sir, I was invited."

"By whom?"

"Sir, by the rumors in the forest, who praised the glory and greatness of your knights. I will not insult Your Majesty by claiming I had any ability to resist such an invitation, sir, since that would imply your glory is less than irresistible."

"You speak in a comely fashion, more elfin than mortal. But why did the rumors lure? What are the knights of Elfinland to you?"

"Sir, I seek to be a knight."

There was a murmur of laughter from the knights there, and even the bear steed snorted. Alberec, however, did not laugh, and his expression beneath his gold-faced mask could not be seen.

Alberec said, "We are Oberon son of Uther, called Alberec and Liosalberec, Elfking and Lightelfking. Child, you address one greater than any monarch of earth. Remove your cap."

"Pardon the discourtesy, Majesty, but I was beset by your knights in an unmannerly and uncouth fashion. I did not have a free hand." Gil brushed the cap off his head with his wrist, not releasing the sword in his hand. The cap fell to the grass.

Gil's silver hair shined in the gloom. The king's eye narrowed, but the other knights saw not what he stared at, for the king's huge mount blocked their view.

The first rider called out, "Sire! Why do you bandy words with this creature made of clay? What is he, that he claims we owe him courtesy?"

Alberec said, "Mortal boy, depart this place. Our world is not your world. Our ways are not your ways. Leave the weapons you took on the ground; Sir Grimnir did not yield them to you. Yet I see, even now he stirs. I hear his groan. You have been gracious enough to spare his life. It would ill beseem if a king of the summer elfs did not return the grace in like kind. I grant you your life."

But Sir Dornar spoke up, "Sire! If I may! That worm spoke proudly to me! I wish to smite him!"

Alberec said, "The eagle does not catch flies, Sir Dornar. Exchange pardons with him and grant him peace."

Sir Dornar said, "Sire! That is a command I cannot obey. Is it not honor that demands a vassal obey his lord the same that cannot accept such slights from lowly born?"

Gil threw down the sharp sword and shining shield he held. "I will obey the word of the king even if his own ruffians dressed as knights do not. Sir Dornar, I both beg pardon from you and grant it."

Sir Dornar sang out a word of rage in a strange language and spurred his steed, which lowered its horned head but could not charge because the king's tall horse was in the way. He began to circle around, trying to find a way to come at Gil.

But Alberec sang a song as well, words that hissed like snakes and climbed note by note through strange warbling pitches. The steed of Dornar staggered and fell, fast asleep, into a heap right at Gil's astonished feet, and the elf knight also sagged in the saddle, toppled slowly, and collapsed to the grass. Snoring came from his helm.

Gil saw what he thought were green snakes writhing and reaching upward, but then he saw they were vines of ivy. The king's song grew wild and strange, rich with passion, and mount and rider alike were twined in vines, hidden beneath ivy leaves.

Gil looked up. A mist blowing along the ground covered up the elfking and his knights. When the mist passed, they were gone, and the winter knight as well, steed and all. Only Dornar was left, breathing softly beneath a shroud of innocent-seeming leaves.

Gil picked up his baseball cap and retreated down the slope. He heard the noise of trumpets and the clash of arms in the distance, but he was not tempted to look.

When he came to the stream, he spent a while looking for Nerea but did not find her. From the stars, he knew it was after midnight, and her charm granting him the power to breathe water was gone.

He hiked across the hilltops beneath the stars, heading home.

Chapter 7

The Glass-Knobbed Door

1. The Shop

He walked without sleep, hour after hour under the stars. He returned first to the waterfall and the cave. By moonlight, it seemed so very empty that Gil knew Bruno the bear would not be back. Ruff was not in the cave. It took Gil only moments to pack his gear.

Gilberec Moth carried the folded-up cot on his back carefully through the empty streets of Blowing Rock, opened the door to the YMCA with his key, left the key and the cot in their proper places, and returned into the night.

He had marched through the night already; and he had another two to go before he reached his mother's apartment above the garage. The streets were eerie without any pedestrians, cars, or noise. Rows of unlit windows looked down blindly on the deserted streets. When the traffic lights all changed in unison from green to red or from red to green, Gil thought it strange that there was no one to stop or go.

He saw lights in one window halfway down the street, in a little shop crammed between two larger buildings. The front door was set back from the sidewalk by a small plot of carefully tended garden, including a line of pots in which miniature bonsai trees grew. Three gold balls hung above the door.

Gil pushed open the door, which set the small bell above the threshold ringing. Inside was a crowded shop that reminded Gil of the inside of the principal's contraband locker. It contained shelves overflowing with gizmos whose names he did not know, but also fur coats, wristwatches, umbrellas, toolboxes, appliances. There was a glass counter displaying jewelry to the left, beneath a line of hanging jars, vials, glasses, and bottles.

An old oriental man with long white hair, longer white eyebrows, his face as wrinkled as a prune, gazed at him with bright eyes. He wore an immaculate black suit with a thin black tie. A pair of pince-nez glasses, tied to his top button by a long black ribbon, was perched on the very tip of his nose.

"Welcome to Yung's Very Good Fortune Pawn Shop. I am Mr. Yung. How may I serve you?" he said in flawless English.

"You're open really late," said Gil. "Or really early."

The wizened old man nodded, his wrinkled mouth puckered into a polite smile. "Some of my customers prefer the nocturnal hours, for they are discreet and wish to avoid indelicate questions."

"Are you human or elfin?"

The little old man nodded again. "This is one of those questions where the question is more interesting than the answer. I am human, most human, sadly so. Are you seeking to pawn or buy?"

Gil unfolded the gold hair needle from his handkerchief and laid it on the counter. The old man tilted his head backward and stared through the glasses balanced precariously on his nose.

"This is fine workmanship, young man. May I?" he said, pulling a very bright goose-necked lamp with a built-in loupe in its hood over to peer at the ornament.

The old man swabbed a fluid from a bottle on the needle and peered again. He took up the needle and weighed it on a delicate balance scale against weights as small as flakes he dropped onto the other pan with tweezers. He placed the needle in a metered flask, drew out some water with an eyedropper, and weighed this against an empty eyedropper. "The alloy is also fine quality. The pearl is unusually large." He rubbed the pearl against his front tooth, licked his teeth, and peered at the ornament closely.

Eventually, he sighed, and spoke: "Aha. I would be remiss, young sir, if I did not tell you that there are others who could offer you far more than I can, such as the acquisition agent for a jewelry shop or a private auction house. Far more."

"A mermaid gave it to me."

The old man nodded sagely, his face showing no surprise. "Jewelry, I hold for thirty days. During those thirty days, anyone who returns with your ticket and the redemption value may take possession. After, the item is mine, and I may sell it to anyone I wish at any price I wish. You understand?" The gaze of the old man became sharp and cold, staring Gil squarely in the eye, unsmiling. "If you return here one minute after midnight on the thirtieth day, young man, the item is no longer yours, but mine, and you have no claim on it. I wish there to be no mistakes, no ill feeling."

"I understand. All charms end at midnight. But I would be remiss myself, Mr. Yung, if I did not warn you that the elfs take steps to hide their existence from men. I do not know if this needle will attract their attention or what they will do if it does."

The old man nodded again, "Sad memories, curses, and misfortune often follow pawned goods or adverse claims of ownership. For this reason, I have adorned all walls and windows, roof and floor, with many talismans and images of good luck, painted in lucky colors on lucky days. But if an elf returns with the ticket and the redemption price within thirty days, it is his."

Mr. Yung used no cash register. He wrote out the receipt ticket in a crisp, clear hand on a slip of paper adorned with frogs and dragons. Then, from a locked metal box in the floor, he counted out five hundred dollars in twenties, fives, ones, and Susan B. Anthony coins, and insisted Gil count the amount again so that there was no mistake. He had Gil countersign the receipt and pushed the money across the counter to him.

Gil put the coins in his pocket and swept the money into his cap, which he plopped on his head. He stepped toward the door, paused, and looked over his shoulder. "Mr. Yung, if I may ask: you do not seem surprised."

"One gets a wide variety of clients in shops like this, at hours like mine. One soon develops an acute instinct for honesty and a stronger instinct not to be curious about whatever strange persons enter the shop on nights when the haunted lights of Brown Mountain are seen." He sighed sadly. "I have lived in many odd corners of the world and met many odd persons, including those who cast shadows that do not match their shapes. I do not ask them if they are not human as you so boldly did. I dare not."

"Why not?"

"Count out the possibilities. Either he lies, or he does not. Either I believe him, or I do not. If he lies and I believe him, I am a fool and do not know it. If he lies and I do not, I know he thinks me a fool, and I am shamed. If he does not lie and I disbelieve him, I am doubly a fool."

"And what if he tells the truth and you do believe him? How is that bad?"

"I may hear an answer that those who walk in the night hours would prefer I had not." The old man took off his eyeglasses and wiped them carefully on his shirttail. "My life is behind me; therefore what little remains, I wish to remain unexceptional and uninteresting. No man can draw the tear back into his eye. Your fate is otherwise."

Gil said, "What is my fate?"

"Your fate is something you cannot pawn. As I said, I have lived here and there in the world. The places where the old tales are remembered are best, of course, but the very oldest tales are very sad. And it may be that the old ones are also found in such places, who draw near to hear what tales men tell of them. It is wise to be polite to all. Good morning."

2. The Homecoming

It was dark, and even the earliest of birds sang no song in the hour when Gilberec Moth returned home. He climbed the creaking, vine-choked stairs, shuddering with the memory of seeing vines something like these close over the snoring helm of Sir Dornar. The gnarled old Cornelian Cherry tree tossed its branches in an unexpected night wind, dropping hard berries on him, and the leaves whispered. Gil flinched with the desire to throw himself prone and to play dead, but he restrained it.

He opened the door with his latchkey, stepped over to the kitchen counter, sighed, and set his knapsack down on the tile floor. He did not turn on any lights. He piled four hundred of the dollars neatly on the counter. One hundred he put in his pocket.

He saw that there were jars on the counter and also on the folding chairs that were now sitting on the kitchen floor. It looked like every cup and bowl they owned was sitting out, all covered with Saran Wrap. In the gloom he could not see what was in them. He picked one up and stepped over to the sink. He put the jar into the beam of moonlight falling in through the window above the sink. A honeycomb floated in the thick fluid inside.

In the sink was a papery shell or broken sphere. He realized it was a beehive that had been hollowed out. It was the wages he had been promised by Bruno the one-eyed bear. No doubt the hive had been left on his doorstep, as promised, and his mom had laboriously put all the honey and honeycomb in containers to preserve it. How she had shooed away the bees, he did not know.

He put the jar on top of the money as a paperweight.

Gil stepped into the corridor, hoping to see the mysterious glass-knobbed door. It was the night of a full moon after all. But the blank spot of wall below the light socket was only a wall. He put his hand on his mother's door and listened. He could hear her soft breathing beyond. He raised his fist to knock, but hesitated, and then lowered his hand again.

He found his room. Already he thought of it as 'his old room.' In the gloom, it seemed too square and too stuffy compared with his cave, and the wooden floor was harder than sand. He carefully avoided stepping on the floorboards he knew squeaked and climbed into bed. The bed was much softer than any cot, and he was asleep instantly.

3. The Next Morning

He woke, bone tired, at the sound of his mother in the kitchen. He sat up and saw that he had forgotten to undress when he had fallen into bed. He was still wearing the same clothes, wrinkled, damp, torn, and muddy, he had worn during the long swim upriver to Brown Mountain and during his fight with elf and bear.

Gil fought off the impulse to roll over and go back to sleep. Instead, he rose, changed, combed his hair with his fingers, and walked into the front room. His mother was dressed in her waitress uniform, her hair hidden in a scarf. She was cutting fruit and bread with precise, delicate motions of her hand and packing herself a lunchbag. The lunchbag already held a jar of honey.

"Welcome home, my son," she said. "Why are you here? Were you fired?"

He said, "No. My boss quit."

"It was not clear from your letters or what you said on Sundays, exactly what your job was."

"Knight," he said heavily. He looked around for a place to sit, but all the folding chairs had bottles and bowls of honey on them. He hopped up onto the counter and sat on that, his shoulders sagging wearily. "I am a knight."

His mother froze in mid-motion, her eyes wide.

He saw her look, and said, "Sorry, Mom! Didn't mean to scare you."

She prodded the scarf with her fingers in a nervous, unconscious gesture, as if afraid a stray strand had escaped. Then, she smiled sadly, "Do not apologize. I have lived with fear for so long I have become friends with it. What lord do you serve? What lands did he grant you?"

Gil put his hands together between his knees, pressing his knees together and leaning forward. "You see, that is what I want to talk to you about, Mom. Any other mother in the world, if her kid came home and said he was a knight, she would ask in what TV show or movie or something. She would not say *what lord do you serve?* Would she?"

Mrs. Moth said in her soft but firm voice, "Other mothers may speak or not speak and may raise their children in whatever haphazard way they wish, but mine has been raised to answer when his mother asks a question."

Gil looked ashamed. "Sorry, Mom. My job is knight, but it was only for one evening. I have not been knighted and have sworn fealty to no one. But I protected a damsel. And she paid me." He nodded at the pile of money lying on the counter.

"What damsel?"

"Her name is Nerea Moth. She is my cousin. She is the daughter of, um, Glaucoma. He is the physician to a queen of the mermaids. Nerea's mom is named Nor'easter. Or something that begins with N. Anyway, we have a great-grandfather in common. Pill Ignore of Listerine. Nerea told me the names of a bunch of my cousins and uncles and stuff, but I did not recognize any of them, including two aunts and an uncle. Ebenezer of the Broken Sword. You have two sisters. Dramamine and Elaine. Elaine of the C. Am I getting any of those names right, Mother? Even one?" And now an angry and sarcastic note began to creep into his voice. "You see, I have not been over to my aunts and uncles every Christmas and Mistmas and Thismas and Thatmas, whose names I *also* cannot remember, so I don't even know what they look like or what their names are!"

"Elaine of the Sea is her name. She is much older than I. She married Garis le Gros, and it was hoped the wedding would calm the quarrel between the Fisher-King of Sarras and the Sea Fairies of the Aegean."

"Sea Fairies! Great! So there is an intelligent species of humanoid supernatural beings living in the Mediterranean that I happen to be related to, and you never mentioned it to me. And there are other groups living under mountains, fighting over the weather, and what day it is going to snow because one side wants to cause starvation and the other side wants diseases."

"No. One side wants pride and envy. The other wants wrath and sloth."

Gil leaped down from the counter and landed on the kitchen floor with a bump loud enough to set the honey jars rattling. "Why did I have to find out all this from a mermaid in sunglasses and getting my butt kicked by an elf-knight riding a bear, and almost get speared by three brothers until Oberon came–"

Her whole body trembled in shock. "Hush! Do not say his name! Titania is gone. He has lost his old crown and now wears a lesser one. Call him Alberec."

"Why, Mother? Why?"

"It attracts less attention."

"No, I mean why did I have to find all this out from talking to stray wolves and random mermaids? There is a world out there, worlds beyond worlds, in the sea and underground and who knows where else? Other hemispheres beyond the mortal two, whatever the heck that means! And I am a member of the largest and best family in the world, and you never told me! Why did you never tell me?"

She said softly, "Do not take that tone with me. I am your mother, and I gave you life. I surrendered my life to save yours."

Gil said, "I am the one you are hiding from them. From the family."

She said, "From the family and from others."

"From the elfs?"

"And from worse than they."

"Why do they want to hurt me? And do not tell me the tale is too heavy for me!"

"Your foes are strong and terrible, my son, my precious son." There was a sob in her throat, and her eyes were wild, but her face remained calm.

"If I cannot face my foes, how can I force my mother to face them for me?"

Ygraine shook her head. "The time is not right for the telling. We must pack, and…"

Gil shook his head. "I am not leaving. I have a bear cave where I can live now… except… uh… well, I am not leaving."

Ygraine picked up her lunchbag. "But I must if I am to catch the bus. Walk with me to the stop."

Outside, the red rays of the newborn sun painted the fields and trees a delicate cherry hue. The heat of the day had not yet come.

Ygraine walked rapidly along the empty road, but her voice was always calm. "Tell me more. Who saw you? What was said? You said you protected your cousin Nerea. From what did you protect her? How did you get this money?"

"From her. She gave me a gold hairpin, and I pawned it in Mr. Yung's shop on Blackstone Street."

She sighed sadly, and he realized that she knew the shop. His mother must have also pawned her possessions.

"Tell me more," she said.

"Nerea and I climbed Brown Mountain. Swam up, actually. We watched the elfs fighting. They looked like something out of a story-book, Mother. Like something from… from… from another universe, a brighter and better universe than this one. From a world where people keep their word, even to their enemies."

"It is the same world as this. Only the falsehoods and illusions differ. But, yes, the elfs are too proud to lie."

"We were found out, and Nerea ran away. I did not run. I stayed behind and fought them! They were armed with spears and swords, but I beat them with just a stick from a tree."

"For what reason did you not flee?"

"They were on horses. Or on something horselike. There were four of them. They would have simply outrun us before we got to the stream to get away. So I had to stand up against them." Gil looked proud of himself, and he put his fists on his hips as he marched along, hoping his mother would praise him.

She peered closely at her son's face. "Did you think of this at the time or later?"

Gil's face sagged, and his shoulders slumped. "Well, later. Much later. But it still counts. Doesn't it?"

"For what reason at the time did you not flee?"

"I could not run away. I saw how brave and noble they were. They would not have run away. I want to be like them. I want to be one of them."

His mother asked no more questions. They walked for a time and came to the sign and the shelter for the bus.

She stood, peering down the road.

"How did you escape?" she asked.

"I am not sure. Their king, Alberec, appeared in a wind of mist. I had crushed one of the Winter knights with a bear hug. The Winter knights belong to—"

"I know to whom they are sworn."

"—And Alberec's three knights were being rude. One of them called you a vile name. I told him I was going to thrash him for that. Maybe Alberec felt ashamed at how his men acted, or he liked that I downed someone on the opposing side. He told me to swear peace with Sir Dornar—"

At that moment, her lunchbag slipped from her fingers. There was a loud snap as glass shattered. Golden, sticky fluid darkened the paper bag and began to seep from it.

Gil looked down sadly and then looked up the road. He could see the bus in the distance. "Well," he said with sigh, "At least you can buy your lunch for once." And he held out a hundred dollars in twenties.

She whispered, "What was on his shield?"

"The shield was divided into blue and silver quarters. In the middle was a gold cup sprouting wings. At the top was an upside-down star. His brothers had the same shield, except for the top part."

She said, "You must forgive that knight whatever hard names he calls me. Any curse he throws on your mother will doubtless return to land on his own. The label is born by the firstborn son, the crescent by the second, the star by the third. It is the heraldry of the Lord of Sarras, the High Country, and they claim descent from the sister of Joseph of Arimethea, who brought the most holy and sacred Grail to England in the days when Nero burned Christians as torches alive in Rome. They are in exile on Earth, for Sarras has fallen. It is most passing strange that Sir Dornar and his brothers should be beneath Brown Mountain only a few miles away. Too strange to be mere happenstance."

The bus was coming.

She said, "Tell me who else knows of you. Either you and I climb aboard this bus, and we go to Spartanburg and leave all things here behind, or else I climb aboard and work my work and return this evening, and all is well."

Gil said, "Why didn't you tell me not to tell anyone my name?"

She said, "I sent you to look for a job in Blowing Rock, not in the woods, nor under the waters, nor under the mountain. I did not foresee that the dog would tempt you to go deeper into the older woods, where the mist is thin."

"How did you know that it was Ruff–?"

"Speak! The bus is nigh."

Gil said rapidly, "Nerea said she was the only one who knows I am alive. The wolf said everyone thought I was dead. After that, I did not tell my name to anyone, not even the bear, because it kind of freaked me out that the wolf knew me."

"What wolf?"

"*Canus rufus*. But he called himself Krasny Volk Odinskyy."

"It is better that you should name any beast rather than they name themselves. But we are safe for now. He has no pack and has no reason to speak to the Elfinking."

"Wait. What? How do you know that?"

"Who else learned of you?"

"A thrush and a mermaid. Oh, and the bear told me he had talked with a man named Francis, who told him I had to go back to my mother's house. He must have told him my name."

"Which Francis?"

The bus pulled up just then. With a shrill squeal of breaks and a dismal sigh the bus came to rest.

Gil said quickly, "The bear told me he rebuilds churches and watches over all the wild animals. Whoa! What is wrong?" And he put out his hand, for it seemed as if his mother were about to faint.

Ygraine took a breath and recovered her composure. Two bus doors swung open, one in the front and one in the rear. They were next to the rear door. A metallic smell seeped out.

"If it were Francis who told the bear to send you home, I dare not gainsay it. I see the hand of providence moving, though I cannot see the deep design. Some call me wise, but all I have learned through all my long years is how little we know. What does the mite who hides in the feathers of a sea mew know of the sea?"

The bus driver honked his horn and called out impatiently.

Gil said, "So, can we stay? Or go? Go or stay? I don't want to move! Mother, I–"

But she stepped aboard and smiled sadly. The bus sighed again, and the doors folded shut. Through the streaks of the door window, he saw her lips move.

Stay.

4. The Stairs

He watched as the groaning bus lumbered off. It was only when he was walking the long walk back to his house that he realized that his mother still had answered none of his questions. That made him feel more angry and more weary at the same time.

This time, as he walked up the rickety, creaking stairs to the apartment, he stomped with his feet very hard, grinning savagely, hoping to break a board or two. Because there was four hundred dollars still sitting on the kitchen counter, and, no matter what else his mother wanted to spend it on, he wanted to spend it on more boards and nails.

He was too tired to walk all the way into his room. He collapsed on the swayback couch and fell immediately asleep.

5. The Visitor

Gil was wakened by a loud noise. Startled, he rolled smoothly to his feet to leap out of bed, or tried to. But he had forgotten he was not in his own bed. The couch was narrower, and the smooth roll was interrupted halfway by an unexpected drop. He fell upon the floor with a painful thud.

Disoriented in the dark, he looked up. Light from the full moon was slanting in through the front window, illuminating the small, chubby faces on the standing radio and making their eyes glisten. Outside the window, in the dim and lunar light, the Cornelian Cherry tree looked like a many-armed monster.

The smaller square window in the door was darkened by the silhouette of a head in a low-crowned wide-brimmed hat. A matching rhomboid of moonlight fell on the threadbare carpet, so the shadow of that unseen face was almost touching his foot.

The sound came again. Someone was knocking.

Gil stared at the shadow in the window, his mind still fogged with sleep. Not only could he think of no one who could be calling at this hour, he could think of no one who would call at any hour.

Was it the police? Had something happened to his mother? Usually, on days when she left early, she returned early. If she had been asked to work a double shift, which sometimes happened, she could not phone home. There was no phone here. For the first time, Gil wondered whether this was due to their lack of money or due to his mother's caution. Perhaps she did not want her name on phone company records.

There was a click. The front door swung open silently and slowly.

Gil rolled to his knee and tensed, ready to spring. He was sure he had locked the door. Sure of it! He had fallen asleep without taking off pants or belt, so he drew his knife, putting the blade in the moonlight and holding it at an angle so that the man at the door would see it.

The moon was behind the stranger. He was tall and broad, in a black hat and voluminous trenchcoat. The reflection from the knife blade fell right across the man's unblinking eyes, which were deeply set and bright as the eyes of a hawk, as green as the sea. The rest of his face was in shadow, as if a mist were clouding it.

"Fear not!" The voice that spoke was as deep and low as the echo heard in a cavern hidden below the roots of a mountain, as timeless and distant as if ancient years and far-off kingdoms were speaking.

"Who are you?" Gil growled.

"Your father sends me. He wanted you to have this."

The silhouette took the lapels of the dark trenchcoat, one in each gloved hand, and drew them apart. On his chest was a fine chain, and hanging from the chain a white and glittering shape no bigger than a table utensil made of green glass. He took the chain in both fists, and yanked them apart, shattering it. The links fled outward in all directions and popped like tiny golden bubbles, vanishing. The glittering green shape was flung forward, spun through the moonlight, and fell to the thin carpet with a distinct chime of noise.

Gil's eyes, against his will, were yanked to the glittering object, but he dared not touch it. It was an old-fashioned key as long as his forefinger, with wards as big as the teeth of a rabbit, and the bow was a cross of Celtic design, made all of intricate interlocking spirals. It was made of green glass. A tracery of gold wire twined through the transparent depth.

"Is this a key? Is this *the* key?" Gil asked in wonder, his fear forgotten.

"What was your father's is now yours. This day you are a child no longer but are come into your legacy. Claim it!"

With a bang, the door slammed shut. The shadow of the head against the window nodded, and the deep voice called out. "Act in haste, before moonset, ere the door you are destined to open is lost!"

Gil jumped to his feet and tugged on the front door, but found it locked. He worked the latch and yanked the door open. The empty night was beyond. The man was not on the stairs nor on the lawn. Gil looked up, wondering if the man had jumped to the roof, or into a tree, or flown away on the midnight wind. He saw no one.

He turned.

The glass key was sitting quietly in a pool of moonlight, glittering and waiting.

6. The Door

Gil touched the key gingerly with a forefinger, wincing, as if he expected
it to give him an electric shock. It was cool and smooth to the touch.
Snatching the key up, Gil ran around the corner to the spot halfway
between his mother's bedroom door and the bathroom door.

For a moment, the wall seemed blank.

Moved by some unknown instinct, he opened his bedroom door behind him so that a rectangle of moonlight from the full moon entering
from his bedroom window fell into the hall. He thrust the glass key into
the moonlight. Immediately, the reflected and refracted beams of silver
light outlined the rectangle of the arched door. Then, like an optical
illusion, he saw or thought he saw a slight discoloration, a hint, a shadow,
forming two uprights, a threshold, like the hint of a door, half hidden in
the texture of the wallpaper. The top was a curved semicircle. The sides
were about an elbow's length apart. There was even a bright spot at the
right height and size to imply a doorknob.

The key grew brighter, as if it were gathering the starlight also and
casting that against the wall. The door was half-visible as if seen through
a fog of mist. As the light from the key played over it, the mist grew thin,
and the door grew solid.

Then it was there.

Gil touched the doorframe and the handle, noticing the little scars and
whorls in the wood-grain and the tiny hole where someone had removed
a nail. He touched the glass knob. Below the doorknob he saw the letters
GPM just where he had scratched them one moonlit evening with his
knife eight years ago. There were also marks about the latch where he had
once tried to pry the door open. There were no hinges visible on this side.
Had there been, Gil would have tried to remove them with a screwdriver
years ago.

He knocked with his knuckles. It was solid. It was real. Finally.

The keyhole was shining with light, and the glass doorknob caught
the reflections in the many triangles of its surface and glowed. He knelt
and put his eye to the keyhole. The staircase beyond was made of dark
wood. The passage was paneled with alternating vertical planks of light
and dark wood. A banister hung from little brass curlicues paralleled the

staircase flight. From this position, he could see only the lowest strip of the threshold above. There was a line of light, brilliant light, white light, coming from under an upper door.

Gil stood. He inserted the key in the keyhole. It fit. He twisted.

The key did not move. It seemed to be jammed.

Gil licked his lips, not sure what he should do. He looked over his shoulder at the window behind him. The full moon was very near the dark horizon and would soon set. It would be another month at the earliest before the door appeared again. And there were months when it did not appear at all.

Gil applied more pressure to the key, trying to turn it. It stubbornly did not move. He twisted even harder.

The glass key exploded into tiny fragments. The loop cracked beneath his fingers. Glass dust fell from the keyhole.

An agony of grief jarred his body, like a hammer blow running from his spine to his skull. His disbelieving eyes were filled with a torment of frustration. He shouted, "NO!" at the top of his lungs and then, a moment later, whispered a little sob of noise that was the same word again, very softly, "...*no*..."

He slumped, banging his forehead against the door.

It opened.

Gil was up the stairs in the moment. The upper door was also arched at the top, but it had no doorknob, merely a sliding bar with a peg in it. Gil yanked it impatiently open.

The attic beyond was filled with sunlight. Gil blinked, blinded, waiting for his eyes to adjust.

Facing him across a dusty floor was an oblong box. It looked like a coffin standing upright on its end.

Chapter 8

Attic in Elsewhere

1. Cabinet

Gil stepped forward nervously. Bright sunlight was pouring in through a set of small holes piercing the closed shutters of two dormer windows to his left. To his right were empty shelves and a pile of broken barrel staves. The floorboards were bare and covered with dust and prints of mouse tracks. Overhead was a main roof beam, with naked beams sloping down to the left and right. Gil noticed the boards were hammered into place with spikes, not carpenter's nails.

He turned first to the windows and found a simple brass hook to flip to open the wooden shutters. There was no glass in the window. He looked out upon the treetops of a rolling, hilly landscape. Below was a valley and a line of mist hinted that a river ran through. The trees were half leafless, half covered with green fur or tender leaves of early spring. Some patches of lingering snow could be glimpsed on the ground beneath the tree canopy. The sun was in the sky, and it was the same size and hue as the sun he knew, so he supposed he was still on Earth.

In the distance was a tower made of a material and set in an architectural style he did not recognize; the blue-green substance of the tower's conical top shined like metal, but there was also a sail or cowl that rose above the tower top to overshadow it, as if the architect were impersonating the look of a Jack-in-the-Pulpit.

Of the house he stood in, he could see nothing but the tiles of the roof, which were painted in a zigzag pattern of white, green, and blue. He saw a bronze roof ornament shaped like an owl at one corner of the eaves and at the other, a falcon carved of black stone.

Gil resisted the temptation to climb through the window and to explore this strange landscape. He did not know how long he had before the glass-knobbed door vanished or what would happen to him if he were trapped on this side when it did.

With both window shutters open to let the sunlight in, he turned back toward the attic room.

He was startled when he saw a man at the door. But no, there was no man. It was only his own reflection in a full-length mirror attached to the back of the upper door. This was not a glass mirror; it looked like a sheet of silver foil, laboriously hammered flat and polished.

The cabinet loomed large in the otherwise empty room. The disturbing impression that it was just the right proportion to hold a man's body did not leave him. It was brightly painted in silver and black, green and gold, with images of white swans swimming in green waters amid tall, thin reeds or flying though the night sky among waxing and waning moons, seven-pointed stars, or silver clouds where an angel bearing shield and spear stood watch.

In the four corners of the doors of the cabinet were carved and painted images: a sword surrounded with fire, a ring in the clouds, a chalice floating on the waters of a fountain, a wand standing upright on a mountain peak. Midmost in the carving, where the two leaves of the lid met at the latch, was an image he had seen before of a golden cup with wings.

Along the bottom of the panels, between the images of the cup and the wand, was a picture of a hairy apelike monster carrying off a screaming maiden by the hair. The hair was silver.

Gil touched the latch. The doors of the cabinet fell open.

2. Armor

Inside was a suit of armor made of a silvery-white metal that shined like starlight-shine on snow. There was a hauberk of closely-woven rings, hasped and clasped at the joints with clews of dark blue. Over this was a solid breastplate, with straps leading to the vambraces, pauldrons, and gorget. Gauntlets hung by the sides. These were made of white metal chased with tracery of black, tiny chips of diamond, and set with gems of jacinth. Beneath the skirts of mail were greaves of jointed metal, likewise adorned with ruddy jacinth stones and tiny diamond chips.

A pair of black leather boots was there with silvery shin-guards or greaves running from knee to ankle. There were straps around the boots to hold a set of spurs in place, but no spurs.

On a mushroom-shaped orb of wood sitting on a shelf directly above the armor rack was the coif and helm. The helm was a single piece without a visor, with eyeholes and noseguard set so close to the cheek-pieces that they nearly touched. The empty Y-shape where the soldier's face was supposed to peer forth seemed spooky, and it gave a grim and frowning aspect to the helm.

An ivory swan with eyes of jet and a bill of gold peered regally from the crest of the helm. From the earpieces of the helm rose silvery swan-wings. Gil could not tell if these were real wings or if a blacksmith had formed each and every separate feather from black and white metal strands. A fan of metal like the tail of a lobster hung down the back of the helm to protect the neck.

Hanging on two pegs on the inside lefthand door of the cabinet was an azure surcoat. On the chest was dazzling needlework. Here was the image of a gold-beaked and gold-footed silver swan with wings outspread, and above the sleek head of the bird hovered a gold crown.

Hanging on two pegs on the inside righthand door was a shield, flat at the top and pointed at the bottom, large enough to cover a tall man from shoulder to knee. The shield was painted blue, made of curved boards over a metal frame, and bore the same image of the crowned and silver winged swan as the surcoat.

Gil had studied in school as a matter of duty but had no love for books. He knew snatches and glimpses of history but not enough to put a name to armor in this style. It seemed half Norman and half Greek. The helm seemed Corinthian, decorated as if by Norsemen but with craftsmanship more like that found in Renaissance Italy.

Finally, in the highest place, hanging on two pegs above the helm, was a belt of silver studs. The buckles were of an unearthly blue-green alloy that shined like a polished aquamarine stone. The leather was tooled with images of flying swans and shooting stars.

He found the linen leggings and tunic quilted with padding folding in a drawer in the foot of the cabinet, and woolen stockings. In another drawer were a set of hammers and studs and pliers, a tin of polish, a shoehorn, and a set of spare buckles, rings, and straps as well as brushes and paint. A small box contained a jeweler's kit.

Gil did not remember deciding to try the mail suit on. Usually, making a decision requires some sort of debate or looking at options, weighing the urge to do something against the reasons not to. In this case, since every part of this mind was unanimous, there was no debate. He took off his pants and shoes and put on the leggings, breeches, and padded tunic first.

He knew that in times of old, knights need squires to help them get into their gear. But whoever had designed this seemed to have wanted to make it possible for a man to dress himself. The back of the mail shirt was drawn together across his spine by a clever system of straps he could yank from his shoulders, something like the straps on a backpack. The mail coif had a leather cap for padding. It went over his head and rested on his chest, shoulders, and upper back. The breastplate and backplate went over the head like the two halves of a clam and likewise tightened with two straps near the waist something like how a lifejacket is donned.

The helm was heavy and buckled with a chin-strap, and he could not turn his head very far left and right. But the weight somehow, in his heart, made him feel taller.

He took up the shield and inspected his reflection in the silver mirror. Both the mere mirth of wearing a masquerade get-up bloomed in him and a much more sober sensation of coming at last to see what it was he was born to do.

A weird feeling troubled him. He was sure he had seen a man dressed like this, the Swan Knight, earlier in his life. It had not been during the battle on Brown Mountain. It had not been in any movie or cartoon about King Arthur. Perhaps it had been in a colored plate in an old story book? Perhaps in a dream?

3. Arms

The sword harness was heavy with studs and buckles, and consisted of a baldric running from shoulder to hip and a belt that wound three times around his waist. He took off the metal-plated leather gauntlets because he needed his fingers free to work the buckles.

He drew the sword. It rested easily in his hand, weighty but well balanced. The heft of it sent a rush of sensation up his arm, as if his nerves and muscles from shoulder to fingertip suddenly were more serious and alert. Gil felt now, looking at this sword, the way he felt looking at the claws of a bear or the jaws of a wolf: this blade was the fang of man.

The pommel was a node of milky aventurine, the leather grip was white and set with silver nails, and the cross-guards were silver plated. The sword itself was a strange material, blue-white and mirror-bright, clear as silver and hard as titanium.

Foolishly, he tested his thumb against the edge, and found it as sharp as a scalpel. This drew a drop of blood from his thumb, but the blade was so keen he did not, at first, feel the cut. He jerked his thumb back in surprise, annoyed at himself. Would he have stuck his thumb into the mouth of a bear to test the sharpness of his tooth? He reminded himself never to take this blade lightly, never to draw it save in some cause grave enough to kill for or to die for.

Then, he saw a wonder. The drop of blood clinging to the very edge of the glassy blade changed color from red to black, hissed, and burst into flame. There was a flash like magnesium burning, too bright to look at, and an angular shape in some strange alphabet appeared in the depth of the blade, burning with blue-white light, and part of a second letter.

He only saw the letters when he blinked and beheld their after-image like ghosts behind his eyelids: The first letter was two triangles kissing, and the second looked like an N with two diagonal strokes instead of one.

The fire was white, not red, and was spreading slowly up and down the shining edge of the blade. The flames did not hiss or roar but made a low whistling noise, almost like a musical note, like what Gil had often heard putting too green wood on a campfire.

Holding off panic, Gil peered in the closet frantically. Surely anyone who owned a fire-hazard would always keep method to douse it close at hand? He saw nothing like a fire extinguisher among the jeweled gear and mystical elfin carvings. Then, his eye fell upon the scabbard. He saw that there was some sort of dark substance, shining like glass but gray as lead, coating the inside of the leather scabbard. He quickly slipped the sword back in place. The hilts slammed against the mouth of the scabbard as he drove it home. The blinding white fire was gone. The deep-toned whistling hum stopped.

In the sudden silence, he heard a noise behind him: a cry of surprise or pain. He spun. There was his mother, her face pale with shock, having come to the top of the stair while he was staring at the sword. She took two steps into the room, her eyes looking odd and unfocused, her pupils like pinpoints, and she swayed and started to fall.

4. Downstairs

Gil shouted in alarm and leaped forward, worried that his mother would fall backward and plunge down the stairs and break her skull. Instead, she slumped forward, and he caught her and eased her to the floor. But now he could see down the stairs the doorway leading into their apartment above the garage, where it was night, was beginning to fade and look blurry.

Taking up his mother gently in his arms, Gil rushed downstairs. The door was wavering like an image seen through water, but it was still real. Across the hall, through the door of his bedroom, he could see his bedroom window. The moon was touching the treetops to the west, but it was not yet out of sight. Was their time for more? He decided to risk it.

Up the stairs he ran. The cabinet itself was too heavy to move, but he yanked out the lower drawer containing the tools and cleaning polish, threw the gauntlets into the drawer, put the shield atop it to act as a lid, and leaped back downstairs three at a time, with the drawer and shield hugged to his chest. The sword and scabbard barked against his legs unmercifully, but the boots, greaves, and long mail skirt saved him.

He leaped back into the hallway just as the glass-knobbed door slammed shut, turned pale and ghostlike, and grew invisible, leaving the familiar blank spot on the wall behind.

Gil sighed. His shoes and pants, complete with his favorite knife and his latchkey, were still in the impossible attic in the other world. And the glass key to open that door was gone forever.

5. Church

Gil laid his mother on the couch, wrapped her in a blanket, and tucked a pillow under her feet. Only then did he remove the winged helm, which he placed atop the standing radio. He wanted to sit on the couch and take his mother's hand in his but found the sword was in the way. He did off his war belt, hung a strap over the nose of one of the cherub faces carved into the old radio, and propped up the shield next to it.

A sigh from behind made him turn. Ygraine had her eyes open, and she was looking at the helm and shield draped over the radio box.

She said softly, "Never lay your sword aside, except only to sleep, and even then, let it be within the reach of your hands."

He stood and stepped over to her. "Mother, how are you?"

She said, "I would be better if my son would heed my words. Never lay your sword aside, except at your lord's command. Keep your blade with you at all times, keep it with you when you sit down to eat or when you dance, and even in the bathroom when you take a shower. You drew it, and you have seen the fire of the blade. It is part of you now."

She closed her eyes. Her expression was one of great grief, and a sob escaped her lips.

Gil knelt by the couch and took her hands in his. "Mother! What is wrong? I am here. Everything will be all right. I will protect you."

She spoke without opening her eyes. "I would be more comforted if my son opened his ears. If you love me, then do as I say."

Reluctantly, he released her hand. Impatiently, he jumped over the end of the couch to where the radio stood, grabbed the sword and scabbard, and jumped back.

She sat up. "I will bind the sword on. It is the custom."

"Whose custom?"

"Our custom. The civilized custom. A mother who does not buckle a weapon onto her son never knows the day and hour when he was a child no longer. Stand and spread your arms." With practiced hand she wound the belts around his waist, and the strap over his shoulder. The weight rested more comfortably and more snugly than it had before.

He put his hands on her shoulders and looked steadily into her eyes. He said, "Mother, if I am no longer a child, now you must tell me."

She sighed. "Walk with me to the church. We will talk there."

Gil thought it was too late in the evening, or too early in the morning, for the church to be opened, but he did not object. He took up the shield in one hand and the helmet in the other and then stared mournfully at the doorknob. "How did people in the old days get around in all this gear?"

"They had servants," she said. "Men were more willing to serve those who protected them in those days." She showed him how to sling the shield properly on his back so that it sat comfortably but could be taken up quickly.

Then she stepped away into her room. He heard her moving boxes in her closet. Out she came again. In her hands was a long gray cloak or mantle with a hood. There were tiny strands of silver and little beads like dew woven into the gray substance of the cloak, and shadows clung to it in a fashion that was baffling to the eye. She threw it over his shoulders and told him to draw the hood up.

They walked in the gloom toward the little church on Westerfield road, less than a mile away. The birds were awake and singing, negotiating territorial claims and gossiping about where the juiciest bugs and worms could be found, but there was no sign of pink in the eastern sky.

Ygraine walked to the main doors of the church, which were not locked, and let herself in nonchalantly. Gil followed uncomfortably.

There was no light in the sanctuary and only starlight in the eastern windows. For the first time, he wondered if his mother had night vision as sharp as his because she did not stumble or hesitate. She knelt facing the altar, made the sign of the cross, rose, and went to sit in the back pew. She undid the scarf around her hair, shaking out the silver tresses, and then took a small lace veil like a doily and laid it across the crown of her head.

Gil followed and stood next to her. "Mom, this is a Baptist church. They don't do those things here."

She said, "If they will forgive me for remembering the old ways, I will forgive them for forgetting them, and Heaven will be pleased with both."

"Aren't we trespassing?"

"The day any town where we have sojourned learns the habit of locking the doors to its church, it is time to depart to find one that has not. There is no trespass where all are welcome."

"Should I leave my sword outside?"

"Never put that sword by you. I have now told you three times."

"And what you tell me three times is true!"

"Don't be sarcastic to your mother in church, young man."

He sat down, putting the helm down on the pew next to him. The scabbard like a big metal tail hung from his hip, and he had to guide it with his hand to lay it down next to him. It stuck out past his knee and bumped the back of the pew in front.

He said, "I just found out everything I thought I knew is false. And you know what is true. Talk to me. Tell me about the elfs, about my father, about you, and about me. Who am I? What am I?"

She gave him a sharp look. "What are you?"

He said, "A knight!" The answer came out suddenly, automatically.

She pointed at his boots. "Where are your spurs?"

"Well… I am a squire then."

"Whom does a knight serve?"

He growled. "Mother, this is not the time for your riddle games. Tell me what I need to know."

She said, "First things first. You asked whether you should leave your sword outside this house of peace, and it is not a foolish question. The Church Militant is and has always been an armed ark in an ocean of deadly monsters seeking to sink her and drown the world in darkness. Show me the sword. No! Unhook the scabbard from the belt and hold it up. The scabbard is like the bridal gown of your bride. No one should see her naked. Do not draw it except when you mean to kill or to sharpen and tend the blade."

Gil held up the sword in its scabbard, scowling.

She said, "All lands have warriors, who fight for their princes, and many a noble and valiant man is found among them. Only in Christendom are orders of knighthood found, who fight for our heavenly prince, who commands you to protect the weak, the widow, the orphan, and the stranger. Knights are governed by a code of sacred honor which sets them apart from soldiers and warriors of other lands."

"Samurai have honor."

"A very delicate and fierce honor is it, indeed, but is it not sacred honor. No Christian knight commits suicide to assuage his shame. Now, look closely!"

She held her finger near the sheathed sword, pointing at the tips and edges, the hilt and pommel, and she spoke as follows:

"All things in this world have a heavenly meaning hidden from earthly eyes. The sword's significance lies in the fact that it cuts two ways and may be used in three fashions. It slays and wounds with both edges and its point also stabs. The sword is the knight's noblest weapon, and he too should serve in three ways. First, he should defend the Church, killing and wounding those who oppose her. Just as a sword pierces whatever it touches, likewise a knight should pierce all heretics, attacking them mercilessly wherever he may find them. Second, the sword belt means that, just as a knight wears his sword girded to his body, so he himself should be girded with chastity. Third, the pommel symbolizes the world, for a knight is obliged to defend his king. The crosspiece symbolizes the true cross, on which Our Redeemer died to preserve mankind, and every true knight should do likewise, braving death to preserve his brethren. Should he perish in the attempt, his soul will go to Heaven."

She paused to draw a breath and to dab at her eyes.

She continued, "A knight should harden his heart against those who are false and impious, but he should be gentle toward those who are peaceful and good."

Gil stared at his mother in confusion and wonder. "Mom, do you need to lie down again?"

She blew her nose delicately in her handkerchief. "I had prayed that the day would not come when I was required to tell you these things. Do you understand the lesson of the sword and the charge I have laid on you?"

"Yes, Mother. Kill heretics, don't sleep around, obey the king. But…

we don't have kings in America, and I think being a heretic is protected by the First Amendment."

She said, "Among men, you must respect the laws of men. But men are the thralls and serfs, the gladiators and poppets, the concubines and cattle, the pets and toys of powers they do not see, do not know, and do not recall upon waking. Those few who by mishap recall truly and do know how truly dark the night is, they are called mad and hauled away screaming. Even the warnings those few who cry out are soon forgotten, sponged away by elfish mist. The laws of men do not reach to the night world, but the lesson of the sword I have told you does: In the hidden world of twilight are enemies of the Church, and fair seductresses, and faithless traitors whom you must slay, or eschew, or renounce." To Gil, the idea that all this was real, that all the mysteries of myth and lore might be out there somewhere, hidden to most but open for him to find, the wonders and the horrors both, was an idea that made him feel lightheaded and yet feel more hard and solid than he had ever felt before.

"Why not tell me before now?"

She said, "I kept you out of the twilight all these years for one sole purpose: the oaths of elfs are not like the oaths of men. They are not mere words but are woven with strong runes and cannot be broken."

"What does that mean, Mother?"

"The Twilight Folk are enthralled by unbreakable oaths to the Night Folk, who are bound in turn against their will to something darker than night, older than years. To have my child bound in service to darkness, I would lay down my life to prevent."

6. Two Worlds

Gil pondered this for a few moments in silence. His mother closed her eyes. Perhaps she was praying, perhaps she was merely waiting patiently for his next question.

He wondered if she were praying for his safety. He had a disorienting moment, as if he were looking at himself from the outside, as if he were just a boy like any other, who could die young as some young men do, in war or in adventure, and leave a mother behind him, grieving.

"I saw a letter written in this sword blade," he said, "What is it?"

"Dagaz, the rune of Day. The name of that blade is Dyrnwen, the fair white-hilted sword. It is one of the Thirteen Treasures of Lyonesse, taken out of the world of man by Merlin and haled to Avalon, kept in the Tower of Glass. It is a wonder and a mystery to see it in this hemisphere again."

"Do all elfish swords burn with light?"

"No, only that one, and only in the right hands."

Gil tapped the pommel of his sword. "You said the pommel represents the king I must serve. What king? I met Alberec last night."

"Would you serve him, my son? Even unto death? A knight does not give half his heart to his liege, nor to his lady."

Gil frowned. "I don't know. He seemed courteous and fair-spoken, as a king should be, but he and Erlkoenig were fighting over which of two evils to impose on mankind, the pestilence of heat or the famine of cold. Do they control the weather?"

"When man rebels against Heaven, nature rebels against man and serves other masters. Influence over nature their charms and songs and wicked sacrifices indeed have won for the elfin kindred, but no lawful authority."

Gil said, "There must be some king nobler than those two, someone who is not an enemy of mankind!"

"All true kingship has passed away from the Earth. You will find no sovereign worthy of your service neither in the daylight, nor in the twilight, nor in the dark."

He said, "Then I will look in more places than those. Speaking of which, where are they? The twilight lands and the night lands?"

She said, "The globe has more hemispheres than merely East or West, Oecumene or Antipodes, for there are more dimensions than the known three. There is a third hemisphere where Troynovant, the New Troy, rears her lofty towers and is the stronghold of the elfs and the other Night Folk."

"Wait. What? That makes no sense, geometrically speaking. There can only be two halves of a sphere, by definition."

"Elfish geometry is different. The mists blind the eyes of men, and they do not see how extensive their world truly is or how generous the creator who made it."

"So is this third hemisphere always twilight? Or how does it work?"

"The twilight is not a place, but a condition, when one has stepped halfway into the mists. There is day and night, summer and winter, for elfs as for men. The twilight of which I speak is of the mind."

"What does that mean?"

"Of the twilight are those folk and those places that the men can sometimes see or to which they sometimes might walk. You and I are of that order, as is your cousin Nerea. We are longer of lifespan than Man, but no less mortal than he.

"The Night Folk," she continued, "are the elfs and others on whom the passage of years lies with a light hand and the laws of nature do not fetter with chains of iron. They were born before Man, with fish and fowl, on the second-to-last day of Creation, and they shall descend into Hell on the first day of the second creation, when Heaven and Earth are remade. They do not age, and few indeed are the weapons that can slay them, but all will perish on the world's last day and be eternally damned. There is no redemption for them. They have no souls that can be saved."

"How many other intelligent races are there? I saw some people last night that looked like foxes or apes."

"There is no agreement of count: elfs and efts, albs and owls, loathes and linderlings, nephilim and nightmare hags, efrits and evil phantoms, man-wolves and vampires, or other Children of Cain whom the waters of Noah's flood did not destroy, mermaids and moorgoblins. Some are monstrous, but more dangerous are those that are fair to the eye."

"Why do they hide from men?"

"I do not know. It was not always thus."

"Why don't you tell people?"

"Whom shall I tell whose minds the elfs will not erase as easily as a palimpsest is scraped free of words no longer pleasing to the scrivener?"

"Since I don't know what those words mean, I can't answer. If there are twelve to fourteen intelligent races on this world, why don't they speak to us? Uh, to human men. Or open trade relations, send ambassadors to the UN, that sort of thing?"

"Those who speak on familiar terms with the dark world, or take gifts from it, are warlocks, and dire indeed is their fate if they repent not. And the elfs have no need to trade when they can steal."

Gil pursed his lips. "I saw a knight slain last night."

"Yes?"

"Was he like us, with some human blood in him? You said they could not be slain."

"No, I only said it was not easy to slay them. They charm their lives. Bullets will not harm any of them whose mother or sister knows the art, nor will any weapon that does not have a shadow to cast into the dreamlands. He may have been a Twilight Man, however, whom you saw slain."

"But Nerea said the elfs would not allow humans among them, except as servants. How could he be a knight?"

"She speaks truly, but at times an elf even of noble or royal blood takes a comely daughter of Eve to wife, and the elfs dare not despise the nobility and royalty of their blood, though it be tainted, and they hide their hatreds."

"Was he a member of the Moth family?"

"Who?"

"The dead knight. He said his name was Callidore."

"Describe his escutcheon."

"It was a red rose with green leaves on a gold field."

"That is the sign of the House of Coll of Tir-n'a-Nog. After Saint Patrick drove all the Nagas and Nagini out of Ireland, the Colls were bereft of all their menfolk, and so the three daughters of Coll, Maeve, Malen and Morgan, rather than see the extinction of their line, lured the heroes Oisen, Anchises, and Arthur to their bridal bowers. Their family is called Le Faye. They are famous for having bold sons well versed in swordplay and dark daughters well versed in sorcery and venom. I do not know if there are any intermarriages with the Moths. We are a very extensive family."

"Where did we come from?"

"Moth was the highest noble in the train of Titania, her seneschal, along with Cobweb, Peaseblossom, and Mustardseed, her chancellor, champion, and chief minister. The fairest Oonagh was merely the first of Moth's many mortal wives from which our family springs, bound to him in solemn rite and proper marriage mass. Some of our mixed blood have climbed by feats of arms or song into the higher ranks of the jealous elfs. Nerea should have said they try to keep us in the servile ranks, often with success."

"So I could be a knight among them!"

She shook her head. "No. I forbid it. There is none to care for me in my old age but you. I have lost three sons into the service of the elfs. No more."

"I have brothers?"

"Half brothers."

"Who is my father?"

"I don't know."

7. Two Lords

"How is that possible?" demanded Gil in outrage. "How could you not know your own husband? My own father?"

"He was not my husband. You were not born lawfully."

Gil was not sure what to say. Anger and curiosity and shame were like a nest of snakes in his chest, fighting and biting each other.

Eventually, she said, "This is the tale: I was once of a higher world than this and the daughter of the Grail King. I fled from the cloud-city of Sarras when Ysbadden the Giant slew the Grail Maiden, my sister, and stole the Grail. In swan form I flew to earth, doffed my robe to bathe, and was caught unawares. A maiden in exile without friend or family, I was wedded against my will to Alain le Gros, a puissant elf-knight of the Hidden Lands. He was sterile, but the charm of the High elfs is that all their daughters are fertile. I bore him three stalwart sons.

"A day came when I went a-Maying and wandered in the greenwood with my ladies and knights. Out from the darkness of the trees came suddenly a Wild-Man-O'-Wood."

"What is that?"

"He is covered from crown to heel with hair like a beast, but he has hands and feet like a man but a face like a jackanape. He is a woses; a wooly man; a yeti."

"You mean Bigfoot."

"I have not heard that name. With his club, his teeth, his great claws, he overthrew my knights, and seized me about the waist, and carried me off. A day and a night and a day he ran without once pausing for breath, and on his shoulders I was battered and shaken and half-dead from grief and thirst, soiled, fatigued, and bruised with great bruises, for he was not gentle as he ran."

Her voice was cool and soft, betraying none of the horror her words conveyed to Gil.

"He brought me to a cave filled with skeletons which served as his larder, carved by dripping water out of a rock on a small island in Goose Lake of California, east of the Modoc National Forest.

"For two years he kept me there, and I was shorn of my silver hair on the Eve of the Feast of Saint Walpurga. He told me his name, which was Guynglaff Cobweb, and he said he had slain Alain le Gros that same hour before he found me in the wood. Verily, he promised he would eat the flesh from my bones as soon as the cloak he meant to weave from my hair was complete, to cover his great carcass and render him immune to swords.

"Many a time I tried to build a raft or brave the waters to escape, but the trees and the waves were loyal to the Cobweb family, and betrayed me.

"On the Feast Day of Catherine of Sienna, whose hair like mine was shorn untimely, I wept and prayed by the shore, for I knew all but a small thatch of the hairy man's robe was patched.

"Then, beyond hope, I saw the shape of a tall knight approaching the island on a boat pulled by swans. He promised to aid and save me if only I swore never to ask his name. He battled fiercely with Guynglaff, but the white-hilted sword could not cut the creature. The Swan Knight nonetheless prevailed, driving Guynglaff into his cave. The ghosts of the dead he had slain rose up, and the bones of the skeletons clutched and bound Guynglaff while the Swan Knight piled rocks before the cave mouth and sealed him within.

"Away the Swan Knight bore me to his manse, which had tall windows of green glass and a roof tiled in gold, and a tall tower for watching the stars. There I was tended by servants whom I never saw. Food and raiment were provided, but there was no seamstress, no cook. Love and gratitude overcame my prudence, and in the darkness of a windowless bedchamber, I yielded myself to him.

"One night I climbed the tower and saw a bearded star and other portents by which I knew I had been betrayed and had betrayed myself, for I was no widow. Guynglaff was false, and Alain le Gros was still alive.

"Without farewell, and taking nothing of his, I departed the castle of the Swan Knight. From a mile away, I looked back and saw the manse had caught fire, and soon after it collapsed, and by this I knew the heart of the house had been broken, and the hearthstone shattered, by my departing.

"Upon my return to the cold and cheerless castle of Alain le Gros, the whispers of scandal immediately came, and at your birth you were called the son of the Wooly Man. I was commanded to give up my child to the tithe; instead, I gave up my crown and my world, and I fled to the world of men.

"Once more I departed in secret and swiftly, but this time I did not depart alone, for you were with me, wrapped in the warm feathers of my celestial cloak. The cold stone stronghold of Alain did not break and burn when I departed, however.

"On that night, within earshot of the stars, I vowed upon the northern star who is constant and stirs not, that my son would never give his vow to the Prince of Shadows, who is the vassal of the Prince of Darkness.

"If you present yourself to Alberec Under the Mountain, you will be required to bow and swear, and when Hell takes its tithe of the Fair People, it is you who will be selected to go into the utmost darkness, whose fires consume but cast no light, where there come no word, no music, and no sound save for the pandemonium of wailing, woeful shrieks, and endless cries of pain.

"For this reason, you may not be a knight."

Chapter 9

Errantry

1. Never

Gil touched his hand to his chest and heard the hard jingle of mail. "This is my father's armor, is it not? This is his sword. That is why you swooned at the sight."

"It is."

"Would you have had him not be a knight? Who then would have saved you? Am I not my father's son? You cast me out without an hour's warning to find honest work, and so I did, for you had faith in me that I could. Can you not have faith that I will find a lord to serve who will not serve the darkness nor offer me to this hideous tithe you fear? The Swan Knight was a knight, was he not?"

She stood, and, for once, her voice was trembling with emotion, and her normal serenity was gone. "We have discussed this matter enough! You will never persuade me to permit this! Never!"

2. A Short Never

As it happened, it took only four months of tireless pleading, promising, arguing, cajoling, wheedling, raging, sulking, storming, and begging for Ygraine to be worn down.

"One promise you must make me," said she. "To reveal your name to no soul, living or dead."

And so Gil promised.

It was an early morning in Advent, and the snow was on the ground, and a week remained before Christmas when Gilberec Moth, singing, and his dog, Ruff, barking, went out.

Gil's heart was soaring like an eagle, for he was armed and armored with his father's sword and habergeon, helm, and shield. The gray mantle his mother had given him was around his shoulders, blowing in the wind. Over one shoulder was his knapsack. Gil with the sun above him in the cloudless sky watched the shadow of himself passing along the contours of the snow, admiring the tall, sharp shadows of the swan wings projecting from his helm. Every now and again, Gil would hold up the shield in both hands, turning it so that he could study the handsome design of azure and silver and gold: a swan of white on a field of blue beneath a crown of gold.

They walked and gamboled through field and wood and back road to the main highway. The armor should have chafed and weighed him down, but in his light-hearted mood, he hardly noticed.

"Where are we going, Gil? Where?"

"Errantry!" shouted Gil. "We are knights errant!"

"Which means what?"

Gil looked up and down the highway. "I think it means we should head for Brown Mountain and look for the elfs. Do you think anyone would give a ride to a knight errant?"

Ruff's ears drooped. "No one picks up a hitchhiker with a dog."

3. A Long Hike

It was a little before noon, and the boy and his dog were trudging up the snowy slopes of Brown Mountain.

Hours passed as they searched. Ruff and Gil were seeking the door into the mountain from which the knightly elfs had come. Ruff cast about, sniffing and hunting, but said the door must not be in this part of the mountain.

Ruff said, "You know, you know, I am pretty sure elf doors move around. You cannot get in unless you know the right words. Besides,

you were probably looking at a postern door, you know? The back door.
I bet the big one is farther up."

"No," said Gil crossly, "I am sure the door was around here. That is the
stream Nerea and I swum up. Or is it swimmed?"

Ruff said, "Mermaids can do both."

"And there is a waterfall farther upstream I do not remember swimming
up."

"Mermaids can find strange shortcuts and go around things even when
there is no way around. We are looking in the wrong spot."

Gil looked at him suspiciously, "Are you afraid of meeting the elfs?"

Ruff said, "Do I look crazy? Of course I am. But I am not sure this is
the spot to look... Look! Look!"

"I heard you."

"No, I mean look! Look over there." And he pointed with his nose.

Gil said, "I don't see anything."

"Human eyesight! Who in the world put you in charge of the world?
Let's go!"

"Wait! What did you see?"

But Ruff was already running across the snow at a gallop, flinging
snowflakes high and wild, barking.

Gil, his armor clanging and ringing at every jarring footfall, pounded
after him.

The two went into a valley and then came up to a rise where a line of
pine trees stood, their branches white. Ruff hunkered low to the ground
and crept forward stealthily, his hindquarters quivering with excitement.
Gil did not need to be told. He threw himself on his face and crawled
forward on elbows and knees, trying not to groan under the weight of
the forty pounds of metal he was carrying. He had to undo his chinstrap
and wiggled the helm off his head because the neckpiece otherwise would
have prevented him from craning his neck, and the eyeholes would have
restricted his peripheral vision.

He looked.

The valley below them was half hidden by clouds of fog crawling like
giant white snails through the scattered trees. Gil saw a set of tracks in
the snow in the near distance, going down the slope away from him and

disappearing into the fog. It was two or three parallel pairs of naked feet, accompanied by paw prints too large to be from any natural creature.

Gil starting crawling forward, trying to get a better look at the prints, but a low growl from Ruff warned him to freeze. Gil held still and squinted, peering.

On the far side of the little valley, emerging from the fog that filled the valley floor, now came furry figures. At first Gil thought it was a troop of apes and a very shaggy pony. He could not see clearly because of the intervening branches.

But then the trio reached the crest of the rise opposite Gil. There were no trees there, and Gil saw the distant figures clearly against the blue sky beyond.

They were covered in hair from head to foot and moved with a rolling gait with knuckles near the ground. The one in the lead was carrying a war axe. The one in the rear turned, and Gil saw a wild beard and blazing eyes. It had fangs like a baboon and nostrils like an ape.

"Bigfoot..." whispered Gil.

Ruff said, "Oh, no! Oh, no! Those are Woses. Their charm is in their fur. You cannot fight them."

Gil recalled where he had heard the name of the creatures before. A tremor of hate shivered through his body.

"I can fight them. I will!"

"No one fights the Abominable Snowmen. And I also smell a wolf around here. A big wolf."

"Ruff, I am going after those guys."

"Okay! Okay! Just... Let's be careful."

4. Ford

It is possible that they were too careful because the afternoon went by, and the yeti eluded them. In one place, two hours later, the trail crossed a stream partly covered with ice, and in the muddy banks was a wolf print twice the size it should have been.

Ruff said, "Are you sure we want to be following these guys?"

Gil said, "I am supposed to be a knight. They do knightly things."

"You don't have a horse," said Ruff. "Can you even be a knight without a horse?"

Gil said, "We already talked about this. I read every book in the library about knighthood, but just reading about fencing and jousting and practicing on my own after work is no good."

Gil had been working as a groom at the local farm of a man named Hoosick. He had made several friends among the horses there but could not remember the names of the other farmhands. That job ended with the harvest a few weeks back and had given Gil more time to pester his mom about being a knight.

"I need money to buy Mom something nice for Christmas. So I am seeking some traitor knight or robber baron to beat up. If I win, I get his arms and armor and his horse. It is called the victor's right. I figure I can pawn the arms and armor at Mr. Yung's pawn shop. Mr. Yung gave me a good price for Nerea's golden hair pin."

"Why not pawn that armor you got on?"

"A dog would not understand."

"Well, I understand we got to go farther upstream to find a ford. These guys are pretty darned tall, and the water neck deep on them would be over your head."

Gil said, "I bet they are heading for Blowing Rock, aren't they? My hometown."

5. Rest Stop

It was night. The two came out of the woods into an oversized parking lot. There were a weigh station, a diesel pump, and a cluster of diners and convenience stores gathered into a rough semicircle around the parking lot. Beyond that were trees with snow on their branches, and beyond them the square shadows of a long-abandoned railway station. Beyond the railway station Gil could see the town square of Blowing Rock. The shops and the courthouse had been decorated with giant snowflakes and neon candy canes. There was a giant pine tree in the square draped with colored lights, with an electric star on the highest bough. The star was taller than the tallest building there.

Gil said, "Seems really strange they would head into my hometown. Won't someone see them?"

Ruff said, "They can hide themselves in a mist."

"Can you find them?"

"Sure! Sure! Just watch me!"

Ruff went carefully around the parking lot once, twice, and then a third time.

He came slowly back, ears drooping and tail dragging. "Nothing. I lost him." And Ruff hung his head.

Gil said, "I am not going home to my mom and telling her my first day out as a knight errant was a bust! We got to think of something. Got to come up with an idea."

Gil and Ruff stood in the snow among the parked trucks beneath a buzzing neon light. Gil said glumly, "I wish there was a squirrel or something I could ask which way they went. I don't like the winter. All the birds stop talking. Animals hibernate. I am used to hearing voices."

Ruff perked up, "Hey! Hey! I got an idea!"

"What?"

"You can talk! You! That way it won't seem so quiet. Dogs like talking. Especially when you say *good dog*! Talking like that is best."

"Great idea," said Gil sarcastically.

Ruff's ears drooped.

Gil sighed, seeing it was unfair to take out his bad mood on Ruff, so he scratched him behind the ears. "Good boy! Good dog!"

"See!" exclaimed Ruff, his tongue lolling. "That was fun!"

Gil found himself grinning. "I guess it *is* fun." Gil looked thoughtful. "Come to think of it, speaking of, um, speaking, I think I should say something when I yell like Bruno taught me. Like words. A battle cry."

"How about '*Go Hornets!*'—?"

"What's that?"

"It's the battle cry of your school you got kicked out of. You know, when you were expelled."

"I don't think I am legally allowed to use that any more."

Ruff said, "How about '*Merry Christmas!*'—?"

"I am not sure if that counts as a battle cry."

"It is something I hear a lot of humans say about this time of year. Whoops!"

"What is it? What is it, boy?"

Ruff suddenly barked and looked excited, "Oh, no! Oh, no! I smell something elfish."

"It is them?"

"No, but it is something!"

"Lead the way!" Gil took up his shield and followed the scampering black-and-white dog across the parking lot, his mail jingling as he jogged.

Ruff sniffed at the glass door of a burger joint. The glass was fogged with condensation. Gil pushed open the door. It was warm inside, filled with the smell of fried meat. Here was a restaurant, but the back wall opened up into a corridor where there were other shops and stands, like a miniature mall. Gil stepped in, scowling at Ruff. "You and your junk food! Did you smell something elfish? Or just a filet-o'-fish?"

Ruff's ears drooped. "The nose knows! How could you doubt me?" So Gil had to kneel and rub his belly by way of apology until he was in a good mood again.

A figure dressed in a Styrofoam outfit of a giant hamburger in a top hat loomed up behind them.

"Excuse me, son. No dogs allowed in here!" came a voice out of the hamburger.

Ruff said, "Oh! Tell him you are blind! Blind men's dogs get to get in everywhere. People feel sorry for them because their humans are blind."

Gil was staring at the hamburger-man in confusion. "Excuse me, sir. This might seem like an odd question, but– you are a human being wearing a costume, right?"

"Very funny. You are advertising for some sort of *Dungeons & Dragons*-themed place moving in, are you? Your outfit looks heavier than mine. Anyway, the manager won't let anyone bring his dog in here."

Just then, Ruff took off at high speed, yapping. The noise of his nails scrabbling on the tile floor was like hailstones. Ruff rushed out of the burger joint into the main section of the mall. He pelted around the corner and out of sight but not out of earshot.

"I'll go get him!" said Gil over his shoulder as he ran after Ruff, his mail clattering and clanging and the hems of his great gray cloak whipping after him.

Ruff turned into a little side corridor past a water fountain. Here were signs for the men's room, the ladies' room, and a door labeled NO ADMITTANCE. Ruff pointed at the ladies' room door with his nose, cocking his foreleg, and barked. "In here! In here!"

Gil skidded to a halt. "I cannot go in there!"

But then a horrifying, shrill scream rang out, and a loud sob of anguish that tore at the heart. Gil smashed the door aside with his shield and barreled into the room, one hand on his sword grip.

There were three woman in the bathroom, two of whom let out shrieks of surprise when Gil entered. The third woman was screaming for another reason. She was a heavyset woman with an overlarge purse filled with diapers and wipes. Next to her was an empty stroller. There was a fold-down changing table built into the wall of the bathroom. On it was a tiny figure wrapped in pink baby clothing, utterly motionless and silent like a dead thing.

Gil squinted, not sure what he was seeing. There was a bright light just above the changing table, and a shadow was cast on the smooth surface. The shadow did not match. The baby's chubby little hands and feet did not cast hand-shaped or foot-shaped shadows. Instead, the silhouette was some sort of root, something like a turnip, but with stalks filling the armholes and foot-socks of the baby outfit. Gil raised his eyes to a motion he saw in the mirror and then looked at the bathroom window. It was a narrow slit, too narrow for a person to fit through, but it was swinging.

Ruff barked, "I see him! I see him! The real baby is over there! The redcap has got him!"

Gil said, "What? I didn't see it–"

Ruff said, "Follow me!"

The heavyset woman was bent over the motionless baby who cast the shadow of a plump plant growth. She looked up, her face wet with tears, and screamed, "Get a doctor! Lubomira! My baby is not breathing! She is not breathing! Little Loobie!" Her wild eyes fell on Gil. She blurted out: "*You have to save her!*"

Ruff, barking like a string a firecrackers, leaped across the bathroom, up to the sink and then up to the sill. A twist of his body and he was out the narrow window and down.

Gil felt a jolt run through his frame when the woman begged him for help, as if his muscles were on fire. He spoke, "I will save the baby, so help me God! Wait here!"

Gil pelted out the door. In the small corridor outside were several men, attracted by the screaming, looking frightened and uncertain.

When Gil in his winged helm and shield and cloak came out of the ladies' room, one of them said, "Hey!" and another, "Stop him!" but Gil slung his shield before him and knocked aside the two men who stood in his way.

He ran out the door marked *NO ADMITTANCE*. Inside was a back room. Here were shelves, boxes, a sink, and another door leading to a loading dock. He leaped off the dock onto the wet pavement, heard his dog barking, and ran that way, his armor ringing like music.

6. Redcap

There was a narrow alleyway between the backside of the mini-mall and the neighboring building. "Here! Here!" barked Ruff. "I see the baby!"

The helm limited Gil's view. He yanked it off, tucked it under his right arm like a football, and pounded down the alley, kicking up snow and melted water with every step.

A sudden turn to the left and he saw Ruff in the distance, on the other side of a small brook, flitting through the trees. Ruff was barking at what looked like a dust-devil or eddy of wind passing along the snow. Gil leaped up a berm of gravel, over some rusted railroad tracks, down the gravel slope on the far side. Then, he sprinted through the trees.

The unseen swirl of wind passed through a thicket of tangled branches, and Ruff was thwarted, held up by the many twigs and jags, barking at whatever invisible thing was skipping away beyond. Gil ran up, smashing through the thicket with his shield and trampling it with his boots. He gritted his teeth and put every ounce of strength into running.

They were now on the common green. No one was around. The lawn of the Blowing Rock town square was empty except for scattered patches of snow and the giant pine tree covered with electric lights in the near distance. Ruff barked, "You go left! I'll go right! Drive him toward me!"

"But I can't see anyone!"

"*He* don't know that! Lesson One! Awe and terrify!"

Ruff ran to one side, teeth bared, barking madly. Gil ran across the little common green of the town square to the right, waving the helm he carried in his hand over head, showing his teeth, and bellowing ferociously.

Ruff barked madly and lunged. Suddenly, Ruff had in his teeth a doll-sized cap of bright red set with an owl feather.

A little blurry swirl of wind suddenly became clear and easy to see. Here was a miniature man, no more than twelve inches tall, dressed in a green doublet and hose, his head bare, with a face as hideous as a vulture's face, eyes bright with glee and malice. The little man was scampering toward the giant pine tree covered with colored lights in the middle of the common green, laughing gaily. His tiny arms, no bigger than soda straws, were able to carry the body of a baby four times his size over his head. It was like seeing a normal-sized man carry a baby elephant. It was the real Loobie, still alive and breathing, and sleeping peacefully despite the jolts and ruckus.

And the little man was leaping a fathom with every stride, his little legs flung out before and behind in a comical fashion, and he bounced like a track and field star on a track made of trampolines. Little sparks and blinks of light came from his feet and calves.

He was able to twist his head around in a half-circle like an owl, and so, without slowing, the redcap stared at his pursuit as he ran. "Slow-foot and slower-foot! Trip on a root!"

"That does not even rhyme!" growled Ruff through clenched teeth, angrily.

"Watch me flee! Just watch me! No mortal hand can catch me!"

"That doesn't rhyme either!" Ruff growled again, even more angrily. "You stink!"

But a swirl of little lights and sparks like fireflies gathered around the legs of the little man. "Rush and hush, the baby sleeps! The boldest redcap whirls and leaps!"

And in a wash of twinkling lights, the redcap left the ground and flew up in a long parabolic arc to a point halfway up the pine tree, far out of reach, and the baby with him.

Gil from below looked up in shock and frustration, seeing the creepy little man so easily escape him. But then he noticed a low-hanging branch with a red-nosed reindeer ornament hanging from it, which would allow him to reach the next branch. His eye marked the path of quickest ascent.

But before he could take a step closer to the tree, Gil heard Ruff bark. "Wow! Wow!" Gil's gaze leaped up.

The little man was about to land on the tree, but before his green slipper could touch the evergreen branch, the branch swayed in the breeze, and an ornament shaped like a singing angel, hanging by the thread attached to its halo, turned toward the little man. It arms were flung out in a T, and its little mouth was open in an O. The white angel had a red cross on its surcoat.

The little man twisted in midair, shrieking in panic, and the sparks carried him backward and away from the tree. He fell headfirst, but landed lightly as a thistledown on the grass. The baby fell as well, but the end of the lowest tree branch caught the baby right where the knot of the big pink handkerchief into which she was tied was placed, so the bundle merely swayed on the end of the branch, rocking the baby.

The redcap yelled, "I thought this was a Kwanzaa tree! I thought it was safe! Wherever elfs and imps have sway, holy trees are outlawed out and done away!"

Gil jumped headlong, dropping his helm, and tackled the little man. The little man was slippery and quick, but not quicker than a fish. Gil caught him in both hands, lifting him to his mouth to grip him with his teeth.

The redcap yowled in woe and horror.

7. Capture

"I yield! I surrender! I *give*! Eat me not! Spare me, and I will grant a boon of equal worth as I prize my very life!" shouted the redcap in his tiny, high voice. Then he muttered, "Er, *live*."

Ruff said, "Oh! Oh! I know this one! I know how this works. Make him swear by his name! His name!"

The little man wailed all the more loudly, mournfully, and terribly. "Thornstab! Thornstab of Lichlamp son of Zahack the Necromant! By my very name I vow the boon you ask to grant! Cruel am I but don't want to die!"

Ruff said, "You can let him down. If he breaks his oath, he loses his name."

Gil, kneeling, spat the little man out onto the grass. Ruff put his nose into Gil's hand and gave him the miniature cap with its feather. "Hold on to that! Give it back when he gives you the boon."

Gil had no pockets in his armor, but his war belt had a pouch of tooled leather adorned with swans, where he kept his whetstone and pliers and tin of polish, and here the tiny thumb-sized hat went.

The little man, Thornstab, was picking himself up, brushing off his green doublet, his ghastly vulture-face screwed up in a scowl. "No Son of Adam erenow has ever *bit* on me! I have man-spit on me! I will get man-germs! Verily!"

Ruff said sharply, "That is a myth! Human slobber is good for you!"

Gil stood, picked up the baby from where she hung, dangling, from the pine tree branch. He doffed his cloaked and wrapped it around her. "First things first. Not as part of whatever boon you owe me, but simply as common decency, you must remove whatever enchanted sleep you put on this child, and the illusion you put on the root you put in her place."

Thornstab said, "If, of whatever boon, it is not part, why should I? Why undo my art?"

Gil said, "Why should I not throw you into this Christmas tree? The boon was only for not biting you in half like a raw fish."

"You eat raw fish? Ugh and yuck. A ghastly dish."

Gil knelt and placed the baby carefully upon the brown grass of winter. Then, he snatched up the little man with a lightning-swift motion of his hand. "Look! There is a nativity scene! Maybe if I put you into the crib next to baby Jesus..."

"No! Not the child! That will burn and scald!"

Ruff said, "Worst rhyme ever."

Thornstab said, "I will be defiled!"

"Much better," Ruff nodded. Then, to Gil he said, "Bite his head off."

"I agreed not to hurt him."

Ruff said, "I didn't. Let's play fetch. Throw him!"

"Harm me no harm! Look! I do undo the charm! The babe will wake without fail, without a wail, when she is once more in her mother's arm." Thornstab rubbed both hands together, producing a palm full of sparks, which he blew with the breath from his mouth to where the baby was wrapped in Gil's cloak.

Gil knelt and put the little man back on the ground, "Thank you."

Thornstab grinned a wicked grin and plucked a blade of grass. "Here is your welcome!" He put the blade of grass to his lips and blew a high, shrill whistle.

Ruff said, "That is not good." And his ears drooped.

Gil buckled the chin strap of his helm.

Chapter 10

Abominable Snowmen

1. Battlecry

The doors of the courthouse swung open. Two furry shapes taller than a man and wider than an ape came lumbering with lurching, sideways steps down the stairs, flourishing great truncheons.

Seen up close, they were horrifying. The hair of their neck and shoulders was thick and dark like a mane, and their skulls were slanted, with receding brows and jutting great jowls.

Behind came a giant white wolf. The red-eyed pale-furred wolf padded down the stairs, claws clicking on the stones, growling and tossing his hairy head. Gil saw the monster's snout was muzzled, and great teeth were biting at the bit.

In a saddle on his back was a hunched and hairy shape greater than the other two, but he was armed with a great double-headed ax, and a cap of bronze metal was on his head.

Gil felt his skin crawling as all his nape hairs stood. A shivering sensation of loathing and hate passed through his body upon seeing the three shaggy ape-faced semi-humans.

"Bigfoots!" he snarled. And, raising his shield, he drew the sword of his father and flourished the blade on high.

"MERRY CHRISTMAS!" he shouted at the top of his lungs.

2. Heretic

Seeing Gil, the mounted woses grinned, showing great yellow teeth. His right fang was broken off short.

"Surprised?" the rider threw back his head to laugh without mirth. Then, tilting his head forward, he intoned in a voice rich with menace, "My brothers and I are in the service of the Winterking, Sir Knight. In his name we gather from the human herd. Beware of us, and stand away!"

The one to the left said, "None stands between the Yeti and their prey."

And the third said, "You are an enemy who greets us so! That word you must not say!"

Gil started toward the huge apelike things and the even more huge wolf, his armor ringing with each step. He met them in the road separating the courthouse from the common green where the Christmas tree was.

Anger crackled in his voice. He pointed the naked sword first at the one, then the next. "I don't care in whose name you do this evil! If you are behind the theft of this child, and her mother's tears, you die! And what's wrong with *Merry Christmas*?"

It was not one of the three apelike woses who answered him, but the great wolf. The monster snarled and spoke through clenched teeth. "God does not rut! He is neither begotten nor begets! There is no Christmas because there was no Christ!"

Gil was so amazed that he stopped and stared at the wolf. "No Christ? How did we get on this topic? Leave the baby alone!"

The wolf said, "The false prophet died in Palestine, two ages ago, forsaken, as he himself confessed in tears, by his heartless God, and never rose again! We wolves know! Our fathers, the wolves of that day, pulled the corpse from the cave of Joseph of Arimethea and gobbled down the rotted meat and cracked the marrow bones! The Roman soldiers stood aside, friends of wolves, for were not Romulus and Remus suckled by a she-wolf?"

Gil felt a moment of sickness and horror overcome him. "You lie!"

The rider said in a slow voice, puzzled, "Are you– are you talking to my wolf?"

The wolf clenched its jaws so that the bit groaned in his teeth, and the eyes of the giant beast were like fire. "No one has ever drunk the blood nor taken the flesh of Jesus, save wolf and wolf alone!"

Without a word, in reckless rage, Gil rushed in straight toward the wolf and struck. The monster reared, his fore-claws tearing at the white swan of the tall shield. Gil stabbed up from beneath the shield, passing the blade neatly between the ribs and into the heart.

Immediately, the blade ignited with a white flame, bright as a lightning-flash. The wolf's blood caught fire; fire roared in the chest-wound; fire billowed from the maw. The wolf screamed a horrid scream, threw his rider, and rolled, trying to smother the terrible burning.

The woses to the left cowered back, squinting and dazzled, his elbow before his eyes. "It is Dyrnwen! The true white blade! It is the lost blade come again!"

The one on the right fell to his face, groveling and crying. "Elfinking! Erlkoenig! Lord of Unseelie! Come to save your loyal slave, for greatly has he need of thee!"

Gil smote the wolf through the neck, and the fiery head rolled free. The burning jaws snapped open and shut with the creature's dying spasms.

The rider with the ax scrambled and clawed himself free from the wreckage of his saddle, bruised and burned where the great monster had rolled atop him in its dying madness. The rider came to his feet and stared in anger at the broken axhandle in his hand, which he cast to the asphalt of the road with a clatter. He roared at Gil, "Why did you kill my wolf?"

"I had to!"

"That was Bolmagnir son of Svartmagnir!"

"Well, his name is Baked Meat now! My mom told me to kill heretics!" Gil laughed, delighted at the strange bright flames leaping and dancing along the blade thrumming in his hand. The letters of strange writing were clear to see, painfully bright. Never before had Gil had permission to answer a liar as he secretly had always wished.

The wide-eyed woses stared at the laughing boy, whose mirth was ringing and echoing eerily from his helm. The hairy man shouted at Gil, "Are you mad?"

"Fighting mad!" Gil shouted back.

3. Skirmish

With these words, Gil drove in at the tall, one-fanged woses in the iron
cap, lunging point-first from beyond the creature's reach. But the point
of the blade skittered off the creature's fur, as if it had struck a steel
plate.

Suddenly, the other two came at him from behind to his left and right
and swung their truncheons. One he parried with the sword, and the
other he deflected with the shield, but the shock of the blows left both
arms tingling and half-numb. He ran, trying to get out of the middle of
the triangle of enemies, but the woses on their crooked legs were more
lithe and limber than a boy in armor, and he could not break free of the
circle.

No matter which way he turned, there was one behind him. One
struck him on the shoulder; another on the helm; the third clawed him
on the legs so that he bled freely. He cut the thick wand of wood in half
with a great stroke of his fiery sword. But the woses to whom he had
turned his back, the one in the iron cap, now grabbed him from behind,
twisting one arm in a wrestler's hold, and the white-hilted sword went
spinning from his hand. The blade dropped to the road, and its light
went out.

Just then Ruff landed on the back of the woses grappling Gil, barking,
jaws slashing. Gil felt the grip weaken, and he twisted free, grabbed the
creature by the hair of his calf, and pulled his leg overhead, sending him
toppling. Ruff grabbed the sword by the hilts in his jaws and ran. Gil
pelted after him, armor ringing. But the woses were swifter than he and
leaped after, trying to circle him again.

The three woses halted suddenly, noses twitching. Gil ran back on to
the common green. A glance showed him the baby was still safe, still
asleep. He ran toward her.

At that moment, a great wind came from behind the courthouse, and
two wings of white mist poured across the road into the town square, thick
and opaque as a stage curtain. Through this curtain a thick and huge shape
moved, coming closer. Gil felt the ground tremble at its footfalls, and he
heard the sounding of trumpets.

4. The Lord of Winter

The mist parted. An albino woolly mammoth walked through the clinging swirls of mist, and the trumpet calls were coming from its trunk. On the neck of the white mammoth rode a slight and slender girl in a black jerkin, skirt and red-peaked cap. She had a narrow face and a wicked smile, wings like an immense dragonfly. Two feathery antennae a yard long issued from her pretty head. In her hand was a goad to drive the mammoth.

Behind and above her, on a tower on the back of the beast was a throne of pallid crystal, and here was a kingly figure wrapped from chin to ankle in a black cloak. A rack of antlers reached from his brow, wider than his shoulders, and little lights danced in them. His hair was a hood as black as night. It reached past his shoulders and, as the night, had small, cold sparks in it. In his hand was a back scepter. The only paleness of him was his face-mask.

"Who calls me? Who calls the King of Winter Darkness, the High King and Caesar over all the Nocturnal World? Who calls Erlkoenig son of Oberon, the King of Elf and Shadows, Lord of Air and Darkness?"

Only one of the three woses still had a club in his hand. It was he that saluted the figure on the mammoth, and crouched, and said, "Sire, this man-at-arms hinders our wooing and slew the wolf, whom you raised from a whelp, to whom you fed unclean meats from your own imperial hand, and over whom you chanted many strange runes and wove them fast! He slew Bolmagnir, the Great Wolf, whom you gave to my brother Guynglaff!"

Gil was now near the Christmas tree, but he stopped, hearing that name. Now he understood the red rage that was thrumming through his body and pouring into his muscles like fire.

Guynglaff was the name of the woses that had kidnapped and terrified his mother before he was ever born. And now Gil stood before him, dressed in the same armor, bearing the same shield, and armed with the same sword as the Swan Knight who had defeated him.

Gil drew a shaking breath. The task of defeating the monster now was Gil's, whether he was ready to meet it or not, strong enough or not.

At his gesture, Ruff passed the white sword to him. Gil petted the dog, straightened, stepped forward boldly, saluted with his sword, and called out, "Your Imperial Highness! I have a quarrel with that creature, who says he is doing your work. These three sent their agent Thornstab to steal and kidnap that child there and replace her with a root. I had not heard erenow that the Emperor of All the Elfin Kind makes war on helpless babies!"

"Thornstab, attend me! Come forth!" called Erlkoenig. But there was no answer. The king kicked the slender driver with his foot. "Glisterwing! Let it be noted that Thornstab is tardy and absent without leave. Send the Winged Nightmare to retrieve his soul in the dream realm, and let the venoms of torment be prepared. Let them be of the ordinary strength; my displeasure is but small as yet."

"Yes, my lord," said the elfin girl, pouting and rubbing the spot where her wing met her shoulder.

Seen this close, Gil could now see the figure did not wear a white mask, or, at least, it was not a mask. It was a slab of ice growing out of his flesh. There was a mouth slit, and a second slit above where the ice was just transparent enough to allow the distant and cruel glitter of the inhuman eyes to gleam through.

"What would you have of me?" asked the figure in the pallid mask and dark cloak, peering down from his white crystal throne.

Gil pointed his sword at Guynglaff. "That one, sire! I seek to meet him in honorable combat to slay him so that he dies the death."

"That one is hard to kill. His name is Guynglaff Cobweb. Here are his two brothers Gulaga and Doolaga, also of the Cobweb clan. What business do you have with Guynglaff? Who are you?"

"Sire, I mean no discourtesy, but I cannot say my name."

The mammoth now stepped with a remarkably delicate motion closer to Gil and lifted its great trunk. The nostrils snuffled and sniffed at Gil, and Gil smelled a warm scent of hay from the breath of the giant creature. With a stab of pity, Gil saw that the mammoth's eyes were coated with a filmy growth. The mammoth was blind.

Erlkoenig said, "Are you human or elfin?"

"Sire, I cannot say."

The ice-covered face of Erlkoenig turned toward the woses. "Guynglaff! Attend me! Is this the same Swan Knight? Or be he another?"

The hairy man louted low. "Sire, I cannot tell."

"Not by voice nor stance?"

Guynglaff said, "He is near enough that it does not matter. We will tear him limb from limb with glee."

Erlkoenig said, "What say you, Gulaga, brother to Guynglaff?"

The one who still held an unbroken club said, "We need the Daughters of Eve as drudges and slatterns, slaves and concubines, for no woman or our kind will wed us, seeing us as hideous, or bear our monstrous get in their wombs. Our race will dwindle and die if we have no mortal women to impregnate! This knight meddles with our very survival! All creatures are allowed to slay others to preserve themselves. And since he must die in any case, it will not matter if the death is merciless, slow, and lingering."

"What say you, Doolaga?"

The second one had a high-pitched voice, wheezing, "Thornstab left a mandrake root in the place of the changeling babe, which is a fair and even trade. We cannot be accused of theft! The mother's eyes were held, so that the root looked like a babe in all ways; unreasonable if she is not satisfied!"

Then, Gulaga spoke again, rearing up and whirling the club in the air. "Once we have him out of his armor, we will gnaw his flesh raw!"

Doolaga said, "Let him die a messy, screaming death with much blood! Too much blood! It will entertain the Winterking!" He also began hooting, and jumping up and down, and pounding himself in the chest.

Gil said, "Sir! I ask for single combat, one on one!"

Erlkoenig said, "The honors given to the nobly born cannot be granted to the base born, for then no reward would be worth risking life and limb to obtain. Knights do not fight for gold nor gain but for such things as have no price and cannot be bought. Can you buy a father for gold? I would sell you mine if I could."

Gil said, "No, sire. But three against one is unfair, and they are invulnerable."

Erlkoenig said, "Unfair? It is unfair to deny you your due, but are you due the treatment owed those born to high estate? Who is your father? If you cannot say your name, then who can say your lineage?"

And, when Gil had no answer, Erlkoenig said, "Guynglaff, Gulaga, and Doolaga, you are dismissed. Be about your business."

The three woses came loping forward.

Gil knew his sword could not cut their furry hides. They were taller and stronger than he was and more agile. Without hope, yet without fear, he raised his sword and readied his shield to receive their charge.

5. Bloodshed

Gil heard a shrill noise above him. "Climb! Climb, you fool!"

In his helm and neckpiece, he could not turn his head without turning his back, and to do that meant to commit himself to running. He had either to trust or not to trust the voice based on the voice alone.

"Take the child and climb to my nest!"

Gil did not hesitate. He had already picked out the path from tree limb to tree limb. He turned and flung away the shield, which he could not hold while climbing. Ruff saw, and barked, and picked up the shield in his mouth by the straps, and ran toward the wood separating the common green from the rest stop, the shield clattering and banging behind him. Not looking back at the monsters rushing so swiftly upon him, with cool deliberation, Gil sheathed the sword, stooped, and picked up the baby. He folded his surcoat in two to make a pocket and used his warbelt and baldric strap to pin the folded fabric against his chestplate, so there was no way for the child to slip out.

Up he went, branch to branch, only banging his helm every now and again. The little lights on their green electric cords flashed cheerfully.

Then, he saw the bird. For a moment, he thought it was a Santa Claus ornament, so bright and red was he. "A cardinal!" said Gil. "You do not migrate, do you?"

"What? Depart the Carolinas? A spot more fair the Creator created not on Earth! My work is here. Now climb! Climb for your life! Do not slack nor stop until I say!"

Gil could hear the breathing and rustling below him and felt the whole tree shake. The woses laughed. One wheezed in a shrill voice, "Who leaps from branch to branch with more ease than a Wild-Man-o'-Wood? He cannot outclimb us!"

"Perhaps he seeks to dangle from a slim branch, thinking we cannot follow?" said the second, Gulaga. "The weight of his armor dooms him!"

"Not so fast, my brothers! Toy with him! Let him despair!" Gil recognized the voice of Guynglaff, which was deeper than the other two. "Let him leap to his death, that he slay himself, and be damned to the dark realm!"

Gil leaped from branch to branch as quickly as the heavy armor allowed, painstakingly careful not to let anything touch the warm burden cuddled against his chest. The pine branches shook beneath his gauntlets and boots as the monsters closed on him. It was maddening that the helm so limited his vision, and he could not turn his head enough to look behind. From the grunts and hisses of the woses brothers, he could tell they were near.

Suddenly, the tree began swaying widely, wildly, dangerously. He was nearing the top, and the branches were getting smaller, less able to bear his weight.

"It is too far!" said Gil. He could not see where the cardinal was.

"Climb! Do not slow!"

Gil could hear the woses behind him. Up he went. The tree swayed alarmingly. Gil saw the star at the crown of the tree waving back and forth dizzily.

"Here!" called the cardinal, flapping before his eyes and landing. "This branch! Here! Out on the branch!"

It looked far too narrow to hold his weight. He decided to trust the cardinal. This branch was near the top, with few other branches within reach. Gil crept on hand and foot along the narrow length. Then, he clung with both hands, for the branch was shaking in his grip. He turned. A woses was coming swiftly and surefootedly along the branch, his prehensile toes gripping the tiny circumference of the branch like fingers, his arms out to either side to help him balance. He had neither club nor iron cap, so this was Doolaga.

The cardinal landed on the next branch up. "Stand up!" The little voice said. The warm little babe was still snugly held against his chest by his baldric and warbelt in an enchanted sleep.

Gil rose up unsteadily, reached overhead, did a pull-up. He kicked his legs away from the tree and threw his leg over the upper branch on the side father from the bole. His weight caused the narrow branch to bend so severely that he sank down below the first branch.

The surprised apelike face of Doolaga slid past his vision, rising, as the thin branch to which Gil clung fell down.

Then, he was below the creature. He saw that the sole of its foot was naked of any fur, bare like the sole of a man.

Clinging to the bending branch with one arm and both legs, Gil drew the sword, and stuck. Both branches were waving, so his aim was thrown off. His blade skittered off the furry calf of Doolaga without cutting. Doolaga, agile as a monkey, leaped neatly down the branch, away from the sword but also away from the bole of the tree so that he was bobbing up and down as Gil was. Gil half-lunged and half-fell, with his left hand grabbing the branch on which Doolaga the woses precariously stood. The motions of both branches, rocking and pitching like a ship at sea made Doolaga collapse to all fours and grab the branch with both hands and both feet.

Gil looked down. The big one, Guynglaff, was yards away, but he was directly below Doolaga, his brother. Gulaga, meanwhile, was at the same height as Gil, having climbed the far side of the tree, and now he was circling, coming toward Gil, leaping swiftly from branch to branch with only three limbs (for he clutched his club in one foot).

Gil let go his legs. The branch, released of his weight, snapped upward and to the left. Gulaga ducked as a lone and thin pine branch of shepherds, kings, and blinking lights whipped passed his head.

Gil, meanwhile, flung by the same force in the opposite direction, did a neat spin around the branch in his hands and landed on the top. It was better than anything he had ever done in gymnastics on the uneven bars, and he could not restrain a laugh of victory. He lifted himself precariously to his feet. "Ta DAH!" he shouted.

Doolaga was before him, and reared up on his hand-like hind paws. "Do not be of good cheer, weak Son of Adam!" he wheezed in an odd, shrill voice. "Your weapon cannot cut the fur of woses!"

Gil said, "It cuts wood!" And he took the sword in both hands and chopped at the branch just before his toes. A large chip of pine flew into the air.

Doolaga, seeing what was happening and feeling the thin branch on which they were both balanced shaking, now dropped to all fours, clutching the wood with hands and feet and ran forward as fast as he could, charging Gil.

Then, he reared up, looming over the boy, tall, broad, and immense in the glittering colored lights. Gil put the point of his blade in the middle of that broad chest and pushed with all his force, shouting, "Merry Christmas!"

The tip of the blade could not penetrate his fur, but the force of the thrust could push on his chest. Doolaga fell in a half-circle and now was hanging upside down by his feet, still directly above Guynglaff, who looked up, shock in his eyes and fear for his brother. Guynglaff began taking prodigious leaps upward and did not see the danger to himself.

Gil carefully put the tip of his sword against the naked sole of Doolaga's foot, where there was no fur, and shoved the blade into the flesh. Doolaga screamed, his foot bloody, his blood catching fire, and he fell.

Doolaga struck Guynglaff, who was in mid-leap, and they were both flung out of the tree by the impact and plunged downward. The sword burst into brilliant white flame, intolerably bright.

Gil turned. Gulaga with his club was now picking his way quickly from branch to branch, once more approaching Gil from the left. Gil retreated closer to the bole of the swaying tree, reached up, grabbed the electrical wires leading to the huge white star at the very top, and yanked. The huge and heavy ornament came free. He swung it by the wires in a huge circle over his head, yodeled, and threw it at the woses. It shattered into a spray of glass. Gulaga staggered, screaming in fear, but caught a branch with a hand and a foot, and saved himself from falling.

Gil now saw a lower, wider branch and jumped down to it with a loud clang and clatter.

Gulaga made an acrobatic flip and landed on the branch just above Gil. The monster smote down with his club with all the power of his thickly muscled leg. Gil's helmet saved his life: it rang like a bell, and he knew a huge bruise would spread across his face, and it felt like his nose was broken, but at least his skull was not shattered.

Gil struck with the sword, but Gulaga parried it with the club, fell prone, and reached down, striking unexpectedly with the claws of his hands. Gil was afraid for the baby and curled his arms before his chest. The claws did not hit the child but tore through Gil's shoulder-armor, mail, and flesh. Blood flowed freely.

Gulaga said, "Even that sword cannot pierce us!"

Gil jumped down another branch, wincing at his wound.

The cardinal was on the branch with him. "Here is my nest. Light it afire."

It was a dry circle of twigs with no eggs in it. Gil wondered why any bird built a nest in winter. He did not see the point of lighting it afire, but he did not question. Gil held his white flaming sword beneath, and the nest ignited merrily. Black smoke poured up. He now saw this one branch was dry and brown, long dead but held in place by its neighbors.

The cardinal said, "The tree will burn."

"This tree is too green to burn," Gil said.

The cardinal said, "The tree says he will help. Do not demean his act of sacrifice. Christmas trees are not like common trees." And the red bird flew away.

Gulaga was baffled by the growing fire and had to climb sideways to go around the burning branch. But he was still coming swiftly after Gil.

Gil descended another branch or two, and he saw that any needles he brushed with his sword, even though they were green and should not have burned, ignited suddenly, as if they had been coated in oil and were blazing like candles.

Gil swung the sword left and right, igniting all he touched. Branches flared into red fire and poured up black smoke. He chopped one thick green cable in half in a spray of sparks and then another. He noticed the blade flared up brightly when it touched a live wire. Perhaps electricity acted like blood? Gil looked up. The fire was spreading far more rapidly than it should; Gulaga was lost in the cloud of smoke. The cheerful lights looked eerie in the smoke, like little bright stars throwing out wavering beams.

He felt sorry for the tree and wondered in awe why it had volunteered to help him and at such a price.

Gil stepped away from the bole to where the branch was narrow and unsteady. He drove the point of the flaming sword through a thick cable and into the branch beneath and left it there. The flame flickered but did not go out, and sparks danced around the tip where it pierced the live wire.

Then, Gil stepped back toward the bole in a spot where the tree lights had gone dark. He waited. Gulaga, coughing against the smoke, dropped down lithely to the branch and saw the light of the sword. This time the club was in both hands, and he was whirling it menacingly.

Gulaga raced quickly toward the brightly burning blade, club held high, as the narrow branch dipped and sagged alarmingly. Gil took a step, put his hands up, grabbed the club, and yanked. Gulaga did not let go of the club, but staggered backward and began to fall. His feet flew from the branch. He let go of the club and grabbed for the branch with arms and legs, twisting in midair.

Gil, finding the club free in his hand, now thrust the wooden length into Gulaga's grasp. The monster's fingers closed about it instinctively. For a frozen second in midfall, Gulaga stared in dumb surprise at the club in his hands, which Gil thrust away from himself with a hearty shove, crying, "Heave HO!"

Down plunged the woses, falling across a line of lights and dragging them with him, bouncing from branch to branch. A shower of glass balls, cows, donkeys, shepherds, angels, and drummer boys fell after him.

Gil crept out to the end of the unsteady branch and recovered his sword, which he sheathed. He inched back to safety, shaking and sweating. He doffed his gauntlet, reached into the fold of his surcoat, and felt the baby. She was still warm and breathing, and her heart was beating. He donned the gauntlet and began climbing down quickly, trying to keep the weight off his hurt shoulder.

6. Noble Blood

Soon he was on the ground. After the glare and fury of the sword, it was dark here, and Gil could only see Gulaga, who had fallen practically at the roots of the tree, with a line of Christmas lights still twined around him, winking and blinking. Instead of the shattered skull and fractured limbs he was expecting, the woses was intact. Gil drew his sword and ran up to Gulaga, who seemed only stunned. Gulaga opened his eyes as Gil stepped over him, and Gil saw the fire of the treetop reflected in the black pupils. He drove the sword point into the eye socket and killed him instantly.

In the light from the sword, he now saw the other two. Both were lying motionless, but they did not seem dead. Guynglaff, the taller one, had fallen farthest from the tree. His bronze cap was lost. Gil saw the light glinting on his bald spot. The bronze cap covered a spot on his head where he had no hair.

The other woses had a bloody foot and a burned calf. The fire had gone out, and there was a splatter of blood on the grass around his ankle. This was Doolaga, and he was stirring feebly.

Doolaga woke as Gil was running up, and he opened his huge ape-muzzle in a yowl, baring his yellow teeth. Gil drove the point of the flaming sword into the mouth and out the back of his neck. The blood in the monster's body ignited and began to burn.

Gil spun toward Guynglaff, but now a tall dark figure in a pallid mask stood in the way. Erlkoenig had dismounted from his mammoth. He raised a pale and slender hand. In his other arm, cradled against his elbow, was Sally, the baby.

Gil reached into the fold he had made with his surcoat. His fingers met a bulbous root bigger than a turnip.

Erlkoenig said, "Gentle right, Sir Knight! In the name of your noble blood, I ask for your courtesy. Allow Guynglaff to ransom his life!"

Gil was panting. "Sir! My grievance against Guynglaff is very great!"

"And you have slain his brothers. Is this not enough? I am Imperator, Caesar, and King of all the Elfin races of the Night World, and many in the Twilight also bow to me. Name what ransom you demand. This is the noble custom."

"Imperial Majesty! How am I so nobly born, now, all of a sudden? Before this, I was chopped liver."

"You fight like one born to kings and champions, and that sword burns brightly indeed in your hands. I will tell my heralds to enroll your escutcheon into the rolls, and all my court will recognize your birth as worthy even if your lineage is unknown. Ask me what I shall give you to ransom the life of Guynglaff."

Gil looked at the baby in Erlkoenig's arms. Had he climbed and fought so fearfully, carrying his precious burden, and it was a root all that time? Or was this the illusion now?

Gil said, "A life for a life. Give me the child, and cast no more illusions, charms, chants, or spells neither on her nor any of her family, sisters or brothers, parents or grandparents, cousins, and, if she weds, on her husband, on her children or grandchildren to four generations. I want Loobie and her family to be immune and sacrosanct to all elfin meddling, tricks, and sleights of hand."

"Granted!" intoned the elfin king. Unseen hands now wafted the baby gently across the air to Gil, who sheathed his sword to take the child. The firelight vanished. The child was in his arms. When he looked up again, blinking, a thick mist was blowing along the ground, and Erlkoenig, Guynglaff, and the bodies of Doolaga and Gulaga were gone.

The cardinal landed on the grass to one side. "Here! Quickly! Daub your eyes and ears and tongue in the blood of the first enchanted monster you have slain. Haste! This time comes but once!"

Gil saw a splatter of blood on the grass, and some burn-marks where Doolaga had been smoldering a moment before. He knelt, put the baby down, put down the root (he put it down gently, just in case it was still Loobie in disguise), and undid his helmet and gauntlets. He plucked the grassblade where a drop of blood had gathered. "Why, exactly, am I doing this, again?"

The cardinal said, "Taste the blood, that all who hear will hear the truth in your voice."

Gil did not hesitate. He always told the truth, and no one believed him. If this charm would make the truth be heard, it was a gift beyond price. He put the grassblade, blood and all, into his mouth, and chewed and swallowed. It tasted terrible.

Gil looked, but the blood was evaporating. On his hands and knees, wishing for brighter light, he saw one grassblade bent double with a red drop dangling from its tip. He wiped it onto his finger and then into his left eye. It stung.

Gil ground the heel of his palm against his eye, yowling in pain. "What does this do again?"

"By its virtue, your eye will pierce deceptions, and elfin glamours fail. Now, find that wolf you slew, for there is virtue in the first battle you fight, and this was all one. Go! You have yet to anoint your ears!"

Gil stood, walked across the common green to the street, and crossed the empty street. The corpse of the vast beast was missing. Kneeling down, Gil could find only a small puddle, which had spread and seeped into the macadam. There was only the tiniest amount of blood left. He touched it to his finger and put one drop in one ear, then in the other. It stung and caused a humming noise for a moment. Then, he heard, or thought he heard, a strange, beautiful noise in the distance like crystal chimes ringing and receding.

"This won't damage my hearing, will it?" he asked the bird in annoyance, wincing at the hot, stinging sensation in his ear and wondering if that noise he heard were real.

The cardinal said, "The songs of elfs and sirens have lost their power over you. You now will speak the truth, see the truth, and hear the truth."

"And what is that ringing noise? No, it is gone now."

"Was it pleasant or unpleasant?"

"Very pleasant."

"That was the armor and harness of your guardian angel, who protected you during this battle, carrying your prayers to a high and hidden tabernacle in the stars, where there is an altar stone."

"I didn't say any prayers."

"None?" said the cardinal in surprise. "The knights of Constantine prayed ere the Battle of the Milvian Bridge, as did those of John of Austria ere the Battle of Lepanto. Do you suppose knights of yore defeated the powers of the Night World without aid? When next you encounter battle, first be shriven, lest you die."

And with a flap of his bright red wings, the little bird flew off.

The Christmas tree was burning rather brightly now, and Gil thought it was time to take his leave. He whistled for Ruff, who came trotting up, still lugging the shield behind him. "We won! We won! I helped! I helped! I ran off with the shield just like you wanted! Did you see me bite him? I bit him good!"

Gil petted him fondly, shaking with fatigue, and hot with sweat. "Good boy!"

"And I guarded the shield! Did you see that?"

Gil said, "Is the mom still at the rest stop? I told her to wait, but she does not even know the baby was kidnapped."

Ruff said, "I think she knows now. Look!" For there were red and blue lights flashing and waving through the trees. Gil could see a police cruiser and a paramedic vehicle had pulled up to the rest stop.

Gil grinned. "Let's go give the mom her baby back!"

And despite all his wounds and weariness, his step was light as he marched through the woods, baby in his arms, shield over his shoulder, and helm hanging from one side of his belt, sword from the other, and a white swan blazing on his chest.

7. Truth and Consequences

As they walked, Ruff said, "Good job killing those Wild-Men-o'-Wood. But boy, are the Cobwebs going to have it out for you! Wow. You're a dead man. I think you made a better bear than a knight. Whoa! What is that?"

There was a crowd of curious onlookers gathered around the loading dock of the mini-mall. To one side were police officers. Gil heard the voice of the mother, shouting and screaming in agony and confusion.

Gil stepped closer. The mother and a medic in white were bent over what looked to Gil like a giant turnip root lying on a pad on the open tailgate of the white vehicle. The medic was trying to give mouth-to-mouth resuscitation to the inert root, but was only blowing raspberries against the upper knob of its gray and wrinkled skin.

Closer, Gil heard her words. "That is not my baby! That is a vegetable!" Gil nodded, realizing that the price asked of Erlkoenig must have been granted. The baby's family was immune to elfish illusions. That included the mother. "That is a vegetable! Where is my baby?"

It was with immense satisfaction that Gil stepped forward from the trees and said in a loud, clear voice. "Here, ma'am. The baby is here. The baby is safe. I have her!"

There was a shout from the onlookers, but it was not a shout of triumph, but of horror. Gil stepped forward to hand the baby to the mother. She rushed to him and snatched the baby fearfully out of his hands, giving him an odd look.

As promised, the baby came awake in the mother's arms and began keening and wailing.

Gil then saw himself in the reflection caught in the window of the police cruiser. He had blood wiped all over his face, in his hair, and all over his hands. More blood, his own, was leaking down his shoulder and arm where his armor was rent. Pine needles were clinging to every part of him. His gear was sticky with sap, sweat, soot, and blood.

And the light from the burning Christmas tree in the town square was visible through the woods behind him.

The police officer said, "Son, can you tell me your name and explain why you took this baby?"

Gil sighed and said in a sad voice, "No, officer, I cannot tell you my name. My mother told me not to. An elf stole the baby, not I. You must believe me!"

The officer said soothingly, "I do. I am sure the judge will believe you, too. Now, I'd like you to come down to the station and make a statement. But first, would you please undo that sword, drop it to the ground, and kick it over to me?"

"I cannot do that either; it would forswear me. Listen, sir: You should hear the truth in my voice from the blood of the woses in my mouth!"

The officer stared at him. "Sorry? What was that about blood?"

Gil explained, "I was fighting a monster. His is the blood in my mouth. The tree I burned too, but all is well. A little bird assured me that the noble pine volunteered himself for the flames."

Later, alone in a jail cell in the North Carolina State Bureau of Investigation facility in Asheville, devoid of both sword and shoelaces, Gil wondered if perhaps he should have answered the policeman differently.

Here ends *Swan Knight's Son*,

Book One of ***The Green Knight's Squire***.

THE TALES OF MOTH & COBWEB continue in

Book Two of ***The Green Knight's Squire***,

Feast of the Elfs

FEAST OF THE ELFS

LITTLE *Ellie in her smile*
Chooses—"I will have a lover.
Riding on a steed of steeds
He shall love me without guile,
And to him I will discover
The swan's nest among the reeds.

And the steed shall be red-roan,
And the lover shall be noble,
With an eye that takes the breath:
And the lute he plays upon
Shall strike ladies into trouble,
As his sword strikes men to death...."

Elizabeth Barrett Browning (1844)

Chapter 1

The Red Cap's Favor

1. An Inauspicious Beginning

The North Carolina police officers in Asheville took away the bright sword and silver armor, swan-winged helm and knightly shield indight with his father's coat-of-arms of Gilberec Parzival Moth when they arrested him. True, he had been covered from head to toe in blood, and he had burned down the giant pine tree that once had stood in the middle of the town square. And it was also true that no one else could actually see the elfin creature who had really kidnapped the baby, or made the other mischief blamed on Gil.

It seemed an inauspicious beginning to his career as a Knight Errant.

It could have been worse. A nurse practitioner, an old woman with a stern face, had been allowed to clean, sterilize, and bandage up his shoulder and stitch his leg wounds. And the police had given him this freshly laundered orange jumpsuit.

Ruff was sitting outside the metal slats of the window of his cell, howling indignantly. *"Let him out! Let him out! It's not fair!"* over and over again. How the dog had followed him along a ninety-minute drive down I-40, Gil did not know.

Gil lay down on the cot, finding it oddly comfortable. He closed his eyes, glad his dog was near.

2. Boon

Gil woke on the cot. He did not remember falling asleep. It was dark. The metal slats covering the cell window prevented him from seeing the stars. He did not know what hour it was, but from the smell of the air, it was before dawn.

He saw a firefly through the cell bars, wandering down the corridor.

The little light passed between the bars and entered the cell. It was Thornstab, carrying a lantern in his hand.

Gil sat up and put his feet on the concrete floor. "What are you doing here?" he said.

Thornstab raised the lantern and peered into the cell. "'Tis the voice, if I hear aright, of the one who called himself the Swan Knight. Be ye he?"

Gil scooted back on the cot to the corner, where it was darkest, hoping the creature would not see his silver hair. "It is I. To what do I owe the honor?"

"You owe nothing to me. I owe you, that I do! Verily." Thornstab held up a ring of metal as large, to him, as a Hula-Hoop. From this metal hoop hung various lengths of toothed metal as long as his miniature arm.

Thornstab smiled his sharp-faced smile. "One of these is the key to your cell. I owe you a boon and would be quit of this debt soon. So take it! And all will be well!" And he tossed the keyring into the cell, where it tinkled on the concrete floor. Gil made no move to rise or pick it up.

"Nope," said Gil. "I would not sneak like a crook out from a place where I have been falsely accused."

Thornstab's smile vanished, and a look of fear took its place on his features. He raised the tiny lantern and peered into the black cell, perhaps hoping for a glimpse of the face of the Swan Knight. "Are you touched by the moon? Ask of me another boon!"

Gil said, "And if I do not? What then? You never get to wear your little red cap again, and you cannot turn invisible and weave the mist into delirium, can you? What happens to your place among the elfs and efts then? You have to clean toilets and wait tables, something like that?"

Thornstab fell to his knees. His eyes had grown to twice their size, and he rolled them back and forth, as if straining for a glimpse. "Noble and gracious knight! I followed your brave dog all this way, and, aided by no invisibility, plain to see, I connived to enter this dwelling of men and took the key from the guard as he slumbered! This, because I knew you would be true and faithful in all your promises, even to your enemies! But how can I grant you your due if you will not ask it? Tell me your heart's desire true!"

Gil frowned. What was his heart's desire? What he really wanted was for the elfs to stop stealing children. "Where is Erlkoenig now?"

"I cannot foretell the comings and goings of the Lords of the Night World. But I know this: he will be present at the great feast of the fairy kings, when he and Alberec meet in solemn court and celebrate the nativity of Him we do not name and squires are knighted, lands and honors granted, and challenges given and taken at that time. And the elf maidens dance, which is a rare wonder."

Gil squinted. "If you are not Christians, why do you celebrate Christmas? It is the birth of Christ."

Thornstab rolled on the floor, emitting a high-pitched keening comical yet horrible to hear, clutching his ears and banging his head against the concrete. Gil stared in disgust and astonishment. Eventually, Thornstab, clinging to one of the bars of the cell where it touched the floor for support, climbed to his feet, trembling. "Would you have me answer those questions as the grant of your boon?"

Gil scowled. "No. Tell me instead, as my boon, how and where to get invited to this feast of the fairy kings. You said they knighted people then?"

"Erlkoenig has told his heralds to record your heraldry. The door guards must admit you, Sir Knight, if you appear. Whether the kings gathered in that place knight you or do not, that I can neither help nor hinder to happen. Who knows what is in the heart of kings, and fairy hearts are wilder then most, like harps with strings of fire! But I can show you the trick of finding the doors and forcing them open. Will that satisfy the boon?"

"Yes," said Gil.

"Before you go to Mommur, remove all cold iron from your person and garb and each crucifix, scapular, or holy medallion. Do not go to mass that day, or they will smell the host or the sacred wine upon your breath. Cut a wand from a willow tree from which no criminal has ever been hanged, strip off the bark, and say these words: *From the straight track let me not vary nor tarry till I be carried to the doorway of the fay*. The wand will point the path. Follow it. Smite the door with the wand and say these words: *The golden doors of Heaven welcome all as do the iron doors of Hell. Delling's Doors of elfin silver wrought ought to unhide and open wide as easily as well.*"

Gil wished his jumpsuit had come with a pencil and paper in the pocket. "Hold it. Say that rhyme again, so I can remember it."

Thornstab sighed a deep sigh. "Actually, you can just say, *Titania is risen*, and the doors will open just as quickly."

"Who is Titania?"

"None of your concern. Now return my cap!"

Gil said, "Fine. But you have to douse your lamp, cover your eyes, and count to five hundred. Don't peek, or the spell is broken!"

Thornstab did not argue, but blew on the tiny lamp. The eerie light winked out. Gil waited until he heard the little man counting. Gil picked up the keyring, felt through the bars for the lock, and found the key on the third try. Then, he quietly opened the cell door and tiptoed down the corridor. A second key on the ring opened the door at the end of it. Beyond was a large green-walled room where two officers were fast asleep. Gil had no doubt this was Thornstab's work, a charm of his.

Gil had seen the evidence room where they had confiscated his gear. It was behind a dark metal door next to a metal desk. One of the other keys let him in. All of his possessions were piled haphazardly in a large box. He picked up the whole box and locked each door behind him as he returned to his cell, which he also locked.

Thornstab still had a large set of numbers to go, so Gil decided to shuck his prison garb, put on the leggings, breeches, and quilted tunic, and don his armor, sword and swordbelt, shield and helm. He winced and hissed at the pain which even simple motions caused his shoulder.

"...five hundred!"

Gil said, "Light your lamp." And he came forward from the shadows of the dark cell and into Thornstab's astonished gaze. The little red cap was still in Gil's pouch where he had put it: Gil flicked it with his thumb into the miniature man's happy hands. With no further ado, Thornstab pulled the cap on his head, and a swirl of mist appeared around him. Gil, however, could still see him, or, at least, see his silhouette. The little man gathered sparks around his ankles, jumped down the corridor, and bounded through a high window and out into the night sky in a single long leap. A trail of twinkling glitter hung in the air for a moment where he passed.

The winter birds outside were singing, a few voices in a wide silence. One of them sang about the noble death of the Christmas tree in the town square and how that tree had been replanted in a land happier and higher than any human land by Saint Boniface. Gil decided not to go back to sleep.

3. Release

The officer found him a short while later, fully armed and armored, sitting on his cot in his locked cell, with the keys to the cell in his hand.

Without a word, Gil tossed the keyring through the bars. The man caught them and stared first at Gil, then at the keys in his hand, and then at Gil again.

He heaved a sigh and unlocked the cell. "Come on. There is someone who wants to see you."

Gil followed, shield on his back and helm under his arm, armor ringing as he trod. The officer led him into a smaller, darker corridor and then up a flight of narrow metal stairs.

"Sir," said Gil. "Who is it who wants to see me? I don't have a lawyer."

"One of our top detectives with the force," said the officer. "He said he could clear you of all charges if you would answer some questions. Don't be alarmed. Just go through that door there."

He pointed to a dark, unmarked door. It was an oak door with no nameplate or number but with heavy triangular hinges of cast iron. There was a vertical band of dark iron running down the center, intersected by a band of equal width running horizontally at chest height.

Something about this door was familiar, however. The top of the doorframe was arched, not flat. The knob was glass.

Chapter 2

The Man in the Black Room

1. The Long-Lived Ones

Gil did not know what to expect, but he did not see any reason to hesitate. He stepped forward, put his free hand on the knob, turned, and pulled.

Then, he stepped back. Whatever he might have expected, it was not this. There was a surface of darkness, as featureless as a pool of ink, standing before him, flush with the threshold. Gil stuck his hand into the blackness and pulled it back. The hand seemed unharmed, and the darkness did not cling to it.

A voice said, "Come in." It was not a voice he had heard before.

Gil thought of two ways he could perhaps ignite his sword to act as an impromptu torch, but he did not want to draw the blade for a frivolous purpose. He stepped into the darkness.

He expected a cool sensation as he plunged into the dark, as if into the surface of an inky pool, but there was not. He heard the door swing shut behind him. From the feel of the air on his brow, he sensed that he was in a room of modest size.

"It is dark in here," said Gil.

"It is useful for ignoring distractions, illusions, and other rumfuddle, my good lad. I also find it terrifically concentrates the mind." The deep voice was both cheerfully merry and gravely serious at once: an odd combination of tones. From the sound of the voice and breathing, the man was large. "The lack of light not only excuses me from the tedium of distinguishing truth from illusion in appearance, but I am also required to memorize the locations of all objects in the room. Your chair is two steps to fore and one step to your right."

"I would rather stand."

"You are a rational being with free will, so naturally that choice is yours, but nonetheless I might suggest seating yourself as the transposition might prove disorienting."

Gil stepped forward twice and once to the right, clasped his scabbard to move it aside, and flung himself down abruptly. His chain skirts rattled on the wooden seat he suddenly found beneath him, and his backplate clanged against the stiff chairback.

The voice said, "You did not grope with your hand. How did you know the chair was real?"

"I did not know, but I had no reason to doubt your word. Unseen things are not necessarily unreal."

"You took my instructions on faith. This is odd since you do not know me."

Gil said, "If you meant me harm, you could have come upon me as I slept, locked in a jail cell, unarmed. If you do not mean me harm, why lie about a chair? A liar would make sure the chair was there so that I would trust him in small things, that he might betray me in large things. Are you human or elfin? What is your name?"

"If I asked you the same questions, would you answer?"

"No."

"I thought not. Like you, I am someone who is aware of a universal system of deception and illusion that clouds the eyes and confounds the thoughts of all mortal men. In times long past, mankind knew it shared the world with creatures as rational as himself, either partly supernatural or wholly. They might be dubbed the *longevitae*, for they are longer lived than men, but not immortal.

"There are three kingdoms and many kinds and clans within them. The oldest are wholly spiritual, and their physical manifestations are mere appearances. The laws of nature excuse them from nature, as immune as a visiting ambassador. Pagan men of old worshipped them as gods and performed impious sacrifices. Call them the Children of Old Night and Chaos. They can die, but not by human hands.

"Next are the Lords of the Night World. These are called *fay* because their fates are not as those of mortal men. The bright sun of day, which counts the times and seasons so faithfully for men, has taken a dislike to them, and for this reason Paracelsus called them *nocturnals* or *nightfolk*.

These are unearthly fair or foul, nymphs or night-hags, light-elfs and dark-elfs, or chimerical between man and beast. Oddly, the sun shines just as brightly on their parts of the world as on ours. The name refers to a spiritual darkness, you understand.

"Four nobles among the elfinkind took the fair daughters of man to wife, as many as they wished, and from them spring the several kinds and clans of the Twilight Folk, neither fully of the day nor dark. These four clans are half human and half superhuman. Much of the glamour, power, and strangeness of faerie still clings to them like clouds about an unvisited far mountain. These Twilight Folk can dwell among men if they wish, cloaked, as predators or protectors of mankind. In time past, some threw their cloaks aside to do great works of wonder remembered forever in song or to wreak great evils never to be forgotten. Many inherit strange gifts and talents from their forefathers, elfish things, and by their nature can do what men cannot; others study unnatural practices, summoning aid from their cousins and uncles in the Night World, and are called warlocks.

"Some Twilight Folk have only a drop of the old blood in them and are very much like men. They keep their youth and strength longer than other men but do not outlive them. A strangeness haunts them, for they see and speak of high, hidden, and far-off things neither feared nor understood by their neighbors. Some dance beneath the stars to music humans cannot hear; some walk by night on strange journeys part in dream and part in waking; some speak into the deep places of the world, and voices answer them.

"And, at last, there are those who have but half a drop. These are called poets and visionaries and madmen, and the world scorns them and ignores them, for their dreams are not strong enough to bend fate or to mend the world. To them the fairy blood, watered and weak, is but a torment, for they yearn to hear the horns of elfland dimly blowing, yet their ears are too dull."

Gil listened, at first impatiently, and then with growing fascination. Here seemed to be a man who would answer his questions, who knew about the hidden world of which Gil's mother spoke either in riddles, or not at all.

Gil said, "How many species are there?"

The voice chuckled. "The laws of nature, to them, are merely strong suggestions. They are not bothered by boundaries between kinds. The Moth family, for example, has mermaid and wolfman in their bloodline, not to mention Minotaur and satyr, swan-maid and fox-spirit, Nagas and Nephilim, Centaurs and cat-women, Borrowers and Brobdingnagians, Brollochan and Brownies, insufferable talking horses called Houyhnhnms, and just about every admixture you could imagine. I have heard of Cobwebs marrying ghosts and ghouls, diseases and delusions, and giving birth to abominations I will not describe; or Peaseblossoms marrying the seasons or the hours, or Mustardseeds, the stars. Love conquers all bounds."

"How can there be so much men do not know?"

"Since I do not know how many mysteries are wandering Creation waiting to be found, I cannot say whether mankind knows a great proportion of them or small, neither can I explain the ratio."

"Why do the elfs hide from men?"

"They love the darkness for the same reason men do: because their deeds are wicked."

"All elfs?"

"Not all. The Old Ones recall brighter dawns, when they sprang shining and strong from the hand of the Creator and rollicked in the sea or rampaged among the clouds and stars, shouting for joy. Some regret the exile. Far too few."

"Who is Titania?"

"Ask rather who she was. The empress and high queen of the elfs and fairest of all her wide realm, which is famous for the beauty of its beauties. She is lost, a fate too terrible to say, and still Alberec grieves and seeks her, paying no mind to the throne he has lost to his ungrateful and treacherous son. Titania is gone from the world and will not be reborn into it, nor shall any likeness of her return."

"Where do the elfs come from?"

He heard another chuckle. "Where do the stars come from?"

Gil tried to remember what he had half-heard in science class. "They were condensed out of a primordial gas cloud by gravity."

"If you say so. Well, for our purposes, the elfs were condensed out of a primordial gas cloud by the Fall of Man."

Gil frowned, cross. "Are you sure you are a police detective?"

"I am, surely," said the voice in a throaty tone, as if holding back a laugh. "But are you sure you know what police detectives do?"

"Solve crimes."

"And what about crimes older than time and larger than the cosmos? Whose business is it to solve those?"

More crossly, Gil said, "You must be part elf."

"What makes you say that?"

"They talk in riddles. I should know."

"But mine was one riddle whose answer you need to speak."

Gil was getting impatient. "What was the question again?"

"Whose business is it to solve the metaphysical crime of men being the prey and playthings of elfs? Men cannot save themselves."

"It's your business. You must be some sort of metaphysical police detective."

A sigh of disappointment sounded. "Ah, well. If you say so."

Gil leaned forward. "You wanted another answer?"

"Did I?"

"Stop answering every question with a question. It is really annoying."

"Is it?"

"Stop that!"

"I will, young man, if you answer me truly."

Gil took a breath and realized he had grown rude. He reminded himself of his manners and said, "I answer truly all questions I may answer, sir."

2. A Larger World

The voice in the black room now took on a more serious tone. "Once there were wide expanses of wood and meadowland, oceans unsailed and mountains unclimbed, walled gardens, cities of alabaster and orichalcum. You were taught man has ruined these things with his industry and logging and hunting. It is not true. You are told that swiftness in ship and airplane makes all parts of the world reached in less time but that the globe is the same physical size it always was. Also not true. The portion of the Earth open to men has dwindled. The mist has merely covered more and more of the globe as the fay take and take all the goods things and good lands meant for man, leaving us the bones and gristle, and shrinking the world, leaving it dull and gray, lacking magic, mystery, wonder, and honor. It is a theft so monstrous that its sheer magnitude makes it invisible."

The voice paused, and the scope and cruelty of what had been done to man's world began to sink in to Gil's imagination.

The man said, "Whose business is it to solve this crime?"

Gil answered firmly, "Mine."

The man in the dark said nothing, but Gil could almost feel a look of warm satisfaction, an avuncular pride, issuing from the blackness.

"Is that the right answer?" asked Gil.

"If you say so. I mean that literally. Only one who truly wills this fight to be his can make it his. You are hired."

"Wait. What? You are not thinking I volunteered for something, are you?"

The man laughed. "If you do not volunteer now, you soon will. It is in your nature."

"I don't have any training. Real training, I mean. And no experience. And to be a detective, I would need to have papers, and be the right age, and be in the policeman's union. Right? Since I cannot tell you my name, I cannot fill out any paperwork. What about boot camp? The police academy?"

"Nothing is required for this line of work but willingness."

Gil was startled. "I have never heard of a job where you do not need any training or experience!"

"I think you have."

"What line of work has no requirements but willingness?"

"Martyrdom."

3. The Light

There was a snap of noise, and Gil's sharp eyes saw a tiny spark. In the light of the spark, he saw a large pair of callused and muscular hands breaking a fine necklace. Every link of the necklace flew apart, and turned into a bubble of tiny gold, then popped. The pendant of the necklace was a glowing object smaller than a credit card, made either of glass or mirror-bright metal, shining with an inner light.

The metal spun end over end, growing larger. Gil caught it in midair. It was not hot, but cool to the touch. It was a badge of white shaped like a miniature shield, divided by two bold red stripes at right angles. Across the top were small metal letters: SCATHED. Along the bottom was written: THE FINAL CRUSADE.

Gil said, "*Scathed*? What is that?"

"Your force and division. You are hereby a member of the Special Counter-Anarchist Task Force, Heterodoxy Enforcement Division."

Gil heard the sound of the big man rising. The footsteps moved to the left, came forward, and then moved to the right again to stand just before Gil. Gil imagined the man must have stepped around a desk or some other large object.

The sound of footsteps and a sense of pressure in the air told him that the man now moved behind him. He felt two large and heavy hands come down, one on his good shoulder and one on his wounded shoulder. Gil forced himself not to flinch or shout.

The man said, "Do you accept this commission?"

Gil thought of the mother whose child had been stolen. It was a crime no human being could see or detect. No one but him.

Gil said solemnly, "I accept the commission."

"Then look!"

A light leaped up from the badge, glistering and clear as starlight, and a beam reached out like a searchlight. The desk and wall Gil had presumed were there were not. Instead there was a cloud of black mist, which, the moment the starlight colored beam fell on it, turned white and rushed away. At the same time, the sounds echoing from the wall, the sense of being indoors, also rushed away, as if the walls and ceiling were expanded to a vastness like the night sky, or as if the chair and floor on which he sat were accelerating backward or tumbling in free fall. Gil clutched the wooden arms of the chair, trying not to faint. Nothing on his gear or garb was moving, so perhaps the rushing sensation was only in his inner ear, not in reality.

Gil found himself in a high place looking out over a vast cavern. The floor was hundreds of yards away. The searchlight beam from his badge reached like a glittering finger across the gloom and danced back and forth on the figure of a crowned king, armed at all points, with his hand folded across his chest.

The king lay on his back on a stone slab. He did not move or breathe. The ensign above him showed the image of a golden dragon; the shield at his feet showed a maiden in blue trampling a serpent.

To his left and right were coffers and vessels filled with gold coins and silver ingots, or other elfin alloys whose names no man knew, and also gems large and small, chalices, drinking horns, and plates, necklaces, rings, armlets, brooches, torcs, and other treasures. A snow-white steed stood at his head, also motionless and unbreathing. At its foot was a cold-black hunting dog of fierce and noble aspect, but standing still as a corpse.

Gil tilted and raised the badge, but the beam would not point at anything else in the cavern save the king on the stone. From the reflections darting from the glittering piles of gold and silver, Gil could see hints and half-shapes of other armored knights on lowers slabs, asleep to one side and the other, with their snow-white steeds asleep next to them. Each knight had a sword in his clasped hands. Only the king's hands were empty.

Gil said, "Where is his sword?"

The man behind him laughed. "I see you are a true knight. A clerk would have asked about his soul, a burgher about his treasures."

"So where is it?"

"That sword was thrown into a lake in Wales. It will not be seen again until that king is healed, opens his eyes, and puts out his hand. Do not wish that hour to come swiftly! Woe to England then, for the hour will be dark indeed for all Christian souls when the true king is needed and is called forth once again."

"How is there a giant underground cave on the second floor of a police station?"

"This is the hollow hill beneath Alderley Edge in England. That is Arthur Pendragon, the rightful King of England and Emperor of Rome. By the unalterable will of Heaven he sleeps in an eternal sleep! By disuse and bad custom, men have forgotten him, but the laws have not forgotten.

It is from him you take your commission. To him and to no lesser lord you must swear your fealty."

Gil said, "How can I swear to a sleeping king?"

"How can you not? The oath is still binding in this world and all others, until Heaven and Earth pass away and are made anew! Go and kneel. Put your hands between his and swear. This hour will not come again. I will tell you the words if you do not know them."

Gil said softly, "I have known them since I was seven years old."

"You must go to him without your sword and helm, bareheaded and empty handed. Let go of the badge. Follow it."

This time, Gil knew, his promise not to set the sword aside did not hold. His mother had said the sword could be set aside when his lord commanded. If he needed to set it aside to get into the service of his lord in the first place, that also counted.

He tossed the badge gently upward, and it hung in midair with nothing holding it aloft. He put the helm and swordbelt on the stiff wooden chair and left his shield behind.

The badge began drifting forward. He followed. The beam of light stayed focused on the king, but now a sphere of light also began to glow from the badge in all directions so that he could see the floor at his feet, which was rough and grew rougher as he descended.

The floor fell steeply. He used both hands to climb down the steep slope of rocks and boulders. Beyond that was something like a bridge or ramp the glowing badge led him down, a narrow path with a steep drop to either side.

Closer to the king, the floor was more even once again, but there were stalagmites here and there, which over a thousand years of dripping water had built up. White horses in their brilliant barding and furniture stood as motionless as marble statues, heads lowered at identical angles. The knights of the Table Round, the fairest and noblest company of knights the world had ever seen, rested in strange and unnatural motionlessness in this vast cave. Gil was almost ashamed of how loud his footfalls were.

Then, he was there.

4. The King

Gil knelt. It was a long moment before he could raise his eyes to look at the unliving and inanimate features. Gil was shy. This was the very man he had selected to be the model and the ideal his real father never was.

Arthur was a handsome man, even asleep. Gil was glad to see crow's feet at his eyes and wrinkles at his mouth to indicate that he laughed often, but there were also lines of care and worry around his brow and nostrils, those of a man who does not smile when he ponders many a hard judgment, or must make in the heat of battle the decision that will win or lose the war, and his men's lives. It was a majestic face.

Gil saw that the hands of the king were not clasped in prayer, for there was a little space between his right hand and his left. Gil put his own hands palm to palm and put their fingers between the palms of the king, so that Arthur's hands were outside his, as if clasping them.

Gil was startled. The king's hands were not cold, but warm. There was no pulse, but the fingers were pink.

Suddenly, like a skyrocket in his heart, Gil realized that all the old and impossible stories he had read and heard and loved as a child were true. This was the once and future king, the Lord of Camelot, who banished the lawless chaos of the land and established peace, justice, and good laws. He was not dead. His laws were not dead. His dream was not dead. He would one day return and with him, a new dawn, a new world. He lived.

Gil said softly, "I, Gilberec Parzival Moth, avow me the liege man of life and limb to Arthur, Emperor and King, against every creature living or dead, now and for aye, to yield him true and faithful service, homage, and earthly worship: to bear arms against the king's enemies; render justice to the king's subjects low and high; defend the faith; uphold the true; honor the fair; and protect the weak. So help me God and the Holy Dame."

The king's hands did not move, but they seemed to grow warmer. Gil took this as a sign that his oath had been accepted.

He stood and climbed back the way he had come. Gil hoped for some glimpse of the man in the dark room, but the light from the badge faded, and the walls and ceiling seemed to shrink down to their previous proportions so that the feel of the air and the sound of the echoes told him he was in a small room again.

"Sit!" ordered the voice.

5. The Gift

"When do I get my spurs?" Gil wound the sword belt around his waist and the baldric over his shoulder, took up the helm, and sat.

The footfalls and sense of pressure from the large man moved around the room again, and Gil heard the scrape of chairlegs against the floor, the creak of a desk as if a heavy elbow now rested on it.

"Officially, you are a squire as yet, but also a man-at-arms, and able to bear weapons in the king's service."

"What about medical care? I seem to get hurt a lot, armor or no armor, not to mention training injuries."

"Show your badge to the desk sergeant at the police station in any nation where the writ of Arthurian Law runs, and if the healing hands cannot be found in that hour, you will be cast into sleep until they can be."

"The writ of Arthurian Law? What is that?"

"You recall he once conquered Rome and assumed the purple as Imperator. Hence the House of Pendragon has lawful claim over all the lands once or ever ruled by the Roman Empire, therefore, also, the Byzantine Empire, the Carolingian Empire, the Holy Roman Empire, the Spanish Empire, the British Empire, and the Austrian Empire. Basically, anything once ruled by Caesar, Kaiser, Czar, or Christian King, from Singapore to Calcutta to Patagonia, from the Bosporus to Australia, from South Africa to Northern Alaska, from Tripoli to Troynovant, still owes allegiance to Arthur."

Gil was trying to figure out which parts of the world that did not cover. His best grades had not been in geography or modern history. He thought maybe the Sahara and Siberia were not covered. He could not remember if any European power had ever conquered Tibet. He knew that Singapore had once been a British colony, and everything in South America was

Spanish or Portuguese, so if he were wounded in Uruguay and could find a police station…

Gil gritted his teeth and told himself to snap out of it and to stop wondering about useless nonsense. What were the chances that a boy without a car, or a squire without a horse, would end up in another hemisphere?

"What about the Revolutionary War?" Gil asked sharply.

"Which one?"

"The American Revolution."

"Elfs don't care about which bull leads the herd. In the end, the rancher owns them all."

Gil was not sure he like the sound of that. "I am an American. We are a free people."

"To be free of good King Arthur's reign is not necessarily a good thing. And you are his subject now, and his loyal vassal," the voice laughed, "no matter which way the rest of America decides to go."

"What was that about healing and sleeping?"

The man's voice said, "My gift is the laying on of hands." The man heaved a sigh, which sounded odd coming from a voice so jovial. "I can heal everyone but Arthur, the only man I truly wish to heal." Then, in a jollier tone, the voice continued, "My office door appears in any police station where the laws of my king still hold, as I explained. When any report that smells of elfwork is filed, I hear of it."

"And you can heal my wounds? By magic?"

"It is not *magic* if, by that word, you mean breaking the laws of nature or trafficking with dark powers. But in the same way federal law at times overrules local ordinance, there is a higher law my gift calls upon. The badge is imbued with starlight, so it will drive the mists away, and you can find or summon my door. It is well trained. Not like some doors I know."

"What was that about sleeping?"

"I have other duties, so if you are wounded, and find my door in an hour when I am absent, enter the dark room, and an enchanted sleep will fall upon you. This will alleviate your pain and prevent the wounds from bleeding or getting worse. And I like to keep my floor clean of stains."

That did not sound very reassuring. Gil said, "I have another question. I put a drop of blood on my tongue from the monster I slew."

"I know."

Gil frowned in surprise. "How do you know?"

"I can hear the truth in your voice."

Gil said, "That's my question. The officer who arrested me did not hear the truth in me. Why is that?"

"What makes you think he did not? He brought you here and held you until I could arrive. You did not want the whole crowd of everyone in earshot to hear about elfs and monsters, did you? They would all end up imprisoned in madhouses, and Winged Nightmare would disorder their brains with alchemy to make sure that each and every witness in the crowd went stark mad, just to keep up appearances. No, I am pretty sure he believed you and acted quickly."

"Who is Winged Nightmare?"

"The witch-king in charge of madmen. He has never been defeated, except by Winged Vengeance. And I cannot call on Winged Vengeance any more, nor heal madness, so you must tell no humans the truth about our world."

"Who is Winged Vengeance?"

"Someone who parted from me not on speaking terms. A foe of the Anarchists."

"Do all policemen believe in elfs?"

"Not consciously. You might say that a metaphysical policeman is allowed a certain degree of authority over physical policemen. But–" and now the jovial tone grew grim and serious "–but you have been granted a great gift and a terrible weapon you carry on your tongue. Use it with wisdom and discretion! The wise grow sad when told more truths than their hearts can hold, and fools grow vain. And, in any case, if you speak a truth too unbelievable to be believed, but your tongue forces your human listeners to believe it anyway, it may go badly."

"Badly...?"

"For one thing, they might think you insane—because they can hear in your voice how you truly believe something they know cannot be true— and throw you in an asylum. Madhouses and churches are the targets of the darkness the elf kings serve. The three folk the enemy does not want to see get better are madmen and sinners."

"That is only two."

"The third is knights, for they return to combat upon recovering their strength."

"Thornstab told me how to find the kings at feast under the mountain."

"The Champion of Air and Darkness will be at that feast."

"Then who should I fight? Him? Alberec and Erlkoenig are both evil."

"Do not blame the elfin kings over much. They are trapped by a maze of oaths without a thread to lead them free. No, there are darker powers at work here: seven who would overthrow all laws of God and angel, elf and man, hollow out the world, and collapse all into Hell! But it is too soon by far to speak of them. The closer foes must be conquered before those from deeper, darker worlds are known. You are meant to fight giants, my lad. But you must first be trained! You must seek a knight to train you beneath the mountain."

"Why there? Do you have any knights on the force who can train me?"

"At the moment, my department is small."

"How small?"

"Quite small…"

"*How* small?"

"It consists of three: one is missing, one is a deserter, and then there is you."

"Wait… what was that?"

"On to other business! Your best bet is to ask the enemy to train you. If you handle the matter correctly, their oaths will require it of them even if it seems…"

"Wait a moment. You mean I am fighting all the forces of evil… alone?"

"I am glad you are eager to begin! Since the crime scene is the entire planet, and the suspects are several races and clans of supernatural beings, I do not need to provide you with any clues, leads, or witnesses. The theft of all human life, the human world, and human happiness is a felony large enough to occupy your time until I contact you with further instructions."

"Go back to the part where I am fighting all alone. Your department is just you, in this room…?"

"When you wake, you will be healed and whole."

"WAIT!" cried Gil, leaping to his feet. But a warm and fuzzy sensation was already making his limbs heavy and making his thoughts float away. He realized that the black room was very dark, but now he was aware of a reddish light coming from somewhere. Or perhaps that was just the sunlight shining on his closed eyelids.

6. Police Dog

He opened his eyes and was immediately rewarded with the sensation of a dog licking his face. Gil snorted in surprise and sat up. He was wrapped in his long gray cloak against the cold, dressed in his quilted tunic and hose, lying under a leafless tree in a little copse of woods. His sword was at hand, tucked into the cloak with him.

Ruff was with him, barking excitedly, jumping, and wagging his tail. Gil's hauberk was hanging from the branches of the tree, with the gauntlets hanging from branches to either side, the boots below, the helm dangling from a leafless branch above. The shoulder plate had been repaired, and all the broken links of his mail made fast and whole once more.

Ruff barked, "You're up! You're up!"

Something was odd. Where were all the pains and aches of his wounds? Gil said, "Was that a dream? Or what just happened?"

Ruff said, "You are a policeman now! Does that make me a police dog? Police dogs are brave! I think I will like being a police dog!"

Gil shook his head, rubbed his shoulder, and then felt his legs. He felt his nose. Nothing was broken. Nothing was torn or even bruised. But he could feel the scars of claw marks in his leg.

The linen had been scrubbed clean of bloodstains, but not perfectly. He could see tiny flecks of brown here and there. Rips in the fabric had been sewn neatly with a green thread with fine, small stitches.

He pulled the tunic off and looked at his shoulder. The stitches made by the nurse practitioner were gone, but the hairs of his skin were missing in a set of parallel stroke-marks from his enemy's claws, and the skin in those lines was pale and thick.

Ruff put his nose to Gil's pouch, which was lying on the brown grass by the roots of the tree. "He left you some food. Cheese and bread. There had been a sausage, also, but, ah, something happened to it."

"What happened?"

"I had to impound it as evidence of a crime."

"What crime?"

"Someone stole the sausage. I saved the cheese and bread for you. You like cheese."

"No," Gil said, talking more to himself than to Ruff. "What happened to me?"

"Eat up! We are in Buncombe County, about seventy miles west of Brown Mountain, and Christmas is only four days away. You told Thornstab. The Necromancer's little son. I was outside the window. That is where we are going, right? So you can arrest people and stab them? When do you get a horse? A police horse! Like a Mountie!"

Gil looked at the big dog intently. "And how do you know I am a policeman now? Can you smell it?"

Ruff wagged his tail, his tongue lolling. "Yes! Yes! Also the fact that you have a policeman's badge hanging on a lanyard around your neck."

Gil looked down. It had been tucked under his tunic. In the sunlight, it looked like it was made of solid diamond, or some other impossibly hard, clean, and precious substance. The word SCATHED was written along the top. At the bottom was the motto THE LAST CRUSADE.

Gil stared down at the badge in his hands. He was not sure what to think. "Was that all an illusion? A joke? A trick by some elf? Or am I Arthur's man now?"

Ruff said, "Can't you see through tricks now? If you saw the king, he was the real king."

Gil looked up. The sky was clear and blue, and the winter sun was dazzling bright on the clouds, but gave little heat. "Then I must fight all the dark powers of the world alone."

Ruff's ears drooped. "Hey! You are not alone. I can be a police dog. I can."

Chapter 3

Alone on Christmas Eve

1. Carrion Bird

The county seat was far from Brown Mountain, and Gil and Ruff were in the county north of there, so the mountain was closer to him than his house. Gil did not even try hitchhiking; if anyone questioned him about his weapons and armor, Gil was unwilling to say he was in a stageplay or visiting a Renaissance fair, but neither was he willing to mark innocent people to be captured and sent screaming to madhouses.

Gil divided his bread and cheese into four parts and ate no more than one part a day. Marching in winter in a heavy hauberk used a lot of energy, and he was hungry and weak most of the time, except at night, when he was cold and wet.

It snowed. Gil had not seen the end of the tournament between the Winter Knights and the Summer, but since the North Carolina December was not supposed to look like a Pennsylvania February, Gil's guess was that the forces of the Summer elfs had been trounced.

Living off the land was not impossible in the cold weather, but it was pretty close. It was not much fun, but no one seemed inclined to offer him a ride, despite the holiday season.

On the second day, Gil found a squirrel that was willing to share some nuts. Ruff wanted to eat the squirrel, but Gil forbade it.

On the third day, Gil had nothing to eat beside his horded morsel of bread.

On the fourth day, they entered a small town and found a dumpster behind a fried chicken stand, where Ruff was astounded at how many perfectly good bones had been thrown out, with meat and gristle attached. Gil was only slightly more hygienic than the dog when it came to what he was willing to eat out of other people's garbage, but he was surprised at how many kids threw out perfectly good cole slaw still unopened in its Styrofoam cup.

On Christmas Eve itself, he was tramping through a small town north of the national park, wrapped in his gray cloak, jangling with each step. Cheerful plastic stars, neon candy canes, and foam rubber Santas glittered from the lampposts and storefront windows, but no one was on the street.

Gil stopped and stared mournfully at a payphone, which was gray and dull under its cap of snow. "I wish I had a dime. I wish my mother had a phone."

Ruff said, "I think calls are a quarter now. Or fifty cents. Or maybe a dollar."

A coal-black crow landed on the phone box. His voice was sharp and crisp. "Your mother is doing fine. She is lonely, but otherwise she is okay. She prays each night for your safety to the angel that stands outside her window with a drawn sword."

Gil said, "You know her?"

"All birds know her. But of her we never speak."

"How do you know her? Why don't you speak of her?"

The crow tapped the box of the payphone intently. "Bah! Never any insects in this sort of tree! Sorry, what? I cannot speak of why we do not speak of her without speaking of her, can I?"

Gil pushed back his coif and plucked a silver hair from his head. "Bring this to her. If she sees it, she will know I am alive."

Ruff said, "Or bald."

The crow looked carefully at the silver hair Gil laid on the top of the hood of the payphone, first with his right eye and then with his left. Then, he put one foot on it. "Nice! Can I keep it after she is done looking at it?"

Gil said, "On one condition! You also have to help me with one other thing."

The crow said, "I would have helped you anyway. Some of us are rooting for you. But, since you offered, I'll take the hair, just to be sociable. What do you need?"

Gil said, "First, what do you know about me that you are rooting for me?"

"You are *her* son." The crow shrugged. "Birds remember the way. That is our talent. We don't get lost on long trips, do we? You were about to tell me what you need."

Gil said, "I am looking for a willow tree from which no felon has ever been hanged. Do you know the trees around here?"

The crow turned his beak to one side to fix his beady black eye on Gil and said, "The trees whisper about the Christmas tree of Blowing Rock that sacrificed himself to aid you in your fight and was burned. Oak and Ash and Thorn-tree are displeased with you, for these trees were worshipped as sacred things in pagan days, and Willow is the witch's tree. Do not fear them! They are asleep this time of year. But Dogwood favors you, for obvious reasons, as do many tribes of conifers and pines, and those trees that do not die in winter. When you walk through these woods in winter, you are surrounded by well-wishers and protectors. The unseen foes do not know where you are. The Cobwebs seeking your life lost sight of you after you were taken into the police station, and the evergreens have used their influence to hide you and lured the Faceless Searching Things far astray."

2. The Witches' Tree

A cold wind blew, stirring up the ground snow. Gil shivered and said, "It is weird to think I was in some sort of danger and did not know it."

The crow said, "Why do you seek a Willow? It is an unchancy tree."

Ruff the dog said, "Some of us think crows are unchancy birds!"

Gil said, "What does 'unchancy' mean?"

Ruff said, "Unlucky. The crow is a bird of ill omen."

The crow raised its yellow beak and said proudly, "It is told among the crows that one of our ancestors landed on the tree the corpse of the Christ was hanging on, and the Virgin asked him not to eat her son's flesh since it was set aside for another fate. My ancestor agreed and fed on the Good Thief instead. Because of that, we crows will be white as doves when we get to Heaven!"

Ruff said, "Some crows liked the pagan gods better and serve the witches. They will stay black! But all dogs go to Heaven!"

The crow said, "Really…? The Barghest, Black Dog of Yorkshire, serves the fay, and so the Cu Shee!" The crow clicked its beak in amusement. "Galleytrot? Hairy Jack? Mauthe Doog? The Yell Hound? What about the Black Shuck of East Anglia?"

"Even Hitler's dog!" barked Ruff. "It is not too late!"

Gil was listening, not sure what to make of this. He said, "Do animals really get to go to Heaven?"

The crow said, "We were in Eden with your first parents. We got kicked out for your sake, didn't we? So why shouldn't we be allowed back in with you? The really bad animals were all drowned in the big flood."

Ruff said, "Dogs did not get kicked out! Adam's dog, Celeb, volunteered to go with him."

The crow said crossly, "You were not the only one! Goat, Ram, Swine, and Kine also volunteered, as did Stallion and Bee. They say Cat was the last of all to leave Eden and was less afraid of the Seraphim than Lucifer, and for that reason, to this day, is permitted to stare at kings, unabashed."

Ruff said, "And the first Crow hung back because he wanted to talk to the snake about death, which was a new invention back then, and find out if it was good eatings! What about that, huh?"

Gil raised his hand. "Look, that's nice and all, but I need some information. I need a willow wand to find the entrance to the elf mountain before Christmas. There is a charm I have to repeat."

The crow ruffled his black feathers so that they stood up. It was a sign that the crow was afraid. He said, "Better not to! It is an elfish trick."

Gil said, "You mean it would not work?"

The crow said, "Certainly it would work! Work like a charm, as they say! And the next charm would work also, and maybe the third, but then the demands for sacrifices would start. Innocent and meaningless things you would be asked to sacrifice at first, and then more doubtful things. And soon, without noticing it, you would be doing criminal acts: misdemeanors; then felonies; then atrocities. You don't think the worshippers of Moloch *started* with child sacrifice, do you? It is all very gradual, and you ground-bound types never see the bird's-eye view and never see the final destination toward which your feet are taking you. Gah! Walking on feet is so unwise!"

Gil said, "But if I don't obey the instructions exactly, how will I get in? I've read fairy tales. You have to obey instructions to the letter in a fairy tale, or things go badly."

The crow said skeptically, "You may have bumped into some fairy tale things, but that does not mean you are in a fairy tale story."

"So says a talking animal!"

The crow shrugged. "So? Balaam talked to an ass."

Gil looked down at his sword hanging by his hip, remembering what his mother had told him about its meaning. He said sharply to the crow, "I am not going to say that was a fairy tale, so don't ask."

"No, I was going to say I know what it feels like," the crow said sarcastically. "What makes you more stubborn than him?"

Ruff said, "More stubborn than which? Balaam or the ass?"

Gil said to Ruff, "You are not helping."

The crow said, "Listen! Aesop interviewed all sorts of birds and creatures back in the day, so I know some of his talking animal tales do not end with the moral of the story being 'obey the creepy elf no matter what.' "

Gil said, "Fine. So how do I get into the mountain?"

The crow said sardonically, "Ask your dog...." And, with his bill snatching up the silver hair lying beneath his foot, the crow flapped away in a flurry of black feathers.

3. Demi-Something

Gil stared down at Ruff, saying nothing. Ruff wagged his tail, tongue lolling, but then, under the relentless gaze, the tail wagged more and more slowly until it came to a limp, sad stop altogether. Ruff's ears sagged, and his eyes were large and dark with sadness.

Finally, Ruff said, "Yes, I can find the entrance for you. It moves around, but I can find it. You have to go farther up the mountain than before, like I said."

"You know where it is?"

"Yeah."

Gil said, "Why? Because you are a spy for the elfs? Is that it?"

Ruff heaved a sigh as if his canine heart would break. "Yeah. That's it...."

"What have you told them about me?"

Now Ruff perked up a little, "I was pretty clever about that! I told them that some human was talking to the rabbits and the wolves, trying to be a knight, and that he wrestled a bear, but I did not give them your name. I figured they would see you were trained by a bear because you roar like a bear and fight like a bear."

"Hmm. You said it was because of who I am. Who am I?"

"I hate to break it to you, Gil. You are some sort of freakish and unusual magical boy. Probably not a demigod, but you are a demi-something. I know you won't believe me."

Gil said patiently, "No, when a talking dog tells me I am a freakish magical guy, it is a good idea to believe it. Were you sent to spy on me?"

"No. They don't know you exist. Not you, you. They know the Swan Knight exists, but they think he might be the one who fought Guynglaff all those years ago in Goose Lake, California, and buried him alive. But they don't know about Gilberec Moth."

Gil felt weary from the hiking he had done that day, the weight of the armor, and the cold. Some of that weariness was in his voice. "Were you sent to spy on my mom?"

Ruff hunkered down and put his paws over his nose. "Yes..."

"Do they know where she is?"

Ruff stood up, his ears and tail suddenly standing up straight. "Nope! Nope! I never told them! I kept them busy with reports on what Mr. Yung was up to because some stuff that he sold had her scent on it, and some of the Headless Hunters found it, so they know she was in Blowing Rock at some point."

"Who are these Headless Hunters?"

"They are the Dullahan. The Headless Horseman of Sleepy Hollow is the one you've heard of. But he was kicked out because he lost his head and has to use a pumpkin with a candle in it. They hold their heads up on poles sometimes, so they can see over hedges and stuff, or they roll them into small places. They don't eat, so they are always hungry, but their hunger keeps them awake, so they never sleep either. The good news is that they cannot eat you alive. The bad news is that they always try. Lots of biting."

Gil said, "*Those* are the creatures looking for my mom?"

"Not where people are! They only come across their victims in lonely places, wastelands, and moors, in the dark, where no one can hear any screams."

"That is not exactly comforting."

"In human villages, or along human roads, especially near a church, the elfs send folk like me. Men love dogs!"

"So why didn't you turn my mom in?"

Ruff looked miserable. "Um. Um. Do you remember how we met?"

"Sure. You were in the road. I was suspended from school again that week and walking home. I had seen you once or twice before. Since I was expelled before lunch, and not really in the mood for a spam and lettuce sandwich, I got it out and tossed a bit of the meat, if you can call it meat, a little way down the road ahead of me. And you ran up and got it. And then I tossed another bit, and I kept walking, and you were still shy, so I did it again and again. After a while, you were walking along with me, dropping the hint that I should throw more food away. And I said I liked walking along with a dog like he was my dog, and you said you liked walking with a boy like he was your boy. I said you could be my dog. And then we had a footrace."

Ruff said, "That was the day I had finally figured out where your mom was, and I was going to follow you home to see if she was there. But then…"

"Yes?"

Ruff said, "Well… Well, you *fed* me! You walked along with me! Side by side! I like walking! Dogs like to walk! And I won the footrace!"

"It was close."

"It was not! I won by a mile!"

Gil said, "How do you know I did not *let* you win?"

"Because we then ran best two out of three, best three out of five, best five out of seven, and then had a wrestling match! And so… and so…" Ruff's voice trailed off, and he heaved a great sigh.

"…And what?"

"…And good golly, Gil! You looked so pathetic and lonely walking along! You had that terrible lettuce in your sandwich! It's rabbit food! How many times had you been kicked out of school for fighting? I had been watching, so I knew. Even when you won, you were still all bruised and scraped. Once you were my boy, we were a pack! I mean, even a wolf would not turn on a packmate! And so…"

"…And what?"

"…and so I lied…."

"What?"

"I lied to Sheila McGuire. She is a mistress of spies for the fortunate elfs. I told them that I had seen a silver-haired woman getting on a bus to Keatchie, Louisiana, which is one place elfs hate to go because of the Confederate cemetery there and all the unmarked graves. Smart, huh? But the Elf King placed a portal to his underground realm here on Brown Mountain anyway."

Gil felt, at that moment, the same way he had felt the first time he was in an elevator in one of the fancy stores he and his mom could never afford to buy anything from, and the motion upward caught him by surprise.

It seemed that his mom had not been too paranoid. In fact, she was not paranoid enough. It was just an accident that she had not been found and caught; a happenstance, a mistake. Gil had been walking the long, tiresome route home with a fat lip and a bloody nose and skinned knuckles, feeling lonesome and not feeling that hungry. And he threw some leftovers to a stray dog.

That was all. That was all that had saved his mom. A spam and lettuce sandwich.

4. Dog and Boy

Gil said, "So the Elf King does not actually live in a cave under Brown Mountain?"

Ruff said, "You told me all about King Arthur in his cave in England. It had a door that led to a police station in North Carolina. The detective said he could put his door anywhere. This is the same sort of trick."

"How does the trick work?"

"By magic. I don't know."

"Who makes them?"

"One of the Old Ones. I don't know."

"And now what? What do you know?"

Ruff looked up, hope and puzzlement warring in his eye. "Uh. Can you repeat the question?"

"Why did you work for the elfs to begin with? Sheila, or whatever her name is?"

"She's a true human, she is. Doctor McGuire, she insists we call her. She just works with them. She read some old books and used a lens to magnify the starlight, so she could see what they really said."

"Why, Ruff?"

"Well…" Ruff whined. He looked as pathetic as only a guilty dog can look. "It was cold! I was hungry! So I ate the elf food. She gave it to me. Free of charge, she said. The first bite is always free, she said."

"And then?"

"Then my taste buds were ruined! Normal, healthy, nutritious food like dead rodents and garbage lying in the gutter began to taste terrible! And, and, then I was trapped! I couldn't force myself to eat normal food. I had to keep going back to her!"

Gil said, "But I saw you pawing through those thrown-out chicken bones like a tiger! And you ate my sausage! And… heck, every time I've seen you eat."

"Your spam and lettuce sandwich tasted good to me. Remember how thin I used to be? It tasted good. All food tasted normal again after that. And I could eat the elf food or leave it alone as I liked. I beg it from Dr. McGuire just like normal and take it in my mouth, and then I go bury it."

Gil said, "I broke the spell… how?"

Ruff looked up at him, with a strange expression in his eye. Ruff said, "I don't know. Magic."

"I don't know any chants or charms or anything like that," protested Gil.

The dog said, "That is not real magic. That is a cheat. What you did was real."

Gil realized what that strange expression was. It was friendship. It was worship. It was love.

Gil sat down in the snow, not caring if it got his mail skirt wet, and he put his arms around his dog, and hugged him tight.

Gil whispered, "Why didn't you tell me this before? Any of this?"

The dog said, "I felt bad. I thought you sort of knew. You know everything!"

"I don't know everything...."

"You know everything important!" said Ruff in a voice of fierce loyalty. "I will show you the way to the door."

"Good dog."

"But I cannot go in with you. I mean, it would be dangerous. For you! I mean it would be dangerous for you. Because they know me."

"I understand."

"You understand...?"

"Yes, Ruff," said Gil. "I understand."

"Do you... forgive..." Ruff choked up, and his voice dropped to a near inaudible whisper. "I mean, is everything all okay? You still... like me?"

"Ruff," said Gil solemnly, "Of course I like you. I would die for you."

"I would die for you, too, Gil."

The boy hugged the dog again, and the dog thumped his tail against the ground in pure canine bliss.

"Gil...?"

"What is it, Ruff?"

"Can I still be your police dog?"

"We are a pack, Ruff. You have to be my police dog."

The dog leaned in closer to him, tongue lolling happily. Ruff said quietly, "You really are a truly magical boy."

Tears had somehow gotten in Gil's eyes. Gil did not want to wipe his nose on his surcoat, so he buried his face in the dog's warm fur so that Ruff would not see him tearing up, and he wiped his nose there.

"Good dog," he whispered. "Good boy."

Chapter 4

The Hall Beneath the Mountain

1. Landmarks

On Christmas Day Gil arose from his sopping and uncomfortable cloak, shivering, and out of bread, and his dog was gone. Ahead and above him was Brown Mountain, including the landmarks Ruff had so carefully pointed out, to tell him where the hidden door to the buried elfin stronghold would be that day.

"Go toward that cleft in the peak. Walk right between a rock shaped like a sombrero and a rock shaped like a beehive and take one hundred steps toward a larch with no branches on one side; then, turn left at a right angle, and take exactly fifty steps in the direction of the spot where the stream falls over a little drop. There is a round spot that had a ring of toadstools growing there where no grass grows. Such rings gather wherever faeries might dance, or their doors might open."

However, as he trudged up ever-steeper slopes, the sun was smothered by gray clouds, and colorless snow filled the air. The snow was heavy, and soon he could not see the cleft in the peak which was his first landmark; and when the snow got heavier, he could not see two hundred yards ahead of him. Then a driving wind came up, blustering and howling, so that the snow seemed almost to be falling sideways, and, whichever way he turned, the wind contrived to turn as well and kept blowing in his face. He was not able to see even twenty yards ahead.

If there were rocks shaped like sombreros or beehives, they were buried in the snow, and any stream, going over a drop or not, was probably iced over and also buried. How the dog had expected him to find in winter a ring of absent grass where toadstools used to grow was a question he wished he had thought to ask. Maybe the dog expected Gil to detect the months-old traces of toadstool spores by smell.

His landmarks lost, Gil kept trudging stubbornly forward, always trying to find whichever direction was uphill. He kept hoping to come across some non-migratory bird or white-coated rabbit to ask directions, but the bad weather seemed to have sent all the wildlife to seek nest, den, or burrow.

The wise thing to do would have been to hole up, build himself a snow shelter, try to stay warm, and wait out the storm. But that would mean missing the Christmas feast of the elfs.

So he kept walking until he lost sensation in his fingers and feet, and every breath was a pain to draw.

Dispirited, Gil sat down beneath a pine tree. The branches hung low to the ground and formed a little space free from the biting wind. Gil sat with his back to the bole, shivering.

He said aloud, "My dog is just dumb. He has got a good heart. I do not believe he would betray me or trick me."

Gil shivered some more, wondering how to make a fire under these conditions or how to survive. He was a little worried that he could not stop shivering.

"That crow said I was not alone when I was in the woods," Gil said. "Well, it sure feels… pretty darned… lonely…" Then, his teeth chattered too much for him to speak. "…but if there is any friend out there listening to me… what was that name the bird outside the jailhouse window said…? Saint Bernard? Saint Boniface? I need some help. Please…"

The wind tossed one of the branches so that it tapped him on the shoulder. Gil looked up. No one was here. The wind tossed the branch again. Its needles were blown and flattened so that the twig at the end of the branch pointed like an arrow to an almost-invisible hump of snow that might have covered a large stone that actually did look a bit like a beehive. The smaller heap next to it could have been the crown of a sombrero. Or it could have been nothing. What did a stone shaped like a sombrero look like anyway?

"Get up, Gil," he said to himself. But his arms and legs were too heavy to move. "Get up!" he said again. "If you want to be a knight, you have to be tough. You have to fight. You can die, but you can't quit. Get up. *Do what is right and never shirk....*"

But it was really cold, and he was starting actually to feel a bit warm and cozy here sitting under the branches.

"If you start to feel warm and sleepy in the snow, that is a bad sign. You are dying. Get up, or you will die! Get up!"

Gil realized it would take his every ounce of strength just to stand up. It would be the hardest fight in his life, just to stand.

If he got up, he would just have some other problem, some other fight to face in the days to come, and one after that, and another after that. Each one would be the hardest fight in his life, and they would just get harder and harder.

He could not be expected to fight each fight with all his strength and all his soul, with nothing left, could he?

"Get up! For Christ's sake, get up!"

The wind did not move, but one of the pine branches came under his shoulder and lifted Gil to his feet. Gil, taken unawares, stumbled a step or two forward and was slapped by the wind so fiercely that it shocked him awake. He looked back, astonished. But the tree behind him looked like it was just a tree. The branches were tossing in the wind, but it was just the motion of the wind. What had happened?

Gil drew his sword and saluted the tree. "Thank you, and may God bless you, Sir Pine Tree." He sheathed the sword again, turned, and marched between the two humps of snow he hoped were the landmarks he had sought.

As he walked, Gil said to the wind and to the snow, "I think I have to decide right now that whenever total *weirdness* happens to me, to treat it like it was real. After all, talking to a tree to thank it might look stupid, but on the other hand a normal tree would not notice and would not care. But if I fail to thank a tree that is somehow awake and took the trouble to help me, that would be downright rude."

With the snow in the air, it was impossible to see which of the trees ahead of him had been the larch with no branches on the side, so he picked one, walked close enough to it to see if it had branches on all sides, turned around, walked back to the two snow heaps he hoped were rocks, picked the next tree in view, and did it again. And then again, and then again. Finally, he found one that looked like a tree with branches only on one side: the huge masses of snow clinging to its branches give it a distinctively lopsided look.

He went back and counted his paces. He was very tired now, and very cold, and feeling lightheaded from hunger and weakness, but he did not give up.

Finally, he stopped in a spot he thought was the right one. He looked right and left. If there were a stream anywhere, it was invisible under the snow. He paced out fifty steps in a random direction and tried to walk in the snow in a circle, keeping the same spot at the center. With each ten steps, he called out, "Titania is risen!" because he could not remember the longer rhyming password anyway.

His voice got weaker and weaker, and his steps slowed. Therefore, as he was standing almost still, or only stumbling along in a slow shuffle through the howling wind blasts and freezing slush underfoot, it was no louder than a whisper the last time when said, "Titania is risen…."

And the ground tilted down under his feet, catching Gil by surprise. He tumbled down the slope thus formed and gathered a sliding rush of snow to tumble with him.

He was fetched up against the bars of a portcullis with a jarring crash, face-downward on the cold marble lip of the threshold. Only the fact that he was wearing his helm saved him from a scalp wound, perhaps a concussion.

Through the bars of the portcullis came a warm and golden light, dancing and flickering like light seen reflected from a pool, and also came the sound of laughter, the echo of strings and horns raised in cheery music, voices raised in song, and, best of all, the smells of freshly baked bread, savory meats, and spices.

He raised his head.

Two tall and splendid warriors in gleaming armor stood to either side of the portcullis, plumes as bright as torches, lance and shield in hand. Both had their faceplates turned toward where Gil lay in a heap, but only one allowed himself to laugh, and it was only a quiet snort.

2. Corylus and Lemur

The one on the left was dressed in black and silver, and on his surcoat was an image of a snowy owl roosting on a scimitar on a blue field under a crescent. The other was dressed in green and gold, and his shield was red painted with a hazel wreath.

Merely the heat from the air escaping between the bars was reviving Gil. He groaned, took the bars of the portcullis in his right hand, drove the point of his shield into the marble with his left, and rose to his shaky legs. The two elfin men-at-arms stood stiffly, their faceplates toward him, watching him from unseen eyes, not laughing aloud, making no move to help or to hinder.

Through the bars, Gil saw a great colonnade driven straight into the living rock of the mountain. The lanterns nearby were dark, and the corridor close at hand could not be seen, but those in the distance were bright. At the far end of the great gallery was an arch whose great doors were twin slabs of pale crystal thirty feet tall, hewn from some unearthly solid diamond. The doors were translucent, and moving lights and shadows could be seen behind as if through a cloud.

Gil turned toward the figure in gold and green. "Soldier of Alberec, admit me, I pray you. The day is deadly cold outside, and the generous hospitality of this court is known to all."

The man-at-arms in green said, "This portcullis cannot lift at my word, sir, but tell me your name, your father's name, and tell by whom you were invited to this festive solemnity, and I will send for the seneschal with all due haste, to learn his will, for he is the governor of the feast."

Gil said, "Is it the custom that the highborn introduce themselves to underlings who do not first give their names?"

The one in green and gold inclined his head. "I am Corylus the fatherless, son of Carya the Hazel Nymph, in service to Alberec."

The one in black and silver spoke. His voice was dispassionate and distant, like one who speaks in a dream. "I am Lemur the fatherless, son of the Queen of the Lilim, whose name it is unchancy to say, and I am the servant of Erlkoenig. We watch the door, a thankless task, while others feast because our fathers are unknown and our mothers dishonored. And you?"

"You have my sympathy and goodwill," Gil said, "I understand your plight; believe me. But I may not say my name."

Said Corylus, "How then? What would become of me if I allowed some unknown whose worth is not proven to enter?"

Gil said, "Send for your master if it is his decision, and not yours."

"How? He sits in splendor with his kings and peers and ministers of highest rank, amid rare entertainments and burning incense brought from beyond Arcturus, meats of long-extinct animals of succulent savor restored by mystic arts to life for the slaughter, and prepared by the late Queen's own chefs and cooks. Music heard only in dreams hangs in ecstasy on the breathless air, and every sight is pleasant to the eye within the feast hall, wonder upon wonder heaped! Should I call him into this drafty space to speak with one whose rank remains an unanswered question? He could turn my head into a boar's."

Gil turned to the other figure, called Lemur. "Soldier of the Winterking, when last I spoke with His Imperial Majesty, Erlkoenig, he told me my heraldry would be inscribed on the rolls of your heralds." Gil held up his shield and tapped it. "He said no one would question my blood. Yet this follower of Alberec here has done just that. Which better serves your master's honor? To agree with Alberec's loyal vassal or to carry out the will of Erlkoenig?"

But before Lemur could answer, there was a billow of white mist from the golden hallway beyond the bars, in the dark part of the hall nearest them. Suddenly, they saw a person tall and thin, garbed in shining white who was walking toward them, and a cloud of fireflies coming with him to light the way. Perhaps he had walked all the way from the diamond doors at the far end and only now became visible, or perhaps he had been fetched by some sudden magic from a distant place.

3. Phadrig Og

His jaw was narrow, and his hair was blue, and in his hand was a wand of ivory. A belt of silver links shaped like lotus flowers bound his waist, and a silver fillet bound his forehead, and there was a blue stone that burned with inner fire hanging between his delicately arched brows. His blue eyes were held in a perpetual squint, as if he were fighting with a headache.

Gil said softly, "Is this your master?"

Lemur said, "No. Erlkoenig's first minister is Gwyn ap Nudd of the Slaugh, dread master of his airy hounds, whose breath is the arctic wind."

Corylus said, "Alberec's minister is the sly and wicked Robin Good-fellow, called Puck. This man approaching is the seneschal of Brian Brollachan, Lord of the Autumn Lands. King Brian is a lesser king. The jealousy of Alberec and Erlkoenig will not permit one to have precedence over the other, so the master of this feast is Phadrig Og, King Brian's seneschal, and to him, for this night only, the keys of the door are given. It is he who seats the guests or turns them away."

But by then the pale-faced figure was near, and the two men-at-arms fell silent.

His voice was high and nasal, waspish and condescending. "The cold air disturbs Ethne, Balor's royal daughter, and I am sent from the revels to seek the cause. Doorwardens! Who opened the ramp? What nonsense is this?"

Corylus said, "Seneschal, here is one who seeks admittance."

But the seneschal snapped his finger impatiently. "I can see that. But who is he? The full roster of all the invited guests is complete. We expect no others. Why did you speak the word of the door?"

Corylus said, "Neither Lemur nor I called the words to open the ramp. The indwelling spirit of the doors did this thing."

"No matter! Who is not called cannot come in! Ask him his father's name. If he be royalty, send him away with gifts and stirrup cup to warm him. If he is of noble blood, send him on his way empty handed. If he is a tradesman, mariner, or crofter, beat him and send him off with a curse, whatever your malice can devise. If he is a churl or serf, kill him for daring to touch our doors." And, with this word, the seneschal turned smartly on his heel, as if anxious to return to the festivities.

But Lemur spoke. His voice was colorless and bloodless, but it cut through other sounds like the winter wind through an ill-made wall. "Phadrig Og! Look well upon this knight and see the shield he bears."

Phadrig Og, the seneschal, turned in surprise and then stared at Gil, his eyes narrowing.

Lemur said, "He slew the brothers of Guynglaff the Wild-Man-o'-Wood with a sword not made by mortal hands, and the Cobwebs are hunting for him high and low and have not found him."

Phadrig Og snapped back, "What is that to me? I am of the Night World. The Cobwebs are half-breeds and half-humans of the Twilight World. What are the half-creatures but troubles and trash, by-blows and cuckoos' eggs?"

Lemur said, "If we send him from these doors, which are watched by the half-born closely, and the Cobwebs fall upon him and slay him, it might be whispered that your master Brian was complicit in his death. And then some will wonder why Phadrig Og was not more curious about the nameless knight whom the headless huntsmen could not find. Some power is aiding him. If it is not my master, it is yours, or there is another player in the game: Alberec of the Summer Lands or Ethne the May Queen."

Phadrig Og turned toward Gil, "Well, sir? State your name and lineage, and tell by what right you intrude where you are not invited and none has welcomed you?"

Gil said, "An oath prevents me from giving my name. And as for by what right–" Gil hesitated. Perhaps he had no right to be here. But then he remembered the kidnapped child and the insane truckdriver. "–I am in service to Arthur Pendragon and am on a great and dangerous quest which brings me here."

Phadrig Og's face changed. His narrow, squinting eyes grew momentarily wide. "Your words ring true in my ear, young man. I dare not doubt them. But can it be that the Pendragon is still alive?"

Gil said, "It is by the unalterable will of Heaven!"

Phadrig Og looked taken aback. "Wh-What?"

Gil lifted his head and said in his most serious tone, "Hear me now! King Arthur's sword was thrown into a lake in Wales and will not be seen again except in his hand. But don't ask for that hour to come too quickly! Woe when it comes! That hour will be dark indeed!"

All three there gasped. Gil wondered if the childhood stories on which his mother raised him were somehow unknown to the elf world. Perhaps the promised return of Arthur was a surprise to them. But if they were spying on the human world, how could they not know that story? It was in books and movies.

Beneath his helm, Gil scowled. If it had been a secret kept from the elfs, might it not have been kept from them for a good reason?

Just then, Gil started shivering again. The cold wind was coming from behind, blowing down the ramp, and the snow was falling down into the little triangle formed by the surface, the upper lip of the ramp, and the lower lip where it met the closed portcullis threshold. Open sky was still overhead. The warmth, the delicious scents and haunting music coming through the bars, and the golden light, seemed unbearably precious to Gil at that moment. He was sure that if he were turned away, even if the Cobwebs did not kill him, the cold would.

Phadrig Og said sharply, "If you are a knight in Arthur's service, where is your horse? Where are your spurs?"

But Lemur said in his icy voice, "The Winter King has enrolled his coat of arms. All the Sons of Winter affirm that this one is of worthy blood, and a true knight."

The music from beyond the diamond doors suddenly crashed into a fanfare, and there was a sound of laughter and applause. Phadrig Og glanced over his shoulder, his yearning to return to the festivities clearly showing in his face.

"Come along! It is time to dine!" He snapped his fingers once more. The bars swiftly and silently lifted up.

4. The Hall of Pillars

Gil stepped forward into the warmth. Gil turned and said, "Lemur, you spoke up for me when there was no one else to speak for me. I will not forget your kindness."

The armored figure in black and silver drifted backward without moving his feet, as if gravity no longer affected him. His voice was as cold as the north wind, "Kindness is not my nature. I obey Erlkoenig with precision, out of fear, and my low birth keeps me far from him. Hence I will not see the fate he will inflict on you as you thrust yourself unwelcome

and unasked into his imperial presence. If your head is not on a platter
with the other rarities offered up at the feast this night before an hour
is past, then the unseen power whose pawn you are plays a deep game
indeed."

Phadrig Og walked at a breathless pace down the long colonnade. At
first it was dark, but the number of lanterns grew as they proceeded. Gil's
sight of the place grew clearer the farther he walked.

The dark part of the hall was full of breathing, and Gil smelled the
scent of hay and horses and heard the growling of dogs. The noise came
from above him. Near the gate were stables and kennels, but even Gil's
sharp eyes could not penetrate the shadows here.

Beyond this, there was more light, and he could see the colonnade was
straight with no arch, no door, and no opening to the left or right, at
least, not at floor level. The floorstones were of white, black, and green
marble, each one carved with the image of a fish or mermaid. The arched
roof above was painted over with songbirds and seabird and birds of prey,
bearded stars and crescent moons.

Every column was carved like a tree with spreading branches, each with
its own distinctive pattern of leaf or fruit: great and stately oak, ash, thorn,
alder, yew, willow; and between them were more slender columns, shaped
like black poplar, holm, hazelnut and chestnut, mulberry, elm, beech, and
fig; and between these were roof designs carved and adorned to resemble
wild grape, wrack, bryony and black bryony. A spiral design wrapped
each tree trunk, but Gil could not at first see what it meant.

The lamps grew brighter as the two approached the diamond panels of
the great door. Now Gil saw a line of narrow windows set in the upper part
of the walls high overhead, with lanterns and loopholes between. These
arches were barred with silver bars shaped into swirling spirals and flowery
designs. Gil saw that any foe forcing these doors could be showered with
arrows or drenched with molten lead poured from these upper places.

The spiral designs on the trees, Gil now saw, were serpents, snakes, and
dragons, each of a different breed, cobra or asp, adder or python. He
also saw carved into the roots of these trees was marble shaped like skulls
or piled bones. The stones underfoot had fewer images of wholesome
fish but now showed sharks and sea serpents or transparent monsters like

living skeletons with eyes like lamps. The stones overhead were adorned with owls.

At the end of the corridor, the doorposts were guarded by two statues, one of black and one of white marble. These were carved and polished idols of two great wolves, one in his summer coat and one in his winter coat. A great rack of swords and spears, with a line of shields below and helms above, filled the walls behind each of the huge wolf statues.

Phadrig Og said, "Take off your helmet and put your sword and shield there and there. Quickly now!"

Gil slipped his knapsack off his shoulder and dropped it on the floor. But he made no move to unbuckle his sword belt.

"I mean no disrespect, but I took an oath not to put this sword from me."

Anger snapped in the eyes of Phadrig Og like blue flame. "I have no time for this folly! I act this night for Erlkoenig and Alberec both: Do you defy the Emperor of Night and the Summer King? I should have you thrown to the corpse-eater!"

Gil said, "I will not break my word. Not even for kings."

Phadrig Og raised his wand. The tall black statue of the wolf now stirred and came to life, and it turned its great, shaggy head of stone and regarded Gil with eyes that were featureless black marbles, seemingly blind.

Gil stepped back, looking at the stone monster pensively. He could see no weakness, no way to attack it. It was not even alive. Gil said aloud, "Seneschal! This is a breech of honor! You invited me in! You said to come along! To come to dine!"

Phadrig Og laughed sarcastically. "Perhaps I meant you should come along to the pit of the corpse-eater! It is time for him to dine, not you! Should he not have his Christmas feast?"

The giant statue of the wolf moved its paw and opened up a marble slab before its feet like a trap door. A vile stench came up from the darkness beneath. No bottom was visible.

Phadrig Og said, "The corpse-eater will swallow even your bones so that Lemur will not fret about what rumors might say if the Cobwebs killed you. An elegant solution, satisfactory to all concerned!"

Gil said, "I am not satisfied!"

"Quite so. I should have said the solution will be satisfactory to all survivors. Alberec will never even know a nameless vagabond attempted to…"

5. The White Wolf

They were interrupted. The statue of the white wolf stirred and lifted its shaggy, stone head, staring down at Gil with smooth stone eyes. "In whose name, child, ask you entrance here, to these dark halls of celebration?"

Gil backed up, hand on sword hilt, eyes carefully moving back and forth between the two wolves. He opened his mouth to admit that he had no invitation here, and then snapped it shut again. Because that was not what he had been asked.

He said, "Titania. It was her name that opened the gate for me."

The white wolf leaned forward on its pedestal, reached out a great paw, and trapped the hem of the cloak of Phadrig Og beneath. The seneschal cried out, tugging at his throat where the fabric choked him.

The white wolf said, "Elfs who dwell in the night cannot see what dwells in the Outer Darkness; nor can the Moths and Cobwebs of the Twilight see the Elfs who dwell in the night; and mortal men are blind before the dawn to come. What dwells in the light? Admit the boy."

Phadrig Og sputtered and scowled. "By what name command you me? I hold the keys of the door!"

The white wolf said, "And I hold the honor of the dead, who cannot speak. I can say the name that commands me, but it would destroy you to hear it."

Phadrig Og, scowling and tugging at his collar, now sneered and sighed, and nodded curtly to the black wolf. "The corpse-eater must go hungry this night. Let him pass."

The black wolf statue shut the marble trapdoor again.

Gil stood a moment, struggling with anger, fear, and puzzlement at how suddenly dangers appeared and vanished in this hell. Then he heard his stomach rumble for hunger's sake.

He put down his shield where he had been asked, and took off the heavy helm and propped it on a peg above his shield, as the other helmets here were arranged, with cloaks or coats hung to either side, hems pinned back to show their colors. His coif covered his hair and head, leaving only his face free.

Now Phadrig Og tapped his white wand on the floorstones. The tall diamond door opened allowing a sounds of stringed instruments and voices lifted in song to escape, and the scent of spices.

Splendor filled the gaze of Gil.

Chapter 5

The Revels of the Otherworld

1. Elf Light

A seductive, wild music of strings, chimes, brasses and reeds, penetrated through his ears to his bones, and he felt his blood flowing to the rhythm of the song, ignoring the rhythm of his heart. The singers sang no words. They were loons and swans and long-necked unicorns whose eerie calls and baying cries were woven through the melody.

Gil's eyes were confused. The scene was swaying to the music, as if seen through the disturbed surface of a pool.

Every person and object here had a strange colored shadow around it. Something was painting colored shadows in his eyes, making the gems in the room more precious, the women more lovely, the men more noble, the polished wood more lustrous, and the light more rich. More than sight was influenced: the smell and savor of the wine and meat were more delicious. It changed hearing as well. Gil heard a hum in his ear that formed other sounds than the real ones, but beneath that, if he listened, he could hear what was really being said or sung.

Was it deception or decoration? Beneath their illusions of grace and beauty, the elfin maidens in their silks and coronets were still graceful and beautiful. The only difference was that the outward illusions had flashing smiles and glittering eyes: their real eyes were cold, and their lips were pale.

2. Beneath the Oak Root Lamps

There was some odd property in the air that made it hard to judge distances. Anything he looked at started looking larger, clearer and closer than it should be.

The ceiling was a vast dome. Around the circumference of the chamber were stalactites and stalagmites grown together to form pillars as great as any art of men could make, with veins of living silver running through them.

Tapestries of blue and silver, black and gold hung between these columns, displaying scenes from tales Gil did not recognize, the doings of wolves and owls, of fallen angels, or babes stolen from cradles, or robes stolen from bathing maidens.

Overhead the roots of a gigantic oak tree were protruding through the domed ceiling like a wide and motionless nest of wooden snakes. Lanterns of many colors were hanging from the lower roots as from a living chandelier.

Below these lanterns, servants no larger than fireflies were flickering and darting through the perfumed air, as graceful as iceskaters, leaving trails of glittering dust behind them as they sped. When they dove and landed, the servants would swell to human size, the manservants bowing and the maidservants curtseying, proffering whatever dish or cup had been called for.

Directly beneath the roots of the ceiling was a firepit where seven fires of seven colors were burning. Roasts on spits, or pies on griddles, or bubbling kettles of copper dangling from hooks were steaming. Cooks in white with ladles and brushes doused the meats with spices or wines or chanted spells. Serpents of fire whose voices were songs of hissing crackles moved among flames of the pit, tending the coals or handling whatever was too hot for elfin flesh to touch.

Maids and potboys armed with meathooks and long-handled spatulas juggled joints and puddings, fish and fowl, or pans or tureens from one hue of the fire to the next, whirling and leaping gaily, stirring the soups and stews with slotted spoons as they did.

The feast tables were trestles and boards covered with white linen which made three sides of a great horseshoe-shaped curve around the fire pit.

The high table on a tall dais to the north was at the far side, where lords in crowns and splendid robes of silk and satin, velvet and ermine sat on thrones of carved and gilded wood. To the east and west were lower tables and smaller chairs where knights and ladies in embroidered linen sat. And, farthest from the thrones, nearest to the doors, were tables with shorter legs. Here were simpler chairs or stools where magnates, yeomen, and humbler persons were.

Around the fire pit was a wide space of marble floor where jugglers and clowns, jesters and harlequins, ballerinas and showdogs pranced and leaped, ostriches bowed or white horses pirouetted or wrestlers struggled.

3. Elf Song

Every motion in the room was all in time with the music. Each time a knight or prince turned a head or princess raised a hand, it was with the rhythm and beat, as if a great and invisible choreographer had mapped out their motions, and punctuated the stanza with their laughter, or the bright clash of wineglasses.

For a long moment, Gil forgot himself, and merely stood and looked. As he listened, enchanted, to their talk, he became aware of how beautiful the voices of the elfs and elf-maidens were, and how easily poetry sprang from their lips, sonnets and clerihews, verses subtle and lovely springing impromptu as if from hidden fountains, or finishing each other's rhymes, or chanting in point and counterpoint simultaneously. How the two voices, weaving their words together in song or speech, could know what the other would say, and match each note or phrase with a balanced answer, Gil could not imagine. What humans could only do in operas or musical theater with a choreographer and lyricist and musician working and rehearsing for weeks and months, these beings could do without effort, as naturally as a man hums a tune or cracks a joke.

It was very beautiful, but to Gil the sensation was creepy: he found he could not walk or swing his arm except in time with the music, and something was forcing him to breathe not according to his own, human rhythm.

His feet began to move without asking him, and followed Phadrig Og.

A pageboy with the head of a monkey blew a blast of sound on a brass trumpet. Phadrig Og sang out, "Majesties and Highnesses! Graces, Excellencies, Eminences, Lords! Ladies and gentlemen of all stations: Behold! The Swan Knight! The Swan Knight is come!"

And the rap of his white wand on the ground was in time with the music, as was Gil's gracefully executed bow.

Gil straightened up. His face was stern, his teeth were gritted. The sensation of being led by elfin music to breathe and bow not by his own will was not only terrifying, it was annoying. He held his breath despite what his lungs tried to do, and did not let his legs move when Phadrig Og twirled lightly, and gestured with his hand for Gil to follow him.

But when Gil did not follow, Phadrig was thrown off his rhythm for a moment, and took an awkward half-step. At the same time, a harpist plunked a sour note.

A rustle of sound, sighs of surprise mingled with annoyance, traveled through the chamber. Eyes like gleaming stars now turned toward Gil, one and all, wondering at the discord. A dancing ostrich raised its head on a long, thin neck and peered. Even the cooks were staring.

4. The Least Seat

Gil stood still. The music was like a wind pushing against him, but he planted his feet like a tree. He was a solid, heavy, human shape in armor, and he did not move.

Phadrig Og said, "A seat has been prepared for you...."

The music slid into a sly and mocking theme.

Gil looked toward the empty seat toward which Phadrig Og gestured. But he saw nothing wrong. The empty seat was at the very end of the last table next to a horse headed man smoking a pipe. But the music was as obvious as the soundtrack on a comedy show: the musicians obviously thought something was funny about the empty seat.

Gil squinted. There was a glamour over the table. The chair he was being offered was not a chair at all, but a stool, and the colored shadow of the seat was half a foot away from where the seat of the stool actually was. Gil strode with heavy step, mail jingling. He put one hand on his scabbard and seated himself on the stool where it really was.

With a burble of penny whistles and muffled horns, the music played a pratfall chord. The music was somehow inside his blood, tugging on his muscles, trying to trip him. But instead of Gil stumbling, the music stumbled, for the horns played one theme, a thrill of brass laughter, and the flutes another, a gasp of surprise. The horn theme stumbled into silence when Gil, instead of falling, was seated serenely. Complete silence fell for a space it might take a patient man to take a deep breath.

Then, gaily, as if nothing had happened, the harpist leading the band, seated with a harp of gold in his lap, led the musicians into a sprightly tune. And the unicorns raised their muzzles and gave voice to an eerie, haunting, beautiful sound as mysterious as the sea seen at midnight.

5. The Beast Table

Next to Gil was a tall creature with the head of a horse. He was smoking a clay pipe and had a red cap on his head adorned with a black feather, but no gloves on his hands, which were hard, calloused, and yellow. He was dressed in an embroidered jacket. It was done up with pearl buttons and had a high, stiff collar that looked uncomfortable.

Next to him was a goat-legged youth in a toga. Then came a goat-headed man dressed in a saffron robe. Next was a scarecrow in a tall green hat and patched shirt with a painted burlap sack for a head, and his place was set with a bouquet of flowers, but no food. Beyond him was a shapely young maiden with the head of an owl, dressed immodestly in a bathing suit of white feathers. Beyond her...

Gil wondered if his eyes were cheating him after all. Next to the owl girl was Ruff, his dog.

Ruff wore a floppy green hat with a wide brim and hatbuckle and a white owl's feather, and he was sitting upright at the table. He was dressed like a musketeer, with a long buff coat and wide pants tucked into green boots. He was wearing a pair of green gloves, and the gloves were shaped like human hands, with thumb and fingers in the proper places, and not like paws at all. Ruff was using a knife and fork to cut the slab of raw meat that rested on his plate, or using a gloved hand to pick up his drinking horn. However, his muzzle was still shaped like a dog's, so he could only lap a little ale from the horn's mouth.

Only then did Gil realize that all the people at this table were probably animals, cast under some enchantment so that they were partly turned into human shape, so that they could sit in human seat and use human utensils. It seemed a strange thing to do, and a little cruel.

Ruff, seeing Gil looking at him, raised his drinking horn in a salute, "Well, hello, there, perfect stranger whom I have never met before! How odd you look to me, since we have never met before! Why are you sitting at the pet's table?" Ruff then coughed, and turned his head the other way, and addressed the figure at the other side of the table, a young woman dressed in a white bodice and long red skirt with a small green cap pinned to her coppery hair, which was piled atop her head. "Begging your pardon, Doctor! Not that everyone here is a *pet*, exactly...."

Gil, seeing her, blurted out. "So this is Sheila McGuire!"

The young redhead looked across the length of the table at him, for she was seated at the head. "I do not recall the pleasure of having met you before, Sir, ah—? What is your name? Do you know me?"

"I know you! You are the spy mistress for the elfs. Ah..." Gil saw the look of shock on her features. Silence fell across the table where they sat, and the animal-headed figures here were staring at her.

Sheila McGuire took a slow sip from her wine glass before answering. Unlike the animals' places, her place had a white cloth laid over the board, her chair had a back, and she was drinking wine, not ale.

She said smoothly, "King Alberec is said to have a magic throne on the side of a high cliff that reaches from Hell to Heaven, and from this seat can see at once all the doings of the mortal men in the mortal world. What need has he of spies? Or why would he have a mere human like myself, the daughter of sinful Eve, serve in such a place?"

Gil sighed, "Riddles, huhn? All right, I give."

Sheila blinked, puzzled, and the music in the chamber stumbled through another sour note. "You give what?"

"I give up. I have no idea why he needs spies or why he hired you."

Some of the animals at the table, those in green caps, snorted or wagged their tails. But there were others here in red caps who were staring at Sheila McGuire with hostile glares, as if surprised to learn her true profession.

Sheila McGuire directed a cold smile toward Gil, saying smoothly. "Young elf, I do not know you, nor whereof you speak. The elfin race is prone to tricks and deceptions...."

The music changed into something soothing and lighthearted, urging everyone to ignore this false step and get back to the festivities. The animals were soothed by the music, and seemed to shrug and nod, sure that Gil was merely an elf playing some trick. The goat-headed man nodded, and the owl-headed maiden reappeared. The soothing tones of music crept into Gil's ears, and mouth, and...

Gil spat, as if spitting the lulling music out of him. "Deceptions!" He realized he was angry. "I do not lie! You are Sheila McGuire! You read the elfin books by starlight and found their world and so were snared."

She tried to raise her wineglass to her lips for another calm sip, but her hand was shaking too noticeably. She tried to speak, but coughed.

The horse-headed creature next to Gil coughed with laughter and muttered. "That's struck the mark!" and blew a smoke ring. The goat-legged satyr next down lifted a drinking horn to hide a wide grin and muttered, "Never seen the Doc so worried! Alberec might turn Granny back to her real age again!"

Sheila McGuire recovered her composure quickly. "You spin an odd tale, Sir Knight.... It is a very amusing, ah, diversion. I am sure that Phadrig Og cunningly prepared many fantastic entertainments for all of us, low and high alike, ah—"

Gil interrupted harshly, "Anyone who hears my voice knows I speak the truth."

Sheila looked relieved when they were interrupted.

6. Salmon and Seeming

A white rabbit in green boots wearing a neck ruff and the tabard of a pageboy stepped up next to Gil and held up a golden trumpet so long and awkward that it took two other pageboy-bunnies in boots to hold it. He blew a blast.

The horn was loud. Gil winced but thought it would be bad form to clutch his ringing ear, so he resisted the impulse. A green boy with a laver of steaming water and a blue-skinned girl with antennae carrying an ewer and a towel appeared in a flicker of magical lights, swelling up from fireflies, to bow and curtsey to Gil.

"What's this?" said Gil.

The horse-headed man next to Gil fiddled with his clay pipe, and whispered. "For washing your hands. Don't take your gloves off. It is dry water."

Gil whispered back, "What is dry water?"

"Water that ain't wet! You are a backward hayrick, or I am no Glashan. What part of elfland mothered you?"

"I was raised all alone, and kept apart from the world." Said Gil, truthfully. He dipped his gauntlets in the water, and saw the frost and grime and pine stains float away, but when he raised his hands from the bowl, the metal of the gauntlet's fingers and the leather of the palm were dry.

A boy set a place for him: a silver knife and spoon, a tiny cube of salt, a silver cup for ale, a fluted glass for wine, a slab of bread to put his meat on, and a shallow wooden bowl rimmed with silver.

Next came a pantler with bread and butter, and then the Butler with wine. The Butler bowed and handed him a fork. A serving girl twirled like a ballerina and placed a dish on a white cloth before Gil.

The delicious smell of salmon cooked in lemon dill sauce and rosemary rose from the plate, and, at first, it almost looked like a fish pan-fried to a delicious golden-brown. But, looking closer, Gil saw that this was another colored shadow. Beneath the shadow was a soggy leather shoe drenched in bog mud, like something plucked from the bottom of a fen.

Gil said to the Butler, "Your Cook has outdone himself in making a dish appear most delicious to the eyes. There is another who might enjoy the dish more than I, however." And Gil smiled at the goat-headed creature in the saffron robe seating a few seats down, and told the pageboy to offer it to him.

The Butler was a handsome young elf with ancient and cruel eyes. He wore a white bearskin draped over his shoulder above his uniform of black. He gestured imperiously. One of the cooks, a round-bellied and big-armed gnome, pale as lichen, came bounding up. He had tufts of hair extending out above his ears nine inches or more. The Butler said, "The young knight dismisses your dish, you villainous churl! Have you nothing worth to set before the worthy?"

The gnomish Cook pushed forward a silver cart whose upper surface was set plates and platters. Twelve dishes of various kinds of filth were there, each one disguised under a glamour of something delicious and savory: joints and cuts of meat roasted or stewed, a paste of chicken and rice boiled in almond milk garnished with fried almonds and anise; meat pounded and mixed with breadcrumbs, stocks, and egg, poached into a dumpling. There were also meat pies, pasties, and fritters. He saw pork, venison, and peacocks, swans, suckling pigs, crane, plovers, and larks.

"Sir?" said the Cook with bland politeness, while the music drifted into a sarcastic tune, "Will you have the blankmanger or the quenelle? The wild boar? Fresh herring flavored with ginger and pepper? Porpoise in mustard? I have also Irish Elk, Passenger Pigeon, delicious Dodo bird legs, haunches from the woolly rhinoceros, and breast of Moa, the sweetest of fowl."

Gil, who could see through the illusion to the dreadful and putrid muck and maggoty corruption beneath, said only, "I have never seen dishes prepared in this fashion. I should think this through before I pick one." Then he noticed what seemed to be a chamber pot on the lower shelf, hidden behind the skirts of the cart. It was a thirteenth dish.

But the Butler said, "Food from the King's own table not good enough for the Unknown Swan who flies in from the land of Who-Knows-Where? Your stirabout and grits offend his delicate tongue!" and he clouted the Cook on his ear.

Gil stood up. He was much taller than the Butler. "Don't speak to him so, master Butler. Clearly a good deal of thought went into that dish to make it entertaining to this royal company."

The young man in the bear skin cloak tilted back his head as if to stare down his nose at Gil. "The gentle born need not intrude on the affairs of servants, Sir Knight. I am not one of King Brian's good-natured and addle-pated underlings. I am fed from the hand of Erlkoenig, and my mother's grandfather is the North Wind, born of Eos and Astreus. The blood of Titans runs in me! Who are you, Sir Nameless of Nowhere?"

Gil said, "I am one who has heard that the Queen's own cooks serve here at this feast. The doors of this place opened of their own accord to me when they heard me whisper the words *Titania is risen.*"

Gil noticed that the musicians had stopped playing a cheerful tune. The song was slow, sad and serious. He looked up. Everyone from the lowest scullery maid to the Emperor Erlkoenig was staring at him. The serving men no bigger than bright bugs who were soaring through the air had stopped, and hovered on silent moth-wings, staring down.

Gil looked back at the Butler, and continued, "For the sake of her memory, the doors were kind to me, and they are made of stock and stone. Should not we, who are flesh and blood, be made of better stuff? She was known to be the fairest of all her wide realm, which is famous for the beauty of its beauties. Titania is gone and will not be reborn into this world again, nor anyone like her. Let us cherish her memory by treating her servants well."

Gil turned to the cook. "Nothing is wrong with your cooking. If sometimes the wrong food is put before a guest, a guest who is here wrongly cannot complain. I will take that dish." And he pointed to the chamber pot.

The Cook bowed, and brought it out, and dumped it on Gil's trencher. He assumed from the gasps and guffaws that everyone else there saw unspeakably vile sewage. Gil saw beneath the ugly glamour a filet of sole baked into a crust of salts and spices, garnished with mushrooms.

But the Cook, as he leaned over Gil's shoulder to deliver the dish, whispered, "*I am Tobias Moth. Some of us remember her. Touch it with an iron nail, and it will be fair and sweet again.*"

The Cook was gone before Gil could thank him.

Gil seated himself, and looked dubiously at the delicious fish painted over with a foul smelling illusion. He was not sure he wanted all these kings and elfs watching him to see him eat filth. The music in the room was sly and mocking, a flutter of strings, as if everyone were holding his breath to burst out laughing when he took his first bite.

But, unfortunately, he did not happen to have an iron nail on his person at that moment. Gil sighed. There seemed to be nothing to do but to sit and eat and let the elfs laugh at him. He was still very hungry and it was still a delicious fish dinner.

Gil crossed himself, folded his hands and murmured, "Bless us, Lord, and bless this food that comes to us from your bounty. Amen." And he remembered also to lay the napkin given him in his lap, as his mother taught him.

The music crashed into silence.

Gil looked up in surprise, not sure what was going wrong now. A low hissing roar of dark emotion ran through the chamber, and many of the ladies there clutched their ears or clucked their tongues.

Several noble women spoke at once, speaking behind their fans, and knights and warlocks murmured to each other, "I don't understand. Whence comes he?" "Who let him in?" "What is he? Man or elf?" "He is not of the Partholan race, nor a Fear Bolg." "I wager he is a satyr walking in elf boots!" "A minotaur with a centaur's head!" "A merman who shed his tail!" "How dares he to speak such uncouth names?" "He insults the Dark. Will no knight here take up sword, and slay him?"

The murmurs trailed into tense silence. The elfin lords were motionless, eyes narrow, teeth clenched, clutching their dinner knives, clearly wishing swords and lances were at hand.

7. The Dish

Gil looked down. The spell had broken. Gil was not sure when the illusion vanished, but it had. The pile of filth before him had resumed its true appearance as a savory dish.

The little red-haired King Brian hammered his goblet on his golden dish, and called into the tense silence. "Niall the Harper! Strike your strings! Now is not the hour when old quarrels should wake! Lull them away! Let play! For now it is the feasting time of kings!"

The purple-haired elf gestured to his company of musicians and singing creatures, and laid his hands on his harp, and filled the air with wonder.

The goat-headed man four seats away was munching happily on the leather boot. "By the blue face of Vishnu! This is the best boot I've ever had!" And he toasted Gil with his mug.

Chapter 6

In Fair and Noble Company

1. Billy Blin of Man

Course after course came, including delicious meats from long-extinct beasts and fowls most succulent, and anointed with spices from Hyperborea or mustard from Utgard or cooked in wine from drowned Atlantis. There were no further tricks: the food was what it seemed.

Except some was too fantastic to be food. One dish held weightless bubbles of iridescent colors, which popped in the mouth releasing a spray of flavor with no substance. Another was a crystal nugget which brought the taste of the last thing eaten back into the mouth as a memory, but made it taste better in hindsight than it had in life: these were eaten with slices of a bitter and salty black fruit Gil did not know the name of, which tasted sweet retroactively.

Most of the wines and brandies came from grapes or peaches, but some were distilled from starlight, and made the soul soar into poetry without intoxicating the blood, or were fermented from the fires of the Northern Lights, and brought warmth to the heart but a cold clarity to the wits. Gil was not sure if he were old enough to drink wine, so he sipped it sparingly, mixed with a double helping of water from a carafe, and it did him no harm.

As he ate, Gil had many questions for the Glashan seated next to him. The Glashan, whose name was Billy Blin, proved to be a willing talker.

Gil glanced at Ruff, who was looking at him with worried eyes. Gil remembered something Ruff had told him, so he asked the Glashan, "I have heard that those who eat of fairy food can no longer take pleasure in the bread and meat of men. Is that true?"

Billy Blin said, "It is part of the art of the come-hither, the Black Spell of Spells, that allows the masters to lord it over men. It is not all elfin food, not at all. It is a venom elfs brew from the tears of witches to put into the food to curse all other foods besides, and beseem them tasteless: but since witches cannot cry, as you can imagine, this come-hither venom is rare. There are other forms of the Great Black Spell: it can be sung as a song or written as letters in a book. This song, once heard, cannot be fully recollected nor fully forgotten: or such an elfin book, when some poor mortal reads it, other books become crabbed and crass, and the joy is gone from them. But let us not blame the elfs entire! Men of good digestion, whose appetites are tamed and temperate, who go to confession and say their paternosters, can drink the come-hither venom by the bucket, and be unharmed. There is no such dark working in this provender here. Do you think these kings would eat such stuffs themselves, in a celebration?"

"What is the point of this black spell? Just to make people unhappy?"

"The Black Spell draws those who place a toe in fairyland back hither, where they work in our mines and fields. In older times, men knew how to strike a harp or an anvil, and the women to sew, but few these days are handy at useful crafts. Ah! I remember years gone by when men could see us, and one note from a churchbell could throw us back, or the smallest bonescrap from a dead saint. Now, the Church is broken in pieces and dying like a pond in the desert, smaller every hour. The Black Spell spreads discontent and makes men forget the past, even what is written in their histories is ignored and rewritten." The Glashan put his muzzle into his mug and lapped up the brew, then leaned back with a sigh. "Why the elfs plays such pranks, no one in the Night World knows. But there are worlds darker than night!"

"You are not an elf?"

"Are you mad? I am of the Night Folk, sure that is as that can be, and ageless, but I am no elf! I am an old Glashan from the Isle of Man, and I know where the Manx cats hide their tails! There lived I, under cold and starry sky, long before the druids crossed the sea or raised their tall, dark stones! I mow for the farmers and mend for their wives, and can do a fortnight of chores in a single witching-hour, when all the clocks stand still. They wrong my name, those who say I wait by fords in the shape of a docile steed to drown men!"

"Do you? Drown men, I mean?"

"It is the scoffers who skip their shriving that I smother in the water's rage. Their sin weighs heavy on my tender spine!"

"It is wrong to kill people."

"Why should that be? They are not like us. Pah! Soon the mortals would die anyway, curse them all, and escape this life of bitter tears."

2. Delicacies

Their talk was interrupted by a blare of trumpets and a round of toasts, and then the butlers brought spiced wine, and maidens brought bowls of pomegranates, raisins, red apples, purple plums, peaches, cheeses, wafers, candied flowers, and what looked like candle flames one could pick up with one's fingers to dance in the mouth and sputter and explode into liquid sugar on the tongue.

While they ate these delicacies, the Glashan said, "Tell me, Swan Knight, what brings you here? Are you on a quest?"

Gil sighed and glanced at Ruff, who was listening intently, while pretending, not very convincingly, to stare at the ceiling and whistle. Gil said, "First, I seek to right a rank injustice, and that task starts here, even if I never live long enough to see the end of it. Second, I seek a master to train me, for I am untested in the arts of knighthood. And third—third, ah!—was simple curiosity."

The Glashan made a sound that was a bit like a chuckle, and a bit like a neigh. "And how has your curiosity been sated, stranger?"

"I have never seen so fair and noble an assembly."

And this was true. Despite that most or all of the creatures and people here were bent either on great mischief or small, Gil could not help but be impressed and amazed at the sheer beauty of the place and those within it.

The men were strikingly handsome, if slighter and quicker than human beings, and the sylphs and nymphs and fairy maidens with their slanting eyes and pointed jaws were as charming as children, as elusive as flame, as graceful as ballerinas, and as beautiful as delusions from a fever dream.

Gil wished Nerea his cousin were here to see this. He smiled to himself, just imagining how a smile of wonder would have brightened her face.

Gil said, "Tell me who is who?"

The Glashan said, "There are seven races of Nightfolk, of which Elfs are the foremost. Seated below the lords and knights are the Efts, whose eyes are lamps and mouths are bright with fire. These are the marchwardens of the elfs, and hold the frontiers against a darker world than night. Next in rank are Nibelungs, who ravish the world for gold, and forge and embellish the elfin arms and ornaments. The Nibelung architects recapture in stone and silver of the elfin palaces the lost glories of the place whereof it is best not to speak! Next are humans among us, warlocks and witches dressed in dark cloaks and hoods. Poor fools! But they perform our rituals and abominations, and they outrank those seated below them: proud six-fingered Nephilim who are children of the Watchers, the Nemedians who are children of the Sea, Fomorians who are the sons of Winter. Lowest of all we sit, Pookas and Bookas, Leonshee and Banshee, and other beastly things."

"That is eight."

"The witches are not a race, but Daughters of Eve adopted by Lilith for a season. And then they are gone. And they are ugly where elf maidens are fair. Gaze upon them all! Who would you say is the most splendid lord? The fairest lady?" asked the Glashan, making a wide sweep of his arm.

Gil thought that this was not the kind of question a true knight would answer, so he said, "Whoever is the bravest lord is best, and the most chaste lady and true is fairest, for what lies within is better than any outward show."

The Glashan squinted at him. "No elf speaks so. There is something strange about you."

"The great lords there. Please tell me their names."

Billy Blin the Glashan pointed with the mouthpiece of his clay pipe at the dignitaries gathered there. "Beneath the canopy of green and gold is Alberec the Summer King, whose house this is: but, as you see, he is put from his seat these twelve days, and must sit in a lower place, to make room for his son, the Emperor."

3. Moths and Villains

Gil looked. When last they had met, Alberec's visage had been hidden beneath a gold mask. As it turned out, the mask was like the man, save for one wound. Alberec was missing an eye. His features were hawknosed, harsh, but handsome. His left eye was emerald green, and changed in hue to blue or silver-gray as the light caught it. The right was covered by an eyepatch.

He seemed neither young nor old, for streaks of gray striped his black beard or touched his temples, and lines of care were etched about his mouth and at the corner of his eyes: and yet the look of him was of a youth entering into his first strength, a young veteran returned unscarred from his first war.

In a taller chair, Erlkoenig sat beneath a canopy of black and silver, images of full moons above him, crescent moons to either side. Gems were in his antlers. Two solemn officers holding axes tied inside reed-bundles stood behind him, and their heads were the heads of black crows. A winged chimera sported at his feet, eating from three golden bowls on the floor, one of oats, one of raw lamb, one of hot coals. Behind him a blind mastodon munched hay contentedly while grooms with golden rakes combed his fur. Gilberec wondered how he contrived to eat with a mask of ice covering his face.

Billy Blin continued: "Alberec is seated with Nimue of the Lake, a queen of the naiads of Broceliande. She acts in the place of his lost wife, as hostess, to pour wine and to sing soprano. Nimue's champion is Bran of Ys, that giant seated opposite from Balor. He is called Bran the Blessed for a reason too shameful to say. He sits in the chair of Sir Bertolac, the King's Champion, who is absent this day. Sir Bertolac has never been defeated in combat, save only by Bran the Blessed. Erlkoenig is seated with Empousa of Tartarus…," Billy Blin's voice trailed off. He drank deeply from his mug before continuing in a subdued voice. "No elf of the Night World is she, but a power from the Darkness, whom the pagans worshipped of old and called a goddess." He shivered and quaffed his drink again.

Gil asked, "Why is Alberec's son Emperor, if he is still alive?"

The Glashan tossed his mane. "Without the High Queen to bless his wars and belt his sword on him, how could Alberec be Emperor any longer? Some say it was wisdom that bade him abdicate the imperial throne to his son, others sorrow. Perhaps the barons and warlocks, grandmasters and villains pushed him off the throne, or a darker power from a deeper place spoke up. We who serve are never told the truth."

"You said the villains helped push Alberec off the throne. Does *villains* mean *bad guys* or does it mean *villagers*?"

"In this case, it means both. The human world is the suburbia and slum of elfin lands, the part outside the walls where all the filth is thrown, to rot in the sun. All the cities of man are but villages to us. We have swineherds to keep mankind in their sty. Halfbreeds and halfwits! They are our churls, serfs, and villains: Peaseblossoms and Mustardseeds, Moths and Cobwebs."

Gil perked up at the name, but then tried to hide his downcast expression. "So the Moths are bad guys? They help the elfs ride herd over Man?"

"I don't know much about the Twilight People. There are four big clans of them, and some little clans. The Moths are the biggest clan. After Titania was lost, they broke faith with the king, and carry on her strange ways."

"Strange ways?"

"Titania would interfere with Alberec—but he was called Oberon then, back when he was Emperor—when he would steal children. Titania would give the children back to their parents, often with gifts and blessings. There was this one Indian lad they still talk about. His mother was a votary and friend of Titania who died in childbirth, and so Titania took the boy for a season, and raised him, but instead of the normal fate of changelings, she granted him the power to conquer many lands, and the name Alamgir. Titania sent visions to the widower to build the Taj Mahal in his dead wife's honor, to allow some of the beauty of elfland to touch the human world. Don't you think that is strange?"

"So Moths are friendly to Man?"

"Of course." The Glashan squinted at him. "You should know that, being Arthur's man."

"What do you mean?"

"Merlin, your Arthur's counselor, is descended from Joseph of Arimathea. Enygeus, Joseph's sister, came with the saint from the Holy Land as the first Grail Maiden, and she wed the Fisher King, from whom all the Moths of England claim descent." The Glashan gave him a suspicious look. "If you are really from the Table Round, you would know these things! Don't you talk to Merlin?"

Gil said, truthfully, "I joined after he was gone."

"Gone? Gone where?"

"Merlin's student seduced and betrayed him. She trapped him under the roots of an oak tree with a spell he himself taught to her. There he sleeps to this day."

The fork fell out of the Glashan's hand. He stooped down to pick it up, and when his horse's head was below the table, at about the level of Gil's knee, he said, "You sound truthful, but don't speak such truths so loudly! Nimue is sitting next to Alberec, and is the hostess of this feast, which might end with your head on a platter if she hears such words!"

The Glashan straightened up again. He whispered, "Did she really do such a thing? Is that what became of Merlin? Iron nails! No, never mind. Don't tell! What I don't hear cannot be plucked out of my soul."

Gil nodded, stealing a glance at Nimue. Was she truly the selfsame Lady of the Lake who had trapped Merlin the Magician? The idea was as strange and dangerous as meeting a saber-toothed tiger. No matter how deadly, it thrilled him to discover things of ancient myth still at large in the world.

But, despite any danger, there were questions he had to ask. "What else can you tell me about the Moths and Cobwebs? And the other clans of the Twilight?"

"Not much. I know that the Cobwebs swore loyalty to Erlkoenig; but the Mustardseeds swore to Alberec and his Nibelungs, and forge his swords and make his clockworks. The Peaseblossoms swore not to return to the human world. Everyone is bound by vow; no one is free. Erlkoenig keeps some Cobwebs as his special servants, as hunting hounds, or to do deeds unworthy of elfin hands."

Gil carefully looked at the knights seated at the King's table. Some were slender, and dressed in silver cloth woven with moonstones and moonbeams, but others were more thickset and slow of speech, and wore silks from the orient over jerkins of linen or wool, or other earthly substances.

"Not all his knights are elfs, are they?"

"Not so loud! But those there seated below the salt were once of the twilight world, or the sunlit world, and have joined their fate to ours, and shed their bad habit of growing old. He in the brown and amber is Sir Breunis Sans Pitie, and he is the most pitiless knight now living, save perhaps for Sir Garlon of Listenoise, who possesses the Mantle of the Mists. Other stalwart knights of Alberec are Sir Ossian the Young, Sir Laundfal the Generous, and Sir Orfeo of the Harp. Sir Sacrapant the Saracen is the one dressed in dragon hide.

"Opposite them are the Winter Knights who serve Erlkoenig. Those who were once men are seated there: Sir Ferracute, whose skin cannot be pierced, Sir Orgoglio, of whom you have no doubt heard tell, and Sir Sansfoy. Sir Cadwallader of the Isle of the Mighty. The tall one is Sir Volkh Vseslavyevich of Kiev, the shape taker. The one in tartan is Sir Maugris who was raised by the fairy Oriande. He is an enchanter, and so wields spear or charming wand with equal skill."

4. Moth Knights

Gil realized he did not know what his three brothers looked like with their helmets off. But then he saw each man had his heraldry behind him, and he looked until he spied the image of winged cup of silver on a blue field. Four men were seated in the lowest place of Alberec's table. Three of them must be the ones who had accosted him the night he had spied on the tournament of the elfs. His brothers.

Gil nudged the Glashan. "Tell of those knights there, please."

"Sir Aglovale, Sir Lamorak and Sir Dornar of Corbenec. Their bastard half-brother there is Sir Tor, the May Queen's son. Sir Dornar still has acorns growing in his hair, for he spent all autumn asleep beneath a tree. They will not answer to the Moth name, for they are shamed. Their mother was Ygraine of the Reeds."

"What kind of reeds?"

"Wise advice, which no one took. They also called her Ygraine of the Riddles, because her wisdom baffled them. Hers is a sad tale."

Gil felt his mouth go dry. He held up his silver wine cup for a passing fairy waitress to fill with wine distilled from the fire of the Northern Lights, and this time he took a mouthful, not just a sip, to clear his wits and brace his heart.

"Tell me the story, please," he said.

And he was proud of how nonchalantly he said it.

5. The Swan Maiden

"The tale tells that Ygraine flew down from a higher realm, and put aside her swan cloak to bathe in a forest pool, for it was April, and the day was hot. Whatever attendants or escorts she brought from the unseen heights she ordered aside, for privacy's sake. Alain le Gros, who was out chasing the Snowwhite Hart, was separated from his hounds and huntsmen and by mishap came upon her bathing. So fair was the skin of Ygraine in the water, that, peering from the reeds at the pond edge, he at first thought it was the Hart he sought and he stalked closer. But then he spied her white cloak of feathers hanging from a thorn, and, taking it in hand, stood over her, and had her in his power and demanded she wed him.

"For three times nine years she dwelled as wife to Alain and Countess of Corbenec, and bore for him three sons, strong in body beyond the strength of men or elfs. A fine and seemly countess she made! It is said she was gracious to all, high and low alike, and that her hands were always open to those in want or distress.

"It is said that, in before times, in Corbenec they remembered the practice of the pagan Romans, and ordered slaves to fight to the death for their sport; but Ygraine by her counsel changed the heart of her lord Count Alain, and convinced him to hold tourneys and jousts. Instead of the great watching the humble fight and grow proud of their might, the great would fight and the humble would be proud of their lords.

"And she said the humans had such a custom in Christian lands, and it ill beseemed the lordly elfs should be less honorable and brave than mere mortals.

"From Alain, all the elfs soon learned the practice and adored it, and wagered on the outcomes. None was more cunning in wagering on tournaments than Alain of Corbenec. He waxed great in name as well as wealth and girth, and so for three reasons is he called Alain le Gros.

"He was jealous and watchful of his wife, for he knew from whom his good fortune sprang. Therefore he would not let her out of the walled mansion, or off the grounds. Then upon a day in her twenty-eighth year of marriage, her sons were offended that their mother could not come a-Maying with them, to sport in the green wood, and each son swore he was strong enough in might and mettle to see her safe: and so Alain's pride in his sons overbore his prudence, and he consented.

"Woe that he did, for the company was beset by a band of Woodwoses from the Twilight world. The weapons of her knightly sons could not bite on the fur of the Wild Men. These champions of so many tournaments were scattered like ninepins, and she was ravished away from their sight.

"Three years later, on a moonless midnight in midwinter, she returned to them but carrying the misbegotten child in her womb. When it was born, it was covered in hair from ankle to crown, and so Alain despised it as the son of the Woses. He ordered it to be given away, as soon as it was weaned. Mother and child were locked in a tower, so none could see the hideous babe.

"Like the beast it was, the child learned to trot and climb far quicker than a true child learns to walk. In its peering and mischief, the wooly child found for her the swan cloak hidden in the chimney, blackened with thirty years of soot.

"Yet it was woven as things are woven in the country above the northern stars, and not years nor smoke nor fire's heat had undone it. Ygraine hid the robe in another spot, and each night for thirty nights, she wept for all hours and did not sleep, until the new moon came, and her tears had cleansed all the stain away, and the robe was bright again.

"Bright cloak in one hand and shaggy child in the other, she crept over the wall and fled into the woods, and the falling snow hid her tracks.

"She threw off her fine and courtly robe, and donned the white cloak, forgetting in that instant her position and pride and children, forgetting all the woes and weariness of Earth, and she flew back to the citadel of Sarras, which the mages called Septentrion, in the circle of the seven unsetting stars.

"For three frantic days, without pause for rest or food, Sir Aglovale, Sir Lamorak and Sir Dornar sought their wayward mother. Her they did not find, but Sir Aglovale came across the abandoned child wrapped in their mothers' cast off court robe, tucked in the roots of a leafless tree.

"The child was silent. It had died of thirst and cold.

"The tracks of the mother went up a hill and not down again, for she had flown away into the air, into a world higher than this one.

"The tracks of the woses-men showed that they had come by the leafless tree, perhaps drawn by the dying child's cries, but they did not take it up, no doubt misliking the mixed blood of the bastard child, and into the wood once more their tracks led, leaving the unloved babe behind to die. So ends the tale."

The Glashan shook its head sadly. "To think! That a woman so wise and of such good heart would consort with her captor in such a wise, and do her lord such dishonor, and put her bastard child before his face one day, and then leave the infant to perish the next! Ah! It just shows how even those the world lauds as good and fine have hidden darkness in the heart! What do you think of the story, eh?"

Gil said, "The story is a damned lie."

Chapter 7

The King of Elfs and Shadows

1. The Truth

The Glashan's horselike eyes were wide and startled.

Gil beat back his anger and spoke in a voice more quiet and more firm. "Ygraine did not fly off and leave her boy to die. There are other untruths in the story: it was not a band of Woses who scattered the knights. It was only one."

The Glashan looked surprised. "In this very hall, I heard the tale! I sat in this very seat where I sit now, fifteen winters ago!"

"Then you heard a lie."

"From the very lips of Sir Aglovale I heard it! He saw the footprints, and after, when he blew his horn and called them, so did his brothers! They all attest to it!"

Gil said coldly, "Sir Aglovale saw no such thing, nor did his brothers."

The Glashan said, "Do not forget yourself, Sir Knight! These are strong and loyal knights, gentlemen and servants of Alberec, the King of Elfs and Shadows! Do you call them liars?"

Gil heard the harpist pluck a triumphant chord, and the brass and woodwinds chuckled maliciously. As if against his will, the music made Gil turn his head toward the high table beneath the green and gold canopy. In the same beat of time, the music seemed to urge Sir Aglovale to stand.

Aglovale called out, "Phadrig Og, seneschal of King Brian! Who is this jackanape that intrudes in our feast, and meddles with his tongue in words he ought not say? What is his name? Who is his father?"

Phadrig now he stepped forth and bowed low. "Sir, I know not his name or lineage."

Aglovale said, "Then why did you admit him?"

Phadrig Og said, "He is from Arthur Pendragon, the King."

There was a murmur of astonishment in the hall. The May Queen, Ethne, spoke out "But—here is quite a riddle!—Arthur is dead. Nimue said so! She did! He died at Camlann, in the shadow of the great stones Merlin reared beneath the circle of the northern stars to mimic them and draw their powers to earth. Sir Mordred, his son and nephew, killed mighty Sir Arthur the King by impaling him on the craven sword Clarent."

Many eyes turned toward Nimue, sitting cold and proud in her diadem and scales of silver and pearl, yet she said nothing.

Gil wondered how these elfs, if they ruled the human world, could be unaware of the stories men told, or the storybooks they wrote. No one was asking him to prove that he was from Arthur, or to prove that Arthur yet lived. That was odd. Beneath the color shadows of their faces, Gil saw expressions, not of surprise, but of guilt and unease.

Even Sir Aglovale's face twitched, but he settled his features into a scowl. Sir Aglovale bowed to Alberec the king, and said, "With your good permission, my lord, let me send a page to fetch my sword from yonder, lest I have need of it."

But Alberec raised his hand. The horns blew a flourish and the music rushed to a resolving chord and fell silent.

"Knight of the Swan!" Alberec did not need to raise his voice, not in this chamber, but all the royalty, nobility, and their servants seated at feast now ceased to speak, but looked on with curiosity.

Gil stood. He bowed to the king, "Your Royal Majesty."

The chamber was so quiet, Gil could hear the breathing of the ladies, and the humming beat of dragonfly wings of miniature servants, and the crackle of fire in the pit.

The one-eyed elf king studied him narrowly. "You have come among us to share our festive solemnity, and cheer us with your presence, and yet we do not know you. There are three orders of beings: the angels, bright or dark, who eat manna, who do not grow old and cannot die; the elfs, fortunate or unfortunate, who eat nectar, who do not age but can die; and the men, Christian or heathen, who eat bread, who grow old and cannot fail to die. Which are you?"

"Angel I am not, my lord, for surely I can die. As for growing old, I have made no experiment of it as yet."

At this remark, some of the elf maidens put sharp smiles on their fair and narrow faces, and their slanted eyes twinkled.

Gil continued, "As for my nature, Sire, until I measure myself against some great task or terrible danger, how shall I know it?"

2. Elfishness

The king did not smile, but he gave a small, almost imperceptible nod, as if that answer pleased him. "I will tell you the nature of the elfs. We are beholden to powers it is better not to name, and yet the care of the earthly world is placed within our hands. Once it belonged to another, but his claim is forfeit, so now the world is ours, our playing ground and battlefield, the garden of our idle hours.

"The green earth saves us from *ennui*, for even the boredom of many thousands of years can be diverted by the grandeur of the woodlands in the summer, the majestic plains and noble peaks, and the gleam of starlight on the midnight sea, and all that flies and swims and walks, hawk and hummingbird, whale and whelk, snake and lynx and slinking cat, renew forever our lost delight.

"And yet there is no foe to imperil our supremacy, no noble deeds yet to be done. And so, for sport, for ire, we fight among ourselves, but the price is too terrible to count: for the death of any ageless fellow robs the world not of fourscore years of his company, but an eternity.

"We await the doomsday, and the doom to come from the Judgment Seat is foreordained. Ours is a melancholy lot: and yet always at hand are means to cheer us, diversions and ballads and chants and the company of maidens, contests and wrestling and games, riding and hunting, wine and whiskey and choice viands, music to smite the coremost part of the soul, and poetry to pursue the bright shadow of beauty's own transcendent self, which cannot be caught. Our youth will never fade, our strength not wane. How can men not envy us?"

Alberec fell silent, frowning, as if musing over his own words.

3. War and Peace

Gil, still standing, was not sure if he was expected to respond. The silence
grew longer, and everyone was looking at him.

Gil said, "Meaning no disrespect to this noble company, Your Majesty,
but if such is the nature of the elfs, I surely cannot be one. My nature tells
me battle is not a pastime. A true knight fights to set right the wrongs of
the world."

Alberec said, "Yet surely peace and luxury will sap the honor from any
soul, mortal or immortal, and rob the spirit!"

Gil said, "Again, I mean no disrespect, and I do not disagree that war
must bring out the courage and fellowship to some. But those who find
no evils in this world to fight have not looked."

Now all smiles were gone. A softly ominous noise was echoing through
the chamber: the elf ladies were hissing through their teeth.

Gil raised his voice and spoke over the noise. "As for sacrifice, my
mother laid down her life for me, and yet her hands have only handled
a sword long enough to belt it about me. At all times, in peace or war,
there are great deeds of love to do."

The hissing grew louder. Gil spoke in the same calm, forthright and
even tone as before, but at a louder volume. "Sire! My mother once told
me that all true courage comes from true love, and all true sight. If the
elfs cannot see, or dare not face, evils that threaten what is beloved, then
they lack love. If elfs lack love, no matter how much else they have, they
have an emptiness that neither the glories of war nor the splendors of feast
can fill. Have I answered Your Majesty's riddle correctly, sir?"

Alberec put his hand on Nimue's hand. Nimue, who led the hissing,
closed her lips. The ladies in the room immediately stopped making noise.

"What riddle?" said Alberec.

"You asked me how men could not envy you."

Alberec's one green eye narrowed slightly.

Gil said, "Sire, it is a difficult one. Since the elfs live forever in eternal
pleasure and diversion, nobly and splendidly, and possess all the earth, it
is hard indeed to say how any man could fail to envy you."

Another moment of silence gripped the vast chamber, and the elfs
glanced out of the corners of their eyes, looking at their lords and princes

to learn how to react. Many an elf was using the colored shadows cast upon his face to make his eyes seem not to be looking where they looked. Gil wondered if anyone saw the deception but he.

Alberec smiled. "Well said."

There was a smattering of polite applause. The elf maidens smiled insincere smiles and the harpist played a glissade of rising notes. The illusions in the air made the smiles look brighter than they were, and the applause was made to sound loud and well-meant, but Gil saw the truth beneath.

Alberec said, "Your mother belted that sword on you, as is the proper custom. Did Arthur clasp your clasped hands, as you prayed to be his man, and swore the oath?"

"Sire, my clasped hands were between his palms, all according to the form."

"And did Arthur bestow those colors upon you? Or by what right do you wear the sign of the swan?"

It took Gil a moment to realize what the Summer King was asking. "Sire, the Emperor of elfs himself, Erlkoenig the Lord of Winter, gave me leave to bear the heraldry of my shield, and the emblem and colors of my coat." Gil bowed his head toward the dark figure with the mask of ice.

The horned head nodded once. Erlkoenig spoke in a voice without passion or compassion. "He speaks the truth."

4. Lies and Silences

Alberec said, "And where did you come by that armor?"

Gil said, "It was bestowed by my father."

"And who is he?"

"As he wore this armor before me, he was the Swan Knight. A better answer I may not give, for an oath closes my mouth."

"And the sword?"

Gil said, "It is called Dyrnwen, the fair white-hilted sword."

There was another murmur in the chamber, but this one was authentic. Gasps of surprise trailed off into a tense silence.

Sir Dornar, Algovale's brother, now stood and spoke to the King. "Sire, if I may?" And, when Alberec nodded, Sir Dornar said, "Swan Knight, have you come to return the great sword to its rightful possessor? The Treasures of Lyonesse to Lyonesse belong, and to our king!"

Gil said, "Sir Dornar, I am its rightful possessor, and it is my hand."

Lamorak flourished his winecup and laughed a mocking laugh. "Not for long. Think you will emerge from this hall alive, carrying so rare a nonpareil?"

Dornar addressed Alberec. "Sire, I see where the cooks have prepared the final course, and place on the silver platter the golden boar of Freyr. It is the long-held custom that the final dish of the yuletide feast must wait until some great deed of arms is done before the company, either to see giants wrestle, or fairies mounted on wasps and armed with poisoned stings tilt in dizzy combats in the air, or knights with sword to clash in duel."

Alberec said, "The custom I well know, since he who held the throne before me enacted it, and faithfully I kept it, as does he who holds the throne after me."

Sir Dornar smiled a cold smile and said, "Here stands an unknown knight, unwary of speech, uncouth, and offering nothing to amuse this noble company. Let me send a page for my sword, let him have a passage at arms with me, and let his strength be tried." The smile grew colder, until it looked like the smile of a skull. "No accidents will happen in the heat and madness of melee, and this boy and I need only fight until one good wound is cut, not deep."

And by this, Gil knew Dornar mean to strike him dead.

5. The Custom of the Feast

Gil scowled. It was not as if he had not been warned that splendor of the elfs was but a trap. Had he been worried that this place was too dangerous for Nerea to visit? It was too dangerous for him to visit. He had no training with the sword, no skill. He was not even sure how to hold it.

He saw the look of fear and sorrow on Ruff's bewildered face: the dog's eyes were dark and wet, his ears drooped mournfully.

Ruff would not even be able to tell his mother what had happened to him, or how he had come to be killed by his own brother. All those years she spent on the road, hiding Gil, instead of living in an elfish palace as a princess, it would all be a waste.

In his mind's eye, against his will, Gil saw the picture of what his mother would look like at his graveside, pale and calm and sorrowing, with silent tears in long silver lines drawn down her cheeks.

Sir Aglovale stood and said to Sir Dornar, "Brother, it is not meet that we should sully our blades on such business during a festive time."

But Sir Lamorak, the second brother, spoke without rising, "A feast is not spoiled if one who spoils it dies. The ladies were sore displeased by his remarks. Is it not a knightly duty to restore their joy?" And he raised his cup to the ladies in the chamber, who giggled gaily.

Sir Dornar smirked and spoke loudly. "Is the stranger who was so unguarded in his speech now wary of the consequences of his untamed tongue? The Swan Knight is most right to be afraid."

Gil said, "Sir, I was thinking of your mother's sorrow should her son die."

Sir Dornar blushed red with anger. "Why keep you talking of her? She has forgotten me and flown back to Heaven! Heaven hates the earth— why else would it place itself so high above us, at such a far remove? She forgot her name and honor as well! A curse on all the Moths!"

Gil said stiffly, "This tale is untrue, and unworthy of you, Sir Knight, and your curse merely curses yourself, and every brother and cousin you have."

Sir Aglovale, the oldest brother, said to Gil, "Pardon me, but you are too free with your speech. Let cooler heads and tongues more discreet prevail. If you were a known knight, I would know your face. Have you ever fought before? The contest is unequal—Sir Dornar is famed for his strength—it would be execution. A contest of wrestling or archery would serve this noble company more fittingly."

Gil wondered whether he should say that he had fought Sir Dornar previously, but thought this would give away too much.

Sir Aglovale continued, "Swan Knight, I bear you no enmity. Apologize, beg my brother for his pardon, and admit you spoke falsely, and I will prevail upon him to spare your life."

Ruff whimpered. Gil dared not look at him.

Gil felt as if two impossible pressures were pushing in on his heart in two opposite directions. He wanted to live: life was sweet, and the world held more wonders than he had even imagined, which, if he died, he could never see. But the opposite pressure was even stronger: he did not want to live as a coward, or a liar.

It was not that he was too proud to apologize. It was that he thought the truth was more beautiful than sunlight, and lies were worse than sewer filth. And what was a liar, after all, but another type of coward, someone afraid of the truth?

Gil said, "I can apologize for disturbing the ladies, which I did not mean to do."

Sir Aglovale frowned terribly. "That is not enough."

Sir Lamorak said airily, "He mocks us, brethren. He mocks us."

Sir Dornar said, "You must say you lied a false and craven and base lie."

Gil said, "No."

Sir Dornar looked surprised. "*No*? Have you nothing else to say but *no*?"

Gil bowed his head, "I should say, *no, Sir Knight.* I do not lie. You do. You and your brothers tell that story to hide your shame. A mother who forgets the world and flies back to paradise makes her absence her fault, not yours."

But now Erlkoenig, the Emperor, held up his black gloved hand. The trumpeter played a flourish. Erlkoenig said, "We ask this Swan Knight if he be a knight in truth. Have you the spurs of a knight, or the lands of a knight given you by Arthur, or by any lord? We know you are sworn to Arthur as his man, but did you swear to be his knight?"

Gil was blushing, ashamed, and he knew his cheeks were red because the saw the expressions in the many cruelly elfin eyes, who all were staring at him.

But he would not lie. "Your Imperial Majesty, I have none of those things."

Ethne the May Queen leaned forward and said in a voice of lilting exasperation, "But then why did you introduce yourself as the Swan Knight? How droll! You are nothing but the Swan Squire!"

Gil said, "But, Majesty, I did not introduce myself as the Swan Knight. Phadrig Og did!"

Ethne smiled and said, "Oh? It is not a knight's place to undo deceits that grant him too much honor? But if you are a churl and not a knight, I suppose you may let falsehoods stand tall, and leave the task for fitter hands. Churls are so very lazy!"

And everyone laughed at that. It was scornful laughter, the sound of disbelief. Gil wondered by what trick he now looked like a liar to them all. Except he saw the champion of Ethne, the giant Bran, did not laugh.

Erlkoenig said, "Knights of Alberec, wisdom counsels you waste not your mettle on this one. He slew two worthless servants of mine, half-breed Cobweb villains I use for uncouth work. This told me their incompetence, which is knowledge I had need of. In return, I extended him the courtesy of enrolling his heraldry in my herald's lists, and extended him the courtesy of knighthood. The courtesy, I say, but not the substance. Let us continue the festivities: the matter will resolve itself, I doubt not, before Epiphany, in some more natural way."

Gil saw Ruff bristle. He knew his dog well enough to read his mood: there was danger here.

Erlkoenig continued, "Sons of Alain le Gros, you see the Swan Knight—so let us call him, for he gives no other name—is of insufficient rank to meet you in honorable combat."

Whispers echoed throughout the chamber, while Gil stood there, feeling miserable. He told himself he should not care what these strange and evil creatures thought. And yet still he blushed.

Gil also heard a dry, cracked, and wheezing voice behind him. It was the merest whisper, but, thanks to the clarity of the air, it sounded as if it were at his elbow. "After the festival, Captain Cobweb, you must mark which way he departs. You have a good nose. Good Doctor Cobweb will employ his terrible weapons."

Then came a second voice, this one lilting, laughing, "What if I take a fancy to the sword, old Professor Cobweb, and keep it myself?"

A deep voice answered, in soft and angry tones. It sounded like words escaping through clenched teeth. "Silence, fool! Be still! Be he man or elf or half-ish like ourselves, die he will. But not by my hand: cousin

Guynglaff has the prior claim to the corpse, Erlkoenig to the sword. More to say is unsafe in this place."

There was a slight hum in Gil's hearing, a sense of pressure in his ear. He realized that no one else in the chamber had heard the voices talking, for they had cloaked their words under a glamour. But somewhere in the room, perhaps among the servants, were three Cobwebs, creatures half-human and half-elfin, seeking his death. He looked carefully left and right, among the lower tables and the gathered servants, but did not see who was talking.

Alberec said to Gil, "Return to your seat, unknightly Swan Knight. You are in the bear's jaws, but you are too small a fish to swallow, so he spits you back. Sons of Alain le Gros! You are fine and loyal knights, but peace and courtesy must keep this feast. I would not have a knight of mine these twelve holy days fight anyone on whom our Emperor, the Erlkoenig, such courtesy bestows, lest I prick old wounds or start new broils between us. Some other event, no doubt, will arise in time to satisfy the custom...."

A horn blew.

It was not a silvery horn like the summer elfs were wont to use, nor the harsher blast of the winter elf horns. It was a bold and ringing roar of soaring sound, bold as the roar of a lion, great as the trumpet of an elephant, loud as an explosion. Gil felt his heart expand and his spine straighten just to hear it.

But the Elfs and Efts, Nibelungs and Nephilim, Sea-folk and Fomorians felt far otherwise, for they flinched and quailed, and the ladies clapped hands to ears and shrieked. Ruff and other canine-faced creatures, pookas or cooshee or lycanthropes, set up a howling wail.

More strange than that, like the bells Gil had once heard chiming, this horn held a dreamlike note, and the sound seemed to come from above the ground, perhaps above the sky, beyond the circles of the world, but also, at the same time, from a tiny spot inside Gil's head, right inside his ear.

The door of diamond shattered, and bright dust was flung to either side.

There in the archway loomed a muscular figure twelve feet tall and green as holly leaves. He was mounted on a hairy steed twenty-four hands high and green as grass. In one fist he held the body of the man at arms who had been guarding the door, Corylus son of the Hazel Nymph. In his other huge fist, was the other, Lemur the son of the Lilim. Whether stunned or dead, Gil could not determine.

With a great shrug, the giant figure tossed the two men aside, and their armor clattered and rang on the marble.

"Is there none to give me welcome? Is there none to give me cheer?"

Chapter 8

The Green Man

1. The Wager

Alberec raised his hand and said to the Green Man, "Welcome, lord, whoever you might be. The discourtesy you proffer my doorwardens I excuse, if you grant your oath that you are come to join in our play and good festivity, no foe to disturb these solemnities. From what world are you, dark or bright?"

The green steed stepped forward, its hoofs clapping loudly on the marble. The rider came closer to the fire pit, and the servants of the elfs, carrying tiny lights like fireflies, now gathered near the horseman to see him better.

The man was muscled like a weightlifter, immense of bone and thew. He wore an emerald mantle, lined within with ermine. Hose of green clung to his thighs, and green stockings to his feet, which were bare of any boots. Emeralds and jade adorned his belt, olive his coat, lime his tunic, which was worked with lizards, beetles and garden snakes.

His face and hands were waxy like holly. And yet, for all this, it was his hair that was most extraordinary. The hair of his head was thicker than a horse's mane, a mass like a hood falling down his spine and hiding his shoulder and arms down to the elbows. His beard was a magnificent verdant bush springing from his cheeks to fall as a full thicket halfway to his broad copper buckle. The hair climbed so far up his check that only his nose was visible, and it was a false nose, made of copper, so large as to make the monstrous figure look like a bird. His mouth was lost in the verdure.

Gil was startled to see the figure wearing dark sunglasses. But nothing else about the huge figure seemed to come from the world of men.

Armor or weapon he carried none, except that from his saddle bow there hung a Frankish ax with a two-yard-tall haft of seasoned oak bound with rings of iron.

But them the cluster of little firefly lights emitted squeaks and insect-cries, and fled in all directions, and the looming figure was dim and dusky, lit by firelight alone.

Next to Gil, the Glashan muttered very softly, "Whatever being that is, he cannot be an elf or eft."

Gil whispered, "Why not?"

"Cold-forged iron elfs will never touch. It is the metal given to Tubal-cain alone, the son of Cain. It is Man's metal."

Gil look at the stranger's height and width and hue. "That is no man."

But Gil stared at the huge green fellow carefully. Not only was he not coated in illusion, the colored shadows that filled the chamber were avoiding him and his ax of iron.

The Green Man spoke. "No shield, no helm, no brazen corset wear I. Not even my feet are shod. If I appeared before you in my war gear, so terrible is my habergeon and war-spear that fully half the hall of these beardless boys would go blind with terror at the sight, and the other half would die of fright. In peace I come, to spread merriment and mirth within your joyless moping halls, O bedamned elfs. I have a wager to propose. Shall we game?"

Alberec said, "You are no elf. Come you from Heaven or Hell?"

"Did not Lucifer himself from Heaven descend, in days gone by? Tell me which way you are going, and I will tell you from which way I come!"

Alberec said, "In this gracious season of merry making and peace, I would welcome even a devil to the feast, if he will do us honor, share our mirth, and do no harm."

"Mirth for myself I shall have aplenty, little king, and any who is worthy to partake of it, let him look to it. As for your feast, I will not chew acorns with swine in your sty. Far and wide both spirits and birds, ghosts and mermaids tell tales of the splendor, bravery and noble courtesy of the elfs, and especially of those who adorn the court of Alberec! I see you seated here with ladies in waiting, serving maids, little girls, and, aha! More girls in fancy dress, disguised as knights and fighters, but with hearts as soft and gentle as any hens'—where are these bold fighters of whom so many tell? Bring them forth! I see only cowards and churls!"

Gil from where he sat could not see who stood up first, but he saw Esclados the Red was on his feet, calling for his sword. Bran of Ys, like a landslide in reverse, was moving upward as he stood, and by magic the chamber seemed great enough to accommodate him. Tethra of the Speaking Sword was on his feet, calling for permission to draw his blade, and in a cold and ringing voice, that same sword, Orn, in the seat beside him, called the same. Sir Aglovale and Sir Dornar likewise had arisen, and were shouting. Then dozens more knight arose, and then all.

All were shouting, demanding to avenge the insult. Only two fighting men there were still seated: Gil himself and Sir Breunis Sans Pitie. Gil sat because he did not really know what was going on. Breunis was leaning back in his chair, fingering his moustaches and peering warily from side to side, moving nothing but his eyes.

The Green Man uttered an enormous laugh, a giant's laugh, placing both hands on his belly and throwing back his bushy green head until his copper beak of a nose pointed at the treeroots in the ceiling.

"Come now!" He roared. "This is a time of peace for elfs and men alike! Your strength is less than the fearful stinging of butterflies to me! No duel of swords, no passage of lances, or frightful wrestling that breaks the bones do I propose! A simple wager, this, a matter of honor. I have heard that the Children of Nox and Aer, Lords of the Night World, you fine princes of the elfin race, were the noblest creatures under the starry sky, superior to men!" With these words, he heaved aloft the iron ax, and, though mounted on his green steed, with one blow smote it into the marble floorstones underfoot, where it struck and rang, and stayed.

The Green Man removed his hand from the axe, and with his knee, commanded his steed to take one large step backward. The iron ax had broken the stones, but Gil saw that the shine and beauty of the marble was gone from them for a yard in each direction. The iron axe seemed to be in the middle of a pool of dirty darkness that spread outward from the blade until it was about three feet in radius.

The shouting died suddenly. The knights and warlords were staring at the ax in horror.

Gil whispered to the Glashan, "What is that? That black pool?"

The Glashan whispered back, "Titania charmed these stones when they were laid not to age and fade with time."

Gil understood. "Where iron touches, the spell is broken, and all the years of wear and tear return. Is that it?"

Ruff the Dog said, "Oh! Oh! Perfect stranger whom I do not know! Whenever the maids are too lazy to sweep and mop the marble floor, they cover it with a glamour to make it bright again. That spell breaks too."

The Green Man bellowed, "My game is simple: an exchange. Let your bravest and mightiest here smite me with this mine axe as hard and hardy a blow as he can muster. I will not dodge, nor duck, nor step aside. Hoolah! I will kneel to the blow! One blow and one alone he shall strike. But this the price I demand in turn: that he then come kneel before me at a time and place of my choosing, that I might return, with this same axe, one stroke and one only."

The silence, if it were possible, grew even heavier.

Alberec said, "This game is not in keeping with the merry and gentle spirit of the season."

The Green Man said, "Not so, O king. Everyone knows the Christmas custom you keep here, not to eat of the golden boar until after some deed of arms is done, or duel, or contest of strength. May not a stranger keep your custom with you? I overheard a moment past you fretting that your elfish warriors and knights grow soft and craven with none but their own brothers to fight, and that over trifles of no worth. You are shallow as shadows, all of you: the outline of knighthood is here, but no substance!"

Alberec said, "There is some contrivance in your wager. How do we know you have not some charm to protect you from your own weapon?"

The Green Man laughed again. "Spoken like a fearful Son of Adam, mortally afraid to die. Where are the elfs? Where are the princes of the elfs? I heard that they kept feast here! But I see no sign of them!"

And with these words he dismounted, strode hugely over to where Gil was sitting, yanked up the dinner fork Gil had been using, a miniature trident nearly a foot long with wickedly sharp tines. The Green Man strode back to where his huge axe was still sticking in the cracked and blackened stones. The Green Man held up his bare left hand and drove the tines of the fork into it fiercely, over an inch deep. He yanked out the fork with a hiss of pain and threw it clattering to the marble floor. Blood came from his palm and dripped to the floor.

"I bleed!" Shouted the huge man. "And I await the knight bold enough to strike at me, if any be here, and honest enough to await the return blow unflinching! But if among you there is even one with strength enough to strike me dead, why, you need fear no answering blow. Is that not the way of elfs? To strike at those who cannot strike back? Do the humans you strike even know you exist? Or do you hide beneath clever charms and weavings of the mist to protect you from their retaliation, immune to their weapons, immune to their eyes?"

There was silence for a full minute in the great chamber, and no one spoke. Gil wondered at the downcast looks in all these bright elfs and brave warriors gathered here.

The Green Man said, "If I walk from here, unanswered, every yule-tide as these Twelve Days come again, from the Nativity to the Feast of Stephen to the Feast of John, you will sit here and remember my words, and then from the Feast of the Holy Innocents to the Feast of Fools, to the Feast of Magicians you shall know how I cast into your teeth my curse, curs and whoresons, rank villains and baseborn caitiffs, and not one of you willing even to muss my hair or bruise my pretty green flesh.

"I turn to go. Let all the world well know there is no one, no, not one, here who is worthy of the name of knight! And let the dark and shriveled raisins you have instead of hearts well know."

The Green Man sniffed a snort of contempt that echoed from the copper beak he wore over his nose, and stepped back toward his tall green steed, and put one foot into the stirrup.

Gil stood up and walked over to the spot between the green steed and the broken doors of diamond, and there he stood, barring the way out.

Gil said, "I return your words to you and call you liar if you say no one here is worthy of knighthood. I accept your wager."

Ruff whimpered, but the noise was lost in the sudden uproar as all the lords and ladies, knight and ministers, princes and princesses, all spoke at once, and Niall, the purple-haired musician, dropped his golden harp with a clang of strings.

2. Final Words

Alberec raised his hand and imposed a glamour of silence on the room.
Gil could still hear, muffled, the voices calling or complaining or shouting
insults or encouragement, but it seemed no one else could.

Into the glamour of silence Alberec spoke, and the glamour repeated
his words, to allow all present to hear. "Swan Knight, you are a stranger
and a guest. The insult was against us, our court, mocking our customs
and our repute. Why perish for our sake? You have no part in this!"

Gil said, "Good Prince, I am the least man here, seated in the seat of
least honor: if I perish, the loss to you is nothing."

Alberec said, "But why? Why? How is the honor of your King Arthur
involved?"

Gil said, "The Green Man slurred not only the knights and loyal men
of Alberec or Erlkoenig, and the retainers of the Ethne, and the vassals of
Brian. He said there was no one worthy of knighthood in the chamber. I
say there is one."

Alberec stared, but there was a small smile in his beard. "For this you
lay down your life?"

"The Green Man also picked up my dinner fork without asking. That
was a discourtesy."

The elfs laughed, but, for once, it was a good-natured laugh, a sound
of surprise.

Alberec said, "We all know this apparition would not offer to stand to
a blow of his axe unless there is a trick whereby he might survive it! He is
surely invulnerable and you are sure to die."

"This means he is stronger than me, sire, not braver. When a vulnerable
squire fights an invulnerable knight, we know who is sure to die. But
which one is sure to be dishonored? The boy who stood up bravely to a
knight, or the knight who opened himself to no danger whatsoever, and
slew a boy?"

Alberec shook his head. "I grant you permission to withdraw from this
wager, and forbid any servant of mine from speaking ill of you should you
do so...."

"I am honored, sire. I decline. Will any elfish knight here take my
place?"

Alberec raised his hand. A pressure in Gil's ear told him the glamour of silence had ended. But the illusion of silence was followed by a real silence, as fearful and sullen elfs, beneath their illusionary expressions of cheerful nonchalance, each waited for someone else to speak.

None spoke.

Gil said, "When I die, no one will hear any boast of the Green Man that he shamed the court of all the elfs to silence, called them cowards, and walked away unchallenged. I challenge him, although I die for it!"

Ruff leaped up on the table of the beasts and howled, "But you are so young!"

Every eye, including those of the Green Man and his green steed, now turned in surprise to look at the dog, who hunkered down to the surface of the table, looking up with big and frightened eyes.

Ruff cleared his throat. "Ahem! Ahem! Not that I know the complete stranger whom I have never met or anything, but he said he had not aged yet. But... won't someone save him? Won't someone stop this? He said he was not trained as a knight yet!"

Gil said, "You are a good dog."

3. Good Dog

Ruff looked sad, but his tail wagged one wag at this good word from Gil. Ruff said, "You have no chance against that huge green monster. This is not a fair fight. I thought knighthood was all about chivalry and bravery and bright color and honor and loud trumpets! Not this! This is an execution! This is butchery! Is this what knighthood means?"

"This is exactly what knighthood means. I would like to live. But I must serve my king. If I live with dishonor, it dishonors him."

Gil looked thoughtfully at Ruff, and chose his next words carefully.

"I thought my service would be longer, and involve some real fighting, or doing some real good. And I had hoped my—the family member who warned me this might happen—I hoped that person was wrong. But none of that matters. I cannot let this Jolly Green Loudmouth walk out of here untouched, even if it is a trick.

"Since you spoke up for me when no one else did, Mr. Dog, I would like you to bring a message to my kin of how I died. Let my arms and armor be put in the keeping of Sir Aglovale, who also spoke up to make peace between me and Sir Dornar. When kin of mine approaches Corbenec to claim them, tell my kin how I died, whether bravely or not. Since you can sit at a table and eat with a knife and fork, I assume you can speak to my kinfolk."

Ruff nodded. "If I wear my green cap with the owl feather, I can talk. I need permission, uh, to wear it outside."

Gil said, "Sheila McGuire, will you give him permission?"

Alberec said, "She will."

And the redheaded woman nodded hastily, staring at Gil in puzzlement. Then she turned and rose, curtseyed to the king, and nodded to Ruff. "Sgeolan of Glen More, do as the Swan Knight says."

Ruff gave her a snappy salute, "Now, and forever, ma'am! Yes, ma'am!"

She snapped, "No, I did not mean…"

Gil said quickly, "Doctor McGuire, yours is a generous gift! No one has ever given me a dog before. Thank you."

Dr. McGuire stole a quick glance at Alberec, who merely narrowed his one eye at her. She said, "Yes, Sir Swan. You are welcome."

Gil said sternly to Ruff: "Now listen to me. Do not abuse the power of speech as men do! If I die screaming and begging, tell that to my kin. If I die bravely and without fuss, tell that. Whatever happens, tell the truth. Do you accept the burden I put on you?"

Ruff stopped wagging his tail, and started nodding, looking more miserable with each nod.

Ruff looked up at all the elfs watching him, and at Sheila McGuire, and looked back at Gil, and said, "Yes, yes, mysterious new master called the Swan Knight. I'll do it. No fail. You'll see. Well, I guess you won't see if you're dead, but, ah, I'll do it."

Gil turned to the three men who did not know they were his brothers. "Sir Aglovale, Sir Lamorak and Sir Dornar, do you agree to keep my arms and armor until the coming of my kin who will claim them?"

Ruff hissed. "Psst! Psst! And the dog!"

Gil said, "My dog goes with my other gear, of course. He will not return to the possession of Sheila McGuire, who once fed him poison."

Sir Dornar said in an explosion of exasperation, "Who in thunder *are* you?! How do you know what Sheila McGuire feeds her dogs?"

Gil said, "Since I am about to die, what does it matter how I know? Let me face this Green Man at peace, knowing my treasures will be cared for by honorable men when I fall. Will you agree, you three sons of Alain le Gros?"

Lamorak said airily, "Why not?"

Aglovale said, "It is agreed."

Dornar said, "It is not agreed! How do we know how you came into possession of that sword? How do we know it was not pilfered, or won by fraud? It is an heirloom and a treasure!"

Aglovale said, "My brother speaks rashly, but will be more soft-spoken, if, perchance, his jaw is broken by some kindly and well-meaning blood relation of his. I will guard your arms and sword and hold it against who comes to claim them. How shall we know him?"

Gil said, "When you find someone known both to you and to this Pooka Dog, and whose hand fed you both, who knows my name and yours and his: this is the one to whom to give the sword, none other."

A looked of obstinate puzzlement grew and grew on the faces of Lamorak and Dornar, but Aglovale lifted up his wine goblet carved of beryl, and raising it, called out, "Let earth and darkness, oak and fire witness, and all this good and noble company, that I swear to do as you have said!" And to the floorstones hurled it with such force that it was shivered to bits. "May my life be dashed out as yon flagon if I am foresworn! So vows the firstborn of Corbenec."

"I thank you, Sir Knight."

4. The Slumbering Crown

The Green Man had waited this whole time with one foot still in the stirrup as if he were one moment away from mounting up and departing. Now he turned his dark sunglasses toward Gil, and peered over the top of the saddle down at the boy in his silver-bright habergeon and blue and white surcoat. Gil was the only person wearing armor in the whole chamber: everyone else was in festive garb. At his hip alone hung a sword.

The Green Man said, "Sir Knight, who are you?"

Gil said, "Should I reveal my name to one who has not said whether Heaven sent him, or Hell? You have given no name, and you bear no shield to show your heraldry. Are you even a knight?"

"I am a knight indeed, and most puissant and terrible. And you?"

"A squire most honest and stubborn."

"I am neither from Heaven nor Hell. And you?"

"I am neither from Avalon nor Atlantis."

"So we know where you are not from, Swan Knight. Where are you from?"

"I am from a house where all questions are answered with questions, but true answers are answered with true answers. Where are you from, Green Knight?"

"Very well, boy. I will answer: I am from the Green Chapel."

There was a murmur of horror from the elfs in the chamber. The name meant nothing to Gil, of course.

Gil spoke: "I am from Arthur, King of the Britains."

"He still lives?" The Green Knight's voice was hoarse with shock.

"He does!" said Gil, honestly. A sleeping man is not dead.

The Green Knight paused as if gathering his wits. His voice trembled when he spoke. "W– What does he want? What does King Arthur want?"

"He wants justice!" said Gil in a voice loud and clear. "He wants the mighty to side with the right, not with the strong, not with the useful, not with whichever side promises the best rewards. Justice! Do the elfs forget what that word means?" The elfin knights and princes wore expressions of astonishment and fear.

The Green Knight asked in a hushed voice, "What does he mean to do?"

Gil smiled wryly. "Arthur did not speak to me. Do kings take squires into their confidence, where you come from?"

The Green Knight had recovered his boldness and bluster, and he laughed. "The world has not heard from Arthur in many a year. Now this wager has zest! We shall see if the servants of Arthur are as bold and true as they were of old. Come, youth!"

And with that, the Green Knight stepped over to the great iron axe, yanked it upward in a spray of sparks and metallic echoes. Then he dropped it with a explosion of clatter at Gil's feet. The stones where it fell grew dark and dusty.

Gil bent and picked the huge green axe up carefully, surprised at the weight.

The elfs whispered among themselves, but in that chamber, every word was clear. *"The iron does not harm him...." "...he must be a human...." "...No human strength could lift that axe one handed...." "...he is an Owl wearing a man-cloak...." "...it is some trick...." "...he is a Yeti who has shaved himself bald...." "...he is a golem of brass, like that which carried off the child of Weyland and the Swanwife...."*

Gil looked at the cutting edge. It was as sharp as a surgeon's scalpel. Gil blew some marble dust from the face. "You treat the weapon with disrespect. Do you want to mar the blade?"

The Green Knight laughed a terrible laugh. "If you knew where that blade was forged, and by whose hand, you would tremble! The iron will stay sharp. 'Twill serve. Oh, aye, my wee bold lad, 'twill serve! Shall I kneel for you?"

Gil looked up at the twelve-foot-tall monster. "You look like Groucho Marx in those glasses, with that nose."

The huge man sank down like green hillside collapsing. On one knee he was still a head taller than Gil. Gil saw no eyes behind the dark glasses, but he knew the giant man was inspecting him.

"You seem not to be afraid," the Green Knight said softly.

"You visited Arthur's Court, or someone like you, long ago," said Gil. "I know the story. So I am not afraid of hurting you."

The Green Knight snorted again. "Odd child! Are you more worried about killing than being killed?"

"My conscience will be clean either way," said Gil.

"And what if the story, as stories tend to do, grew strange in the telling, or had parts lost in the mist, or made into a happier tale fit for children? Does your tale tell that Gawain succeeded? He failed."

Gil now felt a flood of fear come into him. He tried to brace himself against it, but there were no encouraging thought in his head.

But he did not run or flinch, despite that he longed to do just that. Instead, Gil hefted the ax. "Do you want to say your prayers, first?"

Seen up close, the masses of the giant's unruly hair seemed even larger and bushier than could be. With one huge hand, the giant gathered up his green hair into a huge knot, and held it at his shoulder, exposing his neck. With a sardonic snort, he leaned forward, resting his weight on his other hand.

Gil lifted the great axe overhead. His arms trembled under the weight of the huge weapon, but Gil took a deep breath and waited for his arms to get used to the mass. He had only one blow he was allowed, so he did not wish to be hasty.

He wondered what the trick would be. Would the ax vanish in his hands, or turn into a snake and bite him? Or would the Green Knight suddenly have skin harder than steel, or be protected by invisible armor? Or simply disappear?

Gil gave a wordless shout, and the drove the huge blade down.

5. The Blow

He struck through the neck of the monstrous man cleanly. The axe head struck the marble floor and the floorstones turned black.

Blood was everywhere. The corpse slumped and collapsed prone, and the head bounced and rolled across the marble floor, a tumbleweed of hair and beard, and the sunglasses broke.

Gil stepped back from the spreading red pool, feeling lightheaded from the dreadful smell and sight. There was a ringing in his ears which he only then realized were cheers.

The whole huge chamber was shaking with deafening applause. Princesses and lords, knights and ladies, elfin or serpentine, gigantic or miniature, all cheered and clapped their hands, while servants and beasts yelled and banged the table-boards with their fists, or floor with feet.

King Brian, the twelve-inch-tall redheaded king of the Autumn Folk stood and raised his goblet: and when royalty stood, all stood. A toast was called, and trumpets were blown, and King Alberec commanded, "Three cheers for the Swan Knight! He has defended the honor of four kingdoms this day!"

Gil listened to no toasts. Instead he inched backward unsteadily, never taking his eyes from the corpse.

He saw the fingers of the dead man twitch, and the toes on unbooted feet curl and flex. The heavy axe fell down with a clamor from Gil's nerveless fingers to the marble, and more stones turned black.

Someone screamed. It was not an elfin voice: perhaps it was Empousa. Silence fell. Gil could hear the noise like raindrops of the blood falling to the floorstones as the red-stained corpse sat up, and slowly, awkwardly, blindly climbed to its feet.

The chamber was gripped with paralysis. No one moved; no one spoke.

The headless body walked heavily toward the severed head. The body was coated with red from neck-stump to past its belt. The head was a mass of hair and beard, also stained. With clumsy fingers, the body picked up the head, and held it by hairs of its crown, like a watchman holding a lantern, and the red-stained green beard dangled down a yard or more. The hand swung left and right, and the head peered. When his gaze fell upon Gil, the hand ceased moving.

He took a huge step toward Gil, and then two, and then tossed the head lightly from his right hand to his left, and cradled the head in his elbow.

The copper nose-ornament had fallen off. The giant had a straight and surprisingly handsome nose underneath. The sunglasses were also missing, and his eyes were deepset, with irises of a strange coppery color, like pennies.

The head saw Gil staring, and the left hand brushed at the hairs of his head so that his bangs were flung down over the face, so that Gil could no longer see the eyes clearly, but only caught a glimpse of yellow, like the eyes of a tiger seen in the green grass.

Then the huge corpse picked up the axe in his left hand, and held it up in a salute to Gil.

"Well struck, little cygnet!" Roared the huge severed head. Gil wondered how its voice could be so loud when it was no longer connected to windpipe or lungs. Then he wondered how it could be alive at all. But this was no illusion. None of the colored shadows that held the glamour of the elfs dared get near him. "You agreed to receive the return blow when and where I should call for it, did you not? Now is your chance to argue, cajole, cavil, and call your lawyers to go over the fine print."

"I am ready now," said Gil. To his own surprise, that fear which had just a moment ago been washing through him was gone.

The huge man just laughed. "Courage born of rushing blood and the thrill of the moment! We shall see how long that lasts! A month? A week? An hour?"

He turned away, shook the blood from the axe with a heavy shrug of his huge hand, and wiped the axe head rather carelessly on his breaches and leggings, and slung the axe from a loop in his saddle bow. The green steed did not shy, albeit its nostrils twitched. Apparently the monster horse was quite used to the smell of blood. The Green Knight tied his head by the hair to the other side of the saddle bow, where the long beard hung past the horse's knee. Then the headless body mounted and took up the reins. He turned his steed in a half circle, so that the side where his head was hanging faced toward Gil.

"I will grant to you the grace of a year's time minus one day, and will not call you to me to collect my debt for twelve month's time counted from yestereve. Meet me on the last day of Advent at the Green Chapel."

As before, many of the elfin knights flinched with fear at the mention of this name, and many a lady shrieked. Nimue swooned in her seat.

Gil called out, "You have not said how to find you!"

"It is the land beyond the War Poles, beyond the Great Lakes. Set out before the End of Ordinary Time."

Gil said, "End of Ordinary Time?"

Gil did not know what it meant, but it sounded ominous and terrible.

The severed head rolled its eyes and sighed and said, "Well, if greater speed is given you, you may delay, but do not delay past the Feast of Ambrose."

Gil said, "Which way?"

"Any way. Set out. If you seek me, you will be led. If you sit or tarry or give up seeking, you are foresworn and baseborn!"

The Green Knight said no farewell to the elf lords and asked no leave of them, but simply looked on them all and laughed, and dug his heels into the sides of his steed.

The huge green steed with a noise like thunder departed through the broken doors, and down long, dark, high corridor, and out into the snowy night.

Chapter 9

Fate of the Fair Bright Sword Foretold

1. The Queen's Champion

In something of a daze, Gil returned unsteadily to his stool and sat. Immediately there came a clamor of calls and applause.

Gil looked up, wondering what the commotion was about. He saw squadrons of little light flickering around a great roast pig on a grate. The skin of the pig was bright gold, and its tusks shined with dazzling metallic reflections. The little lights were swelling up, and taking on the forms of butlers and serving maids. The proud cook with his giant cleaver sliced meat onto plates and trenchers which the servants took up and flew away with. Gil wondered how one beast, even one as big as a hippopotamus, could feed so great a multitude, especially with servings so lavish.

But he had calculated without taking elfish magic into account. He saw that the plates were handed to the tiny butlers when small, but that when the butlers swelled up to full size, the plates and portions and everything they held grew with them as they grew. Two of the butlers became tall as titans for a moment when Balor of the Evil Eye was served, and so the slice of pork cut from the boar given to him, by the time it rested before him, was larger than the boar from which it came.

But that was not what the calls and clamor was about. The feasters were not applauding the pork.

They were calling for the Swan Knight.

Phadrig Og appeared at Gil's elbow so suddenly that Gil could not tell if the tall, pale seneschal had appeared out of nowhere by magic, or had walked up so softly and swiftly that it was like magic. Phadrig Og threw back his head and spoke loudly, his voice like a trumpet. "The King of Elfs and Shadows, Alberec of the Midsummer, commands to you a better seat; to which Erlkoenig the Emperor, who is first among these mighty peers, and Brian, and Ethne give their consent and add their voices."

Gil realized that his eyes were drooping of their own accord. Gil wondered what hour it was in the outside world. It had been after dark when he entered the mountain, and he had enjoyed no comfort and little rest in the days before. No doubt it was past midnight now.

Thus it was with a weary note in his voice that Gil spoke as he stood. "Ruff must come with me."

Phadrig Og was developing a nervous twitch in one eye. "But of course! You would not be the Swan Knight if you did not make things difficult. Sir Knight, or Master Squire, or however you are called, there is no seat prepared for anyone other than you. And who is Roof?"

Ruff stood up. Gil was disoriented to see the dog in his musketeer outfit standing on his hind legs, but the green boots he wore somehow allowed the animal to stand in a human posture, and he was taller than his real dog legs would account for. "Me! Oh, me!"

Phadrig Og looked down his nose with a practiced disdain. He said to Ruff, "I thought your name was Sgeolan son of Iollan."

Gil said sleepily to Ruff, "You never told me your real name before."

Ruff said urgently, "At dinner, you mean. I did not tell you my name before *at dinner*." Ruff looked back and forth from Sheila McGuire to Phadrig Og nervously.

Gil wondered who in his right mind would ever hire Ruff the Dog as a spy. He was the most transparent fibber of all time.

"You did not tell me your real name before at dinner," said Gil, nodding.

If Sheila McGuire or Phadrig Og harbored any suspicion because of Ruff's tone of voice, the magic in Gil's voice, which allowed others to hear the truthfulness when he spoke the truth, surely soothed those suspicions away, because Gil saw no wary look in either face.

Ruff explained to Phadrig Og, "I did not tell the Swan Knight my name because hearing one of you *sasanach* mangle the pronunciation is rough on my ear. So, I said to the Swan Knight, 'You can just call me Ruff!' That is what I said. It was a name picked totally at random. Rhymes with Gruff. I don't know him."

Phadrig Og said to Gil, "I can see the Hound of Glen More will serve you both as fetch and familiar, but also as jester. Nonetheless, there is nary a seat for him."

Ruff barked excitedly, "Oh! Oh! I'll sit under the table!"

Phadrig Og said, "What?"

Ruff calmed down and spoke in a dignified voice, "I do not need a chair. I will sit and eat whatever scraps my master drops." And, without waiting for any answer, Ruff put his human-shaped green glove under Gil's armpit and urged him to his feet.

Gil stood. Ruff now shucked off the musketeer style coat he wore, and kicked off his thigh-high boots with one swift motion of his legs. He plucked off his gloves with his teeth and put them carefully on the table. Ruff said, "Hey, hey! Lachusa Strega, can you look after my stuff?"

The young bathing beauty with the head of an owl nodded her owl head.

Ruff said, "Thanks!"

The owl spoke in a sweet but husky voice, "Keep the feather in your cap, or else no one will understand your speech."

The music struck up a triumphant and solemn song, and Gil was too weary to resist the pull. He followed Phadrig Og and the waiters carrying the pork dish, and Ruff followed after, prancing and dancing, looking like a dog in a floppy hat. The princes and ladies cheered and the knights and men-at-arms called out.

They marched grandly by the modestly dressed high servants, seneschals and ministers of state, scribes and jurists, and then past the richly-dressed lesser knights, and then the greater.

When he marched past the warlords of the Fomorians, one-legged Morc and one-armed Corb (both of whom glared at him with the one eye in the middle of a frowning forehead) Gil realized something out of the ordinary was happening here. Then they went past the blue-skinned Nemedians adorned in pearls, past the six-fingered Nephilim dressed in fur, and then past sad-eyed human men in dark robes with pointed hats. Gil thought he would be seated here, with the humans, but then they walked past them as well.

He was escorted past the squat and burly Nibelungs and their gem-laden cat-eyed wives. He was escorted past the Efts, men with eyes of dragons, whose forked tongue crawled with tongues of fire.

Gil next thought he would be seated with Aglovale and his other brothers, who sat with the dignitaries and nobility of the elfs. But no, Phadrig Og marched past them solemnly, the wand in his hand tapping the ground as he went.

Gil now thought this whole thing was one more joke of the elfs meant to humiliate him.

But his expectation was wrong. Phadrig led him to where Bran of Ys was seated. Bran the giant was not using a chair, but was crossed legged on the ground. He arose, and bowed to Gil. It was a startling sight indeed to see that huge head like a full moon falling down and going back up as the vast figure made his bow.

Bran the Blessed was the size of a church steeple, sixty feet high. Bran, peering down, said, "It is no shame to yield my seat to one whose heart is larger than mine. Sit here, Swan Knight." Bran reached across the chamber (and his arm was as long as a suspension bridge, and stronger) and picked up a wooden chair with a high, carved back. As Bran drew the chair across the table top, one of the legs bumped and upset the bowl of salt.

Bran held the chair for Gil. The hand of the colossus was two yards from fingertip to wrist, so it was as tall as the chair it held. Gil sat down gingerly, wondering.

Bran now seemed to shrink to half size, so that he was only as tall as a house rather than as tall as a tower. He said, "Excuse my clumsiness...." And he moved his hand (now only a yard long) across the little pool of spilled salt. Gil saw the colored shadows of elfin glamour flicker in his eye when Bran did this.

The illusion showed Bran sweeping the salt to into his palm and throwing it over his shoulder. The reality, which only Gil saw, was that Bran drew a curved line in the salt. It looked like a lower case cursive letter 'l' lying on its side, or perhaps like the outline of a fish.

Bran smiled cryptically and stepped away.

Gil was now served. The pork dish was laid before him, and other butlers and waiters and waitresses, both large and small, set out a goblet, a knife, and all the other finery before him so quickly that it was like a juggler's act. He stared in amazement, and then, only then, looked up and saw where he was sitting.

Next to him, in a seat only slightly higher than his own, was Alberec. Gil was seated at the King's right hand, the place reserved for the king's own champion. Gil remembered Billy Blin had told him the King's Champion was gone today, and that the Ethne's champion, Bran the Blessed, had been given the seat of honor instead.

Ruff had dropped his hat under Gil's chair and took a spot on the floor between Gil's feet. His head rested on Gil's knee.

Alberec raised his glass, and, of course, everyone else did also. Gil started to pick up his goblet, but Ruff coughed a little cough. Gil looked down. Ruff shook his head a tiny shake, and whispered, "*Ixnay on the inkdray.*"

Alberec said, "Here is the only one who places the honor of the sovereign elfs above even his own life. My peers, lords, ladies, and gentlemen, ye wise and ye humble who serve: give your hail and your blessing to the Swan Knight. Weal and long life to him!"

"*WEAL AND LONG LIFE TO HIM!*" roared the voices in the chamber.

Gil listened in shock as the whole chamber of proud and terrible fair folk were toasting him. It should have gladdened his heart; instead he felt obscurely ashamed, for he knew they were toasting the death he had brought upon himself by challenging the Green Man.

Alberec said, "Now hear my decree: This squire will be called at the end of Advent next Wintertide, on this day less one, to appear at a place whose name I will not spoil this feast by naming aloud. Now, if this lad walks forth and is detained, or ensorcelled, or delayed, or maimed or slain in any day of eighteenscore days and four from now until then, rumor will stain and blacken the name of these four crowned heads, and thus stain all our names from highest to least! What squire can walk a pilgrimage so dire?"

Alberec then turned toward Gil. "Young man! It is our royal will that you be trained and taught in all the arts and mysteries of knighthood, sword and lance, the handling of horse, the just laws of courtliness and tourney, and all good practices of war, as much as may be learned in so short a space of time. What say you?"

Now joy did enter Gil's heart. "Sire, such would be my fondest wish." Gil's tone escaped him and leaped up to a high warble as he said this, and his whole face was afire with a silly smile.

And some of the elfs there laughed, for even wicked creatures can be delighted when they hear the voice of young delight.

2. The King's Champion

There came a flourish of trumpets. Alberec betrayed no change of expression, but the dark-haired beauty seated beyond him uttered a gasp halfway between fear and annoyance.

Her gown was samite woven with silver thread, richly figured with images of clamshell and eel, salmon and shad, and she wore a corselet of close fitted scales. Her crown was pearls and abalone. This was Nimue of the Lake.

"What new interruption mars our feast? Green Knights and Swan Knights and knights without limit or let!" she cooed in exasperation. Even when vexed, her voice was contralto music. "Will this evening never cease?"

Now Erlkoenig spoke, "Have you no ears, Nimue? That is the flourish of Hautdesert. The trumpets blow for Sir Bertolac."

Ruff said to Gil, "Hey! Hey! Who is blowing the trumpet? The guards who stopped you were carried off on stretchers."

Into the chamber through the shattered doors now strode a tall and clean-shaven man wearing a coat of mail whose every link and plate was gold, so that sparks and darts of yellow fire seemed to leap from him in every direction as elf light and firelight danced across his form.

Over his shoulders as his mantle was thrown a fulvous lion skin, and with the upper jaw and skull of the lion as his helmet, and a golden mane as his plume. His chain of office was shining amber, and his belts at shoulder and waist were clasped with buckles of chrysoberyl and citrine. His hair, which was cropped short, was startlingly blonde. Even his eyes were yellow. His surcoat displayed the sign of a golden lion rearing. He had no shield in his hand, and his scabbard was empty.

At this side, trotting along, was a tall white collie that seemed more wolf than dog. His flanks and tail were red. From a strap around the dog's neck, in the place a St. Bernard would have carried a cask of ale, hung a hunting horn carved from an elephant's tusk.

Knight and hound came forward, walked past the central fire pit, and stood before the highest table where Alberec and Erlkoenig were seated. The golden man sank down to one knee, and the hound crouched down and lowered his shaggy head.

Alberec said, "Arise, Sir Bertolac of Hautdesert! We had not expected to see your living form with waking eye for many a month."

And when the golden man did not arise, a dark look came into Alberec's eye.

Erlkoenig made a small nod his antlered head. From behind his mask of ice his cold voice came, "To your feet, sir! Address your liege with all due prompt obedience."

Sir Bertolac stood, saluting first Erlkoenig, then Alberec, then Brian, then Ethne and then the other royalty and nobility in order. He then said, "My lord Alberec, by mere happenstance am I returned from my voyage to the abyss to confront the Leviathan. He bade me tell Your Majesty that great Leviathan, king of all the children of pride, hath refused all offers of battle." Bertolac smiled a wry smile. "And I believe it is for this reason now I stand alive before you this night."

Alberec said, "Refused? What of the calamities and quakes that shattered towers in Atlantis and drowned villages along the golden coasts of Troynovant?"

"Leviathan spake a strange tale of a ship made of iron, cold iron, although made of elfin arts and shapen like a manta-ray. This ship passed by secret ways close by him as he slept; not upon, but far beneath the waves. This trespass caused him to stir in his dark slumber, casting up waves in the sea and shaking the world's foundation. He warns the world not to disturb him more. So he bade me say: so I have said."

But Erlkoenig said, "Surely he said more, or else you would not have spoken thus, Sir Bertolac."

Sir Bertolac inclined his head, "Your Imperial Majesty is far sighted. Leviathan leaves it to us to abate this nuisance to him, lest worse befall."

Little King Brian spoke up, "My Emperor, this matter falls in my domain. Let the Autumn People see to it, I pray. And can we not return to lighter matters? The ladies will be vexed if we let the meats grow cold, or diminish the sherbets, sorbets and afterdinner wines, or delay the onset of the dances by one bar of music. Let the champion of Alberec take a seat."

Erlkoenig made a small, impatient gesture with one black finger, which apparently was a sign of agreement, because Bertolac saluted the Emperor.

Bertolac turned toward Gil. "Who is sitting in my seat?"

Gil started to get up, but Ruff from beneath the table coughed and caught his eye and shook his head. Gil uneasily seated himself again.

Alberec said, "This one is called the Swan Knight."

Bertolac squinted at Gil, and then turned and said to the huge black and white dog at his side, "That armor is of strange fashioning…. I seem to recall some rumors from a dozen years ago or so… And, come to think of it, I do not see Doolaga the Yeti seated among us."

Gil licked his lips, wondering if he should say something.

Erlkoenig surprised Gil, and perhaps the whole chamber, by speaking in his emotionless, dry tones. "The Swan Knight in valiant combat slew him, bravely and without any act of deceit or sleight of elfcraft, and the Yeti's brother Gulaga as well."

Bertolac said to Gil, "I salute you, then, as one knight to another! Hard indeed it is to pierce the hide of an Abominable Snowman! 'Tis said they know the secret the Nemaean Lion knew."

Gil said, "I thank you, Sir Knight, but I cannot accept your praise. The name given me is, for now, a form of honor without substance. I am a squire, and not a knight."

Alberec said, "Do not ask him his name or lineage, for he will not give it, nor ask him which knight he serves, for I have decided it shall be you."

Bertolac looked dumbfounded. "Ah… as Your Majesty, um, commands. Is assigning complete strangers of unknown houses to the service of your knights a new custom of the feast? Is it replacing the custom of everyone waiting hungrily while the golden boar-meat gets cold for someone to utter an insult and start a fight, because, if I may, I always thought that such a custom was wasteful of good insults and good soldiers, not to mention good meat."

Alberec said, "That custom was kept this night and most fearfully, and the court was saved from dishonor by this unknown boy. But I see you doubt my wisdom?"

Bertolac bowed, "Never let it be said that any ear ever overheard Bertolac, the King's own champion, utter any doubts about the wits of the King! Doctor McGuire's spies are not that good, for one thing."

Ruff said, "Hey! I heard that!"

The white dog next to Bertolac said, "Sgeolan, is that you under there? Shut your yap. You are a terrible spy."

Ruff said, "Oh? Oh? I should report that you mocked the King's espionage service to McGuire."

"McGuire! The King's pet *mortal*! May the cat eat her and the devil eat the cat!" said the great white dog with scorn. "You are the pet of a pet!"

Ruff said, "Nope! I am out of the spy business. They gave me to the young knight here. He's awesome, so *you* shut your yap!"

The big white dog barked back, "Not my yap! Your yap!"

Ruff barked, "Yap! Yap!!"

Alberec under the table tapped Gil on the knee, snapped his fingers and pointed at Ruff. Gil nudged Ruff with his toe and shushed him. Ruff whimpered, "Sorry, King! Sorry, boss!" and fell silent.

At the same time, Sir Bertolac put his hand on the white dog and said, "Vertifran, heel!"

The big white dog subsided and sat on his haunches.

Alberec said, "Swan Knight, show Sir Bertolac the sword you carry."

Gil stood and unhooked the scabbard from his belt, and held it over head in both hands.

3. The Generous King's Blade

Bertolac said, "Sire…?"

Alberec gestured at Gil to seat himself. Alberec spoke. "You doubt my wisdom in placing this squire in your care, my Champion, but doubt me not. Behold the Fair White-Hilted Sword called Dyrnwen, the sword of Rhydderch Hael the Generous of Alcluith. He was called generous because it was his custom to offer the precious sword to any man willing to draw it and bear it, but knights in those days were wiser and refused. Some call it the first of the Twelve Treasures."

Sir Bertolac said, "Can you unsheathe the sword, and allow me see the blade?"

Gil said, "I cannot, Sir Knight. I was told not to draw the blade in this company. It is peace bound."

Alberec said to Bertolac, "It is the self same blade. I see by signs unknown to you." Then he turned his head. "Knights of Corbenec! Do you recall the riddles Ygraine of Corbenec wove about this far-famed sword? She knew more of the lore of the three worlds than any of us. Do you recall whereof I speak?"

Sir Aglovale stood. "In a way, sire. My lady mother often spoke profound things, and…"

Sir Lamorak, grinning, interrupted, "More often, sire, than we understood them!"

Sir Dornar said grimly, "I paid heed, even if others did not. She spoke in threes. One of her triads was this: Whose is the brand from the king called generous? Which is the brand that should not burn? Where shall it be sheathed when not sheathed?"

Alberec turned toward Bertolac. "These riddles I solve this day in your ears. Brand is an old word for blade. The blade of the generous king belongs to him, Rhydderch Hael. The brand that should not burn is the blade called Dyrnwen, for the burning of the blade is a sign of bloodshed. The final riddle I see things from my throne of wisdom, and my missing eye is in the darkness and knows it. Many shades serve me. The place where this blade shall be sheathed when not in its sheath is the heart of Ysbadden!"

There was a murmur of fear through the chamber.

Since Gil had no idea whose name this was, or what it meant, he could but listen in bewildered wonder.

"Through the contriving of Merlin, the blade Dyrnwen was given to one of Arthur's knights, and it burned as bright as thirty torches in his hand, but after all the Table Round was shattered at Camlann, the blade was taken at Arthur's last command by the King of Cats to Caer Sidi, the Tower of Glass, beyond the sail or sight of the mortal world. Many years ago it was lost, and that it was found again is a wonder."

Alberec nodded to himself, and sighed. He continued: "And of all the wonders in that story, the greatest wonder is that Arthur, the King of Camelot was able to command Carbonel, the King of Cats, to obey him in anything. When before or since has a cat obeyed any order given?"

Bertolac looked doubtfully at Gil. "Sire... if that blade is the only hope against Ysbadden, it should go to the hand of some most stalwart knight, Bran the Blessed, or some other equally mighty...."

Bran, his vast head near the high ceiling, spoke in a mild rumble like summer thunder, "I would not take it. This boy stood before the Knight of the Green Chapel, and defied him to his face."

Sir Dornar spoke up, "Your Majesty, I add my voice to Bertolac's! That this unknown yearling should hold this most potent and magical blade is unthinkable!"

Alberec raised his hand. "Silence! The boy has proved himself worthy beyond any here. Let no one envy his heavy fate!"

Bertolac laughed aloud. He saluted Gil, and turned to Alberec. "Sire, I accept the commission and will exchange oaths with the youth in the sunlight in some bright place where the air is not fogged with wine fumes." He turned to Gil. "Stay in your seat, Swan Knight, and welcome to it! I ask leave of Your Majesty to retire, for the peril and fatigue of my journey has wearied and battered me."

Gil tried to say something polite in return, but he found himself yawning and had to hide his mouth behind his hand.

Alberec said to Gil, "I see weariness sitting on your eyelids like a night-hag. In an hour we mean to clear the tables away and begin the pavane and saraband, cabriole, gigue and sprightly gilliard."

From beneath the table, Ruff muttered, "Those are dances."

Alberec said, "Indeed, they are dances most formidable! If you have not for six hundred years suffered under the demanding tutelage of a haughty dancing master to learn the footing of each of our six hundred figures, bows and graces, flourishes and foot positions, both on the floor and in the aerial maneuvers, the entertainment might fail to display your virtues to best advantage."

Gil said, "I would be pleased if Your Majesty felt free to speak more clearly to me: I am at your service and I don't get what you just said."

A sense of pressure came once more into his ears. Gil realized that Alberec was casting an illusion in his hearing. The illusionary voice said, "You need not stay for our first night of dances. My fairy court, while they might be cajoled to honor the fortitude of a warrior for an hour, cannot be forced to forgive an awkward dance-step in an eon. Depart to your bed, before glory you have gained this night be spilled like wine from a shattered goblet."

But aloud, outside the illusion, what Alberec said was, "Follow Sir Bertolac. He will assign you quarters in his apartments. On the morrow you depart for the training grounds."

Ruff muttered, "The king is getting rid of you as quick as quick can be, so that you do not embarrass him."

Alberec said, "And take your dog with you."

Chapter 10

Training Ground

1. Spy Kit

Gil was awakened by the sensation of Ruff licking his face. He sat up, blinking. It was pitch dark.

"Is it morning?" he asked.

Ruff said, "We're underground, so it is hard to say, but I heard people moving around like it is the beginning of the day watch. I got your pack. You left it in the entry hall. Do you have a flashlight or something in there? Otherwise you have to light your sword on fire."

Gil said, "I am not using Dyrnwen as a torch." He groped around and found the knapsack. One strap was wet from the dog's mouth. His flashlight was hanging from a convenient clip. The beam seemed dazzling in the utter darkness of the room.

Ruff was sitting on his haunches and hands. Hands? Gil blinked, wondering if he were still asleep. But no, Ruff had donned his elf gloves on his forepaws so had fingers and thumbs. Next to Ruff on the floor were some towels, a water kettle, and a basin filled with dark liquid.

"What is that for?" asked Gil.

"I got stuff from my spy kit. I am going to dye your hair. I was thinking black because my hair is black."

Gil said, "With white patches."

Ruff said, "Oh! Oh! Good idea! I can put white patches in your hair, too! Make you look distinguished."

"Or like a skunk. You really have a spy kit?"

"Sure! Sure!"

"What's it got in it?"

"Normal stuff. Disguise stuff in case I want to pass for a terrier or a collie. Gas-powered grapnel and line gun. Bugging devices. Shortwave. Peppery smoke pellets for throwing an enemy off the scent. Tongue antiseptic with a bottle of first-aid spit. A rubber chew toy disguised as a bone that squeaks. A land surfboard for crossing the great deadly desert. Boomerang. You know, normal stuff."

"Boomerang?"

"Sure. Sure. Comes back to your hand when you throw it. I can throw it with my mouth. It is for hunting kangaroos. Dangerous critters! They kick!"

"How often do spies have to hunt… no, never mind…"

"There is a great and powerful fairy kingdom that Alberec cannot enter hidden in the middle of the great deadly desert in Australia. I've had to go there on three missions. 'Ops' we call them. Black dog ops. To gather intel."

"Intel? What's that mean?"

"Yup. That is short for, ah, intel. Anyway, I've got the dye."

"Why am I dyeing my hair?"

"Everyone around here knows your mother, and if they see your magic silver hair, they will know who you are."

"They saw me last night."

"You were wearing your coif the whole time. It covers everything but your face."

"I meant the chambermaids."

"Oh! Oh! Don't worry about them. That kind of fairy is called is pisky: they have amnesia every night at the stroke of midnight. All their short-term memories gone. Poof! They remember how to talk and do their chores, but that is about it. It is some ancient punishment for gossiping. Otherwise the elfs would not trust them not to speak of things they see while cleaning and fetching and stuff."

Gil shivered. "Let's hope the training ground is not as creepy as this place. Go ahead. Dye my hair. Will we have to do this every day?"

Ruff said, "You just have to touch up the roots, depending on how fast your hair grows out."

2. Up the Spiral Tower

Trumpets and bells sounded the hour. There was a knock on the door, and Bertolac, surrounded by a cloud of little lights, came in. His strange yellow eyes glinted in the half-light. He was dressed as he had been last night, in his armor of pure gold and his lion-skull helm and lion-skin cloak, but this time he had sword and shield. At his heel was his giant wolf-faced white dog, Vertifran. Vertifran and Ruff circled each other warily, sniffing.

Bertolac wasted no time on pleasantries, but said only, "Come!"

The tall, golden man led Gil up one dark corridor adorned with scorpions and up a second decorated in centipedes, to an irregular stairway lit by brass snakes hanging by their tails and holding lanterns into their mouths.

The two dogs trotted after, whispering and gossiping in low growls, talking about hunting seasons of days past and days to come, and which dog was bred with which and when, and what litters they had.

They emerged from a sliding panel onto a wide, curving balcony large as a boulevard, gleaming under soft silvery light.

The balcony curved away left and right. Wide, pointed archways facing inward looked upon a vast shaft of air into which captive moonlight poured down. There were ranks of archways, one atop the other, reaching upward and downward as far as the eye could see. It was all one balcony, winding upward like the groove in the horn of a unicorn.

Flitting like motes through this shaft of moonlight were winged servants, bug-sized or doll-sized or child-sized, toting mops or yokes of buckets or baskets of laundry, going from lower balconies to higher or back again. No one of higher rank seemed to be stirring yet.

Gil turned his eyes down. The moonbeam, glinting with motes, stretched down and down like a silver finger into the bottomless well. From far below, Gil heard the sound of thousands of hammer blows on anvils: an army of smiths busily at work.

Bertolac spoke, "Can you fly?"

Gil said, "That is not one of my talents, sir."

Bertolac grunted. "Too bad. I just lost four pence to Puck wagering that you could. Well, I hope you have strong legs. It is quite a climb to the surface."

For a long time they climbed the spiral ramp. There was no one else walking in the corridor except one old lady hobbling toward them. She was dressed in a shapeless black cloak and a tall pointed hat like a dunce cap. When she passed in front of a mirror, Gil saw a line of empty-eyed ghosts, gray as fog, following in her train.

She came closer. The old hag had an owl on her wrist, which she carried as a lady might carry a falcon. Her face was a liver-spotted mass of wrinkles; her hook nose and chin practically touched. Gil wondered at the look of sorrow and despair in her eyes.

Ruff growled, "Don't stare. That is a witch."

But Gil stared nonetheless when the old granny climbed onto a broom and soared up into the beam of moonlight.

Bertolac heaved a sigh of relief. He said, "Do not be so saucy with your eye before your betters. I am taking you to a place where your bumpkin manners, or lack thereof, will neither dishonor you nor put a donkey's head on your shoulders. Elfs are dangerous and fickle people, and their servants more so."

Gil said, "But you are a servant of the elfs."

Bertolac, without any change in expression, clouted Gil on the side of the head. He was not wearing helm or coif, so the blow caught him on the ear and stung like the dickens.

Ruff bristled and growled. "Hey! Hey! Watch the hands! Should I bite him?"

Gil rubbed his ear and gritted his teeth bowed to the knight. "I deserved that, sir." And then he added, "Down, boy!"

Bertolac said, "Do not forget to whom you speak, nor that I am as fickle and dangerous as the rest. My task is to see to it that you become dangerous, too. As much as I can make you in the short span you have." He sighed again and shook his head. "Come! Let us see what wind you have. We will run to the exit."

Gil was strong and sound, but trotting along in his forty pounds of armor up a continuous slope, he was soon wheezing and panting as he tried to keep pace with Bertolac.

They ran past wide gates leading into parks and gardens green and bright beneat small artificial suns, made wide-seeming with illusions. Then, they ran past various doors and gates at which stood sentries, who flourished their pikes in salute of Bertolac, who did not return the salute, but continued trotting onward. They jogged past nicely appointed rooms, indoor lakes of strange fluids, museums, libraries, treasure chambers, ballrooms, and other chambers whose purposes could not be guessed.

Gil developed a stitch in his side, and sweat was running into his eyes. He snatched a glance toward Bertolac. The man was not even breathing heavily.

That earned Gil another sharp blow to the head. "Eyes ahead! Run like the White Christ Himself was after you, manikin!" And Bertolac, whose armor was surely heavier than Gil's own, now broke into a sprint.

Gil ran and ran. Now that they were higher up, the doors opening up onto the spiral balcony were narrower and meaner, unadorned. Apparently, the elfs put their servants and underlings near the surface.

Now they passed arsenals, barracks, and underground stalls or kennels or mews where steeds and hounds and hawks were kept, or creatures odder yet, smilodons and woolly mammoths, Tasmanian tigers, Irish elk, a shining hippogriff.

Gil, wheezing like a broken jalopy, was beginning to look forward to the cold outside and began to imagine, over and over, how refreshing it would be to fall face-first into the snow and never move again.

Bertolac turned around and was running backward now, staring at Gil's sweat-drenched face. He rolled his eyes in disgust, turned a cartwheel or two, leaped like a dancer, kicked his foot against the roofbeam, and still managed to stay well in front of Gil.

Ruff was running, too, his tongue lolling and panting. Vertifran was trotting easily alongside, but his tongue was behind his teeth.

They turned from the main spiral up a narrow and steep stair. Jerking his knees high, Bertolac bounded up the stairs as lightly as a deer, calling on Gil to hurry.

Gil's vision swam. He did not see or notice by what door he exited the underkingdom. He stumbled through the green grass, blinking at the bright sun that blinded him. He saw crooked trees covered in Spanish moss. In the distance were white sand and an expanse of dark water. Nearby on a green hill loomed a large mansion with white pillars holding up a roof of green tiles, all overgrown and blotchy with lichen. Around were several smaller buildings with green moss-covered roofs. Four totem poles as tall as trees carved with leering faces of vultures and goblins, painted in garish colors, stood in a wide square about the mansion.

At his feet was a stream. Ruff jumped to the water and began lapping it up.

Gil staggered a few steps toward the water, panting. His vision swam.

Bertolac said, "Was there something you wanted, squire?"

"Yes, sir," Gil managed to gasp. "Request permission to faint...."

The permission must have been granted because the ground swung up and hit him in the face, and his armor clanged about him. Gil tightened his fingers on the hilt of his sword and scabbard, and, just before consciousness slipped away, wondered in what country he was now, whether this was Earth at all.

It went dark, but he could still hear. Bertolac sighed, just a small sound of disappointment. The hound Vertifran sniffed curiously at Gil's ear and said, "He is stronger than an elf but has less stamina. Maybe a Nibelung?"

Bertolac said, "You trying to sniff out his secrets, Vertifran? It does not matter what he is or where he is from if he cannot perform. I will see him dead before I see him shame me, bury the body beneath some ground where no ghosts walk, and send a changeling in his place to die in his stead in a year."

Gil did not wait for his vision to return. He thought it would be easier, this time, coming to his feet than it had been last night, beneath the tree, when the snow and cold had sapped all his strength.

It was not any easier.

But he did it. It took an eternity, but he did it. Gil stood, swaying, his ears ringing, waiting for his eyesight to clear.

3. Uffern House

The first four weeks were the roughest, and Gil had hardly any sleep the whole time. He was overworked, over-harassed, called, commanded, struck, slapped, and tormented with every cruelty a harsh taskmaster could devise. And it was too cold to sleep at night. New Year's Day came and went without his noticing it.

Uffern House consisted of a mansion housing three knights and a staff of Night World servants and human slaves, some of whom were housed in outbuildings on the hillside. Gil and seven other squires were kept in a wooden barracks at the foot of the hill, hard by the training ground. There were a line of floor pallets on which to sleep, a chest larger on the inside than on the outside in which to stow gear, a single communal chamberpot, and three lamps. One was lit for light, one was lit when smoking tobacco was permitted, and one was lit when returning to one's true form was permitted. The whole barracks was draftier by night and stuffier by day than the stalls where the horses were kept.

Gil was aghast and a little embarrassed when a small troll-face creature showed up at the barracks every day to carry off the chamber pot. Apparently, there were some tasks too humble even for squires to do. The creature's name was Dilk.

Gil's life consisted of three things.

The first thing that made up his life was the practice yard, which included the mess tent, the archery range, and the quintain.

The quintain was simply a pivoting arm standing upright on a sawhorse. One side of the arm was the target, shaped like a shield, and the other was a sandbag dangling from a short chain. When an awkward, overworked, and sleep-deprived squire on an ill-tempered palfrey took a run at the quintain, he would, if he could concentrate and keep his aim, strike the target with the lance that was too big and heavy for him, whereupon the arm would turn on its pivot, and the sandbag would clout the hapless squire from the side or from behind and send him toppling from the horse into the mire and manure of the practice yard, to the neverending amusement of the knights supervising this particular form of devilry.

The second part of Gil's life was the combination of not getting enough sleep, and doing too much washing, wood-chopping, and cleaning.

The third was writing letters to his mother, which he wrapped up and gave to Ruff to mail. How he managed to buy stamps and find a mailbox, Gil never asked. Ruff suggested opening a post office box in the nearest human town beyond the swamp, but without any money, and being a dog, he could not think of a way to do it. So Gil had no way to receive any return letters.

There was no free time and no place to go had there been. Gil learned the stench and location of every bog pool within several miles radius of the house, usually by falling into them. Gil learned to hate the sight of crooked and ancient trees, whose branches were shrouded with hanging moss, and learned to hate the sound of moisture dripping, steadily as a ticking clock, small green drops into midge-infested green ponds.

4. The Servants

From time to time Gil was called into the manor house to do some task there. The place was gorgeous to the eye, decorated in gems and silver and fine woven cloths, but oddly uncomfortable, even for the aristocratic knights.

The elfs did not seem to believe in things like running water or thermostats. When the air was cold, a knight ordered the servants to hang up tapestries, or kindle fires, or breathe out fire. When, months later, the air grew hot, a knight ordered the servants to fan him. When a knight wanted a bath, servants heated water in a kettle over a chimney stove and drew water from the stream which flowed past the foot of the hill, bringing the buckets one by one all the way up the grassy slope. When he wanted light, either a pisky shed it, or the knight had the witch conjure it from the air. There were cooks and kitchen maids a-plenty, but no dishwashing machines.

The witch was a toothless old hag in a dark hood with dark eyes filled with sorrow and helpless rage. In her keeping were the dovecote, where the doves were kept, and the dream library, where dreams were kept. The doves carried messages by day and the dreams by night.

The old witch had an apprentice who slept in the dovecote. This was a nervous girl with frizzled and fly-away red hair, thin-faced and freckled like a strawberry, who, as far as Gil could see, was fully human. The name assigned to her was Foxglove. Gil had few chances to speak with the witch's apprentice, and she was afraid to tell him her real name, or perhaps she had forgotten it.

The stream was fresh and potable and near the hill's foot, but slowed and darkened and sank in a maze of bug-haunted rivulets and inky pools into the marshy land beyond, a place of tall grass, cattails, quicksand, and Bald Cypress groves. Gil would come daily to pound the laundry of the older squires against the rocks, scrub and soap and pound again.

Some of the laundrywomen were also elfs. Others were not. These were old ladies in skirts and aprons and white lacy caps. They did laundry in the same fashion as he did, scrubbing with a washboard and tub at the riverside and stringing the fabric on a line to dry, but at the hour opposite his, so Gil never saw them up close.

He was not sure what he would have done had he seen them up close because he was sure they were human beings.

Ruff confirmed this for him. They were women who were either reported as missing or thought to be insomniacs in the human world, or perhaps victims of UFO abductions. They were summoned nightly by the Black Spell to do work at the mansion and banished, unthanked, back to sickbed or jail cell or asylum, retirement home or gutter, or wherever the elfs saw fit to store their slaves when not needed, with no memory of their labors, merely the weariness. Any who woke partly from the spell to recall, as if in a dream, the nightmare of thralldom, a second elfin charm surrounding the victim would make anyone who heard their tales disbelieve them immediately, discount them as madness, and forget the tales quickly.

5. The Masters

Weeks turned into months. A dozen times a day he told himself he could, should, and must quit, simply flee into the surrounding swampland, and foreswear the elfs, for he had no desire for knighthood after all.

But then, when he noticed he had learned the trick of falling asleep instantly whenever there was available bunk-time and coming awake instantly, alert and ready for more chores, more tilting, more currying, more washing, more whatever, he counted and found he was only wishing to quit half a dozen times a day. By the end of a month, it was down to only three times a day.

The curious thing was that even when he was insulted or beaten, it was always with a certain courtesy and formality. Bertolac could cuss him out when he failed some training task without ever once using a swear word; but Gil told himself to look up the word "jackanape" if he ever got back to human civilization.

There were two other knights aside from Bertolac living in Uffern House, a Sir Dwnn son of Dygflwng, and a Sir Iaen son of Iscawin. Sir Dwnn was the archery master and had the peculiarity that he could swell up to the size of a tree and radiate such heat that everything around him would remain dry when it rained. Sir Iaen taught horsemanship, and his peculiarity was that he was every bit as good a guide in lands he had never seen as in his own country.

Gil could not pronounce either of their names to save his life. He avoided extra punishment by calling them *Sir Dune* and *Sir Yen*, and that seemed close enough.

There had been a third knight there in the first two weeks after Gil's arrival. One of the servants washing his clothing, not a human slave who worked by day but an elf maiden who did her chores by night, found blood seeping from his garments, and she began to keen and wail, before foretelling the third knight's death. And he vanished, either having fled without first asking leave or spirited away unseen by his murderer in another place or world.

Gil never discovered the missing knight's name. The serving girl's name was Gwennmwswgl Bansidhe of the White Moss; another name he could not pronounce. He called her Gwen.

The three ill-tempered palfreys in the stable set aside for the squires to train on were named Hwydydwg, Drwdydwg, and Llwyrdydwg, yet for some reason, Gil had no trouble with their names at all.

He called them High, Dry, and Low for short, talked to them about their troubles, told them jokes and riddles, and asked them polite questions about any aches and the conditions of their hoofs, which he took pains to clean correctly even when another squire was assigned that duty. He was also the only squire who was never bucked off, or bitten, or kicked.

In addition to the palfreys set aside for the squires to train on, there were two Coursers and a Destrier, with glossy coats and fierce eyes, kept in the higher stables, as well as three jennies, a half-tamed gryphon named Gwenglear, and an elf named Selyf son of Smoit who had been turned into a mule.

Sir Dwnn was peppery and erratic and delighted in giving squires contradictory orders so that he always had an excuse to punish failure. He played favorites and simply decided Gil was his least favorite no matter what so that even if Gil executed a maneuver, mucked a stall, mopped a floor, scaled a wall, or shot an arrow into a pikestaff in the exact same fashion as the others, he was punished and they rewarded.

Sir Iaen never raised his voice or altered his tone, and he gave orders in precise detail, expecting them to be carried out in the same detail, just as given. His method was to give tasks it was possible to do but to leave the squires no time in which to do them. If they seemed too close to finishing on time in a satisfactory fashion, he merely added more to the task roster the next day.

Gil could not read the curlicue squiggles of the elf-writing, which, unlike human writing, would change shape depending on whether you looked at it straight on or from the corner of your eye, but he kept Ruff nearby to translate the task roster for him.

6. The Squires

The squires consisted of two purebred elfs as slender as girls but as quick as snakes; a bald boy who wore goggles and had the power of levitation; a surly dark-skinned lad who kept raw meat in a serpent-leather bag which was his prize possession; a seven-foot-tall boy with one eye on the front of his skull and one eye on the rear; a swarthy, squat, and slab-faced lad half Gil's size and twice his strength; and a handsome lad with curly golden locks and eyes of piercing blue. From his hair and skin a cold but refreshing tingle seemed to come like wind from a distant snowpeak.

Ruff identified their race as a Strega, a Fir Bolg, a Fomor, a Nibelung, and Vanir; and Ruff only expressed surprise at seeing a Vanir since they were a people who usually kept apart from elfs due to some ancient enmity between the races.

On the first day, practically the first hour, the other squires knew what had befallen Gil at the Christmas Feast. Each of them, in his own way, made it clear he would not befriend the doomed boy or even take the trouble to learn his name. They called him *manadh-mlwyddyn*, which meant "Year-to-Live" in their particular elf dialect.

In addition to all his other chores and duties, it was the custom here that an elder squire could command any younger to act as his personal servant, doing anything from blacking boots to brushing clothes to bringing tea to cooking breakfast. Gil, as the least senior boy here, suddenly found himself with seven taskmasters, ranging from the unreasonable to the malicious.

There was only a week of pleasant springtime weather. The week before it was bitterly cold at night; the week after it was ferociously hot during the day, and swarms of insects plagued Gil until a group of polite birds asked if they could eat the midges and mites bothering him.

These birds included an Ochre-bellied flycatcher, a Northern Beardless tyrnnulet, a Black-crowned tityra, a Tawny-throated leaftosser, and a Ruddy woodcreeper. They were shy of him, but a Speckled mourner spoke for them. Gil was glad to accept their help and to let them shade him and fan him with their wings. The other squires were nervous seeing these birds flock so close around Gil or fetch him a spent arrow or dropped cleaning rag, so Gil asked the birds to leave him to sweat like the others when he was on the training ground or when Bertolac or the two knights were watching.

He also asked a nightjar to listen after sunset to the talk and gossip of the knights and other elfs, especially anything about him.

Whenever the nightjar reported that Sir Iaen said Gil was being worked too hard by such-and-such a squire or Bertolac said it was "bad form," Gil knew it was time to defy the older boy and to fight him.

He had already fought each of the squires two or three times in the first two or three weeks because, one after another, either in soothing tones or imperious tones, each older boy told him it was against polite custom to say grace at meals. Gil said a prayer aloud at meals nonetheless even though the Vanir lad said it made the beer go flat, and the Owl-boy said it stung his ears.

Gil won more fights than he lost against the Fomorian and Nibelung even though they were stronger than he, but he lost more than he won against the two elfin lads, who were quicker.

Apparently, there was some unspoken tradition about what amount of hazing was allowed and what was too much. It was like an invisible line. Where the invisible line fell depended on a number of things, including the race and relative rank of the squires involved. A boy of an unknown race and lineage, Gil started with this invisible line allowing almost anything. His friends among the birds said the knights were sure he was a half-breed, human mixed with dwarf or eft, perhaps a Moth or Cobweb, who had really no right to be mingling with his betters.

When one of the squires slipped a poisonous snake into his bedsheets one night, Gil politely asked the snake to gather some of his cousins and friends and to return to the squire who had sent him. One of the boys was in the sick house that next day, and Gil had to take on his chores as well as his own, but he could not stop smiling.

After that, the invisible line seemed to move. The gossip now was that since no one knew his parentage, it was best to assume he was of noble blood, a jinn, or a Nephilim.

7. Lessons

They were taught how to scrub and wear their armor. As if he were child again, Gil had to learn how to stoop and rise and stand and walk and run. Gil was embarrassed to discover that knights wore diapers.

"In combat," said Sir Bertolac, "Your body is wiser than you and will expel all uncleanness before any wounds are received. Vision and hearing will close in to a narrow scope, that you may see only what is needed to keep you alive. Your heart will speed, and time will slow."

The training was in horsemanship, sword, battleaxe, mace, dagger, and lance. The swordplay was with sword-shaped wooden batons, called "wasters", which still hurt when they struck and could break bones.

Before Gil ever set foot in a stirrup, he was required to fight on piggyback, at first being the horse, with another squire on his back digging heels into his ribs, and then being the rider. Then there was also swimming, throwing stones and javelins, wrestling, and scaling walls in full armor.

Every fourteen days the knights went out with hounds at their heels or hawks on their wrists, squires trudging dutifully behind, either deeper into the swamp, or on the hillsides beyond the swamp, or on the mountain beyond the hills, or in the arid wastelands on the far side of the mountains, where haunted pyramids and windowless towers brooded above a desert of cactus and thorny trees.

The arts of hunting were useful for honing many aspects of knightly life, from the hardihood of long marches to the making of camp to the patience of stalking prey, the use of horn calls to coordinate maneuvers, and learning to know and use the lay of the land.

The house at times seemed to be closer to the mountain pass, and at other times farther, sometimes deep in the swamp, and sometimes near the edges, so that Gil never formed a clear idea of how far away the western hills were.

Gil from the first was the star pupil during these expeditions. Tree roots would not trip him, thorns not stab, and birds and rodents would tell him how to read the spore or simply say which way the deer, rabbit, possum, or fox had run. Sometimes the deer being chased would simply run toward Gil and come and put his head in Gil's lap. When that happened, Gil felt honor bound to let the creature escape even though it meant he would be punished with mockery and extra duties.

At wrestling Gil also excelled because the quicker boys could not escape his grip, and the stronger boys were not as agile and clever at applying leverage and switching holds. Gil had taken wrestling in school, and from a bear, which these lads apparently had not.

Horsemanship was another matter. No one could understand how a lad his age could have gone through his whole life having never mounted nor ridden a horse. But his lack of basic skills made him not just atrocious, but a laughingstock.

8. Warsteed of the Ghostlord

Then one night as he was sleeping, Hwydydwg, Drwdydwg, and Llwyrdy-dwg came to him in a dream and explained that they could give him extra lessons by night on how to sit properly and post and so on. Gil said, "How is this happening? How can you come when I am asleep?"

Hwydydwg said, "Saint Eloy is a friend of ours, and Saint George, who loves all horses and all horsemen who love them. By their permission we are come."

Drwdydwg said, "Fear not! A fall from a mare in a dream will do you no harm, and no matter your exertions now, you will be well rested in the morning."

And Llwyrdydwg said, "Humans and horse are much alike. Some are maverick and run alone, and some are stallions and run with the herd. Both know how to lead and how to follow. You have yet to find the knight who shall be your true master and teacher; for you have exchanged no oaths with Bertolac and are not bound. You are a maverick still."

Gil said, "What can I give you in return?"

Hwydydwg said, "Be kind to all steeds, both true horses and the elfin Destrier. The fairy horses do not age and cannot be slain, yet none of them is his own master. Beasts lack the power to pray to the Heaven from which their riders fell. Many an elfin steed is tormented by the memories of those high blue fields."

Drwdydwg said, "Do you think humans crave Heaven? Not half so much as we horses; for the shining blue fields run on forever, and the old angelic swiftness which we here on Earth can only foreshadow, there is in its full strength. Running in Heaven, we can outrace the bearded comet. Rarely in waking life can we recall this, and when we do, aha! Swifter than arrows, our hoofs!"

And Llwyrdydwg said, "Do not wonder that there are steeds in Heaven. Is it not promised you that the Prince will return riding a White Horse?"

He awoke refreshed, and, the next morning, when no one, not even Bertolac, could mount up the Destrier, who was bucking and tossing his mane, Gil asked if he could have a try. Everyone laughed and hooted at him, and Sir Dwnn grew red-faced with anger and grew two feet in height, but cold-voiced Sir Iaen said it would be good for the boy to learn humility.

Gil approached the beast, petted his nose, and asked his name, which was Du Y Moroedd. Gil asked about his mother, how she was doing, and other small talk like that. The Destrier said, "I was once the steed of Gwynn ap Nudd, who rules the Land of Ghosts. Should the weight of elfs grown gross and heavy as their spirits slowly become solid be allowed to touch my spine?"

Gil said, "How did you come to be in Sir Bertolac's service?"

"He overthrew the Lord of Ghosts in mortal combat, for he knows the secret of life and death."

Gil turned and looked at Bertolac, a strange look in his eye, for he was puzzled. He wondered what Bertolac was.

One of the squires called out, "Are you just going to pet and nuzzle the beast all day, Year-to-Live? Your time is running short!"

Gil turned back to the stallion. "Let me ride you, and I will tell you a secret."

The Destrier twitched his ears suspiciously. "What kind of secret?"

Gil said, "A good one."

The Destrier said, "I can hear you are telling the truth. A good secret it is!"

So Gil, with some awkwardness, climbed up.

"Put your weight back. No, more the other way," said the horse, and he coached Gil into the proper posture until it felt right on his back. "Now, the secret is…?"

Gil leaned and whispered in his ear, "In Heaven you can run on the shiny blue fields forever, swifter than a comet! Remember?"

The Destrier obviously did remember then, for he reared and neighed and raced away downslope faster than he had ever run before and cleared the stream in one jump.

Bertolac stared after the boy on his speeding steed with a strange look in his eye, for he was puzzled. He wondered what Gil was.

9. Page Pence

Gil asked Du Y Moroedd to bite and misbehave whenever Gil was not around. Gil said, "I'd like to get a reputation for being good with horses."

The Destrier said, "But you are good with horses! I like you just fine. You still don't post properly, but keep trying. No need to be sneaky about it."

Gil said, "I don't think it is sneaky to ask a friend to let you show off your talents, right?"

And so after a few days when it became clear that Sir Bertolac could not mount his prize stallion unless Gil was there petting the horse's nose and holding his bridle, Gil was assigned additional duties as a groom. As it turned out, these additional duties carried additional benefits.

One day, Bertolac on his high war steed and Gil on one of the squire palfreys, Dry, trotted out along the riverside and picked their way from hillock to hillock through the swamp.

Bertolac said, "If you do groom duty, I am expected to give you a silver pence on Michaelmas, or some other like wage. It is called the Page Pence."

Gil said, "Sir, the wage I request is Sundays off. I need to go to pray and to visit the nearest chapel."

Bertolac looked at him askance, then turned, and carefully inspected the surrounding woods. "Aaah. Eh. Prayer is not exactly a normal activity for elfs."

Gil said, "Sir, I am not exactly a normal squire."

Bertolac said, "You know that Alberec has secret police, and spies, and informers, not to mention torture chambers. It is all things that we elfs taught you humans, which you made your own during the Age of Reason, when the final masquerade to hide all trace of elfin overlordship was complete, and all magic and glamour were removed from man. But we also have exquisite variations of our own, nightmare chambers, and witches who can charm the truth out of a born liar, and necromancers who can continue to torment the ghosts of those who die under torture without relent, allowing them no escape."

Gil said, " 'You humans'? You have decided I am a human, Sir?"

Bertolac sighed. "Do you deny that you are human? The Sons of Adam are a sacred race, set apart from nature, and only they can shed tears for their sins. For a time, I thought you were a magician, a human using the black arts to impersonate one of the Night World, but magicians have their tear ducts stopped up when they sign their contract of blood. And you are not a Vanir. You could pass for one, but when you stand next to Fjolnir son of Freyr, the difference is obvious."

"Who?"

Bertolac rolled his eyes. "You blacked his boots last night. The yellow-haired third squire who acts a prefect."

Just then, perhaps by accident, a flock of birds stirred out of the reeds and seeing Gil, rushed up in a clamor of wings and happy greetings. Some of them shaded his head and fanned his brow with their wings; the others dove into the midges, flies, and bugs nearby and cleared the air of them. Birds were sitting on Gil's shoulders and on his head.

Gil carefully moved aside a Coppery-tailed trogon that was blocking his view of Bertolac's surprised face. Gil said ponderously, "Sir, I am not denying that I am a human being."

Bertolac said, "Aha! That means… wait…"

The Destrier said, "It does not mean anything. If he does not say anything about who he is, he is not denying anything either. Use a little horse sense."

Bertolac patted the horse absentmindedly on the neck. "Okay, I suppose that it does not mean anything. But why do you want to go to pray? Are you not afraid of Alberec and his secret police?"

Gil said, "No, Sir. Because it is the King's wish that I stay alive and be trained well enough to comport myself as knight, as much as can be in few months, so that the world will see me go to the Green Chapel."

The wind started blowing at just that moment, and the sun came out from behind a cloud, and the slanting beams fell on and around Gil and Bertolac. Bertolac scowled up at the sun and said, "It is unchancy to say that name aloud, where the sun might hear you."

Gil said, "Sir, nonetheless, I cannot present myself to the Green Knight at the appointed hour if I am in the King's dungeon."

Bertolac said, "Why do you wish to pray? It is a habit that erodes the self-esteem, exasperates friendships, and creates contention and dispute. A true man would stand on his own!"

Gil said, "Sir? Is that your lesson to me as a knight? To be self-serving? If so, I will depart here and now, not even returning to Uffern House for my possessions, but fleeing away from you with all the speed I might."

"And drown in the swamp. It is larger than it seems. The lands we call Yaganechito that stretch from Louisiana through Texas to Mexico are a territory the elfs bought from Napoleon back in the day, but human maps and human minds cannot show it, and the nations and tribes that

Jackson attempted to destroy still flourish here, and the passenger pigeon still flies in myriads along the coasts. How do you imagine to pass through it freely?"

Gil was smiling at this news, for it was the first time he had heard that he was still on Earth and still in North America. How it could be midwinter in North Carolina and the middle of a heat wave in Southern Louisiana, he was at a loss to explain.

Bertolac said, "Why are you smiling? Does the prospect of death in the Sitimacha swamp or Aztec desert amuse you? Hidden from Christian men, the Aztecs have preserved their nations and customs as well, and it is ill to fall into their hands."

Gil said, "Sir, should I perish due to your neglect, I trust you will in good faith report the details of your disobedience to your master, the King. Perhaps you can dress up as me with an illusion and go to the Green Chapel in my stead."

At that moment, the soft, strange, wonderful sounds of church bells ringing in the distance floated across the black pools and reed islands of the mire. Gil asked a quetzal bird, "What bells are those?"

The little bird answered, "The bells belong to Saint Francis de Sales, whose cathedral this is. It is attended by the Sisters of the Holy Cross, who serve Our Lady of the Seven Dolors."

Bertolac clapped his hands over his ears, squinted up at the sun, grimaced, and took one hand off one ear to shade his eyes. He also answered, "Those are the bells of the White Christ. Storms and witches are confounded by the sound. Have you truly never heard them before?"

Gil said, "I have not heard these bells before. Do they belong to the same Saint Francis who is friends with the bears?"

The little bird said, "No, that is a different Francis. This one is the patron of the deaf. We love him because, although we sing along with all creation every dawn all the praises due the creator, there are men who cannot hear us."

Bertolac said, "I don't know to whom they belong. Have you truly never heard church bells before? Count yourself lucky. You must be from Utgard or Ulcoldir or the drowned city of Hy Brasil. What are you? A land-going merman of some sort? A very short giant?"

Gil said, "Sir? I await your answer, Lord. Do you seriously mean to tell me a knight should live for selfish pursuit of self-esteem? Should I dismount and flee from you?"

Bertolac said, "Hmm. I can tell you are not bluffing. Very well: a knight's life is a life of service, as is his death. His life is a life of honor, as is his death. A knight's life is this: never to do outrage or murder; to flee treason; to give mercy to him who asks mercy; to protect the weak and defenseless; always to do ladies and widows succor; never to force yourself upon them, but to respect the chastity of women; not to take up battles in wrongful quarrels for love or worldly goods. And in all things to serve your liege lord in valor and faith."

"Sir, that is well spoken," said Gil. There was a tear in his eye. Hearing such solemn, solid, old-fashioned words, words that affirmed using one's strength to save the weak, to help women, to be true and loyal, and more... weary as he was with the harshness of Uffern, hearing such words made his heart soar.

Bertolac said, "Squire Swan! You have still not told me why you wish to pray. It is not safe for folk of the Night World."

Gil said, "A message from Saint Eloy came to me in a dream and did me a great service. I realized that I am in a deeper danger than I thought, and I want the aid of so mighty a holy man, and of Mary, and the other Saints, and of the Prince of Heaven. Did not King Arthur say once these words? *More things are wrought by prayer than this world dreams of.*"

Bertolac, to his immense surprise, answered him by saying, "*Wherefore, let thy voice rise like a fountain for me night and day. For what are men better than sheep or goats that nourish a blind life within the brain, if, knowing God, they lift not the hands of prayer both for themselves and those who call them friend? For so the whole round Earth is every way bound by gold chains about the feet of God.*"

Gil listened with his mouth hanging open. He had not known the rest of the quote or had not remembered it. It was from one of the books about King Arthur that Gil had read. Up until this moment, Gil had been convinced that the elfs knew nothing of those books. Why else would parts of the story of Arthur that every schoolchild knew be a shocking surprise to the elfs? But here was Bertolac rattling off the words without a pause.

Bertolac nodded sagely. "I had forgotten you were Arthur's man. It is an incredible and unbelievable claim for you to make, but I begin to believe it." Bertolac heaved a sigh. "I cannot stand against one of Arthur's orders. Since he told you to pray for him and for yourself and your friends, I will not contradict him. He once came to Caer Sidi, you know, and the elfs did not triumph in that encounter. I grant you leave provided you take all precautions that the others of my kind do not discover it."

"What precautions?"

"Can you cast the illusions to hide you from prying eyes?"

"I cannot."

"If you are an elf, you must be as sunk in sins as Modsognir to have lost so much. How could you forget all we once knew? Bah! I will have Granny Squannit the Witch arrange to cover you up until you leave Yaganechito. I am no fool to ignore so clear an omen: we are very near the border. You have to cross a bridge of wood and then a bridge of stone, and you will be in the world of men again, where the mists are thin. I reckon it to be seven miles from the edge of the Wildlife Refuge to the center of Houma, where that cathedral is. On horseback you should be able to go and return in the time allotted. I can show you the simple trick all Night Folk use to place their swords and armor partway in the mist so that we can walk among men, without our weapons being seen by them, or recollected if they are. It is our most useful elfwork, and anyone can learn it."

"I am grateful to you, Lord."

"Do not be. You have failed to count the cost. It is already April, and you have proven yourself all but worthless so far. We have eight months left to make you worthy of being the lowliest and most raw of knights. Each day must hold two more hour's worth of work to make up for the twelve hours lost!"

"Yes, sir."

10. One Last Thing

They rode on for a while. Bertolac at one point squinted at Gil's face and said, "One last thing: report to me before dawn tomorrow in the Gentleman's Wardrobe."

"Sir?"

"You have an unlikely growth of hair on your cheek, and it must be scraped clean if you are to be presentable to the humans at mass."

Gil, surprised, rubbed his jaw, and felt the wiry fur of a bit of beard there. He had not looked in a mirror for weeks, and he wondered fearfully if the hair was coming in silver, like the hairs of his head, or dark, like the hair of his eyebrows.

Seeing his look, Bertolac must have misinterpreted it, for said in a soft and almost kindly voice, "You have no father, no uncle, nor grown brother to show you?"

"I have no one, sir."

Bertolac pursed his lips, looking a little grim. "I will have a maiden boil water and bring soap, and I will show you myself the art of shaving. Every boy learns this when he becomes a man. I will have our witch fetch you an oval shard of volcanic glass to strop into a proper razor. It keeps an edge better than a knife of bronze or flint. It is only a shame that..."

He caught himself and closed his mouth, but Gil knew what he had been about to say. It was only a shame that the squire Year-to-Live would only make use of the art of shaving for the year he had to live.

"I am grateful, sir," said Gil.

Bertolac was silent for the rest of the ride.

Chapter 11

Sabbath Day

1. Stockings and Swamp Herbs

Bertolac was as good as his word. Gil was given an extra two hour's worth of work to cram into his eighteen available hours of work, training, hazing, and fatigue on Friday and Saturday. When Ruff read the ever-twisting elf-runes from the duty roster, he growled and said Gil was off duty Sundays.

Friday afternoon, after lance practice, between rushing to thatch the roof of the ice-house, to peel potatoes, to climb a rope in full armor, to put an arrow into a clay pigeon, to haul water buckets from stream to cistern, and to mend an older squire's ripped stockings, he managed to arrange with the older groom (who looked like an ape) and the under cook (who looked like a stump) to have a satchel of bread, cheese, and bologna readied for his Sunday breakfast and to have Ceingalad, one of the two coursers, assigned to his use for that day. The chore of waxing and polishing the saddle, stirrups, bridle, halter, reins, bit, harness, and martingale was added to his load to complete before Friday night lights-out.

He managed this only by asking shy and fidgeting Foxglove, the witch's maid, to swap chores with him. She would sew the stockings for him, as he was no hand with a needle. In return, he would gather purple looses-trife, fennel, henbane, mint, mugwort, and silkweed from the swamp. She did not want to do it because she was afraid of snakes, Will-o'-the-Wisps, and drowning.

Gil, of course, did not have the ability to find these herbs and flowers in the pathless morass, but by a combination of wheedling and threatening, he convinced some opossums, raccoons, river rats, ringtail cats, and woodcocks to help him.

He had to bribe them with his dinner, so he went hungry that night. But by dawn, the animals and birds gathered more into the bag of the poisonous flowers and sweet green herbs than Foxglove could have gathered in three trips. She was so happy when she saw the overflowing bag that she clapped her hands, hopped for joy, and leaped at Gil to kiss his cheek. Then she blushed as red as a beet and ran away.

Gil said, "I hope she remembers to hide it. She is supposed to go out into the swamp from Saturday evening to Sunday morning, or else it won't look like she gathered it."

Ruff, sitting nearby scratching his flees, watched the little witch's maid run off, clutching her bag of swamp herbs. He whistled. "I'm telling Nerea."

Gil said, "What are you talking about? You're crazy."

"Gilberec and Foxglove sitting in a tree... Kay, eye, ess, ess, eye, en, gee...!"

"Other dogs foam at the mouth when they are mad. You rhyme."

"She's sweet on you!"

"Can't be. For one thing, she is thirteen. Or twelve."

"She is older than that. The witch feeds her a drug to keep her from growing up. To keep her too young to breed."

"That's gross."

"Everything witches do is gross."

"Not in the movies. In movies, the witches are always young and cute—they're always good witches."

"Hollywood is run by elfs," grunted the dog.

"Anyhow, I have talked with her maybe once."

"Listen. Listen. If you did not shout at her that once you talked to her, then you are the only who hasn't. You were nice. That means a lot to girls like her. No one bothers to find out her name for the same reason they don't want to bother finding out yours. She is not going to live long."

Gil said, "How do you know?"

"Hey, I am a spy, after all, and I have lots of time to sniff around while you are busy getting hit on the head with wooden swords and falling off your pony."

"What's going to happen to her?"

"The elfs were thinking of giving the witch away at the tithe because the dark powers prefer to take a human in the place of an elf. But the witch will give them her prentice in her place, and they'll agree, because the powers prefer a virgin in the place of a crone."

2. The Dovecote

On Sunday morning an hour before dawn, Gil was in his armor and surcoat on top of Ceingalad, with shield and helm hanging from his saddle. He and Ruff trotted near the creaking old tower used as the dovecote where the Witch slept amid piles of white bird droppings. The moon was down, and the night was cool, and the insects and toads in the swamp were chirruping and croaking.

The snores of the witch could be heard even through the stone walls and wooden cap of the tower. Her nose was like a foghorn.

Gil asked Ruff to sniff around and find the trail of Foxglove.

One of the doves called out in alarm, "Who's there?"

Gil said softly, "Please go back to sleep. If you wake up the witch, everything is lost!"

"Is that you? Gilberec Moth? The trees are talking about you." High above, a small white bird head peered out from between two broken tiles in the conical roof.

Gil said, "Hush! Yeah, I am a friend of theirs. Sort of."

The white dove cocked its head to one side. "A tree-friend! Are you saving Foxglove?"

"Yes, yes, now hush up. Don't wake up the other birds!"

"We like her! We do!" That was a second bird, which also stuck its white, slim head out of the dovecote to peer at him.

And one or two other birds inside the tower cooed, "We do! We do! Dooo!"

The second bird asked excitedly. "Do you like her?"

"Sort of. Not really. Now please be quiet!"

"Why are you helping her if you don't really like her?" piped up a third bird. Now more and more little avian faces with bright eyes were peering down from under the roof eaves. "Who knows what the witch will do to you?" (and other doves cooed, "Do to you! Do to you! Youuu!")

"She's a damsel. She's in distress. It's my job. Now hush up, for Christ's sake!"

The several birds billed and cooed for a moment, and one said, "For his sake, we shall. The spirit who descended on the Christ to baptize him was like one of us, which was a great blessing for all doves. I will go and tell the priest to ready the water, oil, and wine."

And one lone white bird flew out across the night sky. The others, true to their word, returned to their perches inside the tower most silently. No voice was raised in alarm, and there was no clamor as Gil followed Ruff away from the tower. The only sound that followed them was the raucous snores of the Witch.

3. Foxglove

Ruff led Gil directly to the little hillock beneath a moss-covered oak tree where Foxglove sat, shivering. The bag of herbs she was pretending to gather was hanging on a gnarled tree branch. She was sitting in her shapeless brown dress, her red hair a wild mess, her pointed elbows around her knobby knees, rocking back and forth, staring at the oily swamp waters and tufts of grass that hissed and murmured in the night breeze. Gil heard the noise of sobbing and crying.

The twitter of the first bird broke through the susurration of insect whines and toad voices. "Dawn!" the bird cried.

Other birds joined in, twittering. "Hail! Holy light! Offspring of Heaven firstborn! Of the eternal, a co-eternal beam! For God is light! And his first word of creation in his image his own image made, light from light!"

Gil trotted up on horseback, tack jangling.

Foxglove looked up at him, embarrassed, woebegone. Gil saw no sign of tears on her cheeks. She said, "What are you doing here? You are going to get us both in trouble."

Gil said to Ruff, "Good boy. You found her. And there is no one following? No one watching?"

Ruff said, "Nope. The normal elf spies, owls, and pixies and the like, were baffled by the witch-spell Sir Bertolac ordered to cover your tracks."

Gil said to Foxglove, "Are you willing to give up this place forever. I can take you into the human world, and no one will be the wiser. Do you have any folks? Any place to stay?"

She said, "I cannot go back to the human world. I never knew my dad, my mom's boyfriends beat me, and I was in and out of doctors' offices and clinics because I could see things that were not there. A witch woman found me. She was a friend of the elfs. She said she would teach me secrets. Skip was the name of Mom's latest boyfriend. I might have killed him. I was trying to. Skip was screaming in his sleep when I got out of his car, and he got out, too, even though he was asleep. He was sleepwalking in the middle of the road, trying to hit the oncoming cars with a tire iron. I made him drive me in his sleep to the bus station. I can do that to people. Just with words and a stick from a willow tree. The witch taught me. Then, I sent him out into the highway to fight the cars. So I am a killer. Or just as good as one. I cannot go back."

Gil said, "You can find someone to take you in, if you are willing to try. An orphanage is better than this."

She shook her head. "I signed a contract. In blood."

Gil said, "Witches really do that?"

She nodded, miserably. "I sterilized the needle with alcohol first. I learned all about needles from my mother. If I break the contract, the Devil takes me."

Gil raised his head and listened to the birds singing for a moment. Then, he looked down at her, frowned, and said sternly, "I know a prince who is stronger than any demon or devil, but he is bound by his love for you never to help you until and unless you ask. Will you foreswear witches and witchcraft, and her false promises of power, and the elfs and their glamour, and all the deceits and trumpery of the Devil? My prince can protect you."

She looked up. Foxglove must have known some of the gossip about Gil because now her eyes were shining. "Do you mean Arthur? Is he not your lord?"

"I mean the lord Arthur serves. Come. Get up behind me." He leaned down and smiled and extended his hand.

She shook her head, her eyes empty of hope and life. "The elfs will find me."

"No one will look for you. Hand me your shawl."

And, when he had her shawl, he whistled and called for an alligator. After a few minutes, two yellow eyes looked up from the deeper water, and a great red mouth opened.

"What do you want, Son of Adam? My kind has nothing to do with yours! My kind is as old as the terrible lizards who once ruled all the world in aeons long past, when all the world was swamp and no flower had ever opened it face. We were here before you, and we will be here when you are gone and the world is ruled by a coleopterous race of great-skulled beetle monsters, with eyes like lamps, cold and cruel with insect wisdom."

Gil said, "I'd like you to take this shawl, leave some teeth marks in it, and leave it by a deep pool where the witch who lives in yonder tower might find it when she comes looking."

The alligator said, "Is this the witch who has a stuffed alligator hanging in her study?"

Gil said to Foxglove, "Does your witch own a stuffed alligator?"

Foxglove said, "Yes. She makes me push the little dreams down its throat when they don't do as she tells them. The ghost of the alligator is still bound inside the corpse, and it torments them and digests them. They come out the nether parts as nightmares and go to live in the closets and under the beds of little children."

The alligator said to Gil, "I heard her. That witch offends me. Give me a name, and I will do as you ask. We shall fool her."

"You seek revenge?"

"The stuffed alligator was my mate. All her eggs died. I am left without any progeny, without a future. We are a very old race and such a thing is shame to us. I seek revenge."

"Your name is Edmund Dantes, the Croc of Monte Cristo." And Gil tossed the shawl to him. The alligator took it in his great, grinning mouth and without any further words, submerged.

Foxglove climbed up behind Gil, her freckled face wreathed in joy, and she put her arms about his waist and hugged him.

Ruff said, "Watch out! There is a wooden bridge over a river and a stone bridge over a canal where you have to cross! If Nerea sees this, what will she think?"

Gil took out a piece of bologna from the breakfast satchel and tossed it to Ruff. "She will think I am a hero for saving Foxglove."

"Suzy," the redhead said. "My real name is Susannah Winifred Wenk. My mom called me Winner. Get it? Short for Winner-fred. That's how she said it. My mom. Sometimes she had good days. You know. Whenever she was out of money, she could remember who I was." And her face fell, and she sobbed without shedding tears.

4. Mist and Sunlight

The warhorse with its two riders, with a bright-eyed dog leaping and cavorting after, passed two bridges.

The first was a covered bridge that crossed a river of waters dark, deep, and swift. The ground was drier and higher on the far side of this river, but the trees were thicker, and Spanish moss was in the branches, and kudzu was along the ground.

Gil asked, "What is this dank wood called?"

Ceingalad said, "I am a Foal of Equus, the sire of all steeds. It is for the Sons of Adam to name things."

But a ringtail cat in a nearby branch learned down and said, "Gilberec Moth! Is that you? I am sent to tell you that this is called Backswamp of the Backlands. The soil is sterile here, and all the tree roots are shallow. It is an unchancy place for you, where vows are broken."

Gil said, "Thank you, bassarisk! Who sent you?"

"Dominic Moth was his name in life. He was a great explorer, adventurer, and missionary. His is the only known map of the Elfinlands, and even it is not complete." But then the ringtail cat was startled by a noise and fled before he could say more.

Two hours later, under a brighter, hotter sun, they emerged from the wood. Ceingalad's hooves echoed loudly on the stones of the arched bridge that curved lightly over the canal, whose clear waters with idle languor past the feet of the bridge. This bridge was made of many stones in a pleasant variation of light and dark grays, oranges, reds, and ochres. It was so simple and beautiful in design, so well made, that Gil said, "Did elfs build this? Or are we in the human world?"

Ceingalad said, "Elves build nothing. This is something preserved from the old days, when things were built in the old ways. You can tell from the sound and the feel under your hoof if a bridge is sound and will last."

Foxglove said, "I don't think elfs built it. Look: there is a big stone cross by the crossroad right before the bridge. We have left the twilight lands. This is the day world."

Gil was surprised at a feeling, something like shyness or stage fright, he discovered in himself. It had been two months since he had seen any human beings, aside from slaves and servants of the elfs.

The horse halted. Gil sat, staring at the two roads which headed off, one to the north and one to the east, from the big stone cross. He sat on the horse, trying to remember what the noise of a motor engine, or an airplane, or rock music sounded like.

Foxglove said, "Oh! You should not ride around in armor with a sword. People will notice. And if someone takes a photograph, it might get into the newspapers."

Ruff barked, "Hey! She's right. She's right! Elfs run the newspapers. And the madhouses. I think that is where they get the staff."

Just then, the sound of the bells from Saint Francis de Sales came floating and echoing over the trees. Gil pushed with his knees, and jabbed with his heel, and said, "Giddyup!" and snapped the reins.

Ceingalad said sardonically, "Giddy what? Do I look like a cowboy horse to you? I am an elf steed. You are supposed to say *Noro lim! Noro lim!*"

Gil patted him on the neck and said, "Head toward the sound of the bells, please, brave Ceingalad. I'll get you a carrot if you do."

The horse nonchalantly turned that direction, and then began trotting over the fields, and then sped up, charging and jumping any fences or ditches that happened to turn up in his way.

Ceingalad said, "This they call the steeple chase! You pick a steeple in the distance and leap over anything in the way! Only the best steeds dare try this. Hang on!" And he jumped again.

Foxglove clung more tightly to Gil's back. "That is amazing! It is almost as if he understands what you are saying."

Gil said, "A very wise horse, this."

Ceingalad said, "Thank you."

Foxglove said, "See! He neighed. It is like he knows you are talking about him!"

Ruff, running alongside, tongue lolling, yipped, "Tell her is it an optical illusion of the ear."

They came to a dirt road and followed it at an easier pace. They passed a few farmhouses, and then more. The dirt path ran into a paved road. Ahead, downslope, they could see the roofs and telephone poles of the town and the church steeple.

Foxglove said, "But... uh... Mr. Swan. What is your first name? You aren't dressed right to go into the human world. Do you know how to hide your stuff in the mist?"

Gil said, "Sir Bertolac showed me, but he did it rather quickly, and I am not sure I remember. First, you stare at what you want to hide... ah..."

Foxglove chuckled. "So. You are a Son of Adam after all. Haven't you noticed the elfs never need to jot down notes or write books? They memorize everything in their songs and triads. It is the mist that does it. In the old days, when there was less mist, a poet could recite long epics from memory, or a prophet could name his every ancestor back to Adam. So Sir Bertolac would never think of repeating himself. Here. I will show you again."

Gil was not using the reins anyway, so he let them drop, unclipped the sword, scabbard and all from his belt, and held it before him.

She said, "First, it takes mist to summon mist because like attracts to like. Your sword, for example, is a great and ancient artifact, made by Weyland, so its roots reach into the legendary past, which is also in the mist. Close your right eye. Look at a bright part of the sword, such as the pommel."

"Now what?"

"Now find a spot seven times the length from forefinger knuckle to nail down from the pommel. Seven is the magic number. Place your thumb there. Um. Take your gloves off first."

"Gauntlets."

"Then, hold the sword a cubit from your nose."

"What is a cubit?"

"The distance from elbow cap to forefinger. That is the only way to tell a girl is born to be a witch, by the way; only a born witch can kiss her elbow cap."

Ruff said, "No, that cannot be right! I heard the only way to tell was that witches never cry. Or is that mummies? And they have a mark where they suckle their familiars."

Ceingalad said, "I hate mummies! Bertolac always smells like mummy rags when he comes back to Uffern House."

Meanwhile, Foxglove was saying to Gil, "Now, fix your eye without blinking on the pommel, and be aware of your thumb, but do not look toward it, or the spell will be broken. Slowly draw the sword toward your nose until your thumb disappears. Your thumbnail should be in the mist by a very nail's breadth. Draw your thumb down, scraping a tiny wisp of mist after it. Then, quickly take that wisp between thumb and ring finger, and draw again. The mist will be attracted to itself and come trickling out. You can see it with the corner of your eye. Then, you just rub it with your eyesight on what you want to hide."

Gil said, "It is the rub it with my eyesight part I don't get."

She said, "I'll do it this time." Then, she smiled sadly. "This might be the last time I ever do any witchcraft. Will I miss it?"

"If it pains you, think of that pain as punishment for trying to kill that guy you mentioned," said Gil. "But no, I don't think you will miss it."

Foxglove told Gil to close his eyes, which he did. As they trotted along, a cold sensation came up from his hands holding Dyrnwen, like snakes of frost climbing to his elbows, and rapidly spread over his mail shirt, leggings, and coif. When he opened his eyes, he saw a white shadow hovering around him.

"Is this an illusion?" he said.

She said, "No, it is like the base you apply before applying blush. The mist just subtracts from a human's eyesight the things he does not expect to see. If you walked into a Renaissance Fair or a Halloween Party, everyone would see your chainmail."

"It is called mail, not chainmail." Said Gil. "What do they see instead?"

She said, "Well, nothing, really. Sort of whatever they expect to see. Their own mind fills in the background, like it does in a dream. I can weave an illusion for you, if you like, so that everyone would see the same thing. I need something to work with. Oh! I know!"

And to Gil's embarrassment, the girl took a gauzy green scarf out of her apron pocket and draped it over his neck. She sang a song without words or melody, made some passes in the air with her hands, and then took a pin out of her dress seam and thrust it through the scarf. She said, "Green is the best color for illusions. Something about the optical properties."

Gil said. "What do I look like?"

Foxglove said, "It's a Boy Scout uniform."

Sure enough, when they trotted into the town of Houma, the passersby glanced at the horse and gave him a nod, but seemed to see nothing out of the ordinary. A policeman directing traffic gave Gil a snappy three-fingered salute.

5. Church Bells

The cathedral consisted of a tall bell tower with wings to either side, and the main nave running back from the intersection, so the floor plan, if seen from the sky, was a cross.

Foxglove was getting nervous. "The bell noise is bad for me... I... I am not sure I can go on with this. I'm scared."

They were close now. Gil dismounted and raised his hands to her. "Let me help you down."

That made her forget her worries for a moment. But then, when she was in his arms, her whole body started to shake. She said, "It think they put something inside me. When they closed over my tear ducts. It is going to hurt me! This is a bad idea. The witch was not so bad...."

Gil took her by the shoulders and shook her. "Winner, listen to me. The witch was going to sacrifice you to save herself. There is holy water in a little cup by the door. Just take a few steps. Just a few more. Come along."

"I– I'm scared. I don't think I can do it!" Her eyes swam. Tears of panic began to trickle down her freckled cheeks.

Gil said, "Say a prayer."

She said, "What prayer?"

He said, "Any prayer! *Hail, heavenly queen, mother of mercy, our life, our sweetness and our hope...* do you know that one? *Our Father who art in Heaven...*? Come on. Everyone knows that one."

She made a strange gargling noise in her throat, as if she were choking.

Ruff said, "Boss! People are looking at us!"

Gil looked up. There was a crowd of people in their Sunday clothing, who had been filing into the entrance of the church, but now were stopped. They were staring at him holding a girl suffering some sort of choking spasm.

Gil looked and saw a mother with a child. He said, "Ma'am, get help. Go get the Father. Quickly!" The woman turned and ran in the door. Gil said to Foxglove, "Just say, *God is great. God is good.*"

Foxglove wiped her cheeks with the heel of her palm and then stared at her own hand, awestruck. She whispered. "It's wet. I'm crying. But the witch sealed up my tear ducts in my eye. It really hurt. When I signed the contract. It must be... oh, Lord, thank you..."

Foxglove uttered a scream. Her legs went out from under her.

Gil caught her and lowered her to the ground. He looked up and said to the throng of onlookers, "Stand back, please. Give her some room. Would someone lend me a crucifix, please?"

A man in a hat said, "Why do you need a crucifix?"

But the woman next to him said sharply, "He's a Boy Scout! He knows what he's doing!"

The priest came trotting out, smiling genially. He was remarkably young and rather plump. "What seems to be the problem, my children?"

Gil looked up, trying to keep the writhing body of the young girl from banging her head on the brick walkway. "Father? Please say a prayer for her. She is trying to run away from witchcraft, and there may be a bad spirit tormenting her. Can you do an exorcism?"

Gil saw the looks of doubt and disbelief on the faces of everyone there, with one exception. The young, plump priest seemed to have no doubts that witches and bad spirits existed. From the look on his face, he did not even seem to think this was out of the ordinary.

He knelt, whispered in the girl's ear, removed his alb, and laid it around her shoulders. He took the crucifix someone in the crowd held out, blessed it, and put it around her head even though she choked and screamed and tried to bite him.

The plump priest called four men by name and said, "Ralf, Nathan, Bill, Eddy, come here. Eddy, you are the biggest, lay down your coat. We are going to roll her onto it. Let us take her inside. My son, what is your name?"

Gil said, "Call me Swan."

"It that a Dutch name? Svonn, you take her hands. I know just what to do. I have everything prepared. Never thought I would get to use those lessons, but I got top marks in seminary. Gently! Here we go. When I count to three, lift her up."

The four men, with Gil and the priest, grunted and stumbled and lurched, and then carried the girl through the big wooden double doors.

The interior was surprisingly opulent; rows of golden lamps hung from the white arches above the ranks of pews. White pillars marched toward an immense rose window like a brilliant eye, and its beam slanted down to glow across a tall altar of carved wood. Niches to the left and right held saints; niches above held angels. In the center was a suffering figure on a cross. A box of gold, shut with lock and key, was at his feet.

The priest said, "Ah! Sister Marigold! As I warned everyone, mass may be delayed for a time. Could you please lead the congregation in prayer, for the salvation of the soul of this girl, ah…"

Gil said, "Susannah Winifred Worth. The witch tried to take her name."

The priest smiled again. "Her name will be written in the Book of Life, never to be expunged, and she shall be placed beyond the reach of all the powers of darkness."

Gil said, "How can you be sure, Father?"

The plump, smiling young man laid a finger along a nostril. "Let's say a little bird told me. Come! This way! Into the vestry. We can have a little privacy. Did you ever see the movie *The Exorcist*? It is actually not very much like that. There were some technical inaccuracies, you know. Sister Naomi! Bring me my weapon."

Gil said, "Your weapon, Father?"

The nun scurried up, holding out a belt of rosary beads with a shining silver crucifix dangling from the end, bright as a sword.

6. Cynocephaly

It was late in the afternoon by the time Gil, atop Ceingalad, with Ruff
trotting alongside, came back past the crossroads with its tall stone cross
to the old stone bridge leading back into the other world.

There was a man sitting not far from the cross. In one hand was a tall
pole. He wore a hooded sweatshirt and a dented and crushed cowboy
hat, its wide brim pulled low. Over that, he wore a ragged overcoat that
looked like it had been new about the time of the Civil War. In his hand
he held a little square of cardboard with some angular letters in crayon
scrawled on it. Next to him was a shopping cart filled with trash bags.
One bag was open. Inside were vegetables. Gil could see a head of lettuce
and a bunch of carrots.

Ruff sniffed. "I smell a dog."

Ceingalad said, "I smell carrots!"

Ruff said, "I don't trust a guy who smells like a dog. Also, look at his
size. He's really big. Let's keep on."

Gil was not pleased with the smell either, but all he could smell was
wine, and vomit, and months of unwashed hair, dirt, grime, and perhaps
a whiff of some horrible skin disease.

Gil said, "I don't know. We are already late getting back. I don't want
to lose my Sunday privilege."

Ceingalad said stubbornly, "You promised! You promised me a carrot!"

Gil sighed. He saw no other choice. He was not going to break his
word to a horse.

He dismounted. Gil saw that Ruff was right. Even seated on the
ground, the shapeless wide-brimmed hat was nearly the level of Gil's eyes.

The little sign said, *Am a veteran.*

And there were other words, in smaller print, below that. Gil stepped
closer, squinting, wanting to hold his nose.

Served Devil. Bounden in a seat of iron and set afire. Shot by XL arrows.
Almost drowned. Please help. Christ is heavy.

A croaking voice came from under the hat. "Buy some produce? Veg-
gies is good for you."

Gil said, "I don't have any money at the moment. I'd like to buy a carrot. Hang on. I think I can pry one of these diamonds out of my gorget."

The hat brim twitched. "You would mar your father's armor to keep a promise to a beast and bestow a diamond on a beggar?"

Gil with his dagger point had begun the process of bending the little floral tines awry which held one of the dozens of blue white diamonds on his neckpiece. He paused, glancing up at the stinking, shabby figure. "How did you know this was my father's armor?"

"I stare into the face of the Father, and it is a bright-looking glass and holds all the worlds he has made in his gaze; and what I need to see is revealed to me, yes, even in the most secret hearts of men. You are a good lad but prone to anger. I am sent to command you to discipline."

Gil said, "Who is my father?"

"Your mother's lover, true and faithful."

Gil said, "Who are you?"

The foul smell was gone, and a fresh scent, warm and musky, came from the figure. He cast his hat aside, and stood, and grew taller, and then taller again, until he was three times the height of a man.

The pole in his hand grew with him as he grew, and it was as tall as the mast of a pirate ship.

His clothing was torn as his limbs expanded, and the rags cast aside, revealing a shining white garment beneath. Looking up, Gil saw the being had the head of a dog. His skull was black and his mouth was brown, like a Doberman Pinscher.

"I am a messenger, here to tell you three things. First, you have found favor in the eyes of Our Lady, for your compassion toward her lost daughter, Susannah."

Gil said, "By Our Lady, do you mean the Virgin, Mary? Did she have other children after she gave birth to Jesus?"

"All who are baptized in the living water are her children, for she is the Mother of the Church. Susannah was baptized as a baby and does not recall it, but due to this chrism, a champion both bold and kind was sent to rescue her."

Gil said, "What happened to him? Why didn't he show up?"

The dog-faced giant knelt, leaned down, and licked Gil on the face.

Gil jumped back, a little upset, but then he simply had to laugh aloud. "Well! You are a friendly pup, aren't you!" He wiped his cheek with the green scarf and laughed again, for a feeling of lightheartedness had come into him, a spirit of solemn joy.

Ruff said, "Boss, I think he means *you* are the champion."

Gil said, "No way. He must mean someone else…." because the thought that he, Gilberec Moth, might be serving not just Arthur's memory, but also everything for which Arthur fought, was too huge a thought for Gil to believe. Oddly enough, he felt a sense of shame, for he knew himself unworthy to serve so high a cause.

The dog-faced giant said, "My second message is to tell you of Reprobus."

Gil said, "Who is he?"

7. The Tale of the Scoundrel

"His name, Reprobus, being interpreted, means *Scoundrel*. He was of the lineage of Cain, and he was of a right great stature and had a terrible and fearful cheer and countenance. And he was twelve cubits of height.

"So great was his strength it came into his mind that he would seek the greatest prince that was in the world, and him he would serve and obey. Coming to Byzantium, where the king of all the Romans ruled and reigned, the king received him into his service and permitted him dwell in the royal court. So Reprobus served there seven years. Scoundrel.

"Upon a time, a minstrel sang before him a song in which he named oft the Devil, whereat Scoundrel saw the king make the sign of the cross before his visage. Marveling, he demanded of the king what it meant. The king said, *Always when I hear the Devil named, I fear he should have power over me, so I garnish me with this sign that he neither grieve not nor annoy me.*"

Ruff said, "Oh! Oh! I know where this story is going. Is there a dog in it? The dog saves the kid from drowning or something, I betcha."

The dog-faced giant said, "That is not quite the ending. The kid saves the dog. But you must wait for the telling of it."

"Oh! Oh! What happened next?"

"Knowing now that this Devil, whomsoever he might be, was mightier than the king of Byzantium, Scoundrel went to the crossroads where a suicide was buried, far from holy ground, a stake through the heart and the right hand cut off. The ghost arose and told him the way to where the Devil had his Earthly throne, a mighty city called Pergamon on the river Caicus.

"On the road to Pergamon, he came across a rider on a pale horse, and behind him a mighty host; and this rider spoke to him, saying *I am he thou seekest. These in my train are the votaries of Baphomet and Mahound, whom I have deceived with the false prophet Saint John foreknew; and all the Christian lands from Libya to the Levant are red above from the light of the burning cities and red beneath from the blood of the slain. I have commanded the jinn and janna to break up the mountains where hermit folk might hide and commanded the paynim to burn each book to ash and every smallest bone and relict of every holy saint.*

"And so Scoundrel went with him, and served the Devil seven years, and did many cruel deeds."

Ruff sat and scratched his ear. "Hey! Is the Devil the good guy in this story? He is always the good guy in the stories told by elfs."

The giant said, "You must wait for the telling of it."

"Okay! But get to the part with the dog."

"The dog is throughout the tale. Listen: Upon a time as Scoundrel and the Devil passed through a straight highway in the desert, the hosts of Hell came upon a tall and fair cross erected by hermits in the wasteland, and the Devil blanched pale, and turned aside, and could not walk past the shadow of the cross, no, nor so much as look on it. Marveling, he demanded of the Devil what it meant. The Devil answered and said, *There was a man called Christ, who was hanged on the cross, and when I see his sign, I am sore afeared and flee from wheresomever I find it.*

"Knowing now that this Christ, whomsoever he might be, was stronger than the Devil, Scoundrel sought out the hermit who had raised the cross in the wasteland and was instructed by him.

"And the hermit said, *This Prince whom thou desirest to serve requireth this service that thou must oft fast and on Lenten Days abstain from meat.*

And Scoundrel said to him *Require of me some other thing, and I shall do it. For that which thou requirest I may not do.* For the children of Cain eat no grain, but flesh alone, for so our teeth are formed.

"So the hermit told him of a river where many perished and were lost. Because he was high of stature and strong in his members, Scoundrel was made to dwell by the river and bear over all them that passed there. So he did for seven years."

Ruff said, "What is with the 'seven years' jazz?"

"Upon a time a child small and fair came to him and called him as he slept, saying *Wake! And bear me over!* Out of his hut he came, but saw no man. Again, he slept. Again, the voice came, and again, he woke and saw no man. But the third time he was called and came out, he found a child beside the rivage of the river who prayed him goodly to bear him over the water.

"And Scoundrel lifted the child on his shoulders, and took his staff, and entered the river for to pass. But the water arose and swelled, and the child was heavy as lead. As with each step, the water grew wilder and wilder, and the child waxed heavy and more heavy, until Scoundrel had great anguish and feared to be drowned. So he called upon Christ to save him in his distress. Lightly, the child took him up by the hair of his head and bore him across the top of the waves to the shore.

"Scoundrel said *Child, thou hast put me in great peril. Thou weighest as much almost as I had had all the world upon me.*

"And the Child answered, *Marvel thou not. Thou bearest me, who bearest the weight of the sins of the world. Yours also I will bear.*

"Whereupon the eyes of Reprobus were opened, and he knew him, and he prostrated himself along the ground before him, confessing the many crimes and horrible deeds he had done in the Devil's service and also in the service of the king in Byzantium. He said *How can so small and frail a thing as a child carry off from me so many heavy sins? It is no more possible than this dead stick in my hand should bloom to life again.*

"And no sooner was I done speaking these words than the staff in my hand bloomed into leaves and succulent dates. No other food have I needed since.

"So I served the Christ seven years and at the end of that time was martyred by a cruel king after many painful torments. After death, my shed blood healed his wounds, so he was converted and baptized, and now he knows eternal life and joy.

"For I am the Scoundrel of my story."

8. The Reward

The dog-faced giant said, "My third message is this: You have found favor in the sight of the Queen of Heaven, so, as a reward, I am come to impose greater burdens on you and to require of you a greater feat than you have done erenow."

Ruff said, "Hold it! Hold it! How is that a reward?"

But Gil said, "What Our Lady asks of me, I shall perform."

"Will you? There are three duties: first, to eat no meat nor drink no spirits after Shrovetide until Holy Saturday; second, to eat no meat nor drink no spirits between the Feast of Philip and the Nativity of Our Lord."

Gil made a mental note to himself to ask his mother when those dates were. Gil said, "And the third duty?"

"A day will come when one who stands on a bridge you seek to pass will defy you to combat. Answer him with courtesy, meekly, and do not fight. If he strikes you, do not defend yoursel. Do not return the blow, but flee."

"Wait– what?"

The dog-headed giant bristled, and his lips curled back from white, sharp teeth. "The feat is beyond your strength. Shall I tell Our Lady that you refuse her wish? Seven swords of grief have pierced her heart, thou disobedient child. Add you one more?"

Gil bowed low, trying to hide the expression on his face, for his teeth were gritted. "Tell Our Lady that I will obey. I will not fight anyone whom I find blocking my way on a bridge."

And he closed his eyes, sighing, for it caused him a great heaviness in his soul to say such a thing.

Something cold touched the back of his neck, and there was a noise like a fine chain rattling, and something swung and touched his collarbone. "I grant you this medallion, which I bless, that you may finally find your way after being so lost, as did I. Go your way in safety."

When Gil opened his eyes, the saint was gone, and Ceingalad was contentedly munching on a carrot left behind on the grass.

Gil straightened. On a fine chain around his neck hung a Saint Christopher medal.

Chapter 12

The Stone of the Polar Peak

1. First Squire

Months passed. Gil began to notice that the other non-elfin squires, the Owl-lad, and the Fomorian, and so on, although they had been in training for longer than he (some of them since childhood), learned new maneuvers and tricks at a glacially slow pace and had to practice a sword move or a lance exercise over and over again to get it right. It was as if their nerves and muscles had a great innate resistance to what they were being asked to do, but his had little or none. The two slender elfs, however, only had to be shown something once to pick it up. From spring until summer, Gil found he could keep pace with them only with difficulty.

In their mock battles with each other in April and May, and in archery and fencing that occupied July and August, Gil was the last and least of the squires.

But as the weeks passed, when the days were hot and long, something changed in him and grew stronger. He noticed the change only bit by bit; the first time his shield was hung not in the last place, but only second to last, and he was allowed to order the blond Vanir boy to polish his boots for once. The second time when his blunt practice lance struck in the center of the shield of the ferocious Fir Bolg lad, casting him backward out of his saddle.

And then Gil was winning the swordsmanship duels once out of every four or five times; then it was once every other time; and then he could beat one of the elf squires, the shorter and less mercurial of the two, four times out of five.

Only the remaining elf squire, whose name was Llyr of Llell, was slightly taller, slightly older, and much slier. He kept his place as first among them, and his shield was displayed at morning parade at the top of a pikestaff, one rung above Gil's.

Then, a day came when Gil was pounding laundry by the waterside, and he saw a fish leaping in the stream. Hungry, and acting more by instinct than thought, Gil leaped into the stream, bellowed like a bear, and slapped the fish up onto the bank. Here, just by happenstance, Llyr was walking, and the fish struck him in the face.

The elf lad said, "That insult will have to be paid for, Four-Months-to-Live."

Gil said, "Have you changed my nickname without asking? Go find one of the knights to chastise me. You lack the spirit to beat me; I see doubt in your eye."

"Hand me your practice sword," ordered the elf, snapping his fingers imperiously. "And I shall beat you across your back with it, ten good strokes."

The squires were ordered to carry their wasters with them at all times, as real swords would be carried, and to have them by their pallets when they slept. Anyone found at any time without his wooden blade at hand was punished by spending that night atop a greased pole in the center of the practice yard. Gil always had two swords weighing down his hip, one of metal and one of wood, although Dyrnwen he now kept covered in the mist so that the other squires would not see it.

"Quickly now!" said the elf. "Give me your sword!"

Gil drew his waster. The wooden sword was not sharp, but it was thicker than his thumb and could break bones. Only the miraculous medical magic of the elfs had so far saved more than one a squire from dying in training.

With the waster in hand, standing in the middle of the stream, Gil said, "Here it is. Come and take it."

The elf drew his own waster. "You defy me?"

Gil pointed the wooden blade at the elf's narrow eyes. "Today is different. I will beat you, and every day hereafter. You can hear the truth in the sound of my voice. You know it is true."

Rage or fear was in the laughter of the elf as he charged, splashing, into the water, wooden sword high.

Perhaps something in Gil's voice did unnerve him, or perhaps he did indeed somehow sense Gil's growing strength and confidence. Perhaps. Or it could be that fighting thigh-deep in a cold and rushing stream hindered the quicksilver grace of the elf squire's footwork and allowed Gil to use the greater force from his blows to his advantage.

Gil, for his part, felt perfectly synchronized with himself, his soul and body acting as one, his instincts and training somehow fitting themselves in place with an effortlessness he had never known before.

Once and twice the elf blows struck home, cruel and well-aimed. Three times Gil struck the other, shoulder, head, and arm, and the last time, the elf lost his footing in the slippery stream, and Gil grabbed him by the throat and dunked his head under the water again and again, until the poor lad sputtered, coughed, and said, "I yield!"

That night, as he swaggered to the mess tent, Gil had three swords tucked through his belt: Dyrnwen, his waster, and the waster of the elf lad who was now second squire. Llyr of Llell spent the night clinging sleeplessly to the top of a greased pole. It rained that night.

The next day and thereafter, Gil saw his shield was the highest on the lance. He practiced and drilled, fenced and tilted with Sir Dwnn, Sir Iaen, and Sir Bertolac.

Sir Bertolac was the king's champion for good reason. Sir Dwnn and Sir Iaen, when they handled sword or lance, could do surprising feats, beyond what the best Olympic athlete could do, but to the eye, they seemed to be within the laws of what was physically possible.

Sir Bertolac was beyond that. His motions with blade or spear were like a symphony of music. Very, very fast music that always ended with Sir Dwnn or Sir Iaen on the ground and gasping for breath.

2. The Nightjar

The nightjar who spied on the conversations in the mansion house for him reported that the three knights talked of Gil.

Gil was raking brightly colored leaves in the practice yard, and the little bird of prey sat on the bare bough above him, eyes bright, and told him all he heard through the windows.

"The Swan Lad has learned rapidly and well," said Dwnn, "More swiftly than is natural. War is in his blood."

Iaen said, "This settles one wager, at least. He must be an elf, and not human at all. Only we learn so quickly. Humans drill and practice and practice and drill, thanks to all the weariness of sin and rebellious flesh they inherit from Adam, the first in sin! Our flesh is made of ethereal stuff."

But Bertolac said, "Is it indeed? Walk through a locked door, or fly upward like a thistledown, and I will believe your flesh and bone remains ethereal."

"Some elfs retain those arts," Dwnn said crossly. "Cannot the phantom or the jinn through locked doors pass? Or owls can soar the middle airs, or swan maidens the upper?"

"Not you. Nor I." Said Bertolac. "We have all lived on Earth too long and grown heavy and thick with our crimes. As for the Swan, autumn will follow winter, and he will depart for that green place I dare not name. No elf has ever returned from there."

Iaen said in a cool voice, "I fear me there are those among the Twilight half-breeds who seek the lad's life. If he fails his rendezvous with the Green Knight at the Yuletide, the court of elfs will become the scorn of the world. What folly possessed you to allow him off the grounds on Sundays? The Cobweb clan is closing in on him. You know the power of the Cobwebs increases in Autumn."

Or so the conversation ran, as best the nightjar recalled.

Gil pondered a moment, leaning on his rake, pondering.

"This place was as hot as the equator in midwinter," Gil asked the nightjar. "But now it is acting like the temperate zone."

The nightjar said, "You know how the elfs stole all sorts of animals they liked, such as wolves and bears, all the creatures that are succulent or useful they took, leaving none for you, such as Dodo birds, Tasmanian tigers, and Passenger pigeons; but the guilt of exterminating these wild things they put on you. Not only this, they took your territory—the United States used to be maybe twice its size. The states of Absaroka, Deseret, Franklin, Westsylvania, and Kanawha are missing, as are Nickajack and Sequoyah."

"I had not realized they stole so much."

"Well, they also take your nicest weather, leaving you with little ice ages or long hot spells. They put on you the guilt for disturbing the weather also. That is half the reason the weather in the elfin lands is out of step with human seasons."

"And the other half?"

"The distance between the Night World and the Day World changes when the mist gets thick or thin. When you first came here, Uffern House was near Xochimilco, but with shifts in the mist, now it is in Terrebonne Parish, Louisiana."

"How can it move?"

The bird shrugged. "Time and distance are more like suggestions than really strict rules for elfs. Their geometry is different."

3. The Last Sunday

Few leaves now hung from the dry and creaking branches of the Back-swamp Wood of the Backland, and a cold wind blew. One Sabbath day toward evening Gil on Ceingalad rode back from Houma into the elfish lands.

The stone bridge was hours behind him. Before him was the bridge of wood. This was a covered bridge whose roof was green. There were no walls. The pillars holding up the roof were carved and painted to look like oak, ash, and elm trees. In their branches lodged wooden birds, brightly painted, with glass eyes and gilded beaks and claws. Words in the loops and curls of the elfish letters (which twisted oddly in the eyesight unless pinned with a direct gaze) were written over the archway.

Beneath the archway was what seemed to be a hunched shape squatting. It was gloomy, but Gil's eyes were sharp. The figure stirred and stood, rising up and up until the crown of his head brushed the green roof.

Fur like an ape covered his whole body, with a mane of thicker hair like a wolf's on his neck and shoulders. The great collar of fur made his slanted skull seem small. Atop his head was a cap of shining metal topped by a knob of black crystalline rock. He stood on crooked legs which ended in a second pair of hairy hands. In one upper hand was a great two-headed ax of bronze, and the bronze metal caught the light of sunset and flashed like fire.

But Gil could see the one thing he had previously had no power to see: Hidden as if in a colorless shadow of mist, a great silver cloak woven of hair and held in place with three great pins swathed the mighty limbs of the great beast. It was the same hue as Gil's own hair, shining and shimmering like moonlightshine on snow. Only the hood was not complete. Two sides of a tall collar stood up about the ears of the monster and were pinned to the brim of his bronze cap, for the silver fabric was not great enough to meet over his head.

Looking on Gil, he smiled. His left tusk was whole, but the right was missing and gave his lipless ape-mouth a lopsided and sarcastic look, as if he were sneering in mirth.

Gil pulled on the reins. Ceingalad neighed. "What is the meaning of this? We must make haste to outpace the coming night! Why would you halt?"

Gil said to Ruff, "What do you see on the bridge?"

Ruff peered and sniffed. "Oh, no! Oh, no! A woses was here! I can smell 'em! He's near! He's near! I am sure of it!"

Gil donned his helm and took up his shield. "Guynglaff the Yeti is standing before us on the bridge. He is wearing a cloak woven of my mother's hair, and mist and shadow are round about him."

Guynglaff laughed. "Your pooka can neither see nor hear me!" Then, the monster squinted in puzzlement. "How can you bespeak him when he is not in his talking cap?"

Ceingalad snorted. "There is no one here!" and stepped forward, hooves clopping on the wooden slats of the bridge.

Without a word, Guynglaff slashed the ax across the neck of the horse. The horse reared back, slipped on his own blood, and fell. Gil adroitly leaped backward out of the saddle, somehow landing with his feet under him, his heavy mail clanging and clashing. He straightened up and drew his sword. Guynglaff with a second blow stove in the skull of the horse. Ceingalad toppled hugely backward, kicking through the railing of the bridge as he died. Guynglaff put his shoulder to the noble steed, heaved, and threw the dead horse's body into the rushing river. The dark waters swallowed it.

Gil was shocked and sickened at the death of the brave steed. In his heart he was burning with wrath. Gil said to Ruff, "Run. You cannot help me now."

Ruff barked, "Help you! I'll save you! Just watch! Just watch!" But then he turned and pelted away into the leafless trees, running at remarkable speed, barking madly.

Guynglaff smiled his lopsided, one-tusked smile. "It was a long time tracking you down, little Heretic-killer! Had you stayed at Uffern House, deep in the Night World, I might never have found the trail."

Gil put his shield before him. He held his sword as he had been taught, with his elbow high and the blade hidden behind his body, to prevent the foe from seeing whence the blow would come. He began breathing in slow, steady breaths. He set his feet, bent his knees, and began the lightfooted motion, almost like a shuffling dance, preparatory to rushing his foe.

His shield he kept in motion ready to meet the foe's ax head without directly blocking it. He had been taught to imagine the foe's weapon as a lantern and to hold the shield far from his body so that the imaginary shadow it cast covered as much of him as might be. He also remembered the tricks he had learned to use his shield to pull or deflect the enemy blade out of line and to create an opening for the counterblow.

He felt the pebbles and dry grass under his boots. Guynglaff was still on the bridge.

Gil stepped backward then, still with his shield high and sword at the ready. "I have spared your life. It was the bargain I had with Erlkoenig."

Guynglaff said, "Did I yield to you? Did I cry quarter or surrender?"

Gil said, "Your Winter King cried it on your behalf. He cried for the gentle right."

The monster grinned, and its beastly little eyes narrowed in a mass of wrinkles. "The gentle right is to allow me to regain my feet and ready my weapons. I am on my feet again."

Gil said, "You dishonor your lord. He made a deal with me."

"I did not yield, so this is merely a continuation of our first fight, which began before the Erlkoenig spoke. This fight will continue until one of us yields, and only after it is finally ended will the bargain made between Erlkoenig and you apply."

Gil said, "That is rather convoluted logic."

Guynglaff shrugged. "I spoke with my lawyer. He said the reasoning was sound."

Gil blinked. "Bigfoot has a lawyer?"

"Twilight Folk cannot break our oaths anymore than elfs can."

Gil said, "Don't tell me. All the lawyers work for the elfs, too, right?."

"I heard that they work for the Devil, who is their prince. When you see him, you can ask him."

Gil said, "I fear we cannot fight. I am under orders. Unless you would care to step over to those trees, other there? Otherwise, I have to run away."

"You cannot outrun me on those puny little legs. I killed your mount for killing mine. Now I owe you for my two brothers. After I am done with you, I will hunt down your mother!"

Gil opened his mouth to ask how Guynglaff knew his mother, but then closed it again. He himself had just admitted it, right in front of his enemy. *He is wearing a cloak woven of my mother's hair.* Gil felt his heartbeat pulsing his face as he blushed in rage.

Guynglaff said, "I am your true father. Haven't you noticed you are stronger than other boys? Your small patch of fur is invulnerable? Yes, I enjoyed the succulent, sweet love of your mother's fertile body and planted my seed in her..."

Gil heard no more, but rushed him, sword and shield in constant motion.

The monster was crouching with one shoulder nearly touching a pillar to his left. He held the ax high, its head pointed at Gil, in a pose that would let him strike left or right, high or low without warning. There was also a spike at the head of the weapon, meaning he could foin or thrust. The roof would prevent Guynglaff from any over-the-head blows, but his apelike muscles were so strong he hardly needed to employ such a blow. And the bannisters and posts of the bridge would prevent Gil from anything but a straightforward attack. But the creature had both longer arms and a longer weapon.

The first blow Gil deflected with the shield, drawing the ax handle out of line and cutting for the monster's elbow joint, where his invulnerable fur looked thin. The blade bounced off, and Gil bounced back, barely evading the yeti's counter stroke. The yeti tried to catch him about the ankle with a prehensile foot, but Gil was alert for trips and tricks.

Gil tried again, hiding his sword arm behind his shield for a moment, feinting, and then striking at Guynglaff's groin. But Guynglaff also feinted, reversed the ax, and struck Gil's arm with the ax handle while Gil was in mid-lunge. Gil yielded to the blow, so his arm was hit but glancingly, and his vambrace and brassart rang. Diamonds were scattered on the floor as mail links broke. Pain like electricity jumped from elbow to shoulder. The monster spun the bronze ax head toward the spot between the bottom of his mail skirt and his greave, trying to cut off his leg.

The creature was quick and strong and fluid in motion. The fighting style Gil had been taught was also meant to be quick, brutal, and efficient, using strength, speed, parries, and counterblows, indirection and deception. But here he was both weaker and slower, and his silvery armor afforded less protection than the monster's invulnerable fur. Where could he strike? The palms of Guynglaff's hands? The sole of his foot? A lucky shot at eye or mouth?

Gil twisted, deflecting the ax blade with his shield into the floor slats and whipped his blade overtop of the shield at Guynglaff's exposed hand, hoping to sever his naked fingers. His missed. Guynglaff ran forward, yanked the ax upward with a swift jerk, and drove the butt of his ax handle into Gil's stomach, or tried to, as Gil failed to deflect the blow properly with his shield and was rewarded with a blow on his shoulder. He heard a crack he hoped was his father's armor and not a bone.

The pain and rage mingled in his body made him unable or unwilling to notice how hurt he was or what a battering he was taking.

Guynglaff chopped down viciously, disengaged, and then brought the double-bladed ax directly back up. Had the blow landed in Gil's armpit, it might have taken off his whole arm. As it was, he parried with the edge of his shield, but there was a feint within the field, for now Guynglaff had the heel of the ax bit caught on the rear edge of the shield, and Guynglaff yanked Gil's left arm forward and attempted to grapple him.

Gil was too close for swordwork. Gil thrust his shield point first into the monster's armpit to prevent his apelike arm from curling around him. On a man it would have been a crippling blow, but the armpit fur was thicker than elsewhere, so the blow did no harm. Gil also smote Guynglaff in the face with the pommel of his sword and was rewarded with a hiss of pain and the sight of blood running from both of the flat nostrils of the creature, where there was no fur. Gil raised his knee, snap-kicked the monster in the chest, and then danced lightly backward out of reach of those powerful arms.

Guynglaff dropped the ax and attempted a bear hug, trusting his apish strength to crush the boy and his fur to ward off any blows. Gil's shield prevented the monster's arm from circling him, and he drove the silver wings of his helmet into the monster's broken nose, butting like a ram.

Now the cloak which protected Guynglaff was an obstacle because its surface was slippery like silk, and Guynglaff, despite his greater strength and longer arms, could not find leverage. Gil felt his ribs bruise under the monster's hand grip, but he ducked his helmet under the monster's armpit and slid behind him, quick as a salmon. Gil landed a successful blow on Guynglaff's foot, severing two of his hairless finger-like toes. Guynglaff grunted in pain as he spun to face Gil.

The sword ignited. Gil laughed a wild laugh. In the light from the burning sword, Gil now saw two things:

First, that in places the hairs of Guynglaff were gray with age. It was only a little bit, here and there, above his ears or across his chest like salt and pepper mixed.

Second, he saw that when he struck, it was the misty silver cloak, half-unseen like a protective aura swirling about the monster's limbs, that turned the blade: the cloak, not the fur.

Then only did Gil wonder. Why would a Bigfoot with magically swordproof fur have abducted his mother in the first place?

Ygraine's very words came back to him: *to cover his great carcass and render himself immune to swords.* Bigfoot was aging, growing old, and shedding. Gil remembered seeing the monster bareheaded. The crown of his head was hairless.

"An Achilles' head!" Gil muttered, grinning beneath his helm.

Guynglaff lunged and reached for Gil's neck. Gil threw his shield overhead, foining and slashing at Guynglaff's feet to make the monster dance. Gil used several knee blows to the groin. The fur was thick there, and the blows did no harm but kept the monster off balance. Gil swept Guynglaff's feet out from under him and threw him heavily to the bridge slats. The wood cracked. Gil could see the black waters far below rushing past, white where they brushed the feet of the bridge.

Guynglaff rolled with simian grace backward and somersaulted to his feet again, leaving a bloody left footprint behind him. Gil was having trouble breathing from the rib-pain, and some blow to his helm he had not even noticed had given him two black eyes, which were starting to swell. Gil rushed the creature again, but his blows were deflected by Guynglaff's forearm.

Gil bashed him in the face with the shield, deliberately exposing his shield arm for a half-instant too long. Guynglaff immediately grasped Gil by the arm and shoulder. Guynglaff would have twisted it out of the socket, save that the pauldron of elfin steel around his shoulder would not permit it. Guynglaff put his shoulder to Gil's shield and thrust with his feet, pushing Gil off balance. As Gil had hoped, the monster lowered his apelike head while shifting his weight.

Gil now smote down onto the bronze cap of Guynglaff with enough force to break an inch-thick plate of steel, or any harder metal.

He felt a moment of glorious triumph.

But the blow never fell. Instead, an invisible force seized Gil's blade and yanked it against the black crystal knob that topped the bronze cap. It rang and clanged and clung. Gil yanked the sword back; the cap stuck tenaciously, as if magnetized.

Guynglaff's bald head was glistening with sweat, and his whole face a mass of wrinkles around his eyes, bleeding nose, lopsided and leering maw. With his unwounded foot he reached up, grasped the roofbeam, and swung himself onto the roof and out of sight. Only his voice came down, "Helm of Grim, which strengthens thew and limb! Thy cursed brim I pour within, the heavy weight of all my sin! *Hildigrimur hrifr-vithr!*"

Gil was tugging at the bronze cap, wincing as he burned his fingers, but trying to dislodge it from the blade, when Guynglaff spoke these words.

Immediately, the cap grew as heavy as a parked car. A parked car set afire by vandals, that is. The cap fell to the bridge slats, which creaked and groaned under the weight, and he could not pull the blade free. Nor could he sheath the sword, which was the only way he knew to quench the flames.

His helm limited his vision; he could not crane his neck to look upward, not while yanking with both hands and both feet to unloose the magnetized bronze cap from off his sword. His eyes were swollen now, and his lungs stabbed him with pain each time he drew a breath, and both arms were swimming in pain from the monstrous blows and grasps he had endured.

Guynglaff said mockingly, "Here is the stone which comes from the taproot of the magnetic mountain covering the north pole of the world, and it draws all iron to it. Such a stone has power over even such metal as the sword of Weyland. Are you the same man who broke my tooth and took it and buried me alive? The charms that protect me kept my flesh intact, in deadliest thirst the whole time, trapped in a small cell with the ghosts of my victims mocking me. Seven hundred days I was living in my grave before my brothers dug me up. Are you he? Or do I seek another?"

Gil let go of Dyrnwen and drew his waster. He said, "Liar! You said I was your son! Now you ask if I took your tooth…? Coward! Come down and face me…."

But the monster had only been waiting for him to speak to mark his position. Agile as a thunderbolt, the yeti grasped the eaves of the roof with two hands and one wounded foot, and swung himself in a great circle to strike Gil from behind, and with a kick of his unwounded foot, and all the momentum of his body—for he let go of the eave at the nadir of his arc—and rammed into Gil with the force of a pile driver.

The shock of the blow made Gil's vision swim and sent a dizzy sensation through his head. He could no longer feel his feet. But no, he realized dimly that he was in midair, sailing out over the water, broken splinters of his broken wooden blade toppling gracefully through the air with him.

The bridge was a tall one, and the shock of the water was a bludgeon blow. Gil tried to move his bruised limbs, but new pains added to the aches in his arms and ribs made that impossible. Nonetheless, he fought to paddle and kick himself toward the air for which his bruised lungs so badly ached. But then, in the darkness, he could not see in which direction the surface lay. Was he swimming downward?

He struggled.

The cold water ate his strength. The cold armor was too heavy.

He failed.

Down and down he went.

4. The Kiss

Then, he felt nimble fingers at his throat, undoing his helmet buckles. Someone pulled his helmet off. Something touched his head, clung, and spread, and the crown of his head turned cold. It was a cap that had somehow glued itself to his hair and scalp. Little streamers of cold, refreshing, sank into this head and neck, down his throat, and into his lungs.

He drew in a great breath. He could breathe! No, he could not. It was water in his lungs, but somehow it was sustaining him. He still could not see. Perhaps night had fallen, perhaps his eyes had swollen shut, or perhaps he was about to faint from the pain.

Soft arms wound around his chest. "Stop struggling. I have put my *cohuleen-druith* on you, my mermaid cap. Its peculiarity is this: you will not die while submerged, despite your wounds. But more than this! My father, Glaucon, is a great physician, and wove many runes of power into its weaving. Open your mouth. I have herbs to give you, mixed with panaceas of the deep. Lucky for you Daddy makes me lug this bag around."

It was the voice of Nerea.

Gil said, "Can I talk underwater, now?"

She said, "Certainly not! Shut your mouth! Now, open your mouth, like I said."

"...the surface. Have to kill the Bigfoot..."

"Stop talking! Tell me! How did your pooka dog know where to find me?"

"...kill Bigfoot... my mother... he said... kill..."

"That fight is over. I saw him bounding away through the treetops, lighting leaves on fire. Now shut your mouth before I do something drastic!"

"...my sword..."

She kissed him. It was like a lightning bolt of pure pleasure traveled up and down his spine. He could taste the lemon and chili peppers of the bitter herb in her mouth. She breathed life into his lungs, adding the power of the herb to that of the mermaid cap.

He stopped struggling, stopped talking.

The girl took him in her soft arms and soared through the nocturnal waters, swifter than a dolphin, towing him along.

The darkness, the floating weightlessness, the weariness, were too much. His consciousness fled.

Here ends *Feast of the Elfs*,

Book Two of ***The Green Knight's Squire***,

THE TALES OF MOTH & COBWEB continue in

Book Three of ***The Green Knight's Squire***,

Swan Knight's Sword

SWAN KNIGHT'S SWORD

So *down the silver streams of Eridan,*
On either side banked with a lily wall,
Whiter than both rides the triumphant swan,
And sings his dirge, and prophecies his fall,
Diving into his watery funeral!

But Eridan to Cedron must submit
His flowery shore; nor can he envy it
If, when Apollo sings, his swans do silent sit

That Heav'nly voice I more delight to hear
Then gentle airs to breathe, or swelling waves,
Against the sounding rocks their bosom's tear,
Or whistling reeds that rutty Jordan laves....

Your songs exceed your matter; this of mine
The matter which it sings, shall make divine:
The stars dull puddles gild, in which their beauties shine.

Giles Fletcher (1523)

Chapter 1

The Sunlit World

1. The Sunken City

Gil had only disconnected and dazed memories of the next events, like the scattered surviving pages from a burnt diary.

One memory was seeing the lights and citadel and cathedral of a walled city of breathtaking beauty, drowned at the bottom of the sea. He was seeing the city from above. Fish and semi-human forms, some in fine clothing, some nude, darted before the windows in which strange yellow or green glows shimmered.

Between these distant lights and Gil loomed the vast shadow of a human shape, as blue as sapphire, as large as a submarine, more massive than any natural creature could grow on land. If mermaids were half-fish or half-porpoise, this monster was half a whale. The vast shape was speaking to Nerea. "... I cannot offer a nameless knight of Alberec sanctuary in the sunken city of Ys. Our church bells can keep back the elfs of the Night World but not the Cobwebs of the Twilight. Philters and potions I can offer to speed his healing... but..."

Nerea pleaded with him, but Gil did not hear her words.

The vast blue sea-giant nodded his great head, and minnows darted out of his hair. "Before the herb charm ends at midnight, I can open a gate of mist to the nearest streambed or river in the human world. But who is this lad? And why do you trust the word of the pooka?"

2. A Lady's Favor

Another memory was of being dragged ashore over an uncomfortable surface of pebbles and concrete. He could feel the slender, small hands of Nerea tugging at his belt and shoulder, trying to move his weight. He could feel Ruff, teeth gripping his baldric, also tugging. His legs were still in the water. Either because of his wounds, or because of the drugs Nerea had given him, Gil could not move his limbs. The girl and the dog were not strong enough to pull him entirely out of the water.

A tinkling, tingling warm sensation crawled across his scalp. His lungs and stomach ached as he drew in a breath. Gil was shocked to taste air, not seawater, in his lungs. The air seemed somehow too weightless, too frail, to sustain his life.

Gil pried one eye open. He was in a place he recognized: the culvert behind the gas station across the street from the school. He was a dozen paces from the yard of junked cars where he had fought Jeery Wartworth.

It was night in Blowing Rock, North Carolina, and the moon was high and cold.

Nerea said, "Let me put my cap back on him and return him to the water. The charm cannot protect him unless he is submerged."

Ruff was in his dog form, but his green Musketeer hat, with its floppy brim and owl-feather plume, was perched on his head. "Oh! Oh! I called in favors to get help. They are coming. Two of them!"

Nerea said, "I think this is a terrible plan. Why can't I stay with him?"

Ruff said sharply, "She won't let you in the house! She didn't let me in the house! And we agreed not to take him back to Uffern."

"I wish he would wake up! Is he going to die? Does he ever talk about me?"

Ruff said, "No! Yes! He smells pretty healthy at the moment. He told me he was going to ask you for your favor."

"What does he want me to do?"

"No! No! Not a favor. A favor."

"I think your hat is not on right. That sounded like the same thing twice."

"Like a lady gives a knight to carry into battle. A scarf or a snotrag or something. An old sock."

Just then, the noise of a wolf howling sounded in the near distance.

"Okay! Okay! Help is coming. That is the first guy. Here, take my hat, so you can understand his speech and mine. It lets you talk like a person."

"I know how talking caps work! The principle with mermaid caps is the same. You are transmogrified more perfectly into the target world. Why am I doing this?"

"Because I am sneaky and smart. I think we were followed, and I think you need to go! And try to look like a human! Wolves don't like attacking humans."

Nerea said, "I look human!"

"Try to look *more* human!"

Gil heard the noise of an animal paws coming down the slope. He could see the silhouette of a large wolf against the moonlight.

Then, he heard the voice of the Krasny Volk Odinokyy, the Lone Red Wolf. "He looks as bad as you said. Are you sure he will live?"

3. Red Wolf

Gil felt a dreamlike sensation. It robbed him of any desire to speak. He was content to listen.

The voice of Krasny Volk was near at hand. "Hey, Ruff. Still living off scraps and serving Man. Why not join us in the wild, be your own boss, and eat the sheep, not herd them?"

Ruff said, "Why not come into the campfire circle and be warm and loved?"

"I got enough love for myself to keep me warm. Who is the babe?"

"I am one who understands your speech," said Nerea.

"Ah, meaning no disrespect. Are you his mate?"

"His cousin! I am of the Moth family!"

The wolf said, "The Moth family has done me good turns in the past. What needs to be done? He is too big for me to carry."

Ruff said, "No! No! I called someone else for that. I want you to run interference."

"What is that?" There was a suspicious note in the wolf's voice.

Ruff said, "Find men without heads, if any are in or around the town, and rip out their throats."

"If they have no heads, gnawing on their throat stump won't do much. You mean the Dullahans?"

Ruff said, "Can you handle it?"

The wolf laughed. "Ever since Gil Moth gave me that hair, I have been able to go into places and eat things my kind are not supposed to eat, and I have done many dark deeds. I am mighty among my kind and not lonely any more. Got a wife and pups, and I am a respected member of the community, and folks are afraid of me. So I owe him, and, yes, I can set a perimeter, scour the woods and fields, and kill any Night Folk hunting for him."

"Good!" said Ruff.

"Give me a scrap of his clothing, something with his scent on it, and we can set up false trails and deadfalls and tricks like wolves from the Old World used to do, back when Vseslav the Werewolf Prince ruled Kiev, and the wolves ruled all the snowy forests east of the Urals! Those days will come again!"

The wolf threw back its head and howled. Gil heard the answering howl. "*Movement to your east. Large and dangerous. Incoming!*"

Kransy growled. "Smells bad, folks. My pack says someone is already on the trail."

Nerea said, "Help me push him back in the water!"

But Ruff said, "Wait! I know that smell."

Kransy said, "So do I, and I am not going to be here when he comes. Brr! We'll be in front and behind, and on the left and right, hunting and killing. No damned elf is going to fool us and find the Swanmay's house. Always glad to help out a pal." And he threw back his head again and howled. "Come brothers! Come! We hunt! We kill!"

Krasny padded off.

A few moments later, Gil heard the noise of some large, stealthy animal moving upslope. The padded footfalls of the large beast grew closer. Gil smelled a familiar musk.

The voice of Bruno the bear sounded in his ear. "I came when I heard, wolf. I did not know we knew anyone in common. He is good at playing dead. No, wait. He breathed. No one would be fooled by that."

4. Brown Bear

Nerea said, "He is not dead. I gave him a pharmacon to sedate him and slow the blood loss."

The bear grunted. "Well, you may have saved his life. Lend me a hand. Haul him up. Lash him down."

Gil felt himself being moved rather roughly, with Nerea's hands to one side of him and Ruff's teeth to the other. He was half-hauled, and half-rolled, onto the back of the prone bear, who then gingerly stood up. Nerea's hands were needed to unbuckle his belts and baldric, and tie him onto the bear's bowed back so that he would not fall.

Then, Nerea said, "Are you sure I cannot come with you? What if he wants to say something when he wakes?"

Ruff said, "Nope! Nope! Ygraine is super paranoid. If I lead someone she does not know to her house, she will never feed me scraps again. Sorry. It is not my call, you see? I like you! But it is not my secret to give away."

"The bear will see the house!"

Bruno said, "Ygraine and I met long ago, and there is a bond between us hard as iron. Whether she knows me or not, I will do nothing against her. If the dog does not forbid you, I will. She must approach you in her time and way."

"Well... Since you are the bear Gil trusts to knock him silly, I must trust you, too. Let me return the hat to the pooka. But... first... give him this when he wakes, from me."

Gil heard a rustling noise and a tiny metallic chime, but his eyelids were not willing to open. He did not see what she passed to Ruff.

There was a splash of water as Nerea submerged.

Between the rough handling of tying him to the bear's back and the rushing, loping sensation of racing down the road under the moonlight, pain drove Gil's awareness far away, to some dark place where he knew nothing and remembered nothing.

But he thought before he swooned that he heard wolves crying out in the trees beyond the highway. *We hunt! We kill! Always glad to help out a pal!*

5. The Evergreen

Gil's next memory might have been from later that same night, or it might have been from a day or two later. He woke. Before he was aware of anything, he knew his sword was not with him. Somehow, he could tell Ruff was not with him either.

He pried open his eyes. He was on the couch. It was his house. He was home. His head was on a pillow on the side nearest to the old-fashioned standing radio. His feet were toward the door. The moonlight was slanting through the window to his left. To his right, starlight shined in the kitchen window.

An enormous pine tree had grown up through the broken floorboards of the short hall leading to his old room. The roof in that place was broken as well, and the fragrant pine branches were growing throughout the roof beams and stucco of the ceiling, as if embracing the whole apartment in protective wooden hands.

Gil was sure this was a dream, but only at first because the tree did not disappear or change.

He could see stars through the pine-needle-filled gap between the edges of the hole in the roof and the thick pine trunk. He wondered what had happened to the deserted garage downstairs. Was the concrete floor down there broken up into chunks by the knotted pine roots?

Two pine branches moved even though there was no wind to move them, and a beam of moonlight fell down and lit on his mother. She was kneeling next to the couch, and her hands were clasped together above his heart. Her eyes were lowered. Her hair was unbound and fell like a silver waterfall across her shoulders and arms to the floor. Some locks of the hairs were over his arms and chest, a warm blanket.

He looked up. Hanging on a branch in the middle of the kitchen was a long robe made in two parts of white swan feathers. The robe glinted with tiny sparks just at the tips of every feather, and the moonlight shimmered and shined on the threads about the neck and hood, as if these were woven of tiny streams of running water. The cloak pin was a circle divided into four quadrants.

"Mother, I am awake," he said. "Is that your swan robe? I found it for you as a child. They said you left me and flew back to Heaven. They said you left me to die."

"Who said?" Her voice was soft and serene.

"Your sons."

She said, "From which parent did they receive their love of truth, and from which their love of pride? And which of the cities or gardens of those blessed lands above the clouds would receive a mother who abandoned her infant child? And to what world would I flee if I had any hope to meet your father again, when he came to deliver you his patrimony?"

"Please…" his voice sounded weak in his own ears. "No riddles. You promised. No more riddles."

She said, "By certain signs in the heavens I knew you had fallen. I unpacked my celestial robe from the mothballs in a cedar box where I had written runes of power on the lid. I donned it and flew across the face of the world, swifter than eagles, seeking my lost son, and my tears fell into the upper clouds."

"Sorry. So sorry, Mother… I didn't mean to…"

"Hush. I have fasted and prayed as I have never before. Deeply I read in the sacred word, in the Psalms of David and the Wisdom of Solomon. Many things were shown me. My faith erenow was a weak and girlish thing. I see now, only now, what kind of woman Heaven intends me to be. The sculptor strikes a hard blow! I am so imprudent, so presumptuous! Who is wiser: the fool who thinks himself wise or the wise who knows himself a fool?"

"Mom! Please… no riddles…"

"My prayers were answered, but not through any merit of mine." Ygraine blinked and drew in a breath, as if to swallow a sob. "The Virgin is a second mother to you, a heavenly mother. And you disobey her as you do me. One of the seven swords that pierces her sacred heart is her sorrow when her son was lost in Jerusalem, a boy younger than you. A willful child, he went to the temple, seeking his patrimony just as you did yours. She knows what my heart knows; her pain is mine."

"What are you saying, Mother? I don't understand. Did you… see a vision?"

"I saw my son fall. Saint Christopher brought you back to me. You were unwise to break your oath to him. Deep waters claimed you, but the love and loyalty of friends brought you to the light again. Be thankful you lost only your father's sword and your name's honor, and not your life."

Gil had more questions, but the hot sensation of tears stung his eyes, and his mother kissed him on the brow and said to him, "Slumber and sleep! Let the mermaid's potions and panaceas do their work."

6. The Hair of Phanes

When next he woke, his head was clear. He was tucked into a blanket on the couch. To his surprise, the tree from his dream was real. The great pine had broken through floor and ceiling and spread its branches across the roof. The dropped pine needles on rug and floorboards formed a fragrant carpet.

He sat up, smelling woodsmoke. The left and right basins of the kitchen sink had been made into an impromptu fireplace, and the open kitchen window was the only chimney. Firewood and smoking coals were piled under the spigots. The wings of the celestial robe would wave gently in the same breeze that carried the smoke out the window. It took Gil a moment to realize that the breeze came from the robe. The feathers were producing the mild wind. It smelled of mountain air, of ozone, and of the clean atmosphere after a lightning storm.

His mother was in the kitchen, stirring a kettle that hung from the sink spigots over the fire. She was dressed in her beige work-uniform with her nametag, printed with the wrong name, at her breast pocket, her luxurious hair tied up, pinned, and hidden in a dun scarf.

Gil said, "Mom, the Bigfoot knows you are alive. I accidentally told him I was your son."

She smiled sadly. "Perhaps you should not have done that."

Frustration bubbled in his breast. "Dr. McGuire, the chief of the spies for Alberec, put at least one agent in Blowing Rock. So if Bigfoot finds that out, he may figure out where you are and come for you again. I saw his cloak. He still lacks a patch to finish the hood."

She said, "Dyeing your hair with pooka dye diminishes the charm such hair carries."

Gil was distracted. He ran his hand through his bangs, crossing his eyes to look up at a captured strand. It was bright again, a hue more pure than white. He said, "What is the secret of our hair? Why is it silver?"

She said, "Who was the brother of Merlin, but not in blood?"

Gil said, "*Mom!*"

Ygraine said, "Sorry. Elfs are proud and will not hear when you tell them truths in a straight way, but their pride takes all puzzles as a challenge. Humans are different. They are like unto the Creator and see truths only when told as tales and parables." She ladled some tomato soup into a bowl and brought it over to him. "Remember to say your grace."

"I always do, Mother." Gil remembered the drubbings he had taken when the squires told him not to keep the practice of praying before meals. And he smiled because he also remembered drubbings he had given.

Strange. Before Uffern House, when no one beat him to prevent it, he often forgot.

Gil intended to take a spoonful or two and to ask more questions, but his body had other plans. The rich savor and warmth once touching his nostrils and tongue usurped control of his mouth.

She said, "Our hair comes from Phanes, who wed Yglais, the sister of Merlin of Avalon. To her the keeping of the Grail was given after the Hermit King was carried out of this life in a chariot of fire. It is a sign of sanctuary and sanctity. Certain spoken spells or uncouth alchemies can turn that sanctity from its intended purpose and halt one form of death, either the sharpness of a sword, or the speed of an arrow, or the evil virtue in a poison, and so on."

"And when the hair just grows naturally? Yours, mine?"

"It is the sign given the blood of those who watch the Grail. The outward shape of the blessing differs. Yours was given by your grandfather."

"Blessing?"

"I can drink venom unharmed, and take up serpents in my hand, and tread on scorpions. I need fear neither the arrow that flies by day nor the plague that stalks by night." She smiled. "You would be surprised how often a mother with child needs that particular protection."

"And mine?"

"Bullets, shots, and shrapnel will avoid you when allowed, jellied gaso-line, other weapons too recent to have formed reflections in the dream world."

"When *allowed*? What does that mean?"

"If someone pressed the gun barrel to your head, the bullet would have no choice but to carry out its duty. Grandfather knew of the arms and armor your father left and thought this blessing befitting for a knight, to rob unknightly firearms of their fearfulness. If you are shaved bald by a woman, the charm is broken."

"Who is my grandfather?"

"I am the daughter of Pellinore of Listenoise, son of Pellehan, and Danae of Arcadia, daughter of Aegeria."

The names meant nothing to Gil, of course. He wished he had written down what Nerea had told him of his family relations.

"So I am descended from Merlin the Magician?"

"You are the great-great-grandson of his sister, yes."

"Why did you hide all this from me?"

"To preserve your life."

"To preserve my life, you hid my life from me?"

"While your life was under my breast, it was my duty as your mother to preserve it. You are now a man. The duty is yours, now, to fulfill or to fail to fulfill." She sighed. "Your father's armor is well crafted indeed, for not one of your bones is broken. Your dog buried the shield and helmet in the wood, for he thinks you will have need of them again. You must tell him that his foresight proves false."

Gil straightened up. "False? Why false?"

Ygraine looked surprised. "Your father did not come, not even to preserve your life. Why else would I have let you have your way in this, the foolishness of walking in the Twilight World mail-begirt under helm and shield and with a sword beyond your strength and skill to wield?"

"You made that big speech about the meaning of a sword! I killed a wolf because of that! Now you tell me you were kidding?"

She shook her head. "Do not take that tone with me, young man. About such things I do not jest. The mysteries of knighthood run as deep as those of priesthood. Was not Cain the first of knights older than his brother Abel, first of priests? But if your father did not emerge from the shadows to be your liege lord, whom can you serve? The elfs are wicked creatures! Your dream is done. There is no knighthood in your future, surely!"

He said, "I am King Arthur's man."

Her face lit up with the last emotion he expected to see in his mother's eye: joy. Pure, simple, childlike joy, bright as a candle, like what one might see on a toddler's face the first time he climbs into the lap of a storefront Santa, is given permission to ask for his heart's desire, and receives instead more than he dared hope.

But immediately her face fell, first to a quiet look of sorrow and then to a deepening look of dread. She said, "I know Arthur lives and will wake again in day of terror and fire when the Beast shall rise from the sea. But I also know he dreams and issues no orders, and all the chivalry of the Table Round that fell at Camlann slumbers with him, and an archangel watches over them with outspread wings to prevent the passing years from alighting on the sleepers. He has given you no commands."

Gil said, "As best my own wisdom tells me what Arthur would want, that I do. Could Arthur be my father?"

"No. The man who took me in his arms was awake, and Dyrnwen is not Excalibur, and the Sign of the Swan is not the Red Dragon and the White of the Pendragon. Whose ears heard your oath to Arthur?"

Gil said, "He has a servant who is never seen, whose name I do not know. Why is there a look of dread in your eye, Mother?"

"Because I am farsighted, and I see you are foredoomed. If the elfs know you are Arthur's man, they will seek your life, and I do not see how my tender young son, so unwary to their tricks, will escape their malice."

"Why do the elfs hate Arthur?"

"He conquered them and is their rightful lord. Have you kept your oaths to Arthur secret?"

"Not in the least. I told the Emperor, two kings, a queen, and all the nobles gathered of the elfs, and there were Giants and Cobwebs and talking animals, scarecrows and owls, and other races besides, and one deadly creature that was perhaps a Greek goddess."

"She was a messenger of the Outer Darkness, where no music plays and no laughter is heard, but only wails and lamentations forever."

Gil was astonished. "How do you know this?"

Ygraine smiled cryptically and said, "Before your birth, my seat was fifteen seats down from Empousa at Christmastide, for my seat was with Lord Alain le Gros of Corbenec under the banners of Corbenec. She sits beneath the banner of the Great God Pan, who was the first of the Olympians tithed to Hell after Christ struck mute all pagan oracles and sibyls, deceiving man no longer. You walked where once I trod, my son."

"Then you know I must walk to the Green Chapel to face the giant. My father's honor would be stained if I act like a coward."

She closed her eyes, and he saw the glint of unshed tears escaping her downcast eyelashes. "I hear the truth in your voice. You have already slain your first monster and anointed your tongue in the fashion only the Children of Phanes know. Your celestial blood has betrayed you!"

"Celestial? Are you an angel?"

"Hardly. Angels are pure spirit, and their bodies are mere seemings, assumed so that the sight of their glory strikes no man dead with terror. I was a Swan Maiden."

"Was?"

"Swan Matron, now, I suppose. I served in Sarras, amid the fair and white towers mined of stones never stained by sight of sin and far above the woes so commonplace on Earth. Alas! My son is a man and must perish as men do!" She wiped her eyes with a handkerchief and said, "Tell me by what device or trick they snared you. Repeat the whole story from the start."

7. The Doom of Man

Talking to his mother was a wearisome affair, for she often asked the same questions over again, drawing out some added detail, and he had to tell each part of the tale at least three or four times. Her sharp questions often brought to mind nuances he had overlooked.

He finished with, "A wager was made. I struck off the head of the Green Knight of the Green Chapel, and in turn I must report to him in his home in Hautdesert, to which I shall be led, and there he will strike off my head."

Ygraine smiled. "Then there is hope. You must break your word and not keep this bad oath."

Gil was thunderstruck. "When did you stop being my mother? Because you are not my mother! Never before in my life would she tell me to be dishonest!"

She said sharply, "Never before has such folly made it necessary! You accepted a wager, as you call it, known to be impossible, knowing that no one offers his neck to the blade for sport!"

Gil said stubbornly, "There is an old story that Sir Gawain faced this same knight, and he was spared."

Ygraine said, "There is also an old story that Saint Peter walked for seven steps on the sea, before he fell and went under. Did the story say why he was spared? I see a look of doubt in your eye. Did the Green Knight utter the name of Gawain?"

Gil said reluctantly, "Yes. He claimed the old story was misremembered and that Gawain failed."

His mother gave him a withering look.

Gil said stubbornly, "The Green Knight did not say Gawain died. He said failed. So that means, technically speaking, that it is possible that there is one knight who survived the encounter."

Ygraine said, "If no one told the tales of those who did not survive, how could their numbers be counted? This is not a battle, where the victor fends off invaders or gains gold or land for your nation. If you win the wager, the only prize you gain is your life, which is what you possessed before you offered it in wager! For what, then, do you risk a certain death?"

"Honor!"

Ygraine grew angry, and her eyes flashed. "No more nonsense! I strictly forbid you to go."

"Mother, I must."

"Not to the Green Chapel! Not there!"

"What is the Green Chapel?"

"It is the house of living death where dwells a sufferer whose deadly wound cannot be healed and whom to look upon is death. Who has returned from there?"

"The Green Knight, for one."

"Is he alive? Or is his condition other than what men call life?"

"I hate your riddles! I don't see why a chapel can be so dangerous? A chapel is a House of God!"

"Who is Uzzah? How did he die? Who defies the divine wrath and lives?"

"Mo-*ther*! I don't know the answers to your riddles!"

She stood and picked up the family Bible from where it rested in a niche behind the standing radio. Coldly, she flung the book into his hands. "Then read! You have endless hours to fill, for you shall not leave the shadow of this evergreen!"

"And—that is another thing! Why is there a tree growing in our house?"

The pine branches swayed. She looked up. "Thank you for reminding me. I dare not forget the hour. I have to go to work my shift. A double shift: I will not be back until late tomorrow morning." Ygraine narrowed her eyes at him. "I want to hear your solemn oath that you shall be here when I return and that you will break your oath to the Green Knight."

"Mother, how can an oath break an oath? My father's honor would be stained if I turn coward."

She gritted her teeth. "It is not bravery to face certain death; it is folly."

Gil said, "Mother, for all your wisdom, you are not being wise now! All men face certain death all their lives. They only do not know the day. What does knowing the day matter? Living like a knight means dying like one!"

She said, "Stay here. This tree is a friend who came back from the dead to come to your aid and grew thirty-nine year's growth in thirty-nine days. She broke the powerlines and water main with her roots. While she stands over you, the elfs will not see you by any of their black arts. If you get cold, she will cover you in pine needles; if you hunger, she will bear her seeds out of season and show you which parts of the cone are eatable. Stay here; it is my firm and absolute command."

"Mother, I cannot obey it. What day is this?"

"Today is the Feast of Saint Nicholas, when children rule and elders are ruled. But you shall not rule in this! Obey my word, I straightly charge you, or I will have you chained up by force."

Gil said, "I do not have to leave yet. I will stay here until the day arrives when no time and no choice remain to me. That is the only promise I can make you."

Ygraine looked at him with eyes like green stones. With no further word, she turned. She walked out the door.

There were a calendar and a list of feast days in the back leafs of the Bible. The Feast of Saint Nicholas was the sixth day of December. The Feast of Saint Ambrose was the seventh.

Tomorrow. The day when all his choices ran out was tomorrow.

Sitting on the couch, he stared at his feet, lost, bewildered, and wondering what he should do.

Chapter 2

The Crime Spree of Gilbert Mott

1. Hanging Thoughts

The day passed slowly. He stared for a time at his mother's robe, wondering whether it would carry him aloft and out of his life if he put it on.

His thoughts were hung between the two stark and unmovable demands. Back and forth they moved all day, never truly on the ground and never truly in Heaven. Like his mother's swan robe, hung on a branch neither high nor low, swaying and swinging, his thoughts never were silent, but never said anything new.

In the morning he searched through the house, hoping to find something, anything, to settle his restlessness: a secret door or a childhood toy. There was nothing. His old bedroom was destroyed. The walls were still intact, but nine tenths of the floor had collapsed from the intrusion of the tree into the deserted garage beneath, crushing empty shelves and rusted barrels.

His mother's command told him to foreswear his foolish, insane, deadly, suicidal oath to travel to some unknown and accursed place to be struck by an ax. It was so reasonable, so obvious, and so much what he wanted to do. (Was he going to die after only kissing one girl one time only? While underwater? And she had been pushing herbs into his mouth! That did not count!)

Gil spent part of the day reading by the window. There was nothing to read but the Bible, which he turned to in hopes that some clear inspiration would come visit him, as apparently his mother had been visited.

But the words seemed to lie on the page, lifeless, void of meaning. There were endless chains of names broken into syllables which begat

other names. There were obsessively picky instructions on how to deco-
rate some sort of circus tent and serve up the various meats and sacrifices.
There was a story about David finding Saul asleep in a cave while Saul was
hunting to kill him: and David cut a swatch from Saul's robe, but left him
alive and unharmed, rather than break his sworn oath of fealty. But in
another part he found a passage where Christ sternly told his disciples not
to swear oaths: merely saying "yes" meant you would do what you said.

His thoughts turned and turned again. His mother's command was
perfectly clear! But then there was the question of the honor of his
father. If a man vowed to do a hard thing, a dangerous thing, was the
vow nullified if the task was impossible or the danger was mortal? But if
the difficulty of a task excused carrying it out, all swearing of vows was in
vain.

What could he have done differently?

He spent part of the day exercising and recovering from the unexpected
pains of that exercise. He discovered he could not go for a day without
going through his sword drills, for it had become an ingrained habit.
He found two more boards and repaired and painted eight more stairs,
wondering what the landlord thought of the fact that a tree was growing
through the building. Pounding nails did not stop the questions pounding in his head.

What could he have done? Sure, he could have sat in the feast hall of
the elfs, and said nothing, and let the Green Knight fling insults into his
teeth. But he would have been hunted and slain by the Cobwebs in any
case for killing Doolaga and Gulaga the Bigfoots... assuming he was not
killed just for carrying his father's sword.

But suppose he had never gone on errantry? Never recovered that
stolen baby, Loobie. (What kind of name was Loobie anyway?) Well, he
would have been better off, but that particular baby would not have been.

Exercise, drill, and carpentry left him stinking worse than a horse. To
prepare a bath took all afternoon, carrying the water buckets up from a
cistern in the garage below, heating water in a kettle above a fire in the sink,
and pouring it into the tub one kettle at a time. The damage from the
tree had left the bathroom floor at an angle. There were candles in wine
bottles Ygraine had brought home from work to illume the bathroom,
which had no windows.

Suppose he had never wanted to be a knight? What then? His mother had kicked him out to find a job only because he was too foolish to stay in school. If only he had been willing for the schoolboys to commit their crimes, steal their drugs, tell their lies, pick on the weak....

Gil could have learned to be popular, surely. Surely he could have found a way to be like those kids!

He could picture it clearly. He was athletic enough and quick witted enough to handle himself around boys his age, or girls. He could have cozied up to them and joined their world.

He could have learned to wallow in cowardice and falsehood like them, to listen to their banging filthy music, to flatter, and evade, and to tell half-truths and total lies each time he opened his mouth. He could have learned to cower, to lick boots, to laugh at unfunny jokes, and to sneer at all wise and ancient things. He could have learned to answer every honest question with a screaming counterattack. He could have ladled an entire sewer of self pity over himself and played the make-believe game that he was never, ever wrong in the slightest and that all corrections or criticisms were unfair bullying of his delicate, abused, tiny little burnt-snowflake of a soul.

He could have learned to be a coward and fool and so have been so unworthy of an honest life that he would slowly lose even the desire for it.

Bile was in his mouth as he thought these things.

As the sun set, the robe hanging from the pine branch grew brighter, and tiny glints of starlight were caught in the many white feathers and glowed.

That evening he took a walk in the woods. He carried no candle, sure in his night vision. It was cold, and the wind was sharp, but there was no snow on the ground. He asked a raccoon, and then two squirrels who had not yet decided to hibernate if his dog had been nearby. One of the squirrels led him to a recently turned patch of earth, which Gil dug up with a spade. He uncovered his father's helm and shield.

The silver swan of the shield glinted in the starlight. The brave silver crest of the helm seemed to regard him, waiting patiently for some ponderous decision.

He took up his tall helm and tall shield and marched back to the house. His footsteps were firm; his stride was long. Gil paused and stared at his own feet. When had he learned to walk that way, almost a swagger? It was a man's walk.

The only light in the room was from the shimmering swan-robe, softer than moonlight, and from the windows. The smell of woodsmoke from the sink was ever present. He did not bother lighting a candle.

He put the shield atop the armor, which his mother had stowed beneath the couch. The helm he propped up on the standing radio. The tall ornamental wings glistened boldly. The crest reached toward Heaven, nobly trying to fly. Even the cheek pieces jutted like the outthrust chin of a proud and cheerful prizefighter daring a foe to take a poke at him.

The empty eyeholes stared at him accusingly.

"What else could I have done?" Gil shouted at the empty helm. "Lived like a worm? I could have let Jeery go his way, let every bully and crook and lying cheater in this school grow like weeds, or at the school before that or the one before that! Why is it my duty to pluck the weeds? When did it become my job to take out the garbage?"

The helm stared at him sardonically.

"When did it become my job to protect the weak, to help the helpless, to save damsels and widows, to tell the truth, to uphold the law, to serve the King, and to serve the Christ?"

The helm looked unimpressed. Gil knew exactly when that had become his job. When he vowed it to Arthur's noble, slumbering form, and placed his hands between the king's own hands.

Gil said in a softer tone, "Why is it my job to keep my word even when it means death?"

He closed his eyes, not willing to continue the staring contest with the empty eyeholes of a silvery mask after nightfall in an unlit room. He knew why he kept his word: he was born that way.

"Why was I born?"

Gil flopped heavily down on the couch, wincing at his bruised ribs. He stared upward, seeing pine branches swaying in the motionless air. Through the hole in the ceiling, he could see stars. With no lights in his house, they were brighter and closer than stars should be, and they looked down coldly.

But Gil knew why he had been born. His mother, wrongly thinking herself a widow, had bestowed herself in love upon a man who had risked life and limb to save, serve, and protect her and who loved her in return. The cave in which she had been trapped was full of the bones of other victims, and soon hers would have joined them. His father acted as no ordinary man is wont to act and risked everything for a stranger in need.

He was born because his father had drawn a fabled sword both bright and true in defense of the helpless widow against a monster. (That same sword Gil through his own folly had lost into the hands of that same monster.)

In short, he was born for honor. Did that mean he was born to die?

He wished he knew the phone number of someone he could talk to. Gil wished he owned a phone. He was pretty sure there was a working phone in the church a mile or so down the road. He was not as nonchalant as his mother about breaking into a church. There was a payphone at the bus stop in town, eleven miles down the main road. He had no change for a payphone. Perhaps he could pry a gem off his armor and trade it to Mr. Yung, the pawnbroker.

But if he did make a call, what would Gil say? Or ask? What advice was he expecting anyone to give him?

Anyone? Not anyone. The face his longing conjured up was Sir Berto-lac, the King's Champion. What other man did he know who could give him advice on how to be a man?

He stared between the pine needles at the stars. Stars were made to turn and turn again in their courses, rising and setting just where and when they were made.

Stars kept their courses because, like the deathless and sad kings of the elfin lands, they had no power to break their word, to change their destiny, or to select their paths.

He could pick. His choice was simple: either life as a coward or death as a fool.

He wished Nerea had a phone.

2. A Familiar Voice

Gil was awakened in the pitch darkness. The first thing he noticed was that his sword was not at hand. A moment later, he realized what must have wakened him: his mother's swan robe had been shedding a soft starlight from its fabric, enough for Gil's eyes to make out the silhouettes and distances to objects in the room. He could not see any stars through the window. Perhaps clouds had smothered them. He had no idea what hour of the night it was.

A voice spoke in the darkness. It was a rich baritone, full of good humor, but with a strange note of sadness behind the words. "Have you decided whether to resign your commission as an officer in the special metaphysical police force? You have now the training need to be a crusader rather than a martyr, but laying down one's life is a requirement of both professions."

It was the Man from the Black Room. Gil sat up on the couch, and the covers rustled around him. He turned his head left and right, trying to identify the source of the small noises of the big man's breathing and motions.

Gil said, "Who are you, really?"

"Arthur's true and trusted servant."

"Are you Merlin? Bedivere? Gawain?"

"I am neither mage nor knight, nor any post so high and great."

"Baldwin?"

"Nor was I a bishop. My life as an undercover detective involves continual deception and violence and other antics ill-becoming a holy vocation."

"Dagonet?"

"Nor was I the jester. Ah! Is this a test to see how many obscure Arthurian references you can name, hoping I miss one and proving me an imposter?"

"Well..." Gil would not lie, but he did not want to admit that this guess was right.

"Let me help you: Arthur's elf-forged sword was Caledvwlch, his dwarf-forged dagger was Carnwennan, and Carduel was the castle whose stones the eftlings erected for him by harping."

"No, I believe you. You don't need to..."

"I respect your skepticism! Merlin's daughter was Inogen, his master was called Bleys, and his secretary was Bishop Anthony, a Roman who refused

to abandon his flock when the legions marched away, and the eagles of
Rome passed across the sea, and the lamps of brighter days went dark."

"Got it. You can stop now."

"Would you like me to recite the triads of Arthur's ancestry: *Which
three Kings of Arthur's line trod upon the stone of Fal?* Cynvor, Cynwal,
Cynan. *Which lost their true seeming in sin?* Uther in Lust, Cadwalladwr
in Wrath, Cadien in Idolatry."

Gil made an impatient noise. "Fine! Stop! You are from King Arthur's
court!"

"Tuk was the Court Physician."

"Stop! Mercy! I yield!"

"You are wise to surrender since I am expert in the art of irksomeness.
It was part of my vocation and mission at the Court of Camelot."

"And? What was your job there?"

"Kitchen page."

"Wh-What?"

"Pot boy. I worked next to Beaumains. Turns out he was Gareth in
disguise! Who would have thought it! Hard worker, too, and he whistled
like a bird when other boys boasted and cursed and talked about the
Queen's rump. Never a foul word out of his mouth! Too bad he became
a knight because he was the only pot boy who ever got Big Bertha clean.
That was our name for the copper pot Orimonde brought from Persia.
But that was not my main job. I had court duties and wore a tabard! I
carried the cauldron captured from Diwrnach Gawr."

"Who?"

"Dyrnwch the Giant. Please don't tell me that story is forgotten among
men? It was a great and bold adventure, involving miracles and desperate fights by land and sea, and the moon walked backward in the sky.
Forgotten? Ah, time is cruel."

He was speaking of events well over a thousand years ago. Gil was
astonished. "How can you have lived so long?"

The man chuckled. "By being careful. Very careful."

"What?"

"The cauldron I carried acted as a lie detector and would not boil the
meat of men who exaggerated their exploits or cowered before their foes.

I was the most hated man in a court full of cruel and fearless men of war. Do you wonder how I learned to detect crimes and outwit intrigues?"

Gil stood. There was no light from the windows at all, so he could catch no glimpse of the tall man, even by starlight. He could hear and feel that the kitchen window was open. Something in the scent of the air told him it was snowing.

Gil said, "Why are you here?"

"To accept your resignation if you wish release."

"From Arthur's service?"

"I have no power to excuse you from that. But I can excuse you from the Last Crusade if the burden is too great, and I can take back the badge I gave you. And I am also here to beg you not to."

Gil turned his head again, listening. It was really beginning to bother him that he could not pinpoint the man's location. It almost sounded as if the man was equally in every direction. "Beg, not order?"

"Not to me you swore, but Arthur. Technically, that makes you a squire. You outrank the kitchen staff. That is why you have the discretion to select your own case to work on. How are you coming on overthrowing the tyranny of all elfs and evil spirits over mankind?"

"I saved one girl," muttered Gil morosely.

The man cawed with delight. "Susy the witch's maiden, apprentice to Squannit! I thought she was eaten by an alligator! Did anyone tell Saint Cyprian of Antioch? I think witchcraft is in his bailiwick. You have made more progress than I had hoped!"

"How can you know her name?"

"By being very curious as well as by being very careful."

"You were spying on her?"

"Don't be silly. I was spying on *you*. Material was needed for your quarterly performance review! I have heard that you made some initial inquiries at Mommur, doing undercover work."

"Mummery—or what you said—is that Alberec's palace, buried under Brown Mountain?"

"The elf city of Mommur, the Nether Tower, is buried beneath many places and no place so that it can open doors in distant countries. Like my office. Like the cave where Arthur is."

"How can a place have no place?"

"It exists as a cloud of potential locations which only actualize when an observer interacts with the sunlit world. It is a secret of the mists of Everness."

"What's Everness?"

"Merlin's house. His memory. And his arsenal, where the weapons of the Otherworld are hidden. If you go there, the house will simply erase your memory. I assume I have been there many a time, but how can one know? You were in Mommur, and you shamed the elfin court and brought great honor to Arthur, or soon will."

"Yes. I was there. At Alberec's palace."

"You had the sword Dyrnwen with you then."

"Guynglaff Cobweb took it. I fought him."

"Did you yield?"

"What? I mean– I beg your pardon?"

"Did you, of your own will, offer him the sword in return for your life or for some other promise or consideration?"

"No, he took it, and he kicked me off a bridge into the water."

"God be praised!"

Gil reached out with his hands, groping, but encountered nothing. His feet made noise on the layer of pine needles. Why were the big man's feet making no noise?

"Are you still here?" Gil asked.

The voice spoke again, but this time it sounded distant. "Your claim to the sword is still good, and it will serve you when you recover it. You must take up the sword again, for without it the quest to destroy the giant Ysbadden is forfeit, and all the hope of the Grail is lost!"

"Where did that come from? What is the Grail to me?"

"I have recently acquired another agent, working that case. Your mission is to get the training you need to be a true knight. What happens after that? Providence knows."

Gil heard a rustle of pine branches. The voice was overhead. He realized that the big man must be climbing among the pine boughs above him. "Wait! Don't go! Where can I recover my father's sword?"

"Inquire at the Green Chapel."

Gil shouted, "Don't leave yet! Inquire how? Inquire what? It is a death sentence if I go there! The Green Knight is going to kill me!" And then, wretchedly, "My mom told me not to go!"

But there was no answer.

"Where are you? Why are you going?"

The answer was soft and distant. "You have guests."

A moment later, Gil saw a flicker of red and blue lights in the window. He stepped over and looked out, his bare feet rustling the soft pine needles.

Police cars, lights spinning, were coming up the road.

3. A Thickness in the Mist

Gil took the precaution of donning his armor, helm and shield while the federal agents surrounded the building and readied their weapons. He thought it would be wise to render the armor unseen, as he had so often done with his sword.

It turned out that it was easy to coat the armor in mist. The mist came up immediately, much thicker than he had expected. Gil wondered if that meant someone else had summoned up a large and thick cloud of mist in this area, just now.

He looked out the window again. More vehicles were arriving, including a heavy boxy machine on treads that looked like a tank with no cannon. These were not the county police or even the state troopers. He wondered if he should run. He wondered where his mother's swan robe was. He wondered where his mother was.

Gil put his hand against the pine tree. "Hey, listen. I don't think I have time to write a note. If you see my Mom, tell her what happened...."

Then, he fell silent, his stomach knotted. What if his mother had sent the police to capture him? Such a desperate act would keep him alive, would it not? And she had threatened to chain him up, had she not?

The men did not knock and announce their presence, or ask his name, or give theirs. Two hefty men broke in the front door with a battering ram and threw tear gas canisters into the room. The cloud expanded outward. In a moment, Gil was in a smog of stinking smoke.

But it did not touch him. He neither vomited nor did his eyes water.

Gil kicked the gas-emitting can casually through the hole in the floor into the empty garage below, and said, "Pardon me, officers. Do you have a warrant?"

Gil simply had too much respect for the law to resist the men. He ached still from his last fight and was not eager to hurt the innocent. From the dull looks in their eyes, and the dull monotone in which they answered him, he realized that they were under the Black Spell. These were merely human puppets, acting without awareness and without their own will.

The agents were from some bureau of the federal government of which Gil had never heard. They were dressed in bulky bulletproof riot gear and armed with rifles, clubs, grenades, and what looked like bazookas, as if they had come to fight an army rather than arrest a teenager.

But they were able to enter the apartment, step on the pine needles, and stand under the tree without harm. Whatever Cobweb had sent them must have been afraid of the tree. Gil plucked a small twig of pine from the bough and held it in his hand even when the glassy-eyed men handcuffed him and forced him into the back of the police cruiser.

He had slung his shield over his back, and their eyes could not see it, but the tall shape could not fit into the door of the cruiser. Nonetheless, the spell that held their eyes evidently also prevented them from noticing or remarking on how many tries it took them to stuff Gil into the seat. Minute after minute they shoved him toward the opening, only to have the unseen shield clang against the metal door frame. Then, like broken robots, they would stand for a moment with blank expressions on their empty faces and try again and then again.

Eventually, Gil solved the problem by diving headfirst into the back seat, banging his helmet on the far door.

A pinewood scent from the twig in his chained hands filled the back seat. Gil felt an inexplicable intuition that this scent prevented any additional spells or elfin charms from drawing near.

He wondered idly whether they could see his face or not. The mist prevented them from noticing the helm on his head, but it did not turn the metal invisible.

4. The Bureau of Compliance

He had his answer when he was taken to a facility—it was neither the county police station in Blowing Rock, nor the state trooper headquarters in Lenoir, but a blocky concrete edifice hidden off the highway in the middle of nowhere—where he was fingerprinted and photographed. The dull-eyed desk officers did not have him remove his gauntlets for the fingerprinting nor his helm for the photograph.

In a bare side room at a wooden table before a tall mirror sat a tired-looking officer with a five o'clock shadow and jowls like a sad bulldog. He gave Gil a typed confession to sign. Gil asked to see a lawyer. The officer grunted, signed Gil's name, which he spelled as *Gilbert P. Mott*, and slid the confession into a drawer.

"You are a minor, so you do not get a lawyer," the tired man said. "Child protective services has control of your case, and they pled guilty on all charges on your behalf, as this was in your best interest. And you are being held for a military tribunal since you are a serviceman in the armed forces of a hostile foreign power. After that, you will be transferred to a high security mental asylum."

"I am not insane," said Gil. "The asylums are run by elfs."

The tired man grunted. "If you say so, pal."

Gil said, "Which power?"

"What?"

"Which hostile foreign power do I serve?"

The tired man looked at the paper. "Ah. Great Britain. Says here you swore fealty to the English sovereign. Is that true?"

"Why? Are we are war with Great Britain?"

"I am sorry, but since you are a serviceman in the armed forced of a hostile foreign power, I cannot discuss matters which have national security implications."

Gil held up his diamond badge as an officer of the Special Counter-Anarchist Task Force. The words THE LAST CRUSADE caught the light and blazed, but the man's eyes could not focus on it.

Gil said, "This is not a real police station, is it?"

The tired man said, "No, we are the Federal Bureau of Land Reclamation Management, Oceanic Homeland Intrusion, Mental Health, Personal Revenue Seizures, Paperwork Reduction, Alcohol, Tobacco, Fire-water, and Diversity Compliance." He took up a windbreaker thrown over the chair next to him and showed Gil the letters written on the back: FBLRMOHIMHPRSPRATFDC.

"There is no such bureau," said Gil skeptically.

"How could anyone tell? It is not like anyone keeps track."

"I mean you are outside the writ of the law, or else you'd be able to see this badge in my hand. Didn't you take an oath to uphold the law?"

"Oaths? Uphold the what? Are you from the Dark Ages or something?" Gil's eyes narrowed dangerously.

The man glared at him, a cynical smile on his lips. "The president swore an oath to defend the Constitution. Think he means it? His job is to get around it. Doctors take the Hippocratic Oath. Do they mean it? The ones who execute prisoners for us, or do abortions, or euthanasize comatose paralytics? How about witnesses on the witness stand? Promise to tell the whole truth, nothing but the truth. They'd lose their cases if they didn't lie. The lawyers tell them to lie. My wife promised to love, honor, and obey me, in sickness and health, until death do us part, all that jazz. She took up with another guy when I was stationed overseas. And she lied on the witness stand."

That was the only moment when the man did not look tired, and his eyes did not seem clouded by the elfin mists. Gil knew he was hearing the man's deepest, most secret thoughts hidden in his heart. He saw his very soul.

It was like flinging open a buried treasure chest and finding nothing but offal and rotting rodent carcasses within.

5. Piskies and Gremlins

Back in the main office, he saw a slender female figure about four feet tall. She looked like a miniature woman, perfectly proportioned, not like a midget and not like a child. She was dressed in a green shift and green ballet slippers, sitting atop a filing cabinet. She had gauzy wings like a dragonfly and two whiplike antenna issued from her brow. She had a sweet smile and a satanic glint of malice in her narrow eyes.

This fay maiden was surrounded by mist and no doubt thought herself invisible. Gil turned his head to look at her, but he guessed his eyes were shadowed in the eyeholes of his helm, for she did not seem to notice his gaze.

In fact, Gil was not sure she saw him at all. Suzy the witch's apprentice had told him that people saw whatever they expected to see when they looked into the mist. What did elfs see? They were not immune to their own glamour.

Around the feet of the fay maiden danced piskies no larger than lightning bugs, glowing. They were going back and forth between the papers on the sergeant's desk and the filing cabinet, switching photographs, erasing and rewriting entries on forms, and forging signatures. The tiny, swift creatures were infallible forgers since illusions woven of mist hid any imperfections.

He saw his own picture from his yearbook photograph being affixed to some other thick file of crime reports.

Meanwhile, small men the size of mice were toying with two of the computers, dancing on the keyboard, prying open the housing, hooking what looked, at first, like dead insects or dry leaves to the electronic innards. Upon closer inspection, Gil's eyesight could see the small, bejeweled, well-made electronic circuits hidden under the appearance of leaf and bug. The small men were dressed in coveralls and wore tiny baseball caps. They chewed tobacco and spit sparks. Each one had a rag or a wrench in his back pocket, like a cartoon caricature of a plumber or mechanic.

He had not seen this particular breed of elfin creature before, but he heard what name the laughing fay maiden called them as she urged them to their efforts: gremlins.

As Gil was led past the filing cabinet and desk where the fay maiden sat, Gil peered closely. Perhaps the piskies were merely stuffing random unsolved cases into his folder without even looking. Gil was accused of overgrazing on federal land, methamphetamine distribution, gunrunning, subordination of perjury, espionage, witness tampering, bribery, failure to pay licensing tax for class three firearms, campaign finance law violations, jaywalking....

Other crimes listed on the papers he glimpsed seemed to have at least some relation to reality: theft and tortuous conversion of a cot from the

YMCA, trafficking in stolen antiques, arson with a blade of over nine inches, multiple counts of assault and battery, trespass onto federal lands without a camping license, hunting without a gaming license, fishing without a fishing license, keeping a dog without a dog license, obtaining licenses without a licensing license, truancy from school....

6. A Prisoner

The officer gave him into the custody of the jailer, a thin man with long hair grown out from above his ears, and combed over his bald spot. The man seemed not to notice that Gil was dressed in forty pounds of armor, with a tall silver helm, and a four-foot-tall shield. Again, the balding man acted like a broken robot, trying over and over to pat down Gil for weapons, strip him, search him for drugs, force him to shower, and issue him an orange jumpsuit, actions that were impossible to perform on an armored man. Gil merely told the balding man in a soft voice that he had, in fact, gone through the routine correctly.

The man froze. Gil repeated it in a soothing voice, "The prisoner has been searched and showered. Everything is fine. Everything is under control. The prisoner has been thoroughly searched and given an ugly orange suit...."

It was with considerable disquiet that Gil saw the balding man, his eyes entirely dull and dead, nod dumbly. Then, the balding man took up a big, old-fashioned key ring, and unlocked the door leading to the security wing.

Gil found himself wondering if he had committed a crime by trampling on a fellow man's free will and vowed never to do that sort of thing again.

In the upper corner of the door was a spider web. In the spider web one of the piskies had been caught, a tiny girlish imp small as a fly, glowing like a lightning bug. She was wrapped in webbing and called out in a high, thin voice: *Help me! Help meeee!*

Gil was in no mood to help one of the miniature freaks who had been falsifying records and writing lies about him to get him in trouble with the human world. But he did not think knighthood was a matter of moods or feelings. He doffed his gauntlets, reached up with his bare hand, brushed the spider web away, and plucked the sticky strands carefully off the tiny figurine. She snarled, cursed, complained, and flew away after hissing angrily at him.

He watched her go with a sigh of annoyance. He had not saved her for the sake of being thanked, but a small sign of gratitude would have been polite.

Down the gloomy corridor he went with the thin and balding jailer.

The doors were iron, and the ceiling was brick. The dim yellow lights were in cylindrical metal brackets. One after another Gil paced past them. There was no one else in the wing.

An iron door led into a cell. The door had one slit at eye level and another at the foot of the door. There was no thumbprint pad or slot to receive a magnetic card. Light shined in a thin beam through the keyhole, which told Gil the lock was a large and clumsy antique.

Inside the cell, a light fixture was recessed into the low ceiling, above a rusted drain in the floor. A low cot of wooden slats was bolted to the floor.

The window was a plate of iron padlocked shut. The iron plate had holes punched into it, large enough for air to enter, barely, but too small for a finger. Putting his eye to a hole, he saw he was three or four stories above ground. There was a chain link fence topped with barbed wire and, beyond that, wooded hills.

Gil wondered at the obvious age of this building, of his cell. What had his mother said about certain modern weapons being too new to be reflected in dreams? Was it easier for the elfs to cast their spells on people who lived in old houses? Gil had never heard of a haunted house that was brand new or of a haunted skyscraper.

On the other hand, looking once more at the jailor's unblinking eyes, Gil felt such a stab of hatred for the Black Spell of the elfs and their mesmeric tricks, he was not sure if it were safe or healthy for his soul if he learned too much about exactly how it worked.

This much he did know: the mist was a double-edged sword. Apparently, it was thick enough about this federal facility to put all the humans into a sleepwalking state and let the piskies and gremlins forge and fake the records.

But, by the same token, mist that thick allowed Gil to carry forty pounds of shining metal war gear into his cell, unhindered.

In his pouch was a tin of polish, a rag, and a brush. He spent the morning cleaning his armor, closing bent links with pliers, and checking the joints, straps, and buckles.

7. Stegodyphus lineatus

Thus occupied, Gil did not notice the passage of time. Perhaps it was an hour later, perhaps more, when a thin, sinister voice from the ceiling spoke.

"You robbed from me my due prey. I am come to curse you with my deadly curse, you who are so cruel to mothers. I must fatten myself. Must my children starve?"

Gil looked up, but saw no one. "I beg your pardon, ma'am. I have great respect for motherhood. Please don't curse me. My life is hard enough as it is. And short."

"My wrath is great against you! You destroyed my house!"

"I don't remember destroying any houses," Gil said politely, puzzled, wondering why he could not see the woman speaking. He thought he should have been able to see even someone hidden by an elfish glamour. "Besides, we rent from a man named Mr. Umstead. Are you his wife or something? If you are talking about the tree growing up through the rented apartment, my mother did that, not I."

"Do you blame your mother? Your hand smashed my house! How dare you put the crime on her!"

Gil felt anger like a swallow of warm wine spread out from his heart into his chest and guts. "Now, you hold on, whoever you are! I respect and love my mother! I obey her in all things! I listen to all her crazy questions, and... and..." Gil found himself suddenly with hot tears in his eyes, and he wiped his face, sobbing.

The thin voice said, "I hear a dishonest twitch your voice when you lie. It is very obvious. You did not obey your mother, did you? When my eggs hatch, my children, my beautiful children, will issue forth and consume me alive. All children are alike."

Gil suddenly realized what he was talking to. "Where are you?"

"Here. Up here. This crack between the two bricks."

Gil peered, standing on his tip toes.

It was a tiny spider.

Gil could have easily raised his hand and crushed her beneath his thumb. Instead, he wiped his eyes again, and said, "I wanted to obey my mother. But I chopped off a man's head and agreed to travel to the Green Chapel where he lives so that he can chop my head off in turn."

The spider said, "People heads don't grow back. Someone should have told you that."

"No one tells me anything! And I have to leave today! I don't know the way, and I am locked in jail. He said someone would show up to lead me there, lead me to my death. If I run away—I will be less brave than Arthur's knight. Gawain did not run away! He must have really wanted to, too."

Gil drew a deep breath and tried to regain control of himself.

He muttered, "I bet his mother also told him to stay home and break his word."

The spider said, "Your mother gave you life. It is not yours to throw away."

Gil said angrily, "What do you know about it? Your children *eat* you!"

The spider sniffed and said softly, "All mothers suffer for their children. The mercy that the Creator grants to all the mothers of my race that our sacrifice takes place only once, all at once, and our suffering is done."

Gil's anger evaporated. "I am sorry for you, ma'am. That does not sound very merciful to me."

"You pity me? Your estate is no better. I could have stayed a virgin and never known love. You could have stayed a civilian and never known knighthood. My bloodline is preserved; yours dies with you."

"Why do it? Why let yourself die?"

"I promised my mate. He would not come into my embrace until I gave my word."

Gil said, "You believe in a creator?"

She sniffed again. "Of course. I weave webs and place each strand just so to serve me, the capture lines, the control lines, the guy lines. The web is intricate, but I am more intricate, for spiders are higher and better than spiderwebs. Then, I see my life, how wonderfully and fearfully its parts are woven and fitted together, and I know I too was placed just so to serve a higher and a better."

"Ma'am, bless you for saying so! I don't know how to make amends for destroying your house. But... wait..." Gil plucked a silver hair from his head and thrust it into the little crack in the brick. "... I have heard that the hairs of my head are blessed and can grant protection to those who know how to use it. Can it be of any use to you? Wolves and birds I know have found it valuable."

"You are Gilberec Moth, son of Ygraine, of whom the birds never speak?"

"Yes. You know me?"

"Bird are my enemies. I study them and know what they know."

"Do you know why they never speak about my mother?"

"No. They never speak of it."

"Then how do you know– aargh! Never mind. Yes, I am Gil."

"You know not what a noble gift you give, Son of the Swanmay. This hair will allow me to build a web neither man nor brute can brush away and no prey escape. I will cling to a windborne thread and fly to Madagascar, and across a river there raise a web eighty feet wide, and be accounted eminent and famous among my kind for ten generations! That is one generation of men, or two decades. But it would be uncomely of me not to recompense you for so magnanimous a gift. Ask of me three boons, anything within my power, and I will perform."

"First, your forgiveness for destroying your house."

"Granted."

"Can you free me from this cell?"

"I do not know how."

"Could you find a friend of mine? A dog named Ruff. He is also a pooka. His name has an S and a G at the beginning, but I can't remember it. *So go long.* Sounded something like that."

"Am I a flea? They are the insects given stewardship over dogs. I am a spider. I reduce the excess fly population and teach them humility. Ask something else."

"Can you talk to a bird?"

"In peril of my life. But I can summon one here. Carry me to the window and give me your blessing as a Son of Adam. This is your second boon."

And with a bravery that impressed Gil greatly, the spider hung by her thread out the window, and taunted passing birds, using herself as bait to lure one close.

8. Picoides borealis

When a Red-cockaded woodpecker dived at her, the little spider yanked herself back through one of the tiny air holes in the metal plate padlocked over the window, and Gil saw the sharp hammer of a bill follow her.

Gil said, "Picoides, I need your help."

The woodpecker said, "I hear a voice! Are you inside this metal plate? Who are you?"

"Gilberec Moth."

"The pine tree's friend?"

"Uh, yes. I think."

The bird rapped a moment on the metal plate, as if experimentally. "I heard that this very tree got reincarnated and showed up at the house of She of Whom We Never Speak."

Gil said, "Trees get to be reincarnated?"

"They have vegetative souls, so the cherub in charge of pine trees recycles them."

Gil said, "So trees reincarnate back to this world, but humans go to Heaven?"

"Is that where they go? Huh. The world is weirder than I thought. I have seen the ghosts of men lined up on the banks of the river Tiber, and then they get into a boat where a mighty angel stands and uses celestial wings as sails. They go across the sea. I am a nonmigratory bird. I don't go over the sea."

"Then how did you get to the Tiber? It's in Italy."

"That was a one-time thing, a pilgrimage, to pay my respects to Picus, first king of Latium. I don't migrate yearly like a goose does. Geese are crazy. How can they dig bugs out of tree bark with those flat, weird-looking goose bills, eh? Can you send that spider back out? I'm hungry."

"The spider is a friend of mine."

"Well, just keep it platonic. If she mates with you, she'll kill you and eat your corpse. Nasty creature, spiders."

The spider said, "Do I look like a Black Widow to you?"

The woodpecker said, "Step outside, and let me inspect you more carefully."

Gil said to the spider, "Don't be angry. You must admit, eating your own mother is a very disturbing habit."

The spider said, "There is no greater offering of love. You eat your own Lord every Sabbath and drink his precious blood as well."

Gil was not sure if it was wise to get into a theological debate with birds and spiders, so he said to the woodpecker, "Picoides, I am looking for my dog."

"Ruff? He's just outside the fence. Kind of sneaking around. I think I heard him humming some sort of jazz music from a spy show while he was doing it. Watching the trucks going in and out, timing the guard rounds, pacing out the distance and overlapping fields of view from the security cameras, chasing squirrels, sniffing his own buttocks. You know what dogs are like. Disgusting animals, really. Glad they cannot fly. Can you imagine the mess they'd make if they flew? Yikes!"

"You know my dog?"

"Sure. He's a spy for the elfs. A lousy spy. He was asking around about Ygraine of the Wise Reeds. The high parliament of birds was notified immediately. Whenever she goes to or comes from her rotten job in that wine bar, we are supposed to dive bomb the dog, get him to chase us, make sure he never spots her."

"You have a parliament?"

"Rooks do. They form the secular arm. Magpies have congregations, and they form the spiritual orders. Crows are our Execution Branch, and Ravens are our Fourth Estate, on account of their unkindness."

Gil rubbed his temples, wondering why woodpeckers were more talkative than other birds he'd met. "I'd like you to talk to him for me. Ruff, I mean. He has a special glove he can put on his paw to give it the shape and movement of a human hand. I want you to take it from him and leave it on the roof."

Gil picked up the spider on his forefinger. "I have no idea if this will work, but for my final boon, Ma'am, I'd like you to help me with something."

9. A Green Glove

An hour later, Gil lay prone with one eye at the slit that pierced the door, watching a tiny spider, smaller than a dime with seven thin legs and one leg ending in a bright green human-sized glove, walking carefully along the ceiling. Between the finger and the thumb of the glove was the keyring and the keys to this cell.

One of the keys opened the iron plate over the window. It was a four-story climb to the ground, but the spider said that the glove granted her hand human strength while she wore it, so Gil took the glove in both his hands, and she held him and walked slowly down the concrete wall while he held on and prayed and sweated.

As he had been told, the bullets from the riflemen in the watchtowers were able to land to his right and left, making loud, appalling noises, but they simply refused to hit him. The electricity in the fence was evidently also considered a modern enough weapon that it did not harm him. The barbed wire at the top would have been able to cut him, except that his gauntlets were too thick.

After that, he heard Ruff barking. "This way! This way!"

Gil looking behind him at the pursuit, saw how the trees and thorn bushes, which had let him pass by without grabbing his cloak or legs, got in the way of the men with guns coming after.

He found Ruff atop a small snowy hillock, talking to a pair of blood-hounds. These two hounds sniffed Gil carefully. One said, "Fed you a spam sandwich, you said? One of your pack?"

The other hound asked suspiciously, "He is not a cat person, is he?"

Ruff said, "I never sleep on the floor if he has a bed. I never go hungry if he has food."

A silent look of understanding passed between the second and first hound.

The first hound said, "Okay. We'll lead the deputy the wrong way. But you owe us big! Every escaped prisoner makes us look bad on our quarterly performance review. C'mon, Buford. Let's get back to the kennel."

The two hounds loped off. Gil knelt down and gave Ruff a hug.

"Boy, am I glad to see you!" said Gil. "You saved my life at least three times."

Ruff took his green glove back and held it in his teeth. A small cloud of mist gathered around it, turned dark gray, and then vanished, and the glove vanished with it. Then, he licked Gil's face.

"Well? Well? You've decided. Haven't you? You made up your mind," said Ruff, sadly.

Gil said, "You can smell that I have made a decision?"

"Yup. That, and the fact that all you had to do was stay in that building and not risk getting shot breaking out, and you would have missed your date with the Green Knight. I was sure your mom would tell you not to go."

"She did."

"You are not listening to Ygraine of the Reeds? They say she is the wisest woman in the world!"

"Ruff, I talked to a mom in there who is going to give up everything for her kids, even her life. I also talked with a man who did not see the point of keeping one's word. I want to be in her world, not in his."

Ruff said, "You'd live longer in his."

Gil said, "And be just as dead at the end and be called to account for my life."

Ruff nodded sagely, scratched his fleas, and turned in a circle, sniffing. He seemed to be licking or biting himself, but Gil saw a trickle of mist seeping from his teeth.

10. The Token

Gil said, "What are you doing?"

Ruff said, "I hide my stuff in the mist, like you do. It's natural for elfs. It's allowed."

Gil said, "Allowed?"

"Angels don't mind it. Prophets do it, too. It is not actually magic. Here."

And in his teeth was dangling a fine gold chain, at end of which was a tiny glass bead small as the end of his thumb.

"What is it...?"

Ruff said, "*Whoa ho ho* and *Oo la la!*"

"What?"

Ruff laughed in his throat. "You are just a Dude in Distress, ain't you! And then the Damsel had to save you! You know what that means...."

Gil picked up the pendant and held it to his eye. Inside the glass bead were two or three strands of black hair, very long and very fine, frozen in the glass, tied with Celtic intricacy into endless threefold knots.

Gil said, "Ruff! What is this?"

"The favor you asked for. From Nerea. She clipped the hairs off her head with a golden knife. One of Phaethon's daughters is a pal of mine, a nymph named Aetherea; I had her trap it in clear amber to act as a pyx."

Gil said, "First, I don't know what a pyx is. Second, I never asked her for a favor."

The dog said, "Why not? You like her, don't you? I can tell you like her. Humans are in heat all year round."

"She's my cousin!"

"Second cousin once removed. It's allowed. Did you like kissing her? Do you want to kiss her again? Don't lie to me. I can smell the truth!"

"You cannot smell the truth!"

"You going to take it? Or throw it away?"

"Why did you tell her I wanted her favor?"

"I had to ask because you were too stupid to. She sits on rocks all day just watching you exercise. Doesn't that tell you something? And you want her favor to carry into battle. Don't you?"

"I refuse to answer on the grounds it may tend to intimidate me. Beside, what business is it of yours?"

Ruff wagged his head and made a snorting noise. "Look, Gil, I am a smart dog! A good dog! I know things!"

"What do you know?"

"I know that once a girl wins over a guy's dog, it is all over but for the shouting. If you name your firstborn after me, I will be happy to act as his godfather."

"The only shouting is going to be when I kick you down this hill."

"See? It is all over but that!"

Gil slung the chain over his head so that the bead of glass was over his heart. "I cannot throw it away. That would be rude."

"*Ooh la la!*"

"Stop saying that!"

"It is French," said Ruff.

"It is not French."

"It is!"

"If it is French, then what's it mean?"

"It means, '*Whoa ho ho!*'"

"And what does that mean?"

"I dunno," said the dog with a shrug and a flip of his tail. "It's German. I don't speak German."

"Hmm."

"So! So! You know which way to go? Where is this green place? Is it within walking distance? Or do we need to get a boat or something?"

Gil said, "I have no idea at all." So he chose a direction at random and started walking, with Ruff trotting happily after.

Chapter 3

The Headless Huntsmen

1. Green Steed

Gil walked for a day through the snowy hills of Appalachia. Each time he was tempted to quit, he pushed the thought aside. His mother had told him once that temptations were like bugbites: the itch always seemed as if it was sure to last forever. But if you can hold out from scratching for fifteen minutes, the itch might fade. And if it does not, at least you held out for fifteen minutes.

At dusk, he and Ruff were hungry. Only then did he abandon his aimless walking and start to look in earnest for a good campsite. Ruff wended his way downhill, sniffing and searching for fresh water. As Gil was crossing an open meadow, Ruff barked.

"Look! Look! Behind you, there! Behind you!"

Gil turned. He saw above him on the crest of the hill, with the glorious red clouds of sunset like a forest fire behind him, was a steed larger than a Clydesdale and green as a holly leaf. It was the horse of the Green Knight.

The green steed said, "Sgeolan, put on your speaking cap so that you can speak to the young squire. I am to tell him the path to go."

Gil said, "I can understand you."

The green horse's ears twitched. "You speak the speech of horses? That is unusual. It is said that Alexander the Great had that gift, and also Uther Pendragon, Arthur's sire."

Gil said, "How did he come by this gift?"

The green horse flicked its ears again. "We are not here to discuss this. I am come to tell you the way to the Green Chapel."

Gil said, "Tell me."

"First, you are headed in exactly the wrong direction. Go downhill, and follow the springs that feed into the Tennessee River, and sail it to the Ohio, thence to the Mississippi and to the Illinois. Follow this to Calumet Harbor. Then to Lake Michigan, past the Mackinac Bridge, to Lake Huron, to Sarnia, and then to the St. Clair River south to Lake St. Clair. Go to Walpole Island. The war poles after which the island is named will be visible to you, but not the ghosts they drive away. The autochthons call the place Bkejwanong, which, being interpreted, means Watersmeeting."

"Auto who?"

"The Anishinaabeg, which includes the Chippewa, Ottawa, and Potawatomi. These tribes were removed from the human world, brought into the Twilight by shining beings, and hidden behind the mist. Their chief Sassaba agreed to serve and worship the elfs and eschew the Christ of the White Man, and lakes as large as Huron and rivers as long as the Ohio were erased from sight and memory. Untouched woods, and hunting grounds where birds and game thrive in numbers uncounted, were given to the tribes. Here are hills no booted foot has touched, trees that never felt the iron ax. The bold Chippewa range those hidden lands, fighting and raiding and slaving, and keeping all their old ways, and worshiping devils. You must pass through their land: avoid them."

Gil said, "So the Green Chapel is on Walpole Island, which is an Indian reservation? Where is this again? Michigan?"

"Canada. Knights, march-wardens from London and Strathroy, venture to Walpole Island, despite the danger, to do battle with windigo and water-panthers, and corsairs from Algonac and Harsens Island raid there, capturing Pukwudgies to sell to magicians."

"Who are these knights and corsairs?"

"Irishmen, Smithwicks, Moths and Cobwebs, and other Twilight Folk who no longer dwell in the human world. From here, if you sail without rest, and at the speed fit and proper for an elfin boat, you should make the trip in sixteen days. You should not have waited so long."

Gil said, "What if I do not have an elfin boat? Shouldn't I fly?"

The green steed looked doubtful and said, "I was told you lacked the art of flying. That would, of course, be swifter yet. Have you a swan robe? I did not know males wore them."

"I meant by airplane."

"Human contrivances are unlucky as well as unlovely. What became of your swift elfin boat? Are you not the Swan Knight?"

"Actually, I am not sure. There was another who wore this armor before me."

"What armor?"

"Sorry," said Gil. "This armor." Gil stared at one of the diamonds on his armor until the diamond seemed to glow with starlight, which drove away the mist. Sir Bertolac had shown him this means of undoing the glamour.

The green steed reared back, startled. "May the cat eat you and the devil eat the cat! That is very disturbing! Were you hoaxing my eyes? Well, your little elf tricks will not save you from my master's good iron ax!"

Gil said, "I do not have a perfect memory like an elf, so you will have to repeat the instructions."

But Ruff said, "I got it. I know the way."

Gil looked at the dog in surprise. "You do?"

"I do! I do! All pooka know about the northern lakes where knights and Indians battle. It is not London, England. It is London, Ontario. On the River Thames. The other Thames. The March-Wardens of London are famous. The brothers of Lord Simcoe, John and Percy, entered the mist to free the slaves kept by efts and werewolves, and they wed the river women and cannot return to the human world. The fiercest and most famous demi-men of the north are descended from them."

But the green steed said, "That little pooka may not go with you! Sgeolan never struck the head from my master, and he is neither invited to the Green Chapel nor would be permitted to leave alive!"

Ruff said, "No! No! I go with my boy and die with him!"

The steed said, "It is forbidden! I don't want to see you—I mean, the Green Knight will not permit an unclean animal into his lands!"

Gil said to the green steed, "I do not have a boat. How are you getting back there? Can I simply ride on you?"

The green steed said, "As a courtesy, I will carry you to the bank of the river. But the dog must stay behind!"

Gil and Ruff argued about it for a long while while the green horse stamped its hooves in the snow and snorted in its nostrils impatiently.

In the end, Ruff won the argument technically (Gil could not refute the point that if Ygraine could not forbid Gil from seeking death when honor demanded it, Gil could not forbid Ruff) but lost the argument practically.

The green horse could produce a dark gray form of the mists of Everness from its hooves as it galloped, seven fathoms at a stride, or leap half a mile through the roaring air from one hilltop to the next as lightly as a stag. The strange fog streamed backward from the flashing hooves of the flying steed. Ruff was left far, far behind.

As they raced across the Appalachians and into the Tennessee river valley, Gil leaned forward and shouted into the green steed's ear over the uproar of the winds. "Tell me something! How did you know my dog's real name?"

But the green steed gave no answer.

2. Ashore

Gil slept by the waterside, wrapped in his gray cloak. He woke before dawn and started walking north, wondering how he was supposed to find whatever boat the green steed expected him to find.

It was deserted here, out of sight of any human roads or telephone lines or highways. The east was pink and the clouds above bright red. The birds began to sing, "Hail! Holy Light! Offspring of Heaven firstborn...!"

He knelt, crossed himself, crossed his hands, and tried to pray.

Prayer would not come. His thoughts stirred and jumped like a skittish steed. He did not know the way. Surely that was excuse enough to avoid his appointment with the deadly Green Knight? No one in the elfish world knew Gil's name. He could avoid any scandal or dishonor merely by painting his shield with a new design. And it was not as if the elfs had volunteered to take the Green Knight's wager! What right had they to criticism him?

Besides, no one would ever know.

Gil opened his eyes. "I would know," he said.

He stood, and sighed, and began trudging north.

The wind was cold, and the frost was bitter, but there was no snow on the ground here. The sun was a ball of fire, fat and dim, peering over the horizon. The long shadows of twilight still covered the rocks and leafless trees of the shore. Wisps of dispersing fog clung here and there about the river, clouds resting on the waters. In a strip of blue between two cloud banks, he saw a scrap of white, graceful and fair, floating along the waters. After a time of marching, the sun was yellow and almost above the horizon, the fog was less, and the white figure was closer.

Gil saw it was a swan. He had not expected to see swans on the Tennessee River. On the other hand, he did not know whether they were from this area or not.

The creature was far away, but Gil called to it. The swan seemed not to have heard him at first, but, after a while, he noticed it was swimming near and nearer.

She spoke in a very soft voice, "Nobly you bear your shield and nobly high aloft your crest, Swan Knight."

Gil said, "You know me?"

"How could I not?"

"Who is my father?"

"You are the son of the Swan Knight."

Gil said, "And what is his name?"

The swan said, "That I do not know. Why do you walk here, unhorsed and footsore?"

"I walk because I have no horse."

"A knight without a horse is not a knight. Whither go you?"

"To Walpole Island I go."

"Wherefore?"

"I go to be beheaded, and I am late."

"It may not be a thing of sorrow to be late for one's beheading."

"I must be there by Christmas Eve."

"Afoot? It is too far. Shall I bring your boat?"

"I own a boat?"

"You are the Swan Knight, the son of the Swan Knight. Of course you own a boat. Have I your leave to fetch it? Otherwise, you will be late for your beheading."

"You have my leave."

And the swan slowly drifted away.

3. Afloat

Midmorning came and went, and there was no sign of the swan or the boat she had gone to fetch. In the distance he saw a deserted brown shack.

His stomach rumbled with hunger, and Gil sternly told it to shut up.

His power to talk to animals evidently did not extend to the beast called hunger. He went to the shack to see if there were anyone there who might give him a drink or a morsel, but the place was empty, a barn-like place with a dirt floor and dusty rafters. No one was within save spiders, who, learning his name, asked him if he knew the famous spider of North Carolina whose unbreakable webs were yards wide? One offered him fat flies to quench his thirst.

When Gil returned to the shore, he saw there a small boat, no larger than his couch back home. It was painted bright red, and the gunwale was gilded with gold leaf, and the bowsprit was carved in the image of Cupid flourishing his bow.

Here also were a dozen swans arranged two by two in a harness made of vines and flowers like a team of horses, and two long strands of silk thread were the reins.

There were two swans in collars of gold leading the others. The one on the left-hand side said, "We are here, my lord."

Gil said, "Who do you work for?"

"For you, my lord."

Gil said, "Were you the boat, ah, steeds of the first Swan Knight?"

"Are not we the very grandchildren of those who drew him?"

Gil asked, "How did he bind you to his service?"

"He sang and spoke, and his singing was very fine, and his words very fair, and the long lost authority of Adam was in his words, and the glamour of elfin song. He told our grandfathers that he sailed to the rescue of Ygraine the Wise, of whom we do not speak, and what swan would not aid a Swanmay or the son of a Swanmay?"

Gil thought to himself that, for once, he was not going to ask any birds why they did not talk about his mother. "And how are you bound to my service?"

The two lead swans arched their necks and flapped their white wings, and one on the right said, "Swans mate for life. We forget no oaths. Shall we serve the father and not the son?"

"My father—is he man or elf?"

The right-hand one said, "How shall we know this?"

"Why are you here?"

"Do you not need us to carry you to your beheading?"

"Do you answer every question with a question?"

The two swans in the front of the harness looked at each other again in surprise. "Do we?"

"I see where my mother gets it from."

Gil sighed and stepped into the boat. Despite the small size, the boat did not move under his footstep. Before he seated himself (there was a thwart amidships smaller than a camp stool), the boat was drawn into motion by the swans, but it rolled and pitched no more than a steady and massive yacht would have, and Gil was amazed.

To judge from the wind in his face, the little red boat seemed to be moving as slowly and serenely as a swimming swan, but each time he looked at the shore and judged his speed based on the landmarks passing, the pace was as swift as a speedboat.

The elf boat passed slowly and swiftly across the face of the waters with barely a sound, as smoothly as a glass ball rolling along a marble floor, and two white lines of wake trailed away behind.

4. Afoot

Gil followed the sailing instructions of the green steed. Days passed, but from time to time he went ashore to seek food.

Once for his supper he hunted rabbits with a sling and then forbore when the chief of the warren came out of the long grass and turned over a criminal to him for execution. That rabbit, whose only crime was not agreeing with sufficient enthusiasm at whatever the warren was enthused about that week, begged for its life and offered to provide Gil a feast better than coney. Gil agreed and was surprised to find the next morning a perfectly fine heap of asparagus, clovers, chickweed, and pennycress and a bunch of carrots piled near his head. He boiled the leafy mass in his helmet, yet it was not only edible but tasty.

A second time, days later, he went ashore, but headless men in long, dark coats, carrying lanterns from which their eyes peered, hunted him silently through the silent, leafless trees of Monogheia National Park.

A day and night and another day passed as they hunted him. Gil tried ever to return to the river, but the headless creatures were always before him.

Once, when they were close on his trail, Gil hid in a scum-coated leafy bog of freezing water; he saw them close at hand: two cloaked headless men and a headless child on a horse. The men were dressed like dandies, in fine black fabric, with lace adorning their neck stumps. The child carried his head, laughing and hallooing, at the end of a long spear, tied by his hair to the blade. The men would lower the lantern-shaped boxes in which their heads were carried. Gil heard the sniffing and snuffling along the path as they passed him by, seeking his scent. Gil feared the headless men, but he feared the child more.

He slept for two days in a cave above the snowline, beyond where the hunt ranged, eating only nuts a friendly squirrel brought him. The next day, he followed the squirrel's lead and found a high, clear, swift-running mountain stream. He waded in the freezing water, hoping to mask his scent and then came suddenly upon his red boat with the white swans, waiting serenely.

He continued north. Each day he was hungrier, but with the days lost to the headless men, now there was no time to tarry.

It was in the darkness before dawn when Gilberec Moth came to Lake Erie. He looked at the fading stars, saw the date, and realized that no time remained. Perhaps he was too late already to reach Walpole Island by Christmas Eve.

But again he took the silken reins in hand and called out to the swans, urging them to their greatest speed. The birds moved with what seemed slow serenity, but, once again, they passed by the landmarks with deceptive quickness.

5. Aboard

When the sun was at noon, the waters of Lake Erie were clear, and Gil could see to a great depth. He took off his helm to peer closer. He saw a slender, curvaceous shape in a skintight black suit, her black hair caught in a glittering net whose pearls and gems winked in the shimmering underwater sunlight. When she looked up, her eyes were hidden behind the mirrored disks of her sunglasses.

Gil held aloft the locket of her hair he wore at his neck and waved his hand.

Nerea arose and leaped, more graceful than a dolphin, into the air, over the boat, over Gil's head, and into the other side, splashing him. The December water was cold.

She swam down again, and then up, and then leaped again. This time Gil was ready and caught her in his arms. She was surprisingly warm and slippery.

She struggled for a moment and looked exasperated. Gil said, "Welcome aboard. Like my boat? Have a seat. It is the only seat on the whole boat."

He sat on the gunwale in the bow, facing her. She seated herself daintily, and crossed her long legs, and pushed her sunglasses back to the top of her head, which made Gil laugh.

"You mock and sport with me!" she pouted.

"Not at all, miss," he said. "It is just that when a pearl diver comes to the surface, she will push her scuba goggles back on her head just like that. I thought it was funny how it looked the same. You know, because you are... uh... a mermaid. I cannot get over how your glasses don't fall off."

"Inanimate objects hate mortal men," she said, "All carpenters and electricians know that. But they do not hate us. Besides, you cannot call me 'miss.' It is not right."

"What do I call you?" asked Gil, surprised.

"My lady."

"Eh? I mean, beg pardon?"

"You must call me *my lady* so that your unspoken feelings for me will urge you to live through combat, when otherwise your pain and grief would have you give up the ghost." She pointed at the locket winking on his chest. "Is that not the meaning of asking me for my token?"

Gil was too embarrassed to say that it had been Ruff's idea, and then he realized it was an idea he really liked, and he was also too embarrassed to say that. He felt warmth in his face and a burning sensation in the tips of his ears.

He said, "Yes, my lady. That is exactly what it means." And because of the drop of monstrous blood that had touched his tongue, he could hear the honesty in his own voice, and he knew he spoke the truth.

6. Abandoned

Greatly daring, he put his hands on her delicate, black-clad shoulders and leaned down to kiss her, but she ducked under his arm and dived over the gunwale into the water. She smote cleanly into the surface with hardly a splash. The boat, which had seemed so steady and sturdy before, now pitched under his feet, and he stumbled and grabbed the gunwale.

"Hey!" he shouted, feeling foolish.

Her head reappeared above the waters, and a set of ripples spread from her neck. Her hair was black and slick and glittered beneath her jeweled snood. Droplets clung to her eyelashes like little gems and twinkled in the sunlight. "A dog I thought was a collie used the mermaid song to call me from the river water, but then his coat was a wig—his whole coat—and he threw it aside, and it was your pooka.

"This is the second time he called. So I watched your boat, knowing you would call her sooner or later. I did not think you would wait so long. I had been planning to cook you a dinner, shrimp and scallop and meat taken from the belly of the sleeping world-serpent—you have to numb the area with jellyfish venom or torpedo fish before cutting a slice of snake steak free, or else there are earthquakes—and I would have plenty of time! But now! Now! I have no time."

His stomach sent another pang through him. A slice of world serpent steak sounded particularly tasty at the moment. Gil said, "No time for what?"

"You are going off to die!" She shook her head, and the water droplets flew from her eyelashes.

He said, "Yes."

She said, "I conjure you by that token I have bestowed that you shall not go!"

"The rules of knighthood are very simple, but very hard. This is one of the hard ones. I cannot turn back. I gave my word."

"Come to my world! I can lend you my mermaid's cap, and you can breathe the seawater as lightly as air. Come! You can learn a trade and be a shoemaker; we have none of those in Ys."

Gil crossed his arms. "My lady is supposed to make stronger the fortress of my heart, not sap and undermine it. I am in a battle with temptation. If I lose this battle, no victory on Earth in battles of flesh and blood will matter."

Nerea sank down slightly in the water so that it touched her bottom lip. "That is a terrible and heavy wisdom. You are too young for such things. Who taught you these terrible things?"

"A man named Lancelot. He won all his earthly battles and lost the only battle that mattered, for he dishonored himself with his queen and broke the Table Round, and its like has never come into the world again."

She shook her head and wiped her eyes with the palm of her hand, which made her cheeks more wet, not less. "Why can't you put this off and get yourself beheaded ten years from now, or fifty years?"

Gil said, "Nerea, I want you to urge me forward, not back. I want you to tell me to be fearless. That is the job of a knight's true lady."

She looked up at him, and her dark eyes were bright. "Am I your true lady then?"

Gil said, "Are you? It is up to you."

She raised her hand and touched the gunwale, as if she were about to climb aboard again. But a tremble ran through her body. "The duty of a lady is harder than the duty of a knight, for I shall live and think back on this hour. Do you have some plan, or trick, which will enable you to survive?"

"No. Tricks in battle are allowed. Not tricks with one's own honor."

"Oh." Her hand slipped off the gunwale. She drifted away from the boat by a yard or two.

Gil said, "Perhaps the Green Knight will spare me. He spared Gawain."

"Who is that?"

"A man from fifteen hundred years ago. A brave man."

Nerea drifted a little farther away. Now she was ten yards away.

She said wistfully, "Do you think the Green Knight will spare you?"

Gil thought back on the laughter and scorn and insults the Green Knight had spoken during the Christmas feast a year ago.

Gil knew that if he spoke what he did not believe, anyone who heard would know.

He thought of several vaguely worded things he could say, which would not technically be untrue, but then he remembered talking that way to the elfs. Looking down at Nerea's pale and pretty face surrounded by dark and clinging strands of wet hair, he did not think she was as easy to fool as an elf. He also did not think knights were supposed to try to fool their ladies.

So he simply said, "No. I do not think he will spare me."

Nerea was over a dozen yards away. He heard the steel in her voice as she forced herself to speak words she did not want to say.

"Go forward, my knight. Face without fear your fate. Die without dishonor. Go forward!"

Nerea's voice broke into a sob, but he only heard the first half of the sound. Like a dolphin, she reared up halfway out of the water, turned, and dove. Gil saw the water sluicing along her hips and legs and bare feet. She was gone.

Chapter 4

The Knight of the Red Steed

1. The Camp

The small scarlet boat was pulled by the swans swiftly across the lake. They passed up the river to a second lake and then found the mouth of a smaller stream. A leafless oak tree rose on either bank, and their branches commingled overhead, forming a large arch of dry twigs across the stream. Gil saw green balls lodged in the branches, and he wondered if some clumsy children had been playing here. But then the red swan-boat passed under the arch of twigs. Looking up, he saw that the balls were not solid. Rather each was a leafy mass growing in a sphere, green despite the winter season. It was mistletoe.

The stream grew narrower, shallower, and swifter, and for the first time the swans seemed to be straining. Since a dozen swans should not have been able to tow a rowboat at speedboat speeds in any case, Gil hardly blamed them for struggling.

The ground began to slope upward. Ahead rose a cliff like a gray wall. The top of the cliff was fringed with black and leafless bushes. The silver ribbon of a roaring waterfall plunged into a pool beaten into bubbling froth. The rock all around was sprinkled as if with rain drops. This pool was the source of the stream. To either side of the pool rose two more oak trees, dry and leafless in the winter. Here, too, in the midst of the branches were balls of green mistletoe.

The swans beat their wings and pulled the boat ashore. Gil stepped out. Pebbles and dry grass rustled and crunched under his boots. The two lead swans bowed their graceful necks. "No farther we bear you. This cliff, and the higher land it hides, appears on no human maps and in no human eyes nor memories. The Green Chapel is in that high land, but where, no one can say." So spoke the lead swan on the left.

The lead swan on the right said, "Long ago giants cut a stair into the living rock; it is that white line you see in the distance yonder that climbs in zigs and zags up the gray side. However, oak is strong in this place, and evergreen can no longer shield you. If any elf or Cobweb seeks your ill, it must between this pool and the foot of that stair. Call us again when you have need."

Gil said, "How?"

The two lead swans bent their graceful necks and stared at each other a moment, as if startled.

The one on the left said, "The next hunting horn you see hanging from a strap around the neck of any sleeping creature, be it beast or man or angel, take it."

The one on the right said, "It is Roland's horn, and its voice can be heard from afar, for it has an elfish contempt for time and distance. Stand with one foot on land and one in the water, and blow. We will not ignore the far-famed and wide-reaching voice of that horn. Fare you well, and God speed you."

And with no more words, the swans pulled the small red boat into the rushing stream, and the current bore them away.

Gil looked. The foot of the cliff was hidden from view because of the rise and fall of the land and the height of the winter trees. It looked like a long hike. Gil glanced down and stared at his empty scabbard.

Gil went to the oak tree growing by the boiling pool, and, finding a long, straight, and likely looking branch, he cut it free with his dirk. As he walked in the pathless wood, keeping the gray cliff ever to his left, he trimmed and whittled the branch to serve him as a hiking stick but also as a quarterstaff.

He came upon a deer path, which he followed to a streamlet no broader than a footstep. But here he saw prints of moccasins in the muddy bank. He jumped over the stream and passed on, but more warily now.

The ground became rougher, rising and falling in step rolls, as if the earth were a brown blanket wrinkled like an unmade bed. The trees on the high slopes were few and sparse, like hairs on a bald man's head, but the vales between were filled with thorn and brush and had muddy soil at the bottom. This ground there was too rough to push through. Gil walked along the top of one of the ridges away from the cliff, seeking an easier trail but a longer one, trying to avoid the rough ground.

He came suddenly to a place overlooking a wide meadow. Many valleys opened up into a flat and low land of tall grass and few trees. There was water gleaming in the distance on the far side beyond the meadow, no doubt an arm of Lake St. Clair.

On the shore, in the shadow of many tall war poles carved with totems, were canoes of birch bark gathered. In the shadow of the leafless trees were drying racks, wigwams of bark, and tripods of spears and leather shields adorned with feathers, beads, and bright paint. Gil saw the white thin smoke of campfires issuing upward. He was curious, and he grinned, looking for the easiest path he could take to go down and get a closer look. This must have been one of the Indian tribes hidden by the elfs from the eyes of the rest of the world, protected, as it were, from the passage of time.

Then, Gil saw the corpse of a man hanging head downward from an oak tree in the middle of the camp, and the marks of torture on him, and the ashes of a large fire that had been burning directly beneath him.

Gil carefully crept back into the woods and passed even more carefully than before. He found a large stand of fir trees, and, feeling only a little foolish, he asked them for their blessing, and to throw off any pursuit which might be behind him.

Whether or not that worked, he did not know, but as he made his way carefully through the rough land back toward the cliff, no one came upon him from behind.

2. The Stronghouse

A long while later, Gil came free of the last trees and saw the valley that lay before the foot of the giant stair. He saw before him a cloudy fog, filling the valley floor. Across the valley he could see, above the fog, the great steps cut into the cliff face. The stairway ascended a chimney of rock that pressed close to the steps to either side.

As he walked across the valley and started up the slope, the wind blew, and the fog parted and rolled away. He saw before him a green mound covered with what looked like mistletoe, but this plant was growing on the ground, amid the brown grass of December.

At the top of this hill was the foot of the cliff. Here was the giant stair, but the cliff walls to the left had been cut and carved and hollowed out into a squat round tower. To Gil's eyes this stronghouse looked like a rook on a chessboard. Twenty feet of the living rock had been cut and polished into the shape of a half-cylinder. Strong doors ten feet high and bound with brass were in the door-arch, like a mouth half-open in mockery. The portcullis was like a row of iron teeth. Above were two cross-shaped archer's slits, like the merry eyes of a clown. The crown was carved into a crenelated battlement set with corbels of bronze.

Gil walked up the mistletoe slope toward the foot of the staircase. It did indeed look like steps fit for giants, for each step was two or three feet tall and a yard or more deep.

The slope of the hill was so steep, and the weeds were so slippery, that Gil first had to clamber bent double, then sling his shield on his back and crawl. At last, without warning, there appeared a brink, and after that the slope was easy, almost level, running up to the foot of the giant stair.

Just at this brink was a holly bush. On one branch of the holly bush hung a hunting horn. Gil stared long at the horn and then stared long at the stronghouse, frowning. The archer slits were narrow and commanded only a narrow view, and no one was on the roof of the stronghouse. It would have been a simple matter to walk in a broad circle to the foot of the cliff, approach the stronghouse from one side or the other, where no windows were, get to the bottom step unseen, and climb the stair rapidly, eluding whatever guard was posted here.

Gil instead raised the horn to the Y-shaped opening in his helm and blew a loud, long blast. The horn call echoed from the cliffs.

The portcullis ground slowly open. It moved so slowly, Gil saw, that it would have been easy to run past the stronghouse and mount the stairs.

The brass-bound doors swung open. Here on a roan steed was a knight armed at all points. His shield was sable without any charge or design. Above his helm floated a plume as green as ivy. His steed was caparisoned in black silk. A black pennant streamed from the point of his deadly lance.

The steed came forth, stamping its feet. Gil saw that it was a fairy-steed, for it had a tail like a black lion, not a horse's tail, and its hooves were cloven like a deer's. The coat was a dark red, with white markings on the flanks and top of the tail and along the ribs in vertical stripes.

3. The Parley

The black knight called, "Who dares defy me?"

Gil called back, "I am called the Swan Knight. In King Arthur's name, let me pass."

The black knight said, "Arthur? He is king of the dead perhaps. One of his men long, long ago passed this way, but he never returned. You are not his equal. Turn back!"

Gil gripped the quarterstaff in the middle and readied his shield. "Dismount, and let us fight as man to man."

The black knight said, "Who is your family and bloodline?"

Gil said, "Not that nonsense again! Erlkoenig enrolled my name on his lists as a knight!"

"Erlkoenig is damned. I care nothing for him. What does your Arthur say of you?"

Gil said, "Who are you who asks this of me?"

"A man ahorse who blocks your path."

Gil said, "I am the highest ranked of Arthur's court at large in the world today."

The black knight said, "Did he knight you? Where are your spurs?"

"I have no spurs. He did not knight me."

The black knight laughed. "Then why should I dismount and fight you as equal to equal? Withdraw! And thank me that I save your life from the Green Knight. He throws the severed heads of elfish knights bouncing down that stairway behind me. I bury them here and there about my lands so that the elfin ghosts will terrify the savages and keep them away from me."

"Who are you?" and then, with a wild hope in his heart, Gil asked, "Are you a member of the Moth family?"

"No Moth am I. They would not dare assume the privileges of noble blood!"

Gil thought of his half-brothers. "Not openly."

"What does that mean, so-called Man of Arthur with no spurs and no name? Do you hide mixed and mingled blood out of shame?"

Gil ignored the question. "If you are not of Erlkoenig nor Arthur, then of whose court are you? By what authority do you bar my way?"

The black knight said, "By the strength of my right arm! I save your life from the Green Knight. But I will strike you dead myself!"

And with that, the knight lowered his lance and charged.

4. The Charge

Armed only with a staff and a shield, Gil stood no chance. With his lance, the black knight could strike from over a yard beyond where Gil could counterstrike with his green stick. The full weight and strength of the horse was behind the lance point.

The only reason why it did not skewer Gil through shield and armor and all was that Gil was able to deflect the point from his shield at a shallow angle and parry the lance haft with his staff.

Gil lunged toward the speeding horse, trying to get close enough to strike at the rider, but the rider deflected the blow with the point of his shield, twisting in the saddle to do so. Then, the steed reared and kicked Gil. His shield was not in the right position. The world went black with pain, and Gil found himself flying from the brink of the slippery weed-covered slope. Down and down he plunged and slid, aching in all his limbs, and lucky not to be dead. That kick would have slain a man not in armor.

Gil climbed unsteadily to his feet, craning back his head, cursing the narrow field of vision of his helm, but glad the rider was up on the slope above him. No horse could come down that steep slope without breaking a leg.

No horse, but the fairy steed, lion tail lashing, leaped down the sheer slope as nimbly as a mountain goat and made as if to leap onto Gil and trample him as a horse might trample a snake. Gil leaped to one side and smote at the back of the black knight as he thundered by, but the oak staff betrayed him, and the staff broke in two pieces.

The black knight reeled in the saddle and dropped his lance. The steed leaped once and twice more, farther down the slope, and then turned. The black knight drew his sword, a massive straight blade enameled in black, with the cutting edges shining silvery white. It looked like the kind of thing that normally required two hands to wield, but the black knight handled it as lightly as if it were a willow wand.

5. Second Parley

"Do you yield? There is no sport in killing you; you are too small and weak." So said the black knight, and then he roared with laughter.

Gil stepped forward, slipped a bit on the mistletoe weed, and picked up the dropped lance. This did not have the large guard of a joisting lance. It was a length of wood stained black, longer than Gil was tall, with a sharp blade square in cross section like an awl or metal punch. He planted the butt of the weapon in the ground behind him and pointed the head at the steed. "I am tempted to yield to your steed, for it is his strength, not yours, I cannot overcome."

The steed said, "I thank you."

Gil said, "What is your name?"

The black knight said, "I will not tell my name."

Gil said, "I was not talking to you."

The steed said, "Rabicane am I called. Foal am I of Tencendur out of Llamrei. Born of hurricane and flame, I feed on wind and tread so lightly that I leave no footprint in the sand. The arrow from a Tartar's bow I can outpace."

"Who is this man I face?" asked Gil.

The black knight was jabbing the great red steed with his knees. "I said my name is not for you! Onward, my steed! What ails you?"

Gil said, "I told you I was not talking to you."

Rabicane said, "I know not his name."

Gil said, "Why do you serve an unknown master?"

The black knight said, "How– how could you know that? It is true I have never seen his face, but he is– wait. If you know who my master is, then why–? Settle down, boy! Stop neighing!"

Rabicane said, "Fetched here by words of power was I, song of elf and written rune. A faun told me that the Great God Pan required me to serve this knight."

Gil said, "Who raised you?"

The black knight said, "I was raised in a woods on the Isle of Man. Hold on there! Are you *talking* to my horse? Stop that!" He kicked the steed more forcefully and used his spurs. "Charge! Trample him!"

Rabicane said, "Aroint thee! I am *talking* here! Wait your turn!" Then, to Gil, he said, "By the hand of Duke Astolpho of the Paladin was I fed."

The black knight said, "It is an unknightly and unfair trick to bewitch my horse!"

Gil said, "Who is that?"

The black knight said, "My horse? Well, I don't know his name exactly—wait! Stop asking questions! I am about to trample you and cut you to bits!"

Rabicane said, "All men know the Paladin of Charlemagne! His blade is the one who drove back the Paynim and saved all Christendom."

Gil said, "I am in service to King Arthur, a Christian king who drove the pagans from England. Why do you serve Pan, a pagan god and a devil?"

The roan steed was startled. Nostrils and ears twitched. "From deep slumber under Mount Untersberg near Salzburg, I was called. My heart delights in battle and would not stand idle…. Should I dispute with Pan…?"

"The Great God Pan is dead, and the voices of his mourners were heard echoing from a rock in the sea. Pan cannot bind you. Do not serve this nameless knight! Should he not face me on foot, equal in weapons? Horses are said to be of all beasts the best friend of man."

Rabicane said doubtfully, "I heard tell that dogs are man's best friend."

Gil said, "Did the Lone Ranger have a dog? Did he ever say, *hi-yo, Spot*? I have a dog I love, but without a steed, a knight is nothing."

A voice at Gil's feet said, "Superboy had a dog. His name was Krypto."

6. Charadrius Vociferous

Gil moved his eyes without moving his head and saw a medium-sized plover of a breed called killdeer. The brown bird was nestled among the bright green weeds.

Gil said, "Charadrius, greetings and good afternoon to you. You can understand what that man is saying?"

The killdeer said, "What man?"

Gil was thunderstruck, and he laughed aloud. He realized why the rider's plume was green when every other part of his gear was black, "Do me a favor, and go pluck that green plume out of his helmet."

The black knight said, "Wait, are you talking to someone else now? How did you learn the Green Knight's tricks?"

The brown bird flew up. Gil picked up the lance and charged toward the horse and rider, roaring like a bear.

7. Second Charge

The black knight flourished his huge sword and black shield, crying out, "Charge! Charge my bold red steed—fear no spear of his–" Gil understood the words, but the sound of them coming from beneath the helm was "–*hween-neigh-hhhh! Hweeyaww!*"

For the killdeer had landed lightly on his helmet, taken the green plume neatly in her beak, plucked it out, and flown off. The human voice stopped, and a horse's whinny and neigh echoed from the black helm.

Gil cried, "Rabicane! You are deceived! That is no man on you! No son of Adam, he! Should one who bore the valiant Astolpho, Paladin of Charlemagne, carry some unbaptized creature on his back?"

Rabicane reared and bucked. The rider kept his saddle, which had both high pommel and high back, but Gil ran at him with the lance and struck him such a blow that the black knight tumbled to the ground astonished.

Gil ran to the black knight, who was moving his legs feebly and nickering. The black knight raised his boot and kicked at Gil with such force that the lance was snapped in half. Gil was half-dazed by the force of the kick—no human leg could have delivered such a blow—but he had wit enough to step on the man's sword, pinning the black blade to the ground. The black knight tugged on the blade with fierce strength but at such an angle the blade was not meant to take. The tang broke in two with a metallic snap of noise. The black knight, neighing in triumph, raised the blade while Gil staggered back, but then, comically, the heavy blade rattled and fell to the green weeds, and the hilt and handle and pommel all came free in the black knight's fist.

But before Gil could regain his footing on the slippery weeds, the supine black knight kicked Gil's legs out from under him. Gil contrived to fall atop the man, driving an elbow into his neckpiece. The two rolled on the ground, grappling. When the creature raised a foot to kick, Gil took him by the back of the neck and the back of the leg and forced the two together, as if trying to shove the black knight's knee up his black nose.

A strap broke. The black knight's boot and greave came free of his left foot. The left boot was filled with a glittering white sand or paste Gil had seen before.

But the leg that came out and flailed in the air was a horse's leg, and suddenly Gil's grip was not at the weakest part of the leg, the hamstring, but the strongest, the kneecap. The horse-legged black knight broke Gil's grip easily, but could not rise, for now the two legs were uneven. He tried to rise, but he fell, and Gil drove the point of his shield between the shield straps and the black shield, pinioning his arm.

The creature had a kick that could break a man's spine, but Gil had practiced wrestling stronger foes many times in the past year. Another moment or two of scrambling and panting, and Gil was behind him and had the black knight in a neat half-nelson. The shoulder armor prevented the black knight's arm from being broken in this grip, but Gil could hold his opponent motionless, despite the black knight being as strong as a horse, for Gil had leverage.

Gil undid the creature's chin-strap with his free hand and jerked the helm from his head. The inside of the helm was also coated with the same glittering pale cream, like a white molasses made of sparks of light.

The nose and face and head that emerged from the black gorget of the black knight were a horse's. His pointed ears stood up in surprise.

8. The Pook of Glen Meay

Rabicane trotted up. "I had a horse riding me? Another horse? Let go of him. Let me kick and nip him to death. I am the king stallion here!"

"I think it is a glashan," Gil said to Rabicane. To the black knight, he said, "I sat next to one of your cousins at the elfin feast last year."

The other grunted, "If I am a glashan, then your mother's a harlot."

Gil bit his horse ear right in the most sensitive and thin part, but the horse-creature shrieked, "I yield! I give! I surrender, Sir Knight!"

"What was that about my mother?"

"I was just checking to see if you could understand me without my talking cap."

"Why shouldn't I understand you?"

"Pooks and fauns usually cannot be seen or heard by men. Not without a cap."

"Why do you say I am a man?" said Gil.

"You speak with the authority of a Son of Adam. The steed obeys you. The bird did your work. Is she going to use my plume to feather her nest? That could turn out badly. Eggs raised in such nests hatch out magpies or parrots. Do you accept my surrender?"

"Your name?"

"Name have I none. I am the Cabyll-ushtey of Glen Meay and no glashan. Bah!"

"What is the difference?"

"Glashan are Irish! I am Manx. Horrible creatures, the Irish! Boasters and liars!"

"My dog is Irish."

"Except for him... of course... wonderful fellow, your dog..."

"Why do you have no name?"

"No Son of Adam has given me one."

"Your name is Mr. Ed."

"What? No, that's terrible. What about Thunderball Blackstrike?"

"Ed."

"... Or Doomshadow von Stormhoof the Magniloquent...?"

"Ed! Count yourself lucky I did not name you Puddles Pickledrip."

"I am thankful, noble and gracious lord, but I now see why the elfs want for themselves the crown Adam dropped."

"Who posted you here?"

"I was brought over to the New World by Lord Simcoe, who fell into the practice of black magic many years ago and was fed into the fires in the place of the elf who served him as fetch and familiar. I do not know whom I serve now; I have never seen his face. He bade me used the Carabas charm to hide my legs and face and to fend off all comers summoned by the Green Knight to their doom."

"Carabas? What is that?"

The creature pointed at the gleaming white paste coating the inside of his helmet and boots. "This was developed long ago by the Marquis of Carabas so that his cat could walk on his hind legs and dance the jig. One can put a hoof or snout, large or small, into a glove or boot or hat of any size, and all will fit and move as it should. The white alchemy holds the limb, and you move it, and the thing moves as if it were human."

"How do you fit such a big head into such a small helm?"

"It is elfish. Big and small are slippery concepts with them."

"If you are not a knight, how were you able to keep true knights away?"

"Location, location, location!"

"What?"

"Oak is my friend, and my black lance was oak, and this mistletoe weed underfoot was conjured by oakwood nymphs to coat this hill. My skill at joust and blade is not great, but any who comes ahorse will trip on the weeds whereas this red steed is surefooted; any who comes afoot, I run down and trample. But now you have broken my black lance and my great black sword. With what can I ransom my life? I have no other treasures."

"No crock of gold?"

"Am I a leprechaun? I never knew why they are so wealthy until I had to buy this dratted pair of boots from one of them. That leprechaun has all my gold!"

Gil looked at the glittering paste again. It seemed to be made of liquid diamond. The cabyll-ushtey was still talking. "That dratted leprechaun charged me an arm and a leg! I used to have three of each, you know."

"Any food or provision in the stronghouse?"

"I crop the grass and eat the same hay as the red steed, when he is not looking."

"Very well. I grant you your life on two conditions: first, that you give me Rabicane your steed, along with all his tack and gear."

"Done!"

"Second, that you turn yourself in to the mercy of Alberec, King of the Summer Elfs, and tell him that you were overcome by the Swan Knight, whom you failed to bar from seeking the Green Chapel."

"Done! But how shall I pass by the Anishinaabeg? They are no friends of the knights and marchwardens."

Gil released the creature and stood. "That you must discover yourself. It is not my doing that you live in a dangerous land."

Mr. Ed said, "I am a water horse and can pass unseen among them if I am allowed."

Gil said, "Are you asking my permission?"

The cabyll-ushtey nodded its horse head. "You are my master now, Swan Knight, not the magician who called me and set me here."

Gil said, "You may cast your charms and glamour to save your life or the life of another, but not for gain or pleasure or malice, nor may you play tricks on any baptized Christian or his children, nor harass nor harm nor annoy."

The ears of Mr. Ed twitched. "What of infidels? May I bedevil them as I like?"

"And become a devil yourself? It would be wiser to use your powers to do good and become a saint instead."

The creature merely laughed at that. "Well, well, if Ysbadden the King of Giants is agreeable, perhaps I would be as well, but what you seek is impossible, my new nameless master. Yonder stand the stairs leading to your death. Where in that upper land the chapel hides, no one says. Perhaps no one knows. I have never seen anyone, elf or man, come down those stairs again, save those who rejoiced at not finding any sign of the dread chapel. Tomorrow is Christmas Eve. This is your last sunset."

Gil felt a pang. While he had more questions for this creature, he did not know how much time was left. And the prospect of being dead before tomorrow night sapped his curiosity about this world and its miseries.

He wished he had a sword or lance to carry, but there was none to be had. Gil did not bother even to inspect the stronghouse.

Gil mounted Rabicane and bade him climb the giant stair.

Rabicane said, "You do not fear to ride me? Then are you a good knight, bold, true to your lord, and no dastard?"

"Serve me, and see."

They reached the lowest stair. Rabicane paused, gathered his legs beneath him like a cat readying to pouch, and leaped upward.

Gil laughed and whooped like a maniac, for the fairy steed was indeed fast as an arrow and agile as an acrobat. Rabicane shot up the giant steps at two hundred miles an hour, bounding in immense leaps from rock to rock, traveling almost straight up, and the cloak and plume Gil wore, his belts and empty scabbard, and the skirts of the steed's caparison hung streaming behind them in the wind like wings.

Chapter 5

The House of Hospitality

1. The Upper World

As they mounted the stairs, the cliff grew taller. The cliff had seemed perhaps fifty feet tall when looking up from the bottom, no taller than a four-story building. But as Rabicane leaped from one stone landing to the next, up switchback after switchback of stairs built for some race taller than man, the cliff seemed to rise and become larger. Clouds hung against its side, as if against the side of a mountain.

Going upward through the clouds, Rabicane was more cautious, leaping only nine yards at a footstep, not a hundred, for the cloud was a fog bank around them. When they emerged from the top, the air was warm and pure. Gil heard a strange, pure, lingering note as if from a harp with crystal strings echoing down from the wide blue sky above.

At the top of the stairs were two white columns of stone, cracked and dull with age, and the bolts and hinges of some great gates that had once been there hung from the upper and lower parts of the column. Rabicane trotted over the threshold, blowing, sides heaving, head erect and proud.

They stood atop a wall twenty yards wide. On the far side of the wall, three giant steps led down to a green field.

Gil said, "Well done, Rabicane. This was some elfish trick, I assume. It would have taken me forever to climb those stairs!" He looked out and saw from the Great Lakes to the Atlantic Ocean. He saw the curve of the Earth as a blue line of haze tracing the horizon.

"This is not normal," said Gil. "But my eyes are immune from deception. So this has to be real."

Rabicane said, "Time and distance bend for elfs, but not for men. Whither away?"

Gil said, "I was hoping for some bird or beast to tell me." He turned and looked.

Gil could not make sense of the countryside. He saw patches of snow here and there on the ground, and granite outcroppings pale with frost, and the air was sharp with chill; but the tableland was green with summery grass, spangled with small white flowers of a kind Gil did not recognize. Copses of small fruit trees, white with the blossoms of early spring, climbed in gentle hills toward a distant cliff, as gray and stern as the one they had just climbed. There was not a bird in the air, not so much as a rustle in the grass.

Rabicane said, "I am a beast. Ask me."

Gil said, "What is this place? What season is this?"

Rabicane said, "Duke Astolpho once flew to the Moon, where all ghosts and lost things hide, to find the scattered wits of Roland when Roland was mad. He passed through this region. We are above the height where seasons hold sway."

Gil said, "We cannot be in outer space. It would be vacuum."

Rabicane said, "Vacuum no doubt in places where no spirits of the air, no sylph, has thickened the aether and make it wholesome to breathe. How else could the Vanir ride their chariots to Venus for their hunts, or Carter and his sons be brought alive to Mars to fight the beside the Hrossa and Seroni against the Thither Folk, Tharks, and Argzoon?"

Gil said, "A mermaid told me once that Mars and Venus were dead, inhabited by the ghosts of evil beings."

"For all parts men can reach, she speaks true. But there is a third hemisphere to Mars also, and to Venus, just as this world, and many hemispheres reaching out from Jupiter and Saturn into many realms and dimensions, and living things hide there, unseen. You believe in elfs, do you not?"

Gil said, "Look, I have seen elfs. But Martians? Come on."

"Atop a Brobdingnagian pile taller than all mountains is not the place to stand, youth, if you wish your skepticism toward unknown wonders to provoke no laughter! Have you counted every star, and know each mystery creation hides, and therefore know what cannot be? My master flew to the moon on the same hippogriff that carried Lessingham to Mercury. Would you call a Duke a liar?"

Gil felt bad being rebuked by a horse. "So where are we now?"

"Ontario. This is merely a place whose roof is in the upper airs. There be a dozen such on Earth: Olympus and Othrys, Helicon and Helgafell, K'un-Lun and Nandaparbat, Shangrila and Sumaru, Mount Athos and Mount Graham, and Uluru, the accursed rock where dwells the Serpent Being. The great southern mountain in the hemisphere of ghosts which Dante climbed is the tallest, but greater hands than those of Brobdingnag wrought there. The elfs hide the upper reaches of such high places, above the seasons, as they wanted to hide Tahiti so that man would not see and smell and know such kindly weather and good air and remember Eden."

"The air here is cold."

"It is not natural for this elevation, but a curse. Someone seeks to hinder your way."

"Is this the air that strengthens eyesight?"

"Not so. That is from higher yet, if Astolpho told true and I recall aright. Those peaks are shorn from their roots and are as mountains above all clouds."

"What prevents them from falling?"

"What prevents the orbicular Earth from falling? Horses do not fret about such questions or answer them."

"What is that noise? It sounds like ringing chimes."

Rabicane said, "Perhaps it is the turning of the crystals spheres of Heaven! Astolpho told me of it."

Gil felt that very strange moment experienced only by certain scientists or prophets or poets who unexpectedly discover that the shape of the universe is like nothing they had previously believed. But then he said, "No, I think it is the sound of water flowing. The top of the waterfall is near. Let's head that way."

Rabicane leaped the twenty feet to the green grass. The moment his hoof touched the grass, the warm, fresh air turned cold and bitter, as if he had fallen into a meat locker. It was still fresh and pure in his nostrils and lungs, like air that had never known the touch of pollution, but now bitterly cold.

Rabicane thundered across the lawns. It had taken hours for Gil to walk and stalk across a hilly country from the foot of the waterfall to the foot of the stair. For Rabicane to cross green turf as flat as a park meadow took moments. The stream passed between two statues, moss-grown and weathered with age, depicting squat beings with heavy heads in postures of despair. The huge wall ringing this upper landscape grew out of the spine of the two statues. The water ran past their feet and flung itself into the air and down into an abyss of clouds.

The water here was white and swift, running between banks of set stone. There were no fish here, no one Gil could question, or, for that matter, eat. His stomach rumbled querulously.

"I hope he offers me one last meal," he said. Then, "Let us try going upstream!"

Rabicane looked at the stream and snuffled in his nostrils. "I see no stream."

"This creek, or whatever you want to call it. If the Green Knight drinks or takes baths or washes anything, he should be within walking distance of fresh water."

Rabicane cantered along the side of the flowing water. In the distance were gray cliffs.

2. Upriver

Hours passed. The sun was in the west and below the lip of the upper meadowlands. There were no clouds above, but the sky was the deep purple that only astronauts or high-flying pilots saw.

Gil said aloud, "I don't get it. This cannot be an illusion, but it cannot be the truth either. No mountain along the East Coast reaches such elevations, and I doubt even the highest peak in the Rockies or the Andes could either. This must be some parallel dimension or something."

Rabicane said, "No mountain this."

"Then what it is?"

"A tower, as I said."

"What?"

The steed snorted. "Saw you not the cyclopean blocks in the wall as we passed up the stair? From the feel under my hoof, I know that under this soil is roof, not bedrock. This is but a rooftop garden. That which you called a stream is a gutter. This pile was built by the Sons of Brobdingnag."

Gil said, "Then is this whole place the Green Chapel? Are we on the roof?" He looked at the cliffs in the distance ahead of them, which, now that he knew what he was looking at, seemed very much like a wall with crenelated battlements, more imposing than the Great Wall of China, old and sagging in places and overgrown with trees and bushes that hid the straight lines and sharp angles of craftsmanship. He said, "Or is that the roof? Maybe we should head there."

Rabicane said, "Sunset is soon. Even I, with my great speed, could not reach there before dusk, nor am I sure of foot enough to climb such a wall in the dark of night. It will also grow as we try to climb; this is the nature of the masonworks of Brobdingnag."

"Where to then? I have only today and tomorrow to find the guy who is going to cut off my head. So we need to hurry. It is as if the Green Knight was trying to make this hard!"

Rabicane said, "I scent woodsmoke and meat frying. Someone beyond those trees is camped."

It was true. Gil spied a thin trickle of smoke rising against the purple sky.

Rabicane now broke into a trot, which was faster than the gallop of even prizewinning mortal horses. The green lawns and their many bright star-shaped flowers flew past under his hooves. Gil was delighted with the motion and the speed, and he laughed.

3. Red Light

The landscape fled by like a green army rushing backward. Gil still could not understand how he could be seeing cherry trees in blossom but be feeling the bite of the winter wind on his cheek.

Rabicane slowed down suddenly to a canter, and then a walk. The sky was darker now, though it was not yet night. Rabicane stopped at a large upright stone next to the river, marked with the image of a wheel with four spokes.

"Hist!" said Rabicane. "I spy a light. Could that be the chapel?"

Through the trees shined a light, but what he saw was not firelight or lamplight. It was bright, harsh, and garish, and as red as fresh lipstick: it was neon light.

Gil said, "I've never seen a church decked out with flashy neon lights. This could be anything. Let's be careful."

Rabicane's deer-like hooves made little noise on the thick summery grass, and the hiss of the winter wind covered up the rustle of their approach.

The red light was coming from what looked like a drive-thru restaurant. It had a slanted red roof and an outdoor menu for in-car service, complete with microphone and service window, even though there was no road. There were plate glass windows bearing images of hamburgers and hotdogs, meatballs and fried food, cold soft drinks and foaming beer and rich milkshakes.

The neon sign read KNOCKERS.

Below that, a smaller sign read, *Open 24/7. Come In and Knock Back a Few!*

And an even smaller sign read, *Monday night is knight night. Knights eat free!*

Gil said, "I have gone mad."

4. Knockers

There were two waitresses in front of the door. In the gloom, it looked like they were doing some lascivious hip-shaking dance, but, as Rabicane stepped closer, it seemed each waitress was playing innocently with a hula-hoop, wiggling energetically to get the hoop to orbit her waist. The waitresses wore tiny lace hats. Their uniforms were black with a white apron, and left their arms and legs bare, and were adorned with bows at the décolletage and derriere.

Gil trotted up. The two girls squealed, and giggled, and clapped their hands, but never stopped the hip-rotation of the hula-hoops. The one of the left, a blonde, said, "Welcome! Welcome to Knockers! We will knock you out with our low prices."

Gil dismounted and threw his reins over the back of the brightly colored bench.

"Money I have none," said Gil. "May I speak with the master of this house?"

The one on the right, a redhead, said, "You are in luck. Knights eat free on Monday!"

Gil said, "Thank you, miss, but I am no knight. As a squire only I serve my king, this one last night of service."

The two hula hoop girls exchanged a knowing glance. Rabicane said softly, "They think you are an elf because you speak too politely and clearly to be human."

Gil said, "I have heard elf food is venomous and addictive."

Both girls laughed, and the redhead said, "Our fare meets all health regulation standards!"

Rabicane said, "Modest elf maidens would not behave so. These may be nymphs, summoned from the dreams of sleeping streams and meadows by a conjurer's strange song."

Gil said, "How can I tell?"

The blonde one (still shaking her hula hoop round and round) called out, "You cannot tell until you taste and know! Our fare is the finest in the land!"

The redhead called, "It will knock you out!"

Rabicane said, "Inquire of their names. If these are nymphs, they have no names until a human poet grants them one."

Sliding glass doors opened, and a shapely brunette, dressed like the others, strode out the door. Her hair was piled atop her head in a bun or beehive, and she had a pair of eyeglasses shaped like half-moons perched on her nose.

She tilted back her head to look down her nose through her eyeglasses. "I am the hostess here, and I will be serving all your needs this evening. Did you say you wanted to see the manager?"

Gil said, "I seek the Green Knight of the Green Chapel."

Now her head tilted forward so that she could stare over the tops of her glasses. "Well, you really do have to talk to the manager then. This way!"

And she sidled up to him and put her arm through his elbow even though Gil did not need help walking. And he wanted to detangle his arm from his woman, but he did not want to be rude. And it is pleasant to walk with a pleasant-looking woman on one's arm.

The lights within were dim, and the tables seemed mostly unoccupied. The one or two figures he saw sitting at the bar or at a table were young women, dressed in evening gowns, toying with cocktails or smoking cigarettes, looking wistful. To one side were a row of slot machines and pinball tables. In the back was a pool table where two young women dressed as airline stewardesses in mini-skirts were playing pool. A row of booths was to one side.

Gil and the hostess halted at a walk-in closet with a Dutch door. Only the bottom half of the door was shut. Here was a young lady dressed in a top hat and white bow-tie. "Check your armor, sir?"

Gil did not protest as the hostess and the hat check girl helped him out of his helm and armor. The girls carefully hung the mail habergeon on a coat rack and put the plumed helm on a high shelf. "We'll have everything cleaned and burnished before you are ready to leave! I see you have a diamond missing on your neckpiece. We will have a jeweler replace that, lickety-split!"

Gil said, "Well, I…"

The hostess took his arm again, "Don't worry. There is no extra charge. Tailoring, mending, and minor blacksmith repairs are part of the service."

Gil was now dressed in a linen tunic, leather britches, wooden stockings, and black knee-high boots with silver metal shin-guards. The blue surcoat adorned with the image of the silver swan was over all and hung to his knees. His arms were free. Without the weight of the armor, with his arms bare, he felt strangely light and free, half-naked, and almost lightheaded.

Gil said, "If you can just show me to the kitchen, I was thinking I could wash dishes or something. I am very hungry… or maybe a booth in a corner… I am not sure if I, ah…"

The hostess led him to a small table in the middle of the floor, where most of the lights were. The hostess held the chair for him and practically shoved Gil into it.

"Now!" she said brightly, leaning over the table. "What can I get you to drink? We don't card here."

"I am underage," said Gil.

"No, I mean here in Canada, the drinking age is fourteen. Because we're French."

Gil said, "You don't sound French."

"Oo-la-la!"

Gil blinked. "Um, I wanted to ask the manager if, ah…"

A cocktail waitress with honey blonde hair came to the table. She had a silver tray in hand and a mixed drink on it, which she proffered with a flourish.

Gil said, "Miss, I did not order…"

This cocktail waitress said, "The young lady at the bar sends it."

A lady in an emerald silk dress at the bar wiggled her fingers at him in playful greeting. Gil was not sure, but this girl seemed to be the same redhead he had seen outside, playing hula-hoop.

The hostess put her hand on Gil's shoulder, and leaned closer, and whispered, "We Frenchwomen regard it as a terrible insult not to drink when a lady buys!"

Gil said, "I mean no insult. Please explain to the lady that I cannot accept her gift, as I have sworn to drink no wine nor spirits during Advent."

The hostess said, "What is Advent?"

"Four weeks before Christmas. Please, may I see the manager?"

A brunette waitress swayed up to the table and smiled warmly at him. "Would you like to see our menu? Tonight is meat lover's night."

Gil took the menu.

This was a steakhouse. In addition to various cuts of steaks, and spare ribs, and barbecues, and shish-kabobs, there were hamburgers, double-decker hamburgers, triple-decker hamburgers, meatball-burgers, chili-burgers, all-meat chili, chili con carne, chili with meat, and chili with meatballs. They also served fried chicken, grilled chicken, chicken and steak, steak strips, chicken-fried steak, more steak, and another kind of steak.

The special "Chanukah menu" offered various cuts of ham, grilled ham, stuffed ham, pork-hamburgers, ham-hamburgers, chicken tenders wrapped in bacon, and ham wrapped in bacon.

Wine and beer were on the menu, but no soft drinks.

His stomach rumbled, and he asked for a steak and a soda, and the brunette waitress winked at him and skipped away, her fanny bow bouncing cheerily.

5. The Manager

A very tall and muscular man, built like a weightlifter, now came walking across the floor toward Gil's table. The man had a cheerful way of walking. He bounced at every step, as if bursting with energy. His eyes were dancing, he was snapping his fingers, and his grin was infectious.

He was dressed in a dark blue pinstriped suit with a yellow tie decorated with small black dots. On his nose were perched horn-rimmed round glasses of yellow glass that made his pupils seem yellow. On his head was an old fashioned hat, a fedora. Gil thought he looked like Clark Kent.

The man took a chair by the back, tilted it so that it rested on one leg, and spun the chair on that leg like a top. While it was spinning, the huge man leaped into the air and landed on the chair with a great noise. Now he was seated backward on the chair, facing Gil, straddling the chair, with the chair back tucked under his armpits.

"My name is Mr. Bredbeddle!" he said.

He had an odd way of smiling with his teeth parted. He thrust out his hand. Gil shook it. The man had a firm grip and an energetic handshake. The man had calluses in the places on the fingers years of sword practice would cause.

Gil wanted to stand up to greet him, but the hostess and the honey-blonde cocktail waitress had both draped their arms casually across his shoulders and were standing too close, brushing up against him, and he was sure it would be impolite to shoo them away.

"I am the manager here!" Bredbeddle boomed. "Here at Knockers, we have but one motto: We will *knock* your troubles away! Our drinks will *knock* some sense right out of you! We will *knock* our prices down! Our doors are so open you need never *knock*! We aim to please, and our arrows are *nocked*! We have the same enemy, the state, as Albert J. *Nock*! Our girls have the biggest…"

Gil said, "Are you Man or Elf?"

Mr. Bredbeddle threw back his head and laughed as if Gil had made a joke. "We take all kinds and all comers here. Our doors are so open you need never... Wait. Did I say that one already? Our girls are *knock*-outs! They are *noct*urnal! We have but one motto: *Our guests are our guests!*" He laid a finger the size of a sausage aside his nose and nodded at Gil, winking. "This is a tautology, therefore true."

"I have no cash. I could wash dishes, or..."

Mr. Bredbeddle waved a huge hand in the air as if brushing away a fly. "One of the young ladies at the bar has already paid for your meal." He turned and pointed. The same blonde who had been twirling a hula-hoop outside the door was now dressed in a sheer silk dress and smoking a cigarette in a long holder. She now wore a sultry look and a different hairstyle. She gave Gil an enigmatic smile over the rim of her wine glass.

Gil said, "No, I cannot accept charity from a lady."

"That is actually my younger sister. She needs a date for the prom because her last boyfriend dumped her and ran off with the parlor maid to Patagonia."

Gil said, "What's her name?"

"Um. Her name is... Her name is... Younger Sister is her name."

Gil shook his head. "Oh, come on. That cannot be her name."

"Younger Sister Bredbeddle! We call her Y.S. for short!"

"That is a little hard to believe."

Bredbeddle said, "Mom was exhausted giving birth to hecatotuplets and kind of ran out of names. She was in labor for over four years straight from first to last. Can you believe it?"

"It is truly a remarkable tale," said Gil dryly. "What is your mother's name?"

"Her name...? Her name...? Mrs. Bredbeddle, of course!"

"Of course."

"So my younger sister is really broken up about being dumped. She would be humiliated in front of the whole school if she does not get a prom date...."

"I really am not in a position to take anyone anywhere, I am afraid."

"I should explain that my sister made a rash vow that if she could not find a date for the prom, she would join a nunnery. So if you don't ask her out, she will be called 'Sister Sister' for the rest of her life. You can see why that would be humiliating."

Bredbeddle waved at the blonde. The girl in the silk dress sashayed over to the table. Gil was embarrassed when she knelt to him, and twined her shapely arms around his leg, and put her head on his knee, looking up at him with piteous doe-like eyes.

Gil said, "Please stand up, miss. I cannot go to any proms with anyone. I am only here this evening."

The beautiful blonde did not answer, except to smile winsomely.

Bredbeddle said, "Well, fortunately, the school decided to hold the prom right here! We have a ballroom just beyond the gambling parlor, on the far side of the heated all-night swimming pool. There will also be a beauty contest and an all-you-can-drink wine tasting before, during, and after the dance!"

"Aren't proms always held in the spring?"

"Not in Michigan. It is too cold in the spring!"

"This is Canada, or so you said."

"My sister graduated early this year. They moved the prom, just for her."

Gil said, "What is the name of the school?"

"What school?"

"The one holding a prom in your ballroom tonight. Your younger sister's school."

"Um. It is called… It is called…Younger Sister's High School is what it is called."

Gil looked skeptical. "Come on."

"It's true! They named it after her. When they built it. YSHS for short."

Gil said, "No one names a school after a student who goes there."

"Well, they wanted to name it after me because I donated the money for the construction, but I thought it would sound absurd. You see, my first name is Smokedopenget. And I thought a school named Smokedopenget High would send a bad message to the young ones."

"Your mother named you *Smokedopenget*?"

"She was really, really tired after giving birth to me. She was pregnant for twenty-one years, and I was born fully armed and on my horse. So, about my younger sister. Isn't there a rule that knights have to be courteous? And come to the aid of damsels? I mean, it is not like I am asking you to do anything difficult. Dinner, drinks, a dance, a few more drinks, a little bit of snogging...."

Gil frowned, wondering if there were any merit to that argument. A little voice in his heart seemed to whisper that it would be perfectly all right to have a bit of dinner and a dance with a beautiful girl.

He ignored that little voice because a voice even softer voice reminded him who and what he was. Gil said sharply, "Please ask your sister to stand up. It would be wrong and false of me to court her. I am going to be beheaded tomorrow."

The several beautiful girls clustered around Gil cooed and sighed in surprise and dismay. Bredbeddle looked shocked. "What, really? That seems like bad news! Why? What did you do?"

"I gave my word," said Gil.

Mr. Bredbeddle said, "Is that all?"

Gil said grimly, "That was enough."

"Is your life worth so little?"

"Sir, it is not that my life is worth little. But my word is worth much."

Mr. Bredbeddle shook his head. "Well, no one can hold you to that! In the eyes of the law, no man can consent to his own murder, can he? So that makes it suicide! Which is a sin!"

Gil frowned. He was taken aback. It *did* seem an awful lot like suicide to walk toward his own beheading rather than run away, didn't it?

6. The Dish

At that moment, the steak arrived. It was sizzling hot from the kitchen and had been pan-seared in a pepper sauce. Gil's mouth started watering, and his stomach seemed to flip over for hunger.

The honey-blonde cocktail waitress had also gone to the bar and returned to the table, smiling. "And here is your gin and soda!"

Gil said, "No, I ordered a soda, soda. A soft drink."

The waitress looked troubled. "We cannot sell soft drinks to minors. It is one of our Canadian healthcare regulations. Can I bring you an Irish coffee? Or iced tea?"

"Iced tea, please… And…"

He took knife and fork in hand and leaned forward, but the little medal around his neck swung out and clinked against the side of the plate with a sharp, shrill chime of noise.

It was his Saint Christopher's medal. Saint Christopher himself had given it to him. It reminded him of the promise he had made to eat no meat and drink no wine before Christmas.

There was a sinking feeling in his heart. Never had he wanted a meal so badly as this one.

But he pushed the plate away. "Please take it back. I cannot eat it."

The two girls hovering over his shoulders both whispered in his ears. "That is really rude!" said one. And, "You cannot turn down a free meal!" said the other.

Gil ignored them and asked the brunette waitress, "Miss, is there a salad I could have?"

She smiled brightly. "We have our all-meat meatlover's salad, which is ham, pork, and bacon served with ground chuck, spicy meatballs, chicken salad, and cubes of steak fried in wine sauce."

"Never mind. Could you bring me a hamburger instead?"

Gil thought if he ordered a burger, he would put the meat paddy aside and eat the bun, lettuce, and tomato.

The girl smiled again and then scampered off into the kitchen. A moment later she was back. In her hand was a china plate, on top of which was a second, smaller plate made of metal. On this metal plate was a hamburger paddy, sizzling and crackling in its own juices, perfectly cooked and just the way Gil liked it.

Hamburgers were something of a treat for Gil since he and his mom almost never ate out even at fast-food joints. He really, really wanted to take a bite of the burger, just one bite. But instead he said, "Oh, miss! Isn't there a bun or anything? Where is the rest?"

The waitress said, "Well, too much starch is not good for growing boys. Canadian health authorities have outlawed buns for children. Here, we use two slices of breaded ham as the bun. Should I bring you some? The ham has sesame seeds on the top."

Gil winced, and wiped his mouth, and ignored the protests from his stomach, and somehow found the strength to push the plate away. "Please take it back, and just bring me a pickle and some dinner rolls. I am really very hungry."

The brunette waitress looked shocked. "No! I cannot take it back! The cook is very temperamental! She was very offended when you sent back the steak! If you send back the hamburger, too… why… why… she might flip out! Who knows what will happen then? I beg you, kind sir. Please don't make me!"

Gil started. "Miss, please don't…"

This waitress also knelt and grabbed his other knee. "I am so lonely! The cook might kill me if I bring the burger back! At least take a nibble!"

So now there were four beautiful women all around Gil, two at his shoulders and two at his knees, and their perfume was making his head spin.

Mr. Bredbeddle frowned. "I must say, son, I think the restaurant here has been very generous to you, giving you a free meal! Two free meals! You are being very picky."

All the beautiful waitresses and beautiful patrons in the restaurant cried out in loud but very sweet voices that Gil should not be so rude.

Gil stood up and disentangled himself from the lovely sister, the hostess, the cocktail waitress, and the other waitress. "I am sorry, and I wish not to offend anyone, but I cannot eat meat."

Bredbeddle said in astonishment, "No meat… forever?"

Gil said, "No meat until Christmas."

Bredbeddle rolled his eyes. "But you said you would be killed tomorrow! Tomorrow is Christmas Eve! If you don't have any meat now, you will never eat meat ever in your life! The condemned prisoner deserves a hearty meal, does he not? It is a tradition!"

Gil said, "Sir, it is not to be. Importune me no longer."

Yet another waitress came by, this one a dark-eyed olive-skinned beauty, and took Gil's arm, and put a drink into Gil's hand. "Your iced tea, sir!"

Gil was feeling rather hot and very flustered, so he raised the cool glass to his lips, but then his nose tingled. He sniffed. "Is this alcoholic?"

She said, "Long Island iced tea! Just take a sip. One sip."

"What is in it?"

The dark-eyed beauty said, "Vodka, gin, brandy, rum, and triple sec with one-and-a-half parts sour mix and a splash of cola."

"But there is no actual iced tea in this iced tea?"

She said, "If you have never tried it, how do you know if you will like it or not?"

He put the drink down on the table. "Please take it back and bring me a Coke."

The dark-eyed waitress looked frightened. "I cannot bring you a Coke!"

"How about a Pepsi?"

"Canadian health regulations don't allow us to serve oversized sugary drinks to minors! Didn't you hear about the health crisis?"

Gil said, "There is no way that is a real regulation!"

To his surprise and shock the dark-eyed waitress started blubbering and crying. "Please! You don't want to get me in trouble with the law!"

Bredbeddle handed Gil a handkerchief. "Are you just going to sit there and let her cry? That is not very chivalrous of you! Go ahead. Give her a hug. Go on!"

Gil hesitated for a long time because he really, really wanted to put his arms around the dark-eyed girl, who was breathtakingly attractive. She had the same hair color as Nerea, so dark it was almost blue. He stepped forward and touched the girl (who was facing away now) on one shaking shoulder.

She turned so suddenly that her long, fragrant locks dashed against his chest. By some mischance, the girl's hair struck the little glass bead hanging from the chain around his neck so that it flew up, and came back down again, and tapped him sharply just above the heart.

The glass bead was the one that held Nerea's hair, her token to him.

So Gil stepped back out of the girl's reach, and thrust out his hand, and shook the dark-eyed waitress's hand. "There, there!" He said. "Here is a handkerchief." He thrust the hanky into her surprised hand. "Stop crying. It is not very..." He meant to say something like "not very ladylike" or "not very pretty," but what came out of his mouth was "... not very convincing."

A hard hand fell on Gil's shoulder and spun him around.

Bredbeddle's eyes narrowed, and his color rose. The man seemed angry. "What kind of person are you? Coming into my restaurant and upsetting the staff! We gave you free food and free drinks and treated you like a king! And you won't give this poor crying dame a simple hug and a kiss on the cheek!"

Bredbeddle was taller than Gil by a head and half and broader at the shoulder.

Gil tried to keep his face a poker face, but a glint of eagerness escaped from his eyes nonetheless. He was curious how a battle with so tall and strong a foe might go. He stepped back, picked up the steak knife by his plate, fell into a crouch, and measured the distance to his foes with his eyes.

Bredbeddle let go of Gil's shoulder and stepped back out of knife range. Now he smiled again and spoke in a more soothing tone. He said, "Listen. I can see you are not the kind of man who can be pushed into doing anything you don't want to!"

Gil put the steak knife carefully back by the plate.

Bredbeddle smiled more broadly. "But what do you really want? I am not talking about you giving the girl a long, passionate kiss! Just a little friendly peck. On the lips. Following by a wild evening of heavy drinking, dancing, and wanton revelry. *What happens in Knockers stays in Knockers!* That is our one motto! Come on! She feels really lonely right now. Really kind of vulnerable. Just give her a little kiss behind the ear. Cheer her right up! Have you not vowed to help maidens and, uh, widows in distress?"

Gil at looked at the very young lady. "She's a widow?"

"Practically the same as! I did not want to tell you, but—her boyfriend just dumped her, and ran off with the parlor maid to Patagonia!"

Gil raised a skeptical eyebrow. "Really? What is her name?"

Bredbeddle blinked. "Um... um... Her name is... her name is... Knockers Waitress is her name."

"Is that the best you can come up with?"

"They, uh, named the restaurant after her."

"Who did?"

"The, uh, guy who owns this restaurant chain."

"And what is his name?"

"Um... um... He is called Mister... uh... Knockers."

"His first name?"

"Knickers."

Gil said slowly, "So this restaurant chain is owned by a Mr. Knickers Knockers?"

"It's an Irish name."

"I thought you said they named the restaurant after this waitress there?"

"Well, yes! Definitely! But her mother named her Knockers in honor of our owner, Mr. Kickers Knockers, on account of him being such a nice guy. In fact, all the girls here are named after him!"

"You did not say Kickers before. You said Knickers before. Like Kneepants. Don't you know the name of your own boss? That you work for?"

"Knickers Kickers Knockers. And he took the name Kanten as his saint's name at Confirmation."

Gil said slowly, "Knickers Kickers Kanten Knockers. Is that it?"

"Of Knochnasheega! That is it! Right proud of his name, he is! And why shouldn't he be? Now, he would not like it if we sent a customer away hungry, so please sit down again! Sit! Drink! Hey, you, Knockers Waitress! Bring us a pitcher of beer!"

"I am too young for alcohol."

"Not in here in France. The drinking age here is… twelve."

"It was fourteen before. And this is Canada."

"I mean the Canadian part of France, of course. Normandy."

Gil said, "Normandy is in real France."

"Or wherever. Who cares? Listen, friend… you know I have your best interests at heart. There are girls at the bar younger than you who can hold their liquor like sailors. You don't want to seem like some little kid to them? Aren't you all knightly and bold and brave and stuff? If today is your last day on Earth, why not try some earthly pleasures? You are never going to grow up and find out what you are missing."

7. Being Led

The girls tried to gently press him back into his seat, but Gil merely set his feet, stood his ground, and looked stubborn, and the six or eight cooing young women pushing and pulling on him had as much chance to move him as to move a boulder of granite.

Gil said, "I seek the Green Knight! Where is he?"

Bredbeddle said, "Ah! You are in luck. He comes here every few days. This is the only place you can find him! He wanders. We have beds in the back, plenty to eat, and plenty to drink. Games. Do you gamble? So you have to stay here to see him."

Gil said, "I must find him before tomorrow. That was the date set."

Bredbeddle spread his hands. "But listen! You looked, didn't you? You must have already come a far way, right? What more can he expect you to do? If he did not tell you where to go, you have to stay here. There is a dance contest later. And a hot tub. Mandatory for all guests. Health regulations, you know. Nothing we can do. But unfortunately, we are overcrowded right now, so you have to…"

Gil said, "I have to do nothing but keep my word. The Green Knight said that if I sought him, I would be led."

Bredbeddle smashed his fist on the table so that all the silverware jumped. "But why do you trust him? How do you know you are not led here, to have a comfortable night in a comfy bed, a filling and rich steak dinner, spirits as fine as what Mahound quaffs in paradise, and the fairest of companions to warm your loneliness? Maybe you were led here! Don't you want to live?"

Gil gritted his teeth. "I want to live…."

"Aha!" Bredbeddle smiled.

"… I want to live like a knight!"

"Oh." Bredbeddle scowled.

"The Green Knight said that if I gave up or tarried while seeking him, I was foresworn. I lost two or three days when I went ashore and hid from hunters who drove me into the mountains, but that was not my doing, so it is not on me. But if I stay here even another moment, it will be lingering, it will be my doing, and I will have broken my word. So I thank you for your hospitality, which has been remarkable and generous. Too generous. But I must be on my way."

Bredbeddle said, "I tell you, in this house alone will you see the Green Knight! He wanders whither he will, and his steed, Vertifran, is swifter than the sound of the shockwave he sheds as he passes and can put a girdle round the globe in forty minutes. No one can say where the Green Knight goes one hour to the next!"

Gil said, "And the Green Chapel? Unless it is on legs, you can tell me where it is."

Bredbeddle said, "Its portals are locked and guarded by the three-headed hound of Hell itself. No mortal man enters or departs save he that dies!"

"Where?"

Bredbeddle sighed and said, "The stream that runs by this house comes from the fountain that springs up from the threshold stone of the doors of the Green Chapel, for it was there that the most sorrowful stroke that was ever struck was struck, and the waters came up to soothe the wound that no earthly leech can heal."

Gil stood. He looked longingly at the hamburger and the steak.

Bredbeddle said, "You want a doggy bag? You can nibble on it when no one is looking…."

Gil said, "It would be rude of me to refuse so generous a host, good sir."

One of the waitresses wrapped the steak and the burger patty in tinfoil, along with a napkin, silverware, and a brass flagon of Long Island iced tea. He bade his farewell to the waitresses, the hostess, the cook, the sister, the cocktail waitress, and the other lovely young creatures.

Whenever any girl tried to step too close to give him a farewell kiss before his untimely death, he held up the amber bead he carried, and the girl would shrink back, alarmed. It worked like a charm. For all he knew, it was.

He could not stop the three pretty girls who helped him on with his armor, which, as promised, had been burnished and polished and reset with any missing gem of diamond or jacinth.

He went back out into the strange landscape of early spring buds, long summer grass, and biting winter wind. Under one arm was a paper bag with the uneaten meal in it.

Rabicane gave him a sardonic look. "Well? Find out anything?"

Gil said, "We go upstream."

Chapter 6

The Doors No Mortals Pass

1. A Change of Season

At two hundred miles an hour, Gil should have been able to cover three days' travel in thirty minutes. But hours passed as the steed alternated between gallop, canter, and walk. Gil wondered if time were passing normally. He could smell the untouched steak wrapped and packed in his saddlebag, or he imagined he could.

Eventually, Rabicane slowed and halted. "This is a Brobdingnag trick. They have placed their distance-warping stones sidewise in the road to keep the wall an ever greater distance from us. It can only be approached slowly."

Gil said, "No doubt to give anyone attempting to reach the chapel plenty of time to change his mind. I wish I could find out why people are so afraid of it." Then, he closed his mouth and looked around warily, remembering folk tales of people who uttered unguarded wishes in unearthly places.

Despite the cold and his own hunger, Gil took the time to curry Rabicane. There were brushes in the saddlebags, a small and soft one for the face, and a larger one for the body. He was not sure whether to use the winter brush or the summer brush. He tried both, asking Rabicane which he preferred, and being careful around spots where Rabicane said he was ticklish. He picked out the hooves. The black silk caparison was uselessly thin in this weather. Gil threw his heavy silvery mantle over Rabicane.

The night was cold and cheerless. The grass was warm and smelled of summer sunlight, which only made the benumbingly cold wind worse.

Gil lay there, shivering. There was a stir of motion. Rabicane, without saying a word, knelt and rolled, and came to lay on his side, blocking the worst of the wind. Gil huddled up to the great beast's spine for warmth.

In the morning, the landscape had changed. Now the ground was covered with snow as far as the eye could see. The air was now warm and smelled of spring. The trees were covered with the many colored leaves of fall, but Gil, looking for any fruit among their branches, saw tiny knobs of green, unripe fruit, inedible.

The gray walls of the cliff were now close at hand, a bowshot away, or less.

Unlike the outer wall, this one clearly showed the outline of titanic blocks, each the size of an ocean liner, that had been cut and piled one atop the other course by course to raise the immense wall. The cyclopean blocks were fitted so tightly together, Gil saw there was no purchase for seeds nor weeds to take root, yet he saw no trace of mortar.

In the wall rose a pointed arch some forty feet high. It was not a gate, for there was no light on the other side. A tunnel forty feet high drove back into the cliff rock, heading downward.

Rabicane said, "Saddle up."

Gil said, "The door is a hundred yards away. I can walk there."

Rabicane said, "But can you walk away? You may need to run. This place is unchancy. I like not its smell."

Gil decided that a horse ridden by a duke of Charlemagne probably knew the proper habits for knights. Even though his goal was only a short walk away, Gil took the trouble to curry out the grass and snowy slush clinging to the horse's coat.

Gil did not bother with bridle and bit, but merely looped a hackamore around Rabicane's nose. "I appreciate the kindness, master," said the steed, "But I have a bit of a temper. Are you sure?"

Gil said, "When you no longer serve me of your own free will, I am no longer deserving of your service."

Rabicane made a skeptical snort. "Is this a colonial thing? Giving your beasts of war a vote? Lord Simcoe made a great point of keeping the aristocracy intact so that masters rule and servants serve!"

Gil said, "I was taught that the first shall be last and that the servant is not greater than the master."

They approached the archway. The sun was on the far side of these tall cliffs, making their whole face a shadow, which seemed doubly dark compared with the dazzle from the snowy ground.

At the foot of the archway was a great marble slab of a threshold stone. Gil saw the crack from which the waters poured. A spear had been jammed into the crack as if someone had meant to pry it open. Half the spear was iron; half was wood. The head was a long, square blade red with fresh blood. Gil saw droplets of blood falling into the rush of water and being carried downstream so that the first foot of the stream was dark pink, the next foot or so light pink, and beyond that the agitation of the water rushing over the stones of the streambed hid any sign of the contamination.

On the white stone beyond the spear, someone had laid a red cloth. In the middle of the cloth was a circle of green, a wreath woven of pine and adorned with holly, lying like an empty dinner plate. There were four candles in the wreath, equally spaced about the circumference, lit and burning: three purple candles and one pink candle. A white candle, taller and fatter, was in the center of the wreath, unlit.

To one side stood a golden cup. To the other, a loaf of bread.

Gil said, "What does it mean?"

From the darkness of the tunnel beyond the tall arch now shined a pair of green eyes. A deep growl trembled through earth and air. A second pair of eyes, green as poison, opened a yard to the left. Then, a third pair opened up, a yard to the right. Six eyes gleamed menacingly at Gil.

2. Watchdog

A breathy, growling voice issued from the darkness where the central eyes glinted. "Had you not asked of the mystery, your worthless throat would have been torn out already."

A second voice, twin to the first, spoke from the left. "You spoke of the first being last. For this reason, I have not already disemboweled you."

A third voice spoke, "No elf passes this door but that he dies, nor any mortal man, who are born once and then perish."

There came a slithering, massive sound, and Gil saw the muzzle and head of a monstrous dog emerge from the shadows. The distance between his ears was greater than Gil's outstretched arms, and the red mouth was so huge that Rabicane could have been swallowed by those jaws in two bites, Gil in one.

Gil glanced down at his empty scabbard. It was still empty.

When he looked up, he saw the second and third heads emerge from the shadows, and each one seemed larger than the one next to it.

Gil dismounted. He squinted at the three giant dog heads, and took his shield from the saddle bow, and slung it before him. He took up his helm with his right hand and stuffed his head quickly into it while muttering, "Please have three bodies. Please have three bodies...."

But when the eyeslits of his helm fell in place before his eyes, the monster had emerged, and there was but one body. The three necks were longer than they should have been for a wolf, giving it a freakish, disproportionate look. Fortunately, there was a chain around the neck of the middle head.

Gil groaned in disappointment. He and wolves tended to get along. He was not so sure about monsters.

The monster said, "Who are you?"

Gil said, "I am called the Swan Knight. Who are you?"

The monster shook its three heads. From the thick wolf mane coating its three necks and complex shoulders now rose dozens of spotted snakes, their eyes as green as emeralds, tasting the air with their forked tongues. They danced and swayed with a hypnotic motion, two scores of them or more, curling and uncurling restlessly. The patterns of scales on their backs were as bright as enameled mosaics.

Rabicane was trembling. "The snakes with bright colors are bad."

"Cerberus, call me," said the middle head.

"... the son of Typhon," said the left head.

"... the son of Echidna," said the right head.

Gil said, "Pardon me, and meaning no disrespect, is that one long name for the three of you, or does each head have its own name, or how exactly does this work?"

Rabicane nudged him in the shoulder with a nose, saying, "Mount up, and let's get out of here!"

Gil said, "You go. Save yourself. I am staying."

Rabicane shivered and snorted, dancing restlessly, but he did not run.

Gil said, "I seek the Green Chapel."

The monster said, "Then you seek death."

Gil said, "Will you let me in?"

The three heads laughed a horrible, creaking, croaking laugh which sounded like choking, and all the snakes twining and writhing in its mane hissed in a merry fashion, their hundred serpentine eyes never blinking.

"Yes!" said all three heads in unison. "All are welcome to enter here!"

Rabicane said, "Ask of him whether a mortal man might depart again."

The left head said, "Those covered with blood may enter…"

The middle head said, "… those who are dead may enter…"

The right said, "…no elf departs from here, nor mortal man who lives but once then dies."

Rabicane said, "Master, take my reed; this is an evil place. Flee it."

Gil's stomach growled. He said, "You are very generous, Cerberus, to allow me entry. May I eat that loaf of bread? I assume a dog cannot eat it."

The middle head said, "There is no bread."

Gil said, "What is in the cup? If it is not wine, I can have some."

The left head said, "There is no wine."

Gil started to step forward, but Rabicane snorted and said, "Master, they lie. I smell wine."

Gil paused. "Noble Cerberus, what is in the cup?"

The right head spoke, "Blood."

Rabicane said, "Stay back out of its reach!"

Gil said, "Don't worry. It's chained up…."

The monster laughed and raised a paw to its middle neck. The chain opened and slithered to the stone in a bright ringing clatter.

The monster said, "My master requires I chain myself. All who serve him do."

Gil licked his lips, not sure what to do. He had the distinct impression the creature was playing some sort of game with him. "Is the Green Chapel beyond those door you guard?"

The central head said, "No."

The left said, "The Green Chapel is behind you."

The right said, "You walked past it."

Gil was then convinced the monster was lying. He wondered how he could slip past the creature, or, more to the point, once he was inside the Green Chapel, how he could get out again.

Gil was sure there was a way to befriend the three-headed monster. He stepped back, hung helm and shield on his saddle bow, and took the paper bag out of his saddle bag.

The monster sniffed with six nostrils. "What is that?"

Gil said, "Grilled steak. Baked in some sort of pepper sauce. And I also have a hamburger. And some spirits. It's called iced tea, but it is not really tea. I forget what is in it. Vodka, I think. You want some?"

The monster tilted its various heads left and right, squinting and snarling, as if puzzled. "You offer me... food and drink? Why?"

Gil said, "Call it a Christmas Eve present."

"Why did you not eat it?"

Gil said, "I am fasting for Advent. No meat, no wine. Saint Christopher told me so. You'd like him. His head looks like yours. But not so many."

The three heads looked at each other.

"What say you?" said the middle head.

"The ring of truth is in his voice," said the left head.

The right head said, "I smell no deception in his sweat."

The monster raised a great paw and struck the stone before him. The stone was pulverized beneath the titanic paw and left a crater deep as a dish.

"Pour the spirits in there!" "The meat!" "Fetch it forth!" All three heads barked at once.

Gil stepped boldly into the range of the creature's teeth and claws, knelt, and emptied the flask he had been given into the crater. Then, he unwrapped the steak and the burger patty.

Seen in the sunlight, Gil now saw the burger patty was wrapped in bacon strips. Even cold, it looked delicious. He had to wipe his mouth with his wrist as he fed the meat into mouths bigger than coffins.

Gil raised his hand to scratch one head behind the ear, hoping the poisonous snakes would not bite. "Good boy!" said Gil. "Good dog! Er, dogs."

Gil felt a pang of pride as he saw the monster's muzzle unwrinkle. All trace of snarl departed. The monster relaxed.

"Yeah! Really tasty…" said the middle head.

"Where is it from?" said the left head.

Gil said, "This restaurant called Knockers. I was there last night. The manager was this huge… uh… giant."

The right head reared up. "What have you done! What have you fed me!"

The monster raised a paw to strike him, but Gil dodged the blow. The stone next to him exploded under the force of the blow, making a second small crater.

All three heads now drooped. The snakes lashed back and forth, hissing horribly for a moment, and then they hung down and dangled, forked tongues lolling. The three heads sighed. The four legs trembled and folded.

The monster groaned. "Curse you! How did you outsmart me! May the cat eat you and the Devil eat the cat!"

And then the great green eyes closed.

Gil stood a moment, amazed. The creature was breathing slowly and deeply. It was not dead, but asleep.

A strange little smile began to deepen in one corner of Gil's mouth, and his eyes narrowed, not in anger, but in mirth. "*Finest fare in the land,* she said. *It will knock you out!*"

Rabicane looked on, puzzled.

Gil said, "I think I am beginning to figure this out."

He walked past the sleeping monster and under the archway.

3. Darkness and Light

With each step into the corridor, the sunlight was less. Soon he walked in utter darkness.

After a few more steps, he saw smalls lights ahead. Gil came forward cautiously, wondering it these were piskies or some evil magic.

It was candlelight.

The corridor of stone led to a dead end. It was not a tunnel, but a cave. Or rather, not a cave, but a cave-in. The corridor was filled with tumbled rock forming a rough slope from floor to ceiling. The rubble was made of dressed stone. From the debris, some had been mortared together before being smashed apart. It looked as if this corridor had once led somewhere but had been sealed and bricked over; and then the seals broken and the wall battered to open the way again; and then bricked over again. From the different sizes and shapes of bricks in the rubble, it looked like it had happened several times. From the age of the layers of dust, it had been long, long ago.

It was a mystery whose meaning Gil doubted he would ever discover.

The light here came from a rack of candles set before an alcove in the right-hand wall. This candle rack was a hundred steps away from the rubble blocking the corridor. Gil peered.

Within the alcove was a set of figures: to one side were kings in rich raiment, bowing. To the other side were shepherds in coarse robes, hands clasped in prayer. Oxen and asses were kneeling. Midmost were a woman and a man kneeling before a baby in a manger.

Above the scene, at the apex of the alcove, was an august winged figure, garbed in white vestments more devoid of hue than any fabric could be, and above his head hung a coronet of gold. In one hand the figure held a golden trumpet. It seemed neither to be male nor female, but had long, flowing hair that reached to its broad shoulders.

Gil looked and could see no wires. There was nothing coming from the cave wall or ceiling touching the statue. It seemed simply to stand in midair on the toes of its sandals.

Gil felt a weird moment of fear because the eyes of the statue were so realistic that they seemed to be boring into him, looking straight into his heart. Yet, at the same time, the glass eyes seemed to be windows opening up into a sky bluer than the skies of Earth, and larger. It was dizzying.

For a moment, he was convinced the being was alive. But then he noticed it was not breathing, not blinking, not moving.

Gil relaxed. It was just a statue after all. Yet…

A sense of terror and awe smote through him them. There was no change, no noise, no motion, but Gil knew that the entity was alive, more than alive, and watching him. It was not breathing or moving because it did not care to. It did not blink because it suffered no pain, nor fatigue, nor smallest discomfort.

Gil found himself trembling. He bowed to the entity.

BOW NOT TO ME. I AM BUT A FELLOW SERVANT.

The voice was louder than a voice could be, but it did not strike into his soul through his ears. It came directly.

Gil covered his face with his hands. He honestly could not recall having been this afraid before in his life, ever. His knees were shaking.

He said, "Glory be to the Father, and to the Son, and to the Holy Spirit!"

It was all he could think to say. His mind was blank.

FEAR NOT!

The sensation of having meaning without words shoved directly into his mind like a lightning bolt was not the sort of thing which brought calm. But he drew a breath and tried to calm his racing heart, to still his shaking limbs, even though he did not have the nerve to take his hands from his face.

Gil tried to think of something to say. He tried to think of a prayer. "Hail, Mary! Full of grace, blessed art thou above women…" he could not remember the next part.

SO I SPOKE. THE WOMAN SAID: BE IT DONE TO ME ACCORDING TO THY WORD. THAT ANSWER I BORE ABOVE AND PLACED BEFORE THE THRONE, AND IT WAS FOUND PLEASING.

Then, Gil knew to whom he spoke. This was not merely an angel. It was an archangel. It was one of the seraphim.

The strength in his legs gave out. He fell to his knees. He could feel the sting of tears in his eyes. Gil wondered at himself.

Why was he so afraid? Surely this was one of the highest and noblest servants of the Most High! It meant him no harm. Why the terror?

But he knew. He was a killer. He had deceived people. He had been disobedient to his mother, to a saint, to Heaven itself. He walked around in armor studded with gems while poor people starved for a scrap of bread. The insane, reckless, overwhelming love which makes a man love even his enemies was not in him.

It was the sight of a sinless being that frightened Gil to his marrow bones. When a man fails at some merely human task, or breaks a law, he always has a way to lie to himself, to make it seem not so bad. Gil could not do that, not now, not here, not with eyes like those watching.

YOU HAVE BLESSED OUR LADY, SO YOU IN TURN ARE BLESSED.

Gil said, "Here I am. Speak. I will obey."

LET THE LANCE OF THE CENTURION WHICH STRUCK THE DOLOROUS BLOW BE DRAWN FROM THE STONE WHEN THE HOUR IS COME. LET IT BE GIVEN TO THE HAND OF THE GHOSTLY FATHER'S NOVICE.

Gil said, "I don't understand. What hour?"

THE MISTS OF EVERNESS PERISH BEFORE THE LIGHT TO COME. NOTHING IS SECRET THAT SHALL NOT BE MADE MANIFEST, NEITHER IS ANYTHING HID THAT SHALL NOT BE MADE KNOWN.

Gil felt a moment of elation. "Does that mean the elfs will be overthrown? Will I live to see it?"

YOU WILL BE WITH THE DEAD BEFORE THE GATES OF HELL ERE THAT HOUR COMES.

So terrible was this pronouncement that Gil's heart failed him even while his mind was struggling not to accept the meaning of the words. Dead? In Hell?

Gil said, "What must I do to escape the fires of Hell, Gabriel? What must I do to be saved?"

THAT BLOOD HAS BEEN SHED. ON YONDER THRESHOLD STONE HIS FEAST IS LAID: TAKE, EAT, DRINK.

Gil said, "And what must I do to save my life from the Green Knight? Am I going to be alive tomorrow?"

TAKE NO THOUGHT FOR THE MORROW.

Gil waited, but that was all. The angel was silent and offered no comfort.

More words burst out of him, "I don't want to die. Please, I don't! The Green Knight is going to kill me! I wish I was not afraid, but I am! Dear God, I am!"

Ashamed with himself, Gil gritted his teeth and tried to stop the trembling through his body. In a firmer voice, but still not daring to open his eyes, he said, "Let this danger pass me by. Pray to the Lord you serve in bliss, O Angel, pray for me that I be spared. But if–" and now his voice broke out of his control again "–if there is some plan, some purpose to this—if it is the will of Heaven—then let God's will be done, not mine–"

His strength failed him utterly. Gil fell on his face, and faintness entered his brain. How long he lay there, lightheaded and unable to rise, he did not know. But then a sense of immense pressure came into the cave, as if some vast living thing huge beyond all telling had entered there. A warmth passed over him and filled his body like wine being poured into a cup, wine that revived life and brought joy. The silence that came then was like the silence of outer space, or a space even larger and older than that.

After a time, the silence became more like a normal quiet. He could hear the wind outside the cave and hear the drip of wax. The mighty spirit that had passed over him was gone.

He rose to his feet, bowed to the image of the babe, and retreated.

Rabicane was outside, head down, waiting. The giant snake-haired three-headed monster was gone, but in its place, in the exact same posture and snoring the same snores, was a mongrel that looked half-collie and half-wolf. His tail and flanks were scarlet. Around his neck, on a strap, was a small curved cone of ivory. It was a hunting horn.

It was a fairly large dog, but compared to the shape it had been wearing when Gil had entered the cave, it seemed puny.

Rabicane said, "What happened?"

Gil said, "Everything."

4. Breaking Fast

Remembering the words of the swans to him, Gil took the horn about the large dog's neck and the green strap by which it hung. It was carved from the tusk of an elephant, half a cubit long, and bands of dark metal circled near the bell and near the mouthpiece. In a circle around the circumference was scrimshawed an image of two lions facing each other, claws raised as if in combat, but on the other side of the horn's mouth, their tails were tied to each other. It looked as if their eagerness to fight would only draw the knot tighter.

Gil said, "Would you know Roland's horn if you saw it?"

Rabicane said, "No. Horse cannot match the eye of man. Does it depict two lions combatant yet addorsed, nowed, and twined?"

"I don't know what that means."

"A knight unversed in heraldry? Your teachers should have beaten you more. Blow, and let me hear."

Gil put the horn to his mouth and winded the horn. A deep roar issued forth, clear and fair as the chime of a great brass bell, and spread across the land. A sound like it answered him dimly in the distance, as if the cry of the horn had reflected off the sky.

He snatched the horn away from his lips, frowning.

Rabicane said, "That is the horn. By what mischance it came to be carried by a dog I know not, but you cannot leave it in such unworthy hands. Or paws."

Gil slung it about his neck.

Gil said, "Are you strong enough to carry this big dog if I drape him over the saddle?"

"Am I not the foal of Tencendur, Charlemagne's good steed, and Llam-rei, Arthur's mare? I could bear twentyfold that load. Whither bear we him?"

Gil said, "I want to return him to his master."

"Where?"

"The Green Chapel."

Gil prayed, and he ate the bread and drank the wine sitting on the cloth on the stone. It smelled and looked like wine, but he knew it was something more, so he did not hesitate to drink it to the dregs. It cleared his head of all fog, his heart of all fear.

And the bread was so delicious he felt as if he were eating life itself.

Chapter 7

The Lord of Hautdesert

1. The Living Chapel

The fruit trees, which held only tiny and unripe fruit that morning, were rich and heavily laden with apples, plums, peaches, oranges, and pears as he walked back downstream. The snow was melting, and, after an hour, instead of being some spring and winter together, it was spring in the air, summer in the grass, and a very abundant autumn on the branches of the trees. Rabicane walked behind, the big white dog draped over the red steed's saddle.

The trees were taller and thicker than they had been that morning, and the many colored leaves formed an impenetrable canopy overhead.

Now the air was warm and fresh as springtime air yet somehow held the strange and wild scent of autumn. In Gil's mind, that scent was always a time for journeys to new homes because it was always in October that his mother moved and left their old home behind without a word of farewell to anyone. The mingling of the spring wind with the ghostly smells of autumn sent strange longings through Gil, just as if all the beauties in the world, the green trees, the bright waters, the dark mountains, and the mournful cries of geese flying south, were all just a prologue or foreshadowing to some greater and deeper world beyond. Gil breathed in a deep breath, delighting. He wondered if this were indeed the air of Eden.

Gil plucked fruit from one tree after another, eating a different and more delicious fruit every hundred paces, until his stomach forgot even the concept of hunger.

Without the red neon side to guide him, Gil almost did not recognize the spot where the restaurant stood, but he saw the white stone marked with a sign of a Celtic cross and turned away from the bank and went deeper into the trees.

The trees grew taller and closer together. Soon Gil found himself as if in a corridor of pillars with a green roof overhead, green carpet underfoot.

He came into the clearing where the restaurant stood, or once had. It was gone. Instead, there was a bloodstained chopping block set up for an execution.

Here, the trees were larger yet and grown so closely together that the boles touched. Other trees, although still living, had been cropped or trained to grow into the shape of a double row of pillars. Parallel to these were living trees shaped like flying buttresses.

The canopy of leaves overhead in this place was the bright green of late spring, except for a parallel row of archways high above, evenly spaced between the living pillars, where the many colored leaves were translucent, shining with sunlight, and the different colors and shapes of the leaves formed scenes and images: a baptism, a wedding feast, a pilgrim with staff and cockleshell, a figure on a mountaintop clothed in light, a Passover meal. At the far end of the nave, where the lines of perspective from all the living pillars and buttresses converged, was a large, round rose window, made entirely of autumn leaves.

For some reason, the beams of sunlight only passed through the autumn leaves, but the green leaves were opaque so that this spot was as dark as night, except for the many colored beams of red and gold, orange and scarlet, that slanted down through the rose-shaped and arch-shaped designs hanging in the green canopy.

Gil said aloud, "Is this the Green Chapel?"

As he spoke the name, the wind rustled overhead, the leaves tossed, and the many colored beams of light danced. A bell in the living carillon swayed and sounded. The echo of the bell's voice passed across the scenery.

Gil now saw the Green Knight.

2. The Chopping Block

It was as if the voice of the bell had summoned him.

The giant had been standing motionless next to the chopping block, ax in hand. His green hair, kirtle, cloak, and leggings made him blend into the green background of leafy walls behind him. He wore a breastplate of metal, enameled over with green, and his skirts and arms and leggings were covered with many heavy metal scales of green shaped like leaves.

Even as he watched, the Green Knight saluted Gil with his iron ax. The Green Knight now drew on a surcoat of white and pinned it at his shoulders with cockleshell pins. On his chest was the bright image of a red cross.

Gil remembered the Green Knight's boast that the elfs would be terrified if he appeared in his war gear. Now he saw why. It was all iron, which broke the elfin spells and smothered their charms, and the Cross of the Crusaders blazed on his chest.

His hair was as green and wild as before, rising above his head like a breaking wave, and falling past his shoulders to his elbows like a thicket in which a deer might hide. However, this time, between his wild green bangs and wild green beard, he wore an iron faceplate over his brows, nose, cheeks, and chin. There was a mouth slit for the mouth and eyeholes for the eyes. The pupils of his eyes were as yellow as a goblin's teeth.

The echoes of the bell slowly drained away into silence. The leaves ceased to whisper. The air was still.

Gil took the huge white dog from the back of his steed and put it gently on the grass.

He strode over to the chopping block. Without a word, he unbuckled and doffed his helm and set it aside. He stared up at the emerald-colored figure, twice the height of a man.

There was no fear in the eyes of Gilberec Moth as he knelt. He crossed himself and said a prayer. This time he recalled all the words.

Then, he lowered his head and laid it on the chopping block.

Gil felt the touch of cold iron at his neck. It rested there a moment. And then the blade moved to the left and tapped him on the left shoulder. Then, he felt the blade tap him on the right shoulder.

"In the name of God, Saint Michael, Saint George, and good King Arthur, High King of England, Ireland, Fairyland, and France, Emperor of the Holy Roman Empire, I dub thee knight. Arise, Sir Gilberec! Be thou valiant, fearless, and loyal."

3. The Mask of Cold Iron

Gil had suffered as many fears and wild hopes as anyone might on what he thought was his last day of life, but this was so unexpected that he laughed, leaped to his feet, and jumped to the top of the chopping block. From there, he was tall enough and quick enough to leap and grab the Green Knight by the nose.

Whatever the Green Knight had expected, Gil's leap was not it. He cried aloud, half in outrage and half in mirth, and fell to one knee.

Gil landed, and the metal mask, but also the voluminous green wig and beard, all came away in his hand. Gil stood there, grinning and nodding at the vast mass of green hair in his hand.

"I knew it," he said. "I should have figured it out long ago. I am actually pretty good at riddles. But how are you fooling my eyes? You still look like a giant to me, Sir Bertolac. How did you have Vertifran look like Cerberus?"

For, with the iron mask and outrageous wig pulled away, the twelve-foot-tall figure shined with the golden hair, yellow eyes, bronze skin, and handsome face of Bertolac, the King's Champion who had trained him.

Bertolac said, "I will show you, Sir Gilberec. Have you any elfin charm about you? Put them aside and help me off with my habergeon."

Gil aided him. The iron chestplate, iron jerkin, arms, and leggings were removed and put to one side. The iron ax Bertolac smote into the block, where it quivered and stayed. He was now dressed in a green linen tunic and buskins. Bertolac walked past Rabicane, down the corridor of trees to the waterside. There, he knelt for a moment, as if in prayer or meditation.

Little dots or sparkles of light appeared around him and clung to his outline. He began to shrink and the colors of his tunic to fade from green to yellow. He dwindled down from twelve feet tall, to ten, to seven, to the six and a half Gil had seen him wearing all this year at Uffern House.

Bertolac stood. "You see? It is the Lilliputian charm."

Gil nodded. "I see. I saw the serving maids and butlers at the feast of the elfin lords use that charm to make themselves as small as insects. You use it to dwindle yourself to human size. Twelve feet tall is your true height. When you wear your iron, your charm breaks, and you resume your true stature. What about your face when you are Bredbeddle?"

Bertolac said, "It is a similar charm, one that changes the size and proportion of facial features, which coats the inside of those ridiculous eyeglasses I had to wear. How did you know I was Bredbeddle?"

"How did you know my name? My real name? I know I never said it aloud at Uffern House."

Bertolac said, "You said it within my hearing. But, ho! The knight should answer first his master. Why did you come lay your head on the block?"

"You know why. What makes you think I accept you as my master?"

Bertolac said, "Because I am the first knight and the King's Champion, the best tutor in the arts of war you are likely to find. And because I will tell you how to defeat your enemy, Guynglaff of the Cobwebs."

Gil said, "I cannot trust an elf."

Bertolac said, "You are wise not to, Sir Gilberec. But I am no elf."

Gil said, "What are you?"

Bertolac shook his head. "My question first. Then yours. By what charm did you overcome my dog?"

Gil said, "You know by what charm, but I do not."

Bertolac said, "What? Do you play riddles with me?"

Gil laughed. "I suppose it runs in the family. I overcame your dog by sheer accident and kindheartedness. I fed him the steak you gave me. I do not know what charm you put in the meat. I did not realize he was guarding the spear. I thought he was guarding the Green Chapel."

Bertolac said, "This whole mountain is the Green Chapel."

Gil said, "My turn. You are no elf because you can handle iron. How can you have your head cut off and live? What are you?"

"That is two questions, but I only know one answer. Why my flesh is imperishable, I do not know. It is something the Fisher King did to me. I was an elf, but I am no longer such a thing. As to what I am..."

The golden man threw out his chest and raised his head. "I am the knight and true servant of the Fisher King, who lies wounded here in this very chapel, dying but immortal and unable to die. That holy lance which I set my dog to guard struck him, so he is wounded, but the blood of Christ lingers on that lance, and entered his bloodstream, and granted the Fisher King an imperishable nature and deathlessness. Until the Fisher King is cured, I am bound to him."

"Then how can you vow true fealty to Alberec?"

Bertolac wagged a finger. "Not so fast! My question. Your words and eyes when you pulled my mask aside told me you had known or guessed what face would be beneath! How was this?"

Gil said, "You told me yourself."

"That is no answer! Let us agree to give full answers and not speak in riddles, as elfs and prophets do. Agreed?"

"Agreed! Now, my question is—"

"Stop that! That was a bargain, not a question. Right?"

"Right! Now my question is—"

"Are you trying to irk me?"

"Yes! Now, my question is—"

"Very funny! But you gave your word to answer my questions without riddles. How did you penetrate my masquerade?"

"Sir, in your guise as Bredbeddle, you told the name of the Green Knight's steed, whom once I rode. He ran so swiftly that it was plain as day that horse wanted my dog out of harm's way. But why? In your disguise as Bertolac, in the dining hall beneath the mountain, you had him with you in his shape as a white collie, and he spoke to his brother. So if Vertifran is Bertolac's hound, and Vertifran is the Green Knight's horse, then it only stands to reason that Bertolac is the Green Knight. But why are your illusions fooling my eyes, when I can see through all the glamour of the elfs?"

"From the Fisher King, I have the art of forming our bodies into a subtle and ethereal substance that is more fluid than matter and also more permanent and durable. It is no illusion: my shape and size can change, and, as he is my dog, I can to a lesser degree change him. Vertifran was told to warn you away from the Green Chapel. How did he fail?"

"He is too elfin to tell an outright lie as a man would, so he spoke in riddles instead. He said that any mortal man born once could not enter and depart the chapel. I am a baptized Christian so was born more than once. He said a mortal who is born once then dies could not enter. I will die, but I hope to be raised again on the last day, which is more than once. He said I had to be covered in blood to enter and had to be dead. So I was, dead in sins, and covered in the precious blood of the Savior. And other things of like meaning. I was born to a riddler, so I notice the double meanings. And, of course, I finally understood why a chapel is indeed a fearful place, even to men. How much more terrible the chapel must be to elfs, to whom even a far-off church bell is painful."

"Oh? And why is a chapel fearful?"

"My question! What was the point of this rigmarole? This whole charade? You being the Green Knight and pretending to be Bredbeddle trying to stop me and pretending to be Bertolac training me well enough to make the journey. All of it. Why?"

"Because of the sword of your father. It is one of the Thirteen Treasures of Lyonesse, and the Fates never cease to meddle and moil with those who touch them. And do not ask your father's name of me or how he came by the sword! I did not put him to the trial, whoever he is."

"Trial?"

Bertolac nodded. "Whoever your father is, he is a great man if he could hold that sword in hand. I tried Gawain to see if he was worthy, but he was not. But neither did he break his word, so he was allowed to depart from the Green Chapel with only three small scars on his neck."

"And me?"

"You? You are some sort of freak, kid. I have never seen someone who would not break his word, kept his fasts, abstained from cold booze and hot women... Good heavens! What makes you so different?"

"Dumb luck and bad timing."

"Full answers, please! No riddles."

"I'm too dumb to listen when a saint from Heaven comes down and tells me what to do and makes me swear to do it. Because of that, I lost my father's sword and almost lost my life. Every time I take a step, or sit down, or stand up, the empty scabbard slaps against my leg, and I remember what the price is for breaking my oath. He said not to fight on a bridge with the next enemy who challenged me. But I did not see any way to obey since my enemy was Guynglaff, and he had just killed my horse…"

"My horse, if you please," said Bertolac, scowling.

"So the other thing he had me swear was to eat no meat and take no spirits during Advent. I thought it was a dumb rule, but every time my scabbard slapped against my leg, I was reminded…. All this had just happened to me. My scars from my battle with Guynglaff are still fresh. I was not likely to disobey the saint twice so soon. And your temptations were stupid."

"What?"

"I said *stupid*. To come here, I disobeyed my mother, and surely broke her heart, and escaped from jail, and surely broke the law. Do you think a free meal and a pretty face can tempt me? Do you think I can be tempted by a baconburger? I should be insulted by how petty your tricks are."

"Petty tricks oft trip souls too great to be tempted by great sin. Troy was lost over a woman's pretty face, and Eden was lost over a free meal. So lust and gluttony are not so petty after all. But I saw how quick you are to pull a knife. Anger is what tempts you."

Gil said, "Love of battle is no vice in a knight."

"Love of battle? Or intemperate anger?"

Gil said, "Sorry, it is my turn for my question. Between cold winds and black knights, three-headed dogs and no-headed huntsmen, your ever-growing stairway and your ridiculous restaurant, you went to a lot of effort. Why did you try so hard to keep me away from here?"

"I did not want to have to cut your head off."

"Full answers! Would you have?"

Bertolac chuckled a dry, terrible, humorless chuckle. "Darned right. If you had cheated, or lied, or sent a double in your place, or tried any sort of elfish trick or human cowardice? Certainly I would have and kicked your fool head like a soccer ball down the stairs as a warning to others. This is not a game."

"What others?"

"The others who seek to take the great sword Dyrnwen in hand! It was forged by Weyland, and the runes in the blade promise it will shine as bright as thirty torches in the worthy hands of the nobly born, but betray and burn and maim those who are ignoble in birth or deeds. You called me a giant, but you saw Bran the Blessed and Balor of the Evil Eye. That sword, in the right hands, can burn with such fury that it will slay even Titans such as they, or storm giants even taller, who live in the high regions of the air hidden from men, or their king. My question: you speak of huntsmen with no heads. Dullahan, they are called. They were none of mine, not an obstacle an elf would send. Why are the Cobwebs after you?"

"I killed two of them: Doolaga and Gulaga, both Bigfoots, and I wounded Guynglaff. Why won't the sword hurt him? He is unworthy of it."

"He is immune to swords, including that one. His hair is charmed. He fears no retaliation nor curse. Why did you kill them?"

"They stole a child for the Elfking, Erlkoenig."

"So?"

"So... I killed them for it. A Christmas tree helped me."

"The Bethlehem tree? The one that dies, and comes to life again in another land, and blooms every Christmas Eve?"

"It was a tree. It did not give its name to me."

"You talk to trees?"

"Don't be silly. I talk to birds."

"Interesting. That talent is rare. Who is your mother?"

Gil shook his head. "Look, Mr. Changes-his-name. I kind of like you, but you are tricky, and I am not telling you that."

"Then let me ask a different question: why call you the chapel fearful?"

Gil said, "For what reason it was shown to me, I know not, but I saw the Angel of the Annunciation and heard his voice. Never have I known such terror: and after that, all the terrors this little Earth can bring forth will not sting me very deeply."

"What did the angel say? And how did you learn to talk to birds?"

"Is that your question? Because whose turn is it? I have a lot more questions, such as how you figured out my name? And why you serve the

Elf King Alberec if the Fisher King is your lord? And what are you up to? And why do you care who is worthy to wield Dyrnwen?"

Bertolac spread his hands and said, "Well, it is your turn, but this is your last turn because my curiosity is sated. So if I were you, I would ask a really, really good question, like: *how shall I overcome the Yeti Guynglaff the Invulnerable in combat and recover my father's sword?* You'd like the answer to that one, wouldn't you? Or I could tell you some other secret like the name of the Man in the Black Room, or who struck the blow that wounded the Fisher King, or something else you'd like to know more."

Gil said, "I have a lot more questions, but, come to think of it, that one is the top one weighing on my mind right now."

Bertolac smiled and told him.

4. Holding the Bridge

Gilberec Moth, spurs shining on his heels, and carrying in hand a black staff given to him by Sir Bertolac, came one morning to that same covered bridge, whose pillars were carved like trees, above the swift flowing river which formed the border between Louisiana and Elfland. On a tree ten paces beyond the end of the bridge, he hung his father's shield and a small wooden mallet.

The staff was made of hornbeam root, one of the hardest of woods. For his breakfast, Gil fished in the stream by wading into the water with no shirt on, and battering fish onto land with his hand, or catching them in his mouth.

On the first day, he had his first customer. Someone tried to cross the bridge. It was the witch from the dovecote of Uffern House.

Gil merely doffed his helm politely and stepped aside to let her pass.

"You!" she cried. "You sought the Green Knight! Seeking death!"

Gil said, "I am returned. I defeated the foe."

She shrieked, "You? A mere boy? You defeated the Green Knight?"

Thinking of his own fears, his own anger and sin, and the various temptations to which he was prone, Gil said, "The Green Knight was my foe but was not my foe. He set my foe before me, and by being overcome, I overcame. I entered the Green Chapel, where only enter the dead, and ate of the dead who is not dead, and emerged not dead."

The witch, hearing the truth in his voice, but understanding nothing, turned pale and passed on by, muttering.

Gil smiled. "Now I know why my mother does that. It's fun!"

She came back that evening, with some grocery bags in her hands, puffing and complaining, and with two small children, crying, being led by ropes around the neck.

Gil barred her way. "Let the children go."

The old witch said, "Don't stand in my way, or I will boil your spleen with my curses!"

Gil said, "I fear no curses of yours, old mother. I have passed the dog called Cerberus and emerged from the cave mouth he guards. I have eaten the bread of Heaven. I quaffed the blood of God. Let the children go!"

The old witch cowered back. "You would not dare strike me! I am a woman!"

Gil said, "Not against flesh and blood do true knights fight, but also against principalities and powers of the air. In the name of Christ, in the name of the Holy Rood, and in the name of Saint Christopher..."

The old woman screamed and fell on her face. The two children took that opportunity to run the other direction, back toward town and the human world.

At that same moment, the alligator named Edmund Dantes, who sought revenge against the old woman for the slaying of his mate, now stirred and came out of the bushes nearby. His bulbous, cold, bloody eyes regarded her dispassionately a moment, and then the green log-shaped body, low to the ground, came lumbering toward her on stubby little legs at surprising speed.

She dropped her groceries and fled.

On the second day, at dawn, his first opponent was one of the squires from Uffern House. It was the handsome Vanir lad, whose name Gil had forgotten. He came riding up on a horse and banged the shield with the butt of his spear, and Gil stepped up on the bridge and blocked his way.

Because he was on a covered bridge, the Vanir could not come at him without dismounting. Dismounted, the Vanir could not use his lance. He drew his sword and came forward. Gil's staff had a longer reach than the sword, and Gil had quicker reflexes and stronger arms, so all he had to do was dart backward after every blow to his foe's helm, kneecap, stomach, wrist, or neckpiece. After the fifth blow Gil was unharmed, and the squire was laid out cold.

Gil and Drwdydwg (that was who the Vanir had been riding) chatted a while in the friendly fashion while Gil tied the Vanir lad, stripped of his armor, onto the saddle like a sack of laundry.

Dry said, "You'd best take care! Fjolnir son of Freyr came racing here to find you ahead of the knights! But they will be here ere long!"

Sir Dwnn son of Dygflwng came at noon. He swelled up to the size of a tree, but Gil waited under the roof of the covered bridge, which the knight was evidently reluctant to destroy. So he shrank down to human size, but then called upon his other peculiarity, which was that he could issue a tremendous heat from his body. He came at Gil with sword and shield, and his skill was greater than that of any squire, so it was after many hard blows taken and received that Sir Dwnn's foot broke through the smoking and smoldering board where he stood and trapped his leg. Gil stepped on the man's shield, trapping his arm, and smote him on the helm with a blow like a golfer driving a golfball down the fairway. The helm rang like a bell.

As before, Gil spoke with the horse, took the armor, and tied the unconscious body to the saddle.

At dusk came Sir Iaen son of Iscawin, cloaked in invisibility, and riding a jenny small enough to fit under the bridge. He was a skilled and cunning fighter, and if he had fought fairly without fairy tricks, Gil would have fought fairly also, and Sir Iaen might well have defeated Gil.

As it was, Gil stood facing the other way, pretending to be deceived by Iaen's illusion (a convincing image shaped out of colored mist of Sir Iaen on a roaring lion), and he waited. When Iaen charged and was halfway across the bridge, Gil asked the she-mule to halt, which she did, suddenly and stubbornly. Gil asked the many bats beginning to emerge from the swamps to flock around Sir Iaen's head. The man flailed at the bats with sword and shield, ignoring Gil, whom he presumed to be spell-caught. Gil stepped over, took Iaen's left leg in both hands, and threw him off the mule. Iaen's head struck the ceiling of the covered bridge, and the mule kicked him on the way down.

She refused to carry the unknightly elf knight back home, so Gil made Iaen limp home in his linen underthings. He hung the captured armor nicely next to the other suits on the pillars of the bridge.

That night, two headless men and a headless boy on a horse attacked him.

Each man came at Gil from opposite sides of the bridge. Each brandished a knife in one hand and his disembodied head in the other, eyes glowing with eerie light.

Gil was astonished and disappointed at how easy these fearful beings were to defeat. They had no proper fighting stance, no shield, no skill. Aside from the poisonous smoke they blew out of their mouths, Gil was not sure they had any weapons at all.

With a blow like a batter hitting a homerun, Gil knocked the head out of the closest enemy's hand. The screaming head was dashed against a bridge post, and the skull was shattered and cracked. Gil was shocked when the headless body fell down lifeless, but then again he could not see how a headless body could be alive in the first place.

The other Dullahan came at him swiftly with a knife, but Gil's armor turned the blade. As they struggled, the creature stumbled over in the hole left by Sir Dwnn's burning foot. Gil broke both his arms with blows from his staff to elbow and wrist, so the demonic being could not pick up his own head. The headless body stood helplessly near the weeping, blubbering, and wailing head and gently tried to roll it away with a series of small kicks as he retreated, cursing each time he kicked himself in the head, broken arms dangling horribly.

The child, waving in the air the spear on whose end his head was tied, screamed horrible oaths and imprecations at him and spewed up both clouds of poisoned gas and streams of yellow-green venom. Gil made the sign of the cross in the air and called out the names of Saint George and Michael the Archangel. The Dullahan lad screamed as if he were being burned. The horse the child rode reared and plunged and tried to charge and trample Gil, but Gil told the horse to flee and go find Guynglaff Cobweb. The horse ran off, the headless boy clinging to its back and shrieking.

On the third day, Guynglaff came.

5. Knight and Cobweb

Guynglaff pounded on the shield with the mallet. "Come out, come out, Swan Knight!"

Gil stood at the mouth of the covered bridge. In his hand was the sword he had taken from Sir Iaen, a slender, fair-made elfin blade.

Guynglaff was as before, dressed in a cloak woven of Gil's mother's hair which covered all but his head, which was protected by a round metal cap. Atop the cap was a black stone. His face was apelike, with grisly lips and scalding eyes and one broken tusk. But now he carried no ax. Rather, the great sword Dyrnwen was in his hand.

Guynglaff looked Gil up and down. "I see spurs on your heels. Are you the father? For I have slain the son. Here in my hand is his sword. I am now second among the Anarchists because of it, because of the power I wield. Soon Euhemerus Cobweb will be no more, and I shall be first."

Gil said nothing, but took a step backward, onto the bridge. The wooden slats boomed under his boots with a hollow noise.

Guynglaff shouted, "Speak to me! I know you are the elder, for had your son lived, he was doomed to go to the Green Chapel...." All the birds within earshot suddenly sang out and took wing at the sound of that name, and Guynglaff looked startled, glancing right and left.

Gil took another step backward, and raised his hand, and beckoned.

Guynglaff said, "Speak! You are not the son of the Swan Knight! You have been defeating knights and Dullahan and sending them away defeated in hope of calling me, have you not? You knew my hate for you was too great to allow you to live, once I learned where you hid from me! Why did you hide so many years? Who are you?"

Gil said nothing.

"It is no use pretending you are the one who returned from the Green... From that place! You are trying to scare us! Scare the Cobwebs! We are the strength of the world, stronger than the elfs! We are stronger than Erlkoenig and all his court! The spirit of anarchy is loosed in the world and will topple all kings, break all covenants, and end all faithfulness! You cannot stand against us! You cannot! Who are you?"

Gil saluted him with Sir Iaen's blade.

Guynglaff's eyes narrowed into slits. "You are a fool. No sword can harm me. No sword is finer than Dyrnwen, which I took from your son's dying hands." Guynglaff with one stroke cut through one of the pillars of the roof. Wood splintered and exploded under the blow, and the roof tilted. Decorative carved birds with eyes of glass fell to the boards.

Gil took another step back. He was now in the center of the bridge.

Guynglaff said, "Do you know what your son's last words to me were? Begging! He was begging and blubbering for his life!"

Gil laughed. He could not help it. He remembered what the last thing was he had said to Guynglaff when last he stood on this bridge: he had called Guynglaff a lying coward.

Guynglaff was stung by that laughter. "Who are you? Tell me now, ere you die!"

Gil took out of his pouch the ivory tusk of a boar that he had bought in Mr. Yung's pawnshop with a diamond from his vambrace. He had sanded and shaped the tooth as best he could by memory to look like Guynglaff's unbroken tusk. Gil held it up into a beam of sunlight slanting into the covered bridge. The false tooth twinkled.

Guynglaff stared in shock. "Is that my– is that my tooth?"

Gil pitched his voice low to disguise it. "No. Mine."

The Bigfoot, stung both by wrath and fear, now charged at Gil, sword point forward. Gil flung the sword of Sir Iaen aside and picked up the ironwood staff from where it had rested leaning against one of the pillars.

As with the squire, Gil had reach and could strike Guynglaff while dancing back out of sword reach. Guynglaff was not well trained in the sword and kept instinctively using ax moves. Also, he could not maneuver to the left or right in this narrow space and was too tall to make any broad overhand strokes.

And his fur was not immune to wood. Gil struck the monster in the face, chest, neck, wrist, ankle, groin. His foe was unarmored, and Gil was very strong.

Nonetheless, the monster had the advantage of strength, of speed, and of skill. Once and twice he struck Gil, and links broke on his mail under the force of the blows. On the third stroke, he cut through the armor and slashed Gil's upper arm, drawing blood. The blade ignited with a smoky, foul, dim, and stinking fire. Guynglaff cawed in triumph.

The pain was too much: Gil flinched, and a darkness passed before his eyes. Before he could blink it away, the monster grabbed him by the throat and raised the flaming blade over head so that the point scraped the ceiling.

"Tell me now who you are, Swan Knight! Before I kill you with your own blade!"

"Your death," said Gil in his own voice. "I am returned from the Green Chapel, and the Green Knight sent me to kill you."

Now it was Guynglaff's turn to flinch in shock. A look, not of fear, but of supernatural horror was distorting his apelike face. Gil swung his staff with one hand and drove the burning blade so that it banged against the knob atop Guynglaff's metal cap. As before, the blade clung. This time, however, the blazing fire was pressed against the top of Guynglaff's head. He yowled.

Gil said, "Helm of Grim, which strengthens thew and limb! Thy cursed brim I pour within, the heavy weight of all of Guynglaff's sin! In Christ's name, O thou unclean artifice of vile magic, I command you fall!"

The charm had no effect, but Guynglaff, fearing it would, yanked the sword and the cap off his head. Gil struck him in the bald spot of his brow so heavily he heard the skullbone crack. Guynglaff dropped the flaming sword and metal cap over the side of the bridge into the river, and now he clasped Gil in a bear hug, using his great strength, hoping to shatter Gil's armor and break his ribs. Gil, in turn, dropped his staff and wrapped his arms around the monster, whose fur did not protect him against empty hands. He hugged the other with the strength and ferocity of a bear as he had been taught.

Gil was in such pain that he could not breath or think. Guynglaff bit and tried to gnaw on Gil's face, but his tusk slid off Gil's helmet. Gil poked him in the eye with a wing of a swan. Guynglaff screamed.

Rabicane emerged from the wood at that sound and was on the bridge in an instant. He turned, planted his forehooves, and kicked both of them into the river.

Down and down they went. Their arms were locked around each other. Guynglaff panicked and attempted to break Gil's hold. Gil in his armor sank to the bottom, and Guynglaff with him.

Guynglaff struggled and struggled as he ran out of air. Gil clung with hands like hands of iron, without mercy, and without motion.

Guynglaff's struggles grew weaker still. He eyes were wild. His head thrashed back and forth. His invulnerable fur, which no sword could pierce, floated like a brown cloud in the water. Gil clung.

Guynglaff's struggles grew weaker yet. Gil did not let go.

Guynglaff ceased to move. Gil did not relax.

Gil counted to a hundred, then two hundred, then shifted his grip, and took the motionless monster's head in his hands and twisted it so sharply that the neck broke.

He dragged the huge creature to the surface. Rabicane was in the river, swimming, and only his sleek head was above the water. Grunting, Gil managed to drape himself and the monster half across the horse's neck, and the mighty steed carried the heavy burdens toward shore.

Gil said, "You were supposed to wait until I called for you to come kick us into the river."

Rabicane said, "Folly! How were you supposed to call out if you were being strangled? How did you know the many charms that protected the life of Guynglaff did not excuse him from the need to breathe?"

"Nerea told me once the elves have no charms against drowning."

"So? What if he had simply snapped your neck as you fell? Duke Astolpho never made such bad plans!"

Gil had no more strength for talking. Every muscle in his body ached, and his upper arm was bleeding freely even though he could not at first recall when he had been struck.

Gil, panting, tossed the corpse on the bank of the river. He covered Guynglaff in the yeti's own cloak.

On the bank, combing her hair, was Nerea. Next to her was the sword, no longer burning, and also the cap of Guynglaff with its black stone.

The black stone had an iron nail lying atop it. This was an old-fashioned, large square nail, cold hammered into shape by some blacksmith.

Gil stooped, picked up his father's sword, and held it up in the sunlight for a moment, glorying in the look of it, the weight and heft in his hand. He saluted Nerea and sheathed the blade.

She said, "Touching the cursed black stone with an iron nail broke the spell, like you said. Now, come over here so I can look to your wounds. May I have my cap back now? I hate the taste of breathing weed."

Gil removed his helm. His silver hair was covered in the pearly and begemmed meshes of the mermaid's cap. He smiled and said, "Come take it from me."

Nerea sighed with exasperation, but when she stood on her tiptoes and put her hands in Gil's hair to undo the hairpins and recover her cap, he put his arms about her, and caught her, and kissed her.

Chapter 8

The Diamond Wine

1. The Swan Matron

After a short but pleasant eternity, Nerea made a shrill noise in her nose and pulled her face away from Gil's. Her eyes were wide with fear and focused over his shoulder.

Gil, fearing some threat was behind him, spun around, his hand on his swordgrip.

Hanging in midair, about ten feet away and twenty feet above him, was a woman he did not at first recognize. She was dressed in a white chiton which flowed from shoulders to feet in many folds and pleats. It was pinned at the shoulders and belted at the waist with two diagonal straps between. A second garb overtop this ran from shoulder to hip, cloaking one arm but leaving the other bare. These folds and drapes were always in motion, as if the fabric were weightless or alive. On her feet were slippers of pale glass. From shoulder to knees of the robe spread vast silver-white wings with blue-black tips. Little sparks and sparkles of light, gleaming motes, streamed out from the feathers and surrounded her. She wore a jeweled headdress oddly like Nerea's, but adorned with a spray of white feathers. Over her nose and mouth was a veil.

When she pulled the snood and veil aside, the bangs of hair spread out in a weightless cloud of dancing locks, gleaming silver and glittering with sparks. Her ankle-length braid, thick as a limb, floated up and twisted and swayed in midair behind her like a silver river.

She was looking at Gil and at the girl in the skintight black wetsuit. Gil glanced down. He still had his left arm around Nerea's slender waist.

"Uh…" Gil heard his mouth trying to make a noise. He forced himself to speak. "Hi, Mom."

2. The Lady of Sarras

Ygraine landed, looked at Gil's hand around Nerea's waist, and raised an eyebrow. Gil cleared his throat and tightened his grip so that Nerea was pulled up more closely to him. "Mother, this is Nerea Moth. Nerea, this is my mother, Ygraine."

Nerea impatiently squirmed out of Gil's grip and curtseyed. She wore no skirt, but held her hands spread wide to delicately cover her hips as she spoke. "I am the daughter of Narissa, who is the daughter of Nausithöe."

Ygraine said, "Nausithöe is my aunt. I am the daughter of her sister Danaë, who is the wife and queen of King Pellinore of the Grail, Lord, upon a time, of the high and holy city of Sarras before its fall." She looked at the wound on Gil's arm, the bruises on his face and neck, and said coolly, "The boy bleeding on you is my son. How do you know him?"

"I know your son through no fault of his! It was not because of some mistake he made or thoughtlessness. I knew where to seek him out."

Nerea, as she spoke, began to unbuckle Gil's armor.

"Your cousin Narissa, all these years, refused to believe the report of Sir Alain le Gros that you had returned to the celestial fields and palaces of the upper air while leaving a son behind and sent me to look for him. I hired a detective named Elfine from Troynovant."

Nerea pulled Gil's linens over his head. She inspected his wounds while he stood there, embarrassed and trying not to show it.

"While she was often less than helpful, once she discovered a wolf protected by the ghost-dance, whom human bullets could not harm, and from him learned a silver-haired boy had been seen walking in the woods near Brown Mountain."

She rubbed a poultice on his swollen bruises, and bound up sprained limbs, and cleaned and stitched and bandaged the cut in his arm. As before, Nerea's herbs and crystals acted remarkably quicker than any human medical arts, sometimes instantaneously.

"I knew the lights of elfin wars had been seen there, and I supposed that the spies of the elfs also sought the boy. I found him near the smallest of the Four Pools that lead by buried portal into the subterranean Lost River, which runs from Cacapon to the wellsprings of Atlantis."

Ygraine said, "And now that you have found him?"

Nerea blushed. "I mean him good, not ill. He is… not what I was led to expect. I have told no one, not even my own father."

Gil, now cleaned and bandaged, stood up, and pulled his linen tunic on. He said, "Mother, Nerea saved my life the first time I fought Guynglaff. There he lies: the one who abducted and mistreated you. I have avenged the wrongs done you!" Gil drew the cloak of mists from off the face of the corpse.

Ygraine was startled because her eye had not seen through the misty cloak, so the body prone on the grass had been invisible to her. Now, in the raw sunlight, was the broken and motionless corpse of the monster clearly seen.

Ygraine was overcome with emotion. She sank down to her knees, crossed herself, and clasped her hands in prayer.

Gil looked on, wondering. But when Ygraine raised her eyes and Gil saw the gratitude and joy shining in them, he realized his mother was praying a prayer of thanksgiving. "May Heaven be praised for granting you this victory over so terrible a foe!"

Gil said, "You doubted me…?"

Ygraine said, "Of course. It is a mother's joy and burden to care for her son. Guynglaff is cunning and fell, and had he used his wits and called upon the many terrors that serve him, you would not have survived. Even the Swan Knight, your father, could only fight him to a standstill, and that was by a miracle, for the ghosts of the dead rose up to aid the Swan Knight in battle and pulled the roof of the cave down over the cave mouth. Did either of you yield or call halt during the combat?"

Gil shook his head a curt shake.

Ygraine smiled again. "It is as I hoped."

Gil said, "Why?"

She said, "It means that, although over a year and many miles sever you when first you slew his vile steed from beneath him in the shadow of the Christmas tree, that this is still the same battle, still one."

Gil said, "So?"

Nerea said, "So therefore the charm which comes from the first blood shed by a hero is yours."

Ygraine gave Nerea a look of respect. She smiled. "I see Glaucon's daughter is not unwise! She speaks truly. The charm is yours. But you must use it prudently, for such good fortunes are fleet of foot, nor do they tarry, nor do they come again."

Gil said, "Will I gain some new blessing, like the gift of my eye to pierce illusions, my ear to resist the wiles of elfsong, my tongue to convince skeptics that I speak the truth?"

She said, "No, but you will share a gift you have, for weal or woe. What is the difference between a blessing and a curse?"

"Please, ask me no riddles. Just tell me what would you have me do, Mother? That is all I need to know."

"The kings of the elfs have met in feast, as is their custom, from Christmas to Epiphany. Nine of the twelve days of Christmas have passed, but my sons and husband keep the feast. You must go to them." Ygraine brought out a bottle that was carved from a single gigantic diamond, and the liquor within was as bright and clear as moonlight on a cloudless midnight. "Here is wine irresistible to elfs, for in it is distilled the nimbus light of higher realms before their exile and contains the taste of hope their tongues know not on Earth."

Gil said, "I take it back. You have to tell me more than just what to do. Where did you get that bottle? For that matter, where did you go? The night I was arrested, I mean."

"I was warned by certain signs that the Faceless Man was breaking into my house and that the pine tree in my house could not keep him away, but I knew no servant of Arthur would hurt you. I dared not let him see me, so I donned my celestial swan-robe and fled. Among the shattered towers of Sarras I came upon a hermitage, where a company of holy sisters dwell in prayer, widows of the dead city, weeping for the sins of man. From the hand of the abbess, who often in dreams has concourse with angels and knows things Heaven hides from men, I was given this precious gift of wine."

"What is the wine for? It is not for me."

"It is for your honor. I would have you win your due from them and the honor you are owed."

Gil said, "You told me not to reveal my name."

"Reveal it now."

"What has changed?"

Ygraine said, "Beyond all hope of mine, you have found Arthur and swore to him, not to some lesser and wicked lord; and won your spurs from the Green Knight, which is an excellence and a dignity even elfs will not dare scorn; you fought all comers on the bridge; and overcame your deadliest foe; and my nightmare of so many restless years is put to rest forever and aye. You once boasted that I would need no longer protect your life, as you would protect mine. That day is come. My doubts are done."

Gil felt a strength enter his heart and settle into his bones at his mother's words, and it did not depart from him.

Ygraine said, "Now then! All that remains is the world pay you your due honors."

"Do I need honors from the world?"

Ygraine said, "You are not a monk, but a knight, and the fear of your name is half of your might in arms. The Night World will not meddle with you hereafter if all is done as I advise. Take a drop of blood from the heart of the dead yeti and mingle it into this wine bottle."

Nerea said, "Allow me." From a medical pouch filled with simples and crystals she took a hypodermic needle.

Nerea rubbed the iron nail over the chest of the yeti. Her metal razor would not cut the hair, so she used a sharpened clamshell to shave a small circle above the heart. She raised the needle in both hands and drove it into the chest in a blow as straight and true as Gil had ever seen a knight to do.

Nerea spoke as she worked. "For a pericardiocentesis, the needle is inserted between the fourth intercostal space between the ribs. That is done to remove excess fluid from the pericardium putting pressure on the heart. I suppose it would be the same in this case. There is no medical procedure where a living patient has a puncture made in his heart."

Ygraine whispered to Gil, "Saved your life, did she? You are fated to be happier in matters of the heart than I, it seems. Cherish this one, and do not let indifference, or jealousy, or folly come between you."

Gil heaved a huge sigh of relief he had not realized he had been waiting to sigh.

He had not known that he had feared his mother might dislike his girl.

3. The Peppercorn

Ygraine took out from her bodice a small silk purse, which she passed
to Gil. She said, "Now there are a few more matters to decide. Despite
having lived a life of despicable poverty among low and uncouth menials,
lady am I in great landholds, appurtenances, and rents, and fealty is due
me in my own name. For seven years and more, Lord Alain le Gros,
my lord and husband, has declared me dead. When Elaine of the Sea
wed Garis le Gros, her issue was Alain, who is my nephew. I have
flown across the sea and appealed to the Pope in Rome, and my case
was well received by the Jesuit Clerk Regular the Holy Father has set
aside to receive petitions from the Twilight Folk, Father Ramon Ruiz-
Sanchez. So my false marriage is annulled *ab initio*. Do you understand
me?"

Gil said, "No. I liked it better when you talked in riddles. You married
your nephew, but not my father?"

She said, "How can one scarlet with sins be yet innocent as the unblemished snow? Why is it unlawful to call any living man damned? Why is
it lawful to call even the best of living men damnable?"

Gil said, "Stop, please. Go back to talking in declarative sentences
peppered with archaisms, obscure references, and law Latin."

"In this pouch is the peppercorn due and owed to Erlkoenig of
the Elfs for the sustenance of the land, and I have here a writing
describing the metes and bounds. Once my name is cleared of the
falsehoods and felonies blackening it, demand of Alain le Gros the
keys to the Tower Dolorous, so called for my weeping when I was
first abducted to be his bride. It is set far from the heart of Corbenec, in the dismal waste called Terregaste, that none would hear and
pity. That tower and the lands and rights appurtenant thereto were
given me as my bride-price. By your hand I shall have again what is
mine."

Gil said, "How about declarative sentences that declare things more
simply?"

She said, "Alain le Gros both was never lawfully wed to me and also
abandoned the marriage by the pretense and false accusation that I had

fled from it, driving me out by threatening you, so his rights lapse. The Tower Dolorous and lands surrounding are yours. With this peppercorn, I pass my rights to you."

And she handed him the little bag.

Gil said, "After this day, it will be the Tower Dolorous no more, but its name shall be called the Tower Joyous, in remembrance of this one evil that was made right: that my mother who wept there was vindicated."

Ygraine said, "While the world endures, such small victories are given us only to remind us that joy is not native to this world and cannot long here endure. Such moments of triumph are meant only to strengthen our hearts against sorrows to come, as foreshadow and surety of the final triumph, when the bars of time are snapped, and we shall enter into eternity with endless rejoicing."

4. Four Last Things

She said, "There are last things to do: first, you must go to confession and be shrived."

Gil nodded. The cathedral of Saint Francis de Sales, where Foxglove the Witch's prentice had recovered her own true name of Susan, was but a few moments away at the speeds Rabicane could run.

She said, "Second, you must summon your father's swan boat and arrive at Mommur in her. For only thus will the doorwardens be unable to deny you entrance."

Gil said, "The boat is too small to port my horse, Rabicane. Where can a horseman go without his horse?"

Ygraine said, "You must summon the swan boat nonetheless."

Other preparations were made and other words said, but finally the hour came when Gil put one foot into the cold and rushing stream and lifted the horn of Roland to his lips.

The sound rang as loud as the shock of a thunderclap, echoing off far mountains, but as sonorous to the ear as the peal of the church bell and as bracing to the heart as only the voice of the trumpet crying out to all brave things to defend all fair things can be.

5. Hound, Steed, Skiff

The swan boat was there in less time than it took for Ygraine to pray her rosary. The boat was more than thrice the size it had been before and now had a poop deck and canopy, and now the number of swans pulling it was thirty-six. Their necks were arched with grace; their wings shined with beauty; their eyes gleamed with pride.

Ruff the dog was in the bow of the boat, his forepaws against the head of the cupid bowsprit, and he was barking.

"Hey! Hey! I knew it was you who was holding the bridge here! But I was in Canada! Do you know how hard it is to hitchhike as an unaccompanied dog? I had to clobber the dogcatcher and steal his truck! And they all drive on the wrong side of the road in America! My legs were too short, so I just put a brick on the accelerator, and that worked just fine for a while, I guess. So I knew it was you! I knew! I know everything!"

Gil made a trumpet of his fingers and called across the waters, "The Green Knight's green horse is your brother Vertifran in disguise."

Ruff's ears drooped. "I didn't know that! Is he a better spy than me?"

Gil shouted back, "Everyone says you are a terrible spy! Give it up and get an honest job! Knight's hound."

Ruff's ears perked up. "Wait! What? What? Have you got spurs? Are those spurs on your feet? Have you got spurs on your feet? Are you a knight?"

Ygraine said, "He seems agitated by your remarks. Tell him his counterespionage deflected the attention of Dr. McGuire and preserved me from harm. Dr. McGuire was my guest once at Corbenec, and she feared me."

Ruff would not wait for the boat to make landfall, so he jumped over the side and splashed noisily to the bank, shaking himself enthusiastically and spraying everyone with water. Then, he leaped up and put his muddy paws on Ygraine's beautiful white robe so enthusiastically that she toppled backward. The dog licked her face.

Ygraine, on the ground and looking upward, said with perfect dignity, "We shall get along famously, Sgeolan son of Iollan. You have my blessings for the good you have done my son and the loyalty you have shown him."

Gil grabbed Ruff by the scruff of his neck and hauled him off his mother. "Bad dog! Bad!"

Ygraine sat up, her clothing now muddy, but her face as serene and calm as ever. "Chide him not. Without him, what would have become of you? Dirt washes out. Trueheartedness runs to the core of the soul."

Gil helped her to her feet.

Ygraine said, "This was the third thing. I had to meet your hound before I dared send him with you. I do not know how you found it in the heart of a sneaking spy of the enemy, but where you have found it, keep it. More precious than gold is faithfulness. He walks among men. Can he touch iron, cold iron, unharmed?"

Ruff said, "Is this your mom? Is this her? Oh, I am going to like her."

Rabicane said, "Who is this mongrel?"

Ruff said, "Him, not so much."

Gil said, "Hush! Rabicane, this is Ruff. A knight without a horse is nothing, and a boy without a dog is less than nothing, so I forbid any quarrel between you two. If you love me, you will love each other...."

Horse and hound looked at each other warily.

"Or at least find a way to fake it."

Rabicane said, "Am I not the steed of Astolpho, foal of the steed of Charlemagne? The ways of courtesy are known to me. I can falsify good will as well as a cat."

Ruff said, "With me it's all or nothing. If you are in the pack, you are all the way in, and we live and die as one."

Rabicane looked away. "Your simple, vulgar honesty shames me, brute."

Ruff said to Gil, "He'll come around. A few fights against bad guys, once he sees how smart and brave I am, he'll come around. I am smart! I am a smart dog!"

Gil said, "And you know where the court of the elfs is being held? Where is Mommur this year?"

Ruff said, "I know. I also knew you would call your boat again, so I got the swans to let me have a ride. I told them I was yours."

Gil looked at Ruff and Rabicane, Ygraine and Nerea, and said, "You are all mine. Nerea, you want to come watch?"

Nerea shook her head. "Into Mommur itself? I will stay and talk with your mother."

Ygraine said, "Do you have anything to wear to pass unremarked among men?"

Nerea looked down at her skintight black diving suit. She lifted up one of her small, well-formed naked feet and pointed at her toes. "I have feet!"

Ygraine said, "Come. I will find something. You can come with me to the coffee shop after we visit my apartment. I have to change for my shift. Have you ever ridden in a motor vehicle, child? One called a *bus*? It is most exhilarating. Even after all these years, the speed and the noise, the smoke and commotion are quite thrilling!"

Gil said, "What? What are you talking about? You are not going back to work at that cruddy little job! I have gems studding my armor that could buy a mansion!"

Ygraine said, "I want to give Flo enough time to find a replacement. It is only polite. Should I leave her shorthanded? How shall it be if my good fortune becomes her misfortune?"

Gil said, "Who is Flo?"

Ygraine said, "Ah! That is a deep question. Who is any immortal soul? Will she not outlast the stars themselves? I see I taught you well...."

Gil said, "No, that was not a riddle. Who is...?"

Ruff was licking his own back leg. He looked up and said, "Florence E. Grundy is your mother's manager and part owner of the coffee house and wine bar where she works. You want I should tell you her social security number? Since your mom is paid in cash, off the books, she cheats her."

Gil said to Ygraine, "You are now a lady of Elfland again! You have a tower and everything! All the glories of Elfland are yours again for the asking...."

Ygraine said, "I am a Moth. I am of the Twilight, neither of the Day nor of the Night. I belong to neither world. The glories of Elfland are snares and falsehoods for the unwary. I send you there not that you should gain glory but that you should gain strength. Why your father put that sword in your hand, I do not know, but I can see that a high and terrible destiny is yours. But that is a worry for another day. Let us do well this day the duties given us now. You must go to Mommur and I to the coffee house."

Gil said, "And then?"

"That is the fourth thing I came to say. And in a week, or when Flo has a new girl, I will return to Sarras in the Summer Stars, to where the abbess holds reign over the ruins."

Gil said, "But, Mom! But... but... I mean, I am sure there is room in this tower you are giving me, isn't there? So I thought..."

She said, "You thought that you and I would share a roof? That I should tend and mend, and guard and guide? Those days are past.

"You are a man.

"I knew you were a boy no longer the day you were cast out of school because on that day you chose for yourself, prudently, open-eyed, and not recklessly, to disobey the law in the name of higher law, to do right and damn the cost.

"You chose the life of one who flees from no fights, but finishes them and renders justice with his strength. That is a man's decision. You gave your fealty to Arthur, and your body will die in his wars. That is also a man's decision."

Ygraine drew up a corner of her white robe and daubed her eyes. "I could not be more proud. For so many years I lived in fear. Now my name shall be washed clean and yours made known, and I shall return to my home in the airy realms."

Gil looked as if his guts had been kicked out by a horse, and his voice sounded as empty as someone speaking from a coffin. "Mother, you cannot mean to leave? To leave me? Forever?"

She smiled. "No mother would forswear the chance to visit her son. I will return to North Carolina on Easter, Christmas, at Embertide, quarter and cross -quarter days, and you and I shall go to mass together. A mother must take care her young do not drift into paganism and apostasy. What days shall these be?"

Gil smiled and said, "*Fasting days and Emberings be: Lent, Whitsun, Holyrood, and Lucy.* The quarter and cross-quarter days are the Feast of the Presentation of Jesus at the Temple; the Feast of the Coronation of Mary; Lammas; All Saint's Day; the Feast of the Annunciation; Saint

John's Eve; Michaelmas; and the Nativity of Our Lord. These are the days, my lady mother, when the mists are thin, and doors between the worlds open."

Ygraine raised both eyebrows, looking pleased. "At one time, you did not know this lore."

Gil said, "My interest in the old ways grew quickly once I sat at table and supped with monsters, sprites, and devil, and shook hands with a winter-vampiress who deadened my arm to here." He tapped himself on the shoulder. "Mother, I tell you, nothing focuses a man's attention on the theology of things like holy water and crucifixes faster than meeting a vampire."

She said, "Then you will welcome my blessing. I have been saving it unspoken since the day I first wove wings in Sarras, and learned the art of flight, for a child born of love I would one day have."

Gil said, "Mother, why do the birds never speak of you?"

She said, "That is obvious. They will not lie, but they cannot be trusted, if they speak, not to reveal clues to my position or to say whether I was alive or dead. Therefore they were commanded to silence."

Gil said, "By you?"

She shook her head. "I have no such authority, nor can I speak to birds. By your father."

"Who is he that the birds of Heaven obey him?"

She said, "He is a great man, but, more than this, he is a good and kind one. Even after so many years, I love, and I know not the name of who I love."

Gil sighed a deep sigh and looked up at the bright blue-white winter sky. Too many emotions to name were in his heart then. "When shall I know who my father is?"

She said, "Not soon. Be worthy of him, no matter who he proves to be."

He knelt, and she put her hands on his head and blessed him.

Chapter 9

Arise, Sir Gilberec

1. The Gates of Mommur

Gil was drawn swiftly by the swan boat over many strange waters, and he passed places and sights he did not believe were part of Earth: a cliff of solid beryl shining strangely in the rays of a rising moon, a beach whose sands were ground dust of countless pearls, and a colossus of bronze as tall as a skyscraper who stood with one foot on either headland, that any ship departing his harbor must pass between his knees.

He saw strange towers of white metal, covered with vines from which nightshade and poppy and drowsy orchids glared; he smelled the wondrous scent of perfumed jungles, among whose shadows and colored blossoms elephants pale as death walked silently, with lanterns hung on either tusk, eying his boat with cryptic, cold gazes as he passed.

Perhaps the time passed less harshly than in human lands, or perhaps Rabicane was no ordinary horse, Ruff no dog, for as the hours passed the two neither stirred nor complained, nor grew hungry nor weary. Horse and hound spoke in low voices of ancient things, wars lost long ago or won, losses and victories alike eroded by time to nothingness, and of sad things of forgotten years. Gil stood in the bow of the boat, sword at his hip, wine bottle in hand, and his foot atop the corpse of Guynglaff, wrapped in a large leather bag sewn shut.

The next day the weather turned colder, and Gil passed mountains of ice floating on the water. Gil knew from books and pictures that these were something from the human world, but when he saw an iceberg sailing serenely past, with the winds blowing long spumes of snow from the upper peak so that they seemed like swan wings, he rejoiced that there

were still many elfin wonders and things of beauty and strangeness left for
men to see and recall. Flocks of seamews as pale as ghosts screamed thin,
high, harsh cries and circled the ice peak. Gil called them down, and
spoke to them, and was told by the quarrelsome birds that he had crossed
an unseen meridian and now sailed in a sea appearing on no human maps,
called the Sea of Tethys.

At last Gil came to a black mountain rising with its roots in the sea, its
crown in the snow, but behind it, as a cloak of black and white, spread
a forest of icebound leafless trees. The forest reached to the far horizon
without break. The wood was ancient, as if it had never known man, and
the trees were giants.

Each titanic tree was coated in clear ice, and from the wide-spread
branches hung icicles as delicate as lace, and down from the thicker
branches came icicles four feet long and thicker than a woman's leg. In
other places huge spires of ice rose up like stalagmites. In places where
the branches of one titanic tree mingled with another, bridges of ice ran.

The sun was setting behind the black mountain when the swans found
the mouth of a swift-flowing river. The swans swam strongly against the
stream so that white curls of spray flew back from the boat. To his left
and right, he now saw towers looming above the icy-white trees. The
towers were made of a shining blue-green metal Rabicane said was called
orichalcum. Each tower top was shaped something like a hood, for it had
a sail or canopy shaped like a triangle rising over its single window.

On the crests of hills to either side of the river, in places where the trees
of white crystal were few, Gil saw strange and ancient houses, perhaps
half a dozen, whose walls were bricks of opaque white glass with doors
and windows painted blue. The roof tiles were laid in crooked lines of
green, white, and blue which Gil now recognized as the curls and knots
of elfin letters, which always seemed to change in the corner of one's eye
into new shapes.

There were two peculiarities of architecture: first was that the buildings
had no corners, for each was built on round or oval foundations or curves
more complex than these.

Second was that each building had a mix of doors of several sizes and
types: small doors near the ground no larger than mailbox doors; tall
doors as large as church doors with knobs and locks six feet off the ground;

doors in the roof with neither stair nor ladder leading to them, fit only for winged things to use; and barred doors leading into buried pools into which canals filled with frozen waters reached.

Gil's sharp eyes also saw silhouettes of hawks and owls and other birds decorating the eaves and window arches, and now he knew in what land he passed and what river he sailed. He had seen it once before, from a distance, from one of those very windows. Which one, he could not guess.

Gil came to an ivory wall. It was shattered in one place, and the waters of the river streamed forth there. The swan boat passed between the broken panels of the wall as if through two cliffs of dazzling white. Here was a wide lake held within ivory walls. Leafless trees coated with frost circled the walls in all places but one. The swans swam there.

Here was a stair of ivory steps that ran straight up the black mountain to a black rock. Each step had tall and thin statues looming one to either side, but these were so coated with snow as to be indecipherable.

Gil disembarked, and thanked the swans, and slung the covered corpse of Guynglaff over Rabicane's back. Ruff jumped out of the boat. With Ruff at his heels, Gil mounted the stairs.

The sun was setting, and the western sky was as red as fire, and Gil made as if to hurry. But Rabicane said, "Pace these stairs slowly so that they will not expand beneath your feet."

Gil heeded the advice, and as the twilight darkened into night, he walked with a solemn pace, step by step, past statues smothered and coated in snow.

The two figures on the topmost stair, however, were not statues, but soldiers with silver lance in hand. The lances were twice as tall as the soldiers holding them, and the blades gleamed in the clashing, silver-white shadows of the leafless trees with their own captured starlight.

One was dressed in the green and gold livery of Alberec; the other in the sable and silver of Erlkoenig. It was Corylus and Lemur.

Gil approached. Lemur said, "Long ago, we were told to admit any who came hither in the Swanskiff without question or challenge." And he inclined his head.

The black rock rolled back with a grinding roar, disclosing a buried gate below. Golden light and the blare of elfin trumpets came from underneath. Gil saw through the bars of the portcullis the same long hall he had seen one year ago, leading beneath Brown Mountain in North Carolina.

Lemur smote the silver bars with the butt of his lance and called out, "The golden doors of Heaven welcome all as do the iron doors of Hell. Delling's Doors of elfin silver wrought ought to unhide and open wide as easily as well." And the bars rose up.

Gil said, "Tell me, Corylus, have they eaten of the Golden Boar yet?"

Corylus said, "This year, Alberec commanded that the custom of the feast be kept not on the Eve of Stephen, but this night. They will not feast of the golden meat until some great adventure or deed of arms is done."

Gil doffed his helm, and now he drew back his coif, so that his silver hair caught the light of spear and star and shined. Corylus stared at the silver hair with awe, and even Lemur seemed impressed.

Gil said, "Please escort me to your lords, good and loyal Corylus and Lemur. I have returned alive from the chapel where the Green Knight holds vigil, and I wish not to surrender sword and gear as I pass in. Come with me. The sight will be worth seeing."

Lemur said, "Torments to vex even the most stalwart await those who abandon their posts without leave, but I will send my spirit ahead of you, and none will bar your path."

2. The Wine of Truth

Down the long corridor adorned with trees and serpents, skulls and owls, walked Gil. The diamond doors at the far end had been repaired and opened as he approached, and fanfare rose up.

Gil mounted his steed.

The black wolf and the white wolf made of stone watched him wryly as he came but pretended to be statues, and neither moved nor spoke as he rode in.

Above were the roots of a great oak on which lanterns burned, this time in the pattern of the Southern Cross. The strangeness of the air was here so that any object far away was clear in his eyes as if close at hand, and any distant whisper, when he wished it, loud. All the lords and ladies of the elfs and the dignitaries and grandees of the night world were here, sad human wizards dressed in black hoods, owl-headed figures in white robes, splendid Fomorian women with their ghastly men, knights in livery, counts in crowns, dukes in diamond cloaks, and other beings in robes woven of liquid fire, or of butterflies, or in mantles of opaque and solid music, or in robes of living snakes as bright as gems.

Gil inhaled, and now he recognized the scent here. Behind the wine and the sizzling meats and fresh bread and pastries baking merrily was an odor he had smelled last when the angel spoke to him. As if a small, still voice spoke in his heart, he knew this was the odor of the air of eternity, the perfume of timelessness. The inner intuition told him to take a slower, deeper breath and to savor it more carefully. Gil did, and now he tasted a sour taste at the back of his tongue. Compared to the breath of the angel, this was somehow stale, as if eternity had rotted or gone bad. It was a disturbing sensation, and he suspected he knew what it meant.

But the air also gave a pall of timelessness over the whole scene, for here was Erlkoenig in his faceplate of ice, his eyes like malignant stars; there was Alberec in his eyepatch; little King Brian, no larger than a doll, sat on his same small throne atop the feast table; Ethne the May Queen, with candles in her hair, was next to her giant, Bran the Blessed. The elfs and Night Folk were ranked by dignity beneath their canopies from the bow of the horseshoe-shaped table, to the aristocrats, high-ranked servants, and viziers, warlocks, nibelungs, craftsmen, and poets, and yeomen. Beyond this were Twilight Folk, and at the tail ends of the table, to one side was the beast table, and to the other, Gil saw the three Cobwebs: Rotwang with his metal hand, Lucian dressed like a Cossack in a fur hat, and Zahack in a turban, gray and groaning with age. In the center of the table, in the wide space, were the colored fires where the cooks and bakers toiled, and tiny butlers, no bigger than bumblebees, flashed through the air. Here jugglers tossed, and captive unicorns and loons cried and sang. Here a harpist with a golden harp put the song directly into Gil's bloodstream like a drug, and, as he had before, Gil had to brace himself not to fall into its seductive rhythm and have it set the set the pace at which he moved and spoke.

And there was the golden pork, being kept warm in a dish by a fretful cook.

All was the same, except for one thing alone. In the seat where once Gil sat, the place of honor next to Alberec, Sir Bertolac in his gold livery was, a goblet in his hand.

Gil did not hide the scowl on his face. For it seemed to him almost as if the elfs were frozen like the figures in a stained glass window.

So into the feast chamber of Mommur, where the elfin lords kept revel, Gilberec Moth trotted on horseback, atop one of the most magnificent steeds in the world. And Rabicane lashed his lion's tail and held his head high.

Gil could hear their murmurs and whispers perfectly. All were wondering at his silver hair, at who he was, and at what he was. That made him smile. The hour was now come when all would know.

Gil hated the mesmeric elf music, so he put the horn of Roland to his lips and blew. The whole chamber trembled at the sound like an explosion of brass, clear and bold and shocking as being dashed with cold water.

Niall the harpist put his hands over his ears and off his strings. Gil said to the loons and unicorns, "Please cease your calls." And when the beasts stopped singing, the musicians allowed their music to die in mid note.

Alberec said, "Swan Knight, you have returned. You have preserved the honor of the court and won our admiration. You must tell us the adventure."

Gil said, "There is little to tell. I kept the fast of Advent and did all the things a Christian gentleman must do, and Heaven protected me from various and sundry temptations I am too ashamed to name. The Green Knight, for reasons known only to him, instead of striking off my head, dubbed me knight in Arthur's name. I learned then that no feats of knighthood are possible, and no victory secure, without the help of Heaven, so I pray all you good knights in this chamber who seek to survive the toils and ruin of hideous war put aside your pride and seek first victory in unseen things, before any battle of flesh and blood be fought, and kneel to Christ!"

He had to raise his voice toward the end because the choir of hisses and howls and mocking laughter erupting from the silver throats and perfect lips of the elfs was growing louder. And many of the pookas and animals yowled at the sound of the name of Christ.

Erlkoenig tapped on the table before him with his fingertip, making no noise, and all fell silent upon the instant, save one young knight in blue and gold who did not stop his laughter in time, so Erlkoenig pointed the same finger at him, and this young knight was struck mute, clutched his throat, and fell over the table.

Alberec nodded politely to Erlkoenig, and turned to Gil, and said, "Forgive the discourtesy and continue, Sir Knight."

Gil said, "The Green Knight counseled me wisely how to overcome my foe and the foe of my father. You know the rest, or else Sheila McGuire is no spy."

Alberec looked at the covered body draped across the saddle. "And who is this foe of your father?"

Gil dismounted, and drew the body down, and placed it carefully on the floor in just the way his mother had instructed him. The Helm of Grim was inside the leather sack, and Gil contrived that the helm and its lodestone were on the underside of the corpse.

Gil said, "I slew Guynglaff wrestling with him, and we fell in the water, and he drowned. Here is his body!"

Gil now drew his sword, Dyrnwen, and in one stroke he cut the upper flap of the leathery bag and exposed the face and neck of Guynglaff.

The apelike face and balding skull looked particularly harsh and ugly in the leaping colored lights of the elf chamber.

Through the corner of his eye, Gil saw Lucien Cobweb, the Cossack, was hissing in detestation and anger, and he opened his mouth and displayed an impressive pair of fangs. Rotwang Cobweb kept his face impassive, but the solid gold goblet in his metal hand shattered into a dozen shards. Even Zahack was moved. The ancient man opened his bleary eyes and gritted his few, crooked and yellowing teeth in anger. Drool leaked out and stained his scabby chin and straggling wisps of beard.

Gil shouted, "And here is the sword!"

Gil stabbed the great sword Dyrnwen through the leather, ribs, body, and back of Guynglaff, carefully inching the sword tip until it touched the Helm of Grim hidden in the bag beneath the body.

The body was dead, but some trickle of life, the thing that makes the nails and hair of corpses still to grow, was in it. There was a flash as bright as lightning from the sword.

Gil felt a jerk in his arm as the lodestone gem adorning the helm clung and stuck to the blade. Gil let go of the blade, and the fire from the blade became dim, turgid, smoky, and yellowish, no brighter than a red coal.

Gil said, "I returned in triumph to my mother, and she gave me this bottle of wine, but charged me strictly not to open it except that I share it with the knights of Corbenec, Sir Aglovale, Sir Lamorak, and Sir Dornar! Your Majesty, Your Imperial Majesty…" Gil now bowed to Alberec and Erlkoenig. "… I would like your permission to offer a toast, for this victory of mine, over both the Green Knight and the foe of my blood, would not have been possible had it not been for the courtesy and noble dealing of Alberec, the hard training by his Champion, Sir Bertolac, and all done at the behest of Erlkoenig, Emperor of all the Elfs, Lord of Shadows!"

The chamber gave a gasp of wonder when the diamond bottle in Gil's hand came out of his poke. A quick-thinking serving girl flew down and proffered a corkscrew.

Gil now drew the cork, and he discovered that the wine, bottled in the high country from which his mother came, had the same property as the air in this chamber, except that it was not stale. The scent and savor of the wine, delicious, irresistible, stole through the wide chamber like a spring wind, and each soul there felt as if the drink were only an inch beyond his tongue.

Without waiting for permission, Gil stepped over to the table where his three brothers sat. As before, there was no sign of the father. Here was Sir Aglovale, cool-eyed and intent; here was Lamorak, smiling lazily, as serene as a panther half-asleep in the sun; and there was Dornar, eyes narrowed in perpetual anger. Gil took up their three goblets from the table and dashed the wine to the floor in a splash of purple.

All three knights stood, offended at the effrontery. Gil poured the delicious scented wine from the upper world into their goblets one by one. Gil then looked toward Mathuin Moth, Alberec's butler, and smiled. Without a word, the butler handed him a goblet, into which he poured some of the wine.

Gil shouted, "A toast to Erlkoenig!"

Erlkoenig said in his cold and emotionless voice, "Hold, Sir Knight. Do you seek to insult me by throwing a corpse before me, befouling his body with a savage blow, and calling on my vassals and followers to drink your triumph? What if this hairy man had been a servant of mine? Or had been someone you swore you would spare?"

Gil bowed, "I proffer no insult of any kind, Imperial Majesty. For I made certain that this wild and hairy man was no servant of yours before I slew him. Indeed, he boasted of his disloyalty to you in my ear while we fought."

A rustle went the chamber, the noise of many small sounds of surprise.

"A loyal servant of yours would not have drawn this sword to slay me, who just this fortnight did a great and memorable service for your Imperial Majesty. A loyal servant would have laid it at your feet. Moreover, had you sent him to fight me, I would be dead, for you would not have allowed foolishness and anger to decide your tactics, but Guynglaff allowed nothing but. And any oath I might have made to spare him was foresworn by Guynglaff, who betrayed the terms his master laid on him. Why did he not present that sword to you if he thought I was dead? For whose hand did he keep it?"

Gil pointed at the dimly burning sword piercing the corpse on the marble floor. "There is a sword that can slay giants. Can it not slay kings?"

There was much murmuring and muttering at this question.

Gil raised his voice, "These were the very words of Guynglaff to me before he died! *We are stronger than Erlkoenig and all his court! The spirit of anarchy is loosed in the world and will topple all kings, break all covenants, and end all faithfulness!*"

Now the musical voices of the elfs held a note of rising anger, and there was a hushed note of fear behind it.

Gil said, "My dread lord, all in this chamber hear the truth in my words. I deceive no one. So Guynglaff spoke. Was he your servant in truth?"

Erlkoenig raised a finger. All in the chamber fell silent so quickly Gil wondered for a moment if he had been struck deaf.

Erlkoenig said in a cold, soft voice, "You recall, Sir Knight, what words we exchanged when we met outside this chamber and the bargain we struck? A loyal servant of mine would have kept my word whole and offered no dishonor to me, to make me seem a liar."

Gil said, "Neither will I offer you dishonor, lord."

He had been schooled by his mother to say this, for Ygraine predicted Erlkoenig would not admit in open court that his servants disobeyed him. She predicted also Erlkoenig would be grateful for Gil's silence.

Erlkoenig said, "Guynglaff Cobweb was no servant of mine."

Gil saw that three colored shadows now occupied the spots where the three Cobwebs had been seated. He alone could see Rotwang and Lucien, each with an arm under the thin shoulders of decrepit Zahack, silently sneaking out of the hall.

Gil said, "Guynglaff will not strike against anyone again. Have I permission to call for a toast to your Imperial Majesty? I was first enrolled on your lists as a knight before any other power recognized me. It was by that courtesy I was brought into the chamber last year, and by this good hap I was present to defy the Green Knight, who shamed all chivalry gathered here, your knights as well as those of the other kings and lords at this feast, from greatest to humblest. It would be base indeed were I to claim all honor to myself and forget Alberec and Erlkoenig, at whose behest and high command all these things were done."

Erlkoenig said carefully, "I know you to be a very honest man, and a stalwart knight, and such as ye be hard to turn from their purposes. Why do you offer the wine to those three knights of Alberec, instead of to us? For its savor is very sweet."

Gil said, "First, I ask to serve the wine to the knights of Corbenec as I was commanded by my mother, whom I dare not dishonor nor disobey, not even for fear of kings."

The elfs laughed.

Gil said, "And second, these were the three knights of all knighthood I first saw when I climbed a mountain to see the elves. I wrestled Sir Dornar and overthrew him fair and square even though I was unarmed and unhorsed and him armed at all points. Because of that, I knew I had the strength to be a knight, and a good one."

Another murmur of laughter ran through the chamber, and the music of the elfish laughter seemed to effect Dornar like a charm. He grew pale and trembled at the sound of shame.

Aglovale said, "You? That was you? That boy was the Swan Knight?"

Dornar, pale and shaking, said, "Of course it is not him! He is the Swan Knight's son. Look at the hue of his hair! Look at his eyes, the shape of his jaws and lips, and then look in a mirror, you fools! The lies arise to haunt us!"

Aglovale said, "Brothers, do not say in this place anything we cannot unsay!"

Lamorak said in a voice of lilting nonchalance, "Oh, come! It cannot be! This man is dressed in disguise to impersonate a character from a story! The Swan Knight is a fiction, a false tale invented by our mother to cover her shame! She slept with the Wild-Man-o'-Wood and bore to him a hairy whelp, more monkey than human...."

Aglovale put his hand on Lamorak's shoulder to warn him not to speak, but it was too late, for Gil in anger drew up Lamorak's goblet carrying the celestial wine and dashed it into Lamorak's face.

A few drops must have entered Lamorak's mouth because his whole demeanor changed. Instead of wrath at the great insult done him, he grabbed for the goblet and sought to bring it to his lips, yearning for other droplets of the heavenly wine. Gil politely handed him his own goblet, which Lamorak drained.

Erlkoenig turned his mask of ice toward Alberec, as if expecting him to object or intervene when one of his own knights had been insulted, slung with wine. But to the surprise of everyone there, Alberec said, "A toast to the Swan Knight! A toast to the Emperor! Blessings and honor and glory and power upon them!" And he picked up his own cup and put it to his lips.

But King Brian, the diminutive red-haired red-faced king next to Erlkoenig said, "Hold and halt! Sir Lamorak acts strangely. See how he guzzles and laps at the wine. Perhaps it is enchanted—or poisoned!"

Gil said, "Each time I speak a lie, every ear within earshot knows. I swear by Heaven that the wine contains no venom, but only a blessing." And he poured wine from the bottle into his mouth and swallowed.

Gil turned to his brothers, "Drink the toast! And I offer one toast more! Gentlemen: a toast to the mother of the knights of Corbenec, Ygraine the Wise, Ygraine of the Silver Locks, the gentlest, best, most truthful, truehearted, and kindhearted mother under Heaven! Drink! Will you not drink to your own mother, gentle knights, or will you insult her before all this fine company? Drink!"

Aglovale said, "Sire, I suspect some deceit is here! Excuse me from this toast."

But Alberec said, "Drink!"

Aglovale and Dornar both warily sipped the wine but, finding it savory beyond all measure, drank heartily and deep.

Lamorak said gaily, "That is the finest of wines ever I drank! I taste the courage of heroes burning like fire in this wine! Where does it come from?"

Aglovale said soberly, "I taste tears in this wine. The smell and savor reminds me of when I was a small child and my mother held me. What is in this wine?"

Dornar said sullenly, "I taste blood! You who forced this wine down our throats. Who are you?"

And then the brothers looked at each other in horror, and the chamber looked on in wonder, for every word out of the mouths was true, and everyone heard and knew it.

Alberec said, "Swan Knight! Answer the questions asked of you."

Gil raised his head and spoke in a voice like a trumpet.

"The wine comes from Sarras, the City in the Summer Stars, the home of Ygraine of the Swan Wings.

"Those wings your father, Alain le Gros, stole and thereby forced Ygraine into his marriage bed unlawfully, uncouthly, and against nature, for Ygraine is the sister to Alain's mother, Elaine of the Sea. Nonetheless, in return for his hand, Alain rendered to her the Tower Dolorous in Terregaste.

"When the Wild Man stole Ygraine, you were too weak to stop him, so you concocted the tale that she ran off willingly with him; and when she returned with babe in arms, you concocted the tale that the babe was the child of Guynglaff.

"Your father threatened to have the child done away with, so to protect it, Ygraine took the boy and fled through the trackless air, for the boy had unwittingly discovered for her the hiding place of her swan robe.

"You searched and found proof that this was so, that she would surrender name and fame and titles and all to preserve the babe at her breast.

"But you were so ashamed that she protected your brother, whom you did not protect, that you declared the child dead and her a murderess for having abandoned him, and also called her adulteress and traitress to her lord husband, and many worse things beside.

"She flew back not to paradise, but to a life of menial chores, unthanked labor, and constant fear and uncertainty, knowing that if she were found, the child's life was forfeit.

"But the child's true father armed and equipped him for battle, and the child slew the Wild-Man-o'-Wood you failed to slay, and with that charm, which only comes to a hero when he slays his first monster in his first fight, three blessings were given to me.

"You ask what is in the wine? What is in this wine is the last and the greatest of those blessings, which is that all who hear you can hear the truth you speak so that no man can pretend to doubt your word! It is a princely gift, and freely I share it with my brothers. It will be your blessing until you die!

"Who am I you knew the moment you saw for the first time the hair of my head, which I have kept hidden all this year. I was born Gilberec Parsifal Moth, son of Ygraine of the Wise Reeds and the Swan Knight; and now I am the Swan Knight in my own right, and Sir Gilberec of the Court of King Arthur.

"And I am one thing more: the Lord of the Tower Dolorous and possessor of all the rights and lands that go with it, for I have here in hand the peppercorn which is due and owing to Alberec, the King of the Fortunate Elfs, by whose law those lands are mine."

He stepped over, bowed, and placed the silk bag containing the peppercorn before the plate of Alberec.

Alberec said, "How shall I accept this token since you have not sworn fealty to me?"

Gil said, "I swore to Arthur. Ygraine told me that would satisfy you."

Alberec's one eye glinted strangely, and he laughed. "I had forgotten the sensation of what it felt like to be outsmarted by Ygraine! The memory returns. Knights of Corbenec! How do you answer all these charges and calumnies heaped upon your name by the Swan Knight of the Tower Dolorous?"

Gil said, "Begging your majesty's pardon. It is the Tower Joyous now, for Ygraine no longer weeps tears there."

Alberec nodded, and a small, tight smile slightly made his lips thin. He called out, "Corbenec! Answer him!"

Aglovale said, "None of his accusations can be proved."

Alberec said, "A nicely worded answer, but one which says nothing."

Lamorak laughed, "They say there is truth in wine. Wine this good must have truth more potent! I will bring no curse on myself. I have no answer, my lord."

Alberec said, "This wording is even nicer, and even less was said."

Dornar shouted, "I say the Swan Knight lies! He is a base knave and…"

And all the elfs laughed because the falsehood that rang from his voice was obvious and clear to one and all.

Dornar gritted his teeth and said, "If we have lost the power to tell lies, then we cannot live among the elfs!"

The elfish laughter died at these words because their truth was also obvious.

"So my only answer is this!" And Dornar drew his dirk and came over the table toward Gil.

But Gil was wearing armor from heel to neck, and had not spent the last nine days drinking, and was not maddened with wrath. He coolly caught Dornar by the shoulder, and toppled to the ground with him, driving his armored elbow joint into his solar plexus, and in a trice had him in a bear hug, as he had been taught. He banged Dornar's head against the marble floor, until it was bloody, and Dornar in misery called out, "It is true! It is all true! What the Swan Knight says is true!"

Gil growled in his ear, "Swear it! Swear in the name of Christ that it is true and Mother is innocent!"

Tears drew trails in the blood covering his face. Dornar shouted and sobbed, "I swear by the name of Christ that all my brother said is true! And that Ygraine was innocent of all we claimed! Everything we said was a lie, a damned lie!"

And all the animals in the chamber yowled in pain at the name of Christ.

Gil let go of Dornar, but the other knight did not get to his feet. Instead, he knelt. "I beg your pardon, too, Sir Knight. You have defeated me in combat. How may I ransom my life?"

Gil realized, to his shock, what Dornar meant. He said, "You are my brother, and I would not kill you."

Aglovale said, "You must ask something of him, or else it dishonors him, that you think his life worth nothing."

Gil said, "Arms and armor I have, and finer than any I have seen, and a horse and hound I envy no man's. So I will ask my brother for something more painful to surrender: go, be baptized, go to confession, and seek the forgiveness and peace and pardon found there."

Alberec said, "You render him worthless to me."

Gil said, "To the contrary, sire, he will be a better knight than before."

But Dornar, ignoring Alberec, looked up from the floor and spoke. "Yes. I agree. By tree and fountain, star and blood, I swear it...."

Gil held up his hand. "I hear the truth in your voice. Your *yes* is enough. You need swear by no pagan things."

And he helped him to his feet.

Gil turned to Alberec, "Sire! I believe I have provided the adventure and the deed of arms you require to feast on the golden meat...?"

But Ethne the May Queen interrupted them, her voice filled with hauteur, "Not so fast! There is a law that no Moth and no son of Twilight can enter this land without binding himself with unbreakable oaths to the Lord of Elfland! I have heard no oath given to Erlkoenig! And how dare a mere half-breed wear those spurs and carry that sword! They are treasures of our world!"

But Erlkoenig said, "Was it not I who first ordered Sir Gilberec enrolled as a knight on my rolls? All the proper forms and legalities have been satisfied." He pointed his finger at the diamond wine bottle, which still had some left in it. The bottle flew threw the air into the central fire pit, where it shattered in the tiny, glittering shards, and the precious wine with its lovely scent of Heaven was split and mingled with the ashes, and perfumed steam rose up hissing.

Erlkoenig raised his hand, "But the May Queen raises a question not to be turned aside. Sir Gilberec is a Moth, a lesser race, wherein dirty and diseased human blood is mingled with the ethereal ichor of finer beings to produce a mongrel race that is welcomed nowhere. How should one of our finest treasures be found in his hand? What do my lords and gentlemen advise we should rule?"

Gil said, "Begging your Imperial Majesty's pardon, but I believe a higher power has already adjudicated the matter."

Erlkoenig said, "What mean you?"

Gil pointed again at the dim and smoking blade protruding from the corpse. "Let him who is worthy draw the sword from the belly of the beast."

3. The Trial of the Fair White-hilted Sword

Nothing of Erlkoenig's face could be seen but the glitter of his eyes, so, when he did not speak, it was unclear what thought held him back. He said slowly, "What is your counsel, oh ye sovereigns sworn in fealty to me?"

Little king Brian Brollachan of the Autumn Elfs said, "Some spry trick or turn is here, my lord. This little boy has returned as a squire of the Green Knight and knows his tricks!"

Sir Bertolac's gold eyes flashed, and he spoke up, "Forgive me, lords, if I speak out of turn, but let some volunteer, unasked and uncommanded, step forth to grasp the blade and take it up. Then, if that one fails, it was not at the command of any king. In such as wise no knight will be shamed should he fail."

Balor of the Evil Eye, the giant coated in rime and frost with four men standing on his knee propping up his horrid eye in a beam now called for a fifth to step onto his knee, and put his back into pushing the pole so that Balor could lift his eyelid more widely open and glare. "What? I will volunteer!"

Erlkoenig said, "No, let this be done in order. I call forth my champion, Pwyll Penannwn, who once clasped living arms about the queen of the dead."

The knight who stood was white-haired, and his face was lined and scarred with grief and wound, and his eyes haunted with strange things. His cloak and cloakpin were of plain wool and green copper. Adjacent tables, as if by an inner spirit, moved their legs to make a space where an elf could step without flying over or ducking under. Pwyll put his hand to the great sword Dyrnwen.

Immediately, the blade burned with a blue-white flame, bright as twenty torches, and the elfs put their hands before their eyes, the efts hissed, the Nephilim cursed, and the pookas and lesser servants squinted and yowled.

A terrible stench rose up from the corpse of the yeti as Guynglaff caught fire.

Pwyll pulled. The sword moved by not so much as a hairsbreadth. He put his foot on the corpse, put both hands on the hilts, and yanked again.

He turned to Erlkoenig and spoke in a voice as cold and dry as Erlkoenig's own, with no change of tone or expression. "I feel the weight of my sins pulling my hand. Naught can move the blade."

Erlkoenig merely turned his mask of ice toward the next knight seated one seat lower than Pwyll, who was Bertolac, the champion of Alberec. Bertolac said, "I will not venture it. I smell the magic of the Green Knight at work here. I trained this boy, and in a year he learned what most squires learn in ten. For his reward, I gave him my own horn, which once was Roland's. How, then? If I come into possession of so great a treasure as that sword, will not the noble company gathered here suspect me of being party to deceit? And I do not wish Ysbadden to rip my arms off, as he did to Rhydderch Hael, who last held that blade!"

Then, Ethne smiled in her anger and spoke in a lingering drawl. "That blade is too fine to be found in the hand of a Moth, a mere Twilight creature, a half-breed! Bran, step forth!"

But Bran said, "Sir Esclados the Red is your champion, O Queen! Let him be first before me."

A tall figure in scarlet, azure, and gold brocade, set with figures of fiery serpents and swimming eels strode forth next. When he touched the sword, it burned with a yellow flame no brighter than two or three torches. He tugged in vain. The fires spread, and more of the corpse was burning now.

He scowled and gnawed his moustaches in fury, tugging and pulling with both hands, and then lying on the floor and pushing on the hilts with both feet. He would have been there pushing forever had not Ethne, scoffing, called him back.

Bran, without moving from his position, reached with his mighty arm to the center of the chamber. He could only grip the sword with finger and thumb, like a man plucking a toothpick. It burned blue-white for him, not as bright as it had for Pwyll, but brighter far than the fire Esclados the Red had called forth.

King Brian called forth his champion, who had the shape of a horse whose coat changed color from white to red to black and back again. "Blackahasten!" called the king, "Not often do I call you to fight and fret on my behest, but I've a potent hankering to have that sword me own! And, wallaway, how it will vex the giants if the wee folk have the giantkiller's white sword!"

The horse stepped over to the sword, and his neck grew like a giraffe's neck, and he clamped powerful teeth on the hilts, and sparks and flickers of multicolored power shined in his mouth. Tug as he might, he was no better than any man-shaped knight.

Knight after knight made the attempt, and the corpse burned and burned.

When it came his turn, Sir Aglovale said, "I will not attempt it!"

Some near him jeered, but he said, "I am unafraid. But I know too well that if my mother gave this, my bastard brother, his advice, she has already outsmarted us all."

From the hushed and whispered remarks (all of which could be heard in the strange, high air of that enchanted chamber), it was clear that everyone heard the truth in the voice of Aglovale and believed him.

The knight smiled a small, sad smile at that, as if the loss of the power to lie or be accused of lying might not be such a curse after all.

But Dornar his brother jumped up. "What? Shall Queen Ethne say no Moth will carry such a blade? For twenty years I have hid that name and called myself Dornar de Corbanec, but no more! I claim my due!"

When he touched the blade, it was white with heat and fire and burned like ten torches, but he could not stir it.

More than half the body of the corpse was consumed by now, and bones protruded from the ashes and burned flaps of leather, but still the horrible stench rose up.

Lamorak laughed and said, "Come now! If this little bastard dropped from the wrong side of sheets stained with the sweat of Mother cavorting with some strange fellow can hold the blade, can I not? Am I not better born than he and in wedlock to boot?"

"Incestuous wedlock and unholy rape," said Gilberec coolly. "But I blame you not for the sins of the father. Take it and hold it, if you can!"

Again, the blade burned white with heat, bright as it had under the hand of Dornar.

There now began whispers and titters in the chamber, and a pressure in Gil's ears told him that the elfs were speaking but maintaining an illusion of silence. Some ladies were glancing sidelong at Esclados the Red.

After the elfs, the cry in the chamber rose to let others come. Without waiting for Erlkoenig to speak, Gilberec called out that all were welcome.

Dragon-faced or snaked-eyed efts in their baronial coronets and shirts of gold tried next, and the blade burned white for them. Dark Svartalfar with muscles like knots of iron tugged, and for them the blade burned yellow.

Two of the knights who wore the goggles and owl-feather cloaks of the Striga attempted, and each one walked counterclockwise thrice about the sword before attempting it, as if to break the charm. They each used the strength of the wings as well as arms, flapping furiously, but could not budge the orange-yellow blade.

Only one human warlock was young and hale enough to attempt it, a man with iron-gray hair who seemed very fit and strong for a man so old. He called out blasphemous names and touched the white hilt with mistletoe, and for a moment Gil was worried. The blade burned orange at his touch like a hot coal, but did not stir.

A woman warrior of the most ancient race of Cessair, dressed in the white tunic and red cloak like a Spartan maid, attempted the blade. Sparks and shimmers of power, which gave her the strength of a man, came about her slender and fair limbs, and she groaned and strained. The blade burned dull red under her touch, a smoky and poisonous color no brighter than it had done in the hands of Guynglaff. A scornful laugh trickled through the chamber, and the Amazonian girl blushed in shame.

When Balor of the Evil Eye came, fairies landed on his head and shoulders, and shed sparks and sprinkles of light on him, and shrank him down to the size of a tall man. A servant led him to the sword, for his one eye was closed, and he could not see. He pulled with such strength that the marble broke under his heels, and he pushed himself two inches into the floor. But the sword did not move.

By now the corpse was a great heap of ash, burnt meat, and blackened bones, and it was a great dark pile on the marble floor.

Other Fomorians, creatures hopping or hobbling on one leg and reaching out with one arm, came next, and the blade shined with a dull orange hue for them as well.

Red it burned for the proud Nephilim, who yanked at the blade with their six-fingered hands.

When pooka or servants attempted, the blade shed heat like might be seen above a pavement on a summer's day, but did not grow brighter than a black frying pan and did not burst into flame.

The corpse was now a soft black pile of bones and charred debris, smoking and smoldering, and still the helmet clutching the sword was unseen beneath heap of ash.

Not every knight or strong man in the chamber made trial of the blade. The elfs were hissing and whispering openly now, for they had noticed at whose touch the blade burned more brightly or less.

Sir Esclados the Red was blushing with shame and glaring at the serpent-faced efts, for the sword had betrayed his birth to be less than theirs. Before the last attempt was made, so many had seen the low births and high presumption of several knights and nobles betrayed, or an eft who touched the blade and turned it orange, not gold, or a Nephilim for whom it would not ignite at all.

Gil called out asking to step forward anyone to endure the test of the sword. No one was willing.

4. The Swan Blade

Silence hung over the chamber.

Gil smiled thinly, remembering what the Man in the Black Room had told him about being a kitchen page in Arthur's Court, and how the magic cauldron could detect lies and betray boasts as false, and how dangerous such an instrument could be among those who whole lives were based on reputation, glory, and honor. How much more desperate and dreadful for a race of beings whose lives were based on illusion and vainglory.

Erlkoenig said, "Your mother has counseled you well, Sir Gilberec son of Ygraine and an unknown sire. But that treasure is too precious to take from this chamber. No man passes into the Elfinlands unless he bows and swears to serve me, or one of these my vassal kings, Brian or Alberec, or the queen Ethne, or some other lord of Elfland."

Gilberec said, "Nonetheless, the sword is mine, as it was my father's before me, and I shall take it."

Alberec said, "But what if your father is baseborn, or a traitor, or a damned soul condemned to Hell? You cannot assume your blood is fine enough to let you take up that sword!"

Little King Brian said, "Tell us on the quickstep how you tricked us! Neatly it was done, I say! And it is fair sport and fine to match wits with you."

The May Queen, Ethne, said cooly, "You have earned your place here, Sir Gilberec. If you put aside the name of Moth, we will forbid any to call you bastard and halfbreed to your face. Immortality, endless strength, the beauties of fair women, and the secrets of magic can all be yours; a castle made of ivory with sirens and lamia to sing from the sea beneath your casements! Bow and serve us, and the elfs will reward you."

Gilberec laughed. "Noble offers, sovereigns of elfinkind! I will ask you three riddles in answer: first, who was king in Elfland before Alberec took the throne?"

Alberec said, "Arthur, for in the power of Excalibur, he conquered Troynovant, the Third Troy, as easily as he conquered Rome, the Second Troy."

Gilberec said, "Your law is that I must swear fealty to a King of Elfland. So I have, for Arthur is not dead, nor is Merlin, for he was betrayed, but the charms he wove about his life were too strong for his false and traitorous student who betrayed him to overcome. Lady Nimue! Perhaps the sword will serve you! Come and take the hilts in your hand."

Nimue shook her crowned head so that the clamshells of her coronet rang. She shrank back in her seat. "You cannot prove any crime of mine! Take that dreadful sword away! How did it come to be in the hands of a Moth?"

Gilberec smiled, "Even so, milady? Is there any here who doubts that I am Arthur's Knight, duly knighted and sworn, or must I call here to testify the Green Knight himself of the Green Chapel?"

And at those words, there was a mighty roar and rushing of winds in the corridors and doors outside the chamber, and the diamond doors were battered, and the bar broke, and they were flung open. Yet when the doors opened, no man was there, merely the roaring winds that swept through the chamber, making all flames blow and tremble and all the feasters shiver with cold.

Sir Bertolac stood up and cried, "No! No! Knights and gentlemen! Sovereign kings and queens! You know me to be the most fearless fighter of this generation, undefeated save only by Bran the Blessed! I am no coward, but I tell you, let not this lad call the Green Knight here again! Who can withstand his terrible wrath?"

Other voices in the chamber took up the cry. Alberec looked at Erlkoenig and shrugged. Alberec said, "Let us acknowledge that fealty sworn to Arthur will suffice. The Swan Knight surely will not hurt the realm that Arthur rules, not and be a true knight. And Arthur might never wake."

Erlkoenig said nothing.

Gilberec said, "Answer me my second riddle: *what is louder than a horn, or what is sharper than the thorn; what is heavier than lead, or what more blessed than the bread?*"

The kings and princes looked at each other in confusion, but little King Brian snapped his fingers, "This one, 'tis known to me! 'Tis an old one, but sound and hard, like all old saws should be. *Shame is louder nor the horn, guilt sharper than the thorn, heavier than lead is sin...*" His bright, ruddy face now collapsed into a sullen frown. "Aye, ah! I forget the rest..."

Gilberec said, "*More blessed than bread is bread the Savior's flesh is hid within.* Do you see know how you were prevented from drawing up this sword? Even struck through a heavy body, none of you could stir it an inch."

Gilberec now took the sword in hand. It ignited with a brightness of thirty torches, burning with white-hot heat. Sharp black shadows leaped back from every object in the room. As before, the elfs cried out and hid their eyes, for the sword in his grasp outshone them all.

He lifted up the sword. The charred and black remains of the body of Guynglaff fell away. Gil stood with the blazing sword overhead, with nothing but scraps of leather about the hilts, and a few burned and blackened ribs, which he shook onto the floor. At the tip of the sword, unharmed, still stuck to it, was the Helm of Grim. In a moment the bright fires Gil's hands called forth burned all the ash away. The helm glowed red hot.

Earlier, during the bright flash when Pwyll had attempted the sword, Gilberec had knelt and petted his dog. As they had practiced, Ruff spat the iron nail he had been carrying in his mouth—the pooka could indeed carry cold iron unharmed—and Gil hid the nail in the palm of his hand as Ruff had shown him how to do.

Hiding and passing small objects was apparently one of the skills Ruff had learned in spy school. Gil had not wanted to carry any cold iron earlier because he was not sure whether it would denature or disenchant his mother's wine or the yeti's helmet.

Now Gil reached up and yanked the Helm of Grim free of the sword, for he allowed the tiniest unseen tip of the nail peaking between his fingers to touch the iron crystal topping the metal cap.

As before, the touch of cold iron broke the charm, and the stone from the lodestone mountain released its grip.

Gil dropped the red-hot helm clanging to the marble floor in a spray of red sparks. He sheathed the sword to quench its fire and allow the blinking and half-blinded elfs to see what he had dropped. The helm had lost its roundness, and its crown sagged, and steam poured upward from it.

Gilberec said, "Here is the Helm of Grim, which Ygraine of the Reeds called upon to gather to itself all the sins of any man who tried to pull my sword from its grip. None of you was strong enough to pull against your sins, your years and centuries of sin, sins unrepentant, ugly, and proud. Have none of you ever asked for absolution, as befits a knight before combat? Ere I came here, I was shrived, and all my sins were forgotten. For me, this cursed cap was feather light. For you, heavier than lead, sharper than thorns, louder than horns. None here is worthy to bear this sword, and so none of you will dare take it from my hand."

A silent chamber answer him with no words at all.

Gilberec said, "Here is my third riddle: in whose hand burns Dyrnwen the brightest withal? The most base or the most nobly born in the hall?"

The elfs and nobles looked on silently. The Glashan, pipe in his horselike mouth, was seated at the lowest table farthest from the fire. He laughed aloud, and the laugh was the only noise in the great chamber. And the Glashan began to clap his hands in applause.

Gil said, "Have I any art this great sword to deceive? My father is the equal of anyone here; so vows the brightness of the blade. Do you still not believe?"

Others joined the applause. First, it was only the maids and butlers banging cooking pans together, then the pookas barking and neighing, then the Fomorians banging their fists on the table, the Nephilim striking the floor with their feet, the Nibelungs tossing coins, and the elfs making clever rhymes and songs.

To Alberec Gil looked. The one-eyed man was wiping at his one eye.

Gil drew the sword and saluted Alberec, holding the sword before his eyes and looking over the hilts toward the elfking. There being no blood on the blade, it was shining metal only, quiet and waiting.

"Sire, I have done you service in defying the Green Knight and returning alive. I ask this boon in return: although I do not know his name as yet, and perhaps never shall, I wish your decree to go out to all your subjects, that the honor and blood of the Swan Knight cannot be questioned. Is this so?"

Alberec said, "The sword burned in your hand as only it would for a prince. Higher born are you than nobles and wisemen, and all burghers and serfs. In you is the royal blood of some high kingdom, and you are above your brothers, who boast a family line no greater than a count and a swanmay. Yes. I shall decree as you have said, and I grant as well my prayer that if some day you meet the elder swan who is your father, you will be pleased and happy rather than ashamed of him. He may not be as good a man as you."

Ethne said, "Have you no riddles for me, you saucy son of Ygraine? Have you no answer? I offered you all the glory of Elfland if you will stay, and serve, and do as you are bid by one of these sovereign lords, including all pleasures of the flesh and all the glory of the world."

Gilberec said, "Yes, ma'am. Here is my riddle. *Four things have eyes but can never see: one in the tailor's hand is found, one in sky and one in ground, the final one in thee.*"

She said, "I don't know that one." But at the same time, wee King Brian laughed and slapped his knee. Ethne glared through half-closed eyelids at Brian, and her skin glowed pale and terrible.

Gilberec said, "I will ask an easier one. *Ever more and ever more at end of days you have of me. The more you have, the less you see. What am I?*"

Now Brian ceased to laugh and looked stricken, even frightened.

Gilberec bowed to the kings and nobles of the elfs, and saluted the warlocks and mastersmiths, the sea-folk and winter giants, and turned to go.

He saw that someone had closed the diamond doors before him. He said, "Open! In the name of the Green Chapel!" And with a roar that blew the fires behind him out, the doors were kicked open by the wind.

He mounted and rode to the end of the long corridor. The doors before his face were closed. He said, "Titania is risen!" and the gates rose, and the great black rock drew back.

Sunlight was pouring in. Time was strange below ground, for even though less than an hour had passed, the sun had set and risen again into the sky above. Gil looked left and right. He had passed these doors in the dark of night twice, and heard the breathing of the beasts in the kennels and stables, but now he saw them. Wooden doors were above him, and ramps wide and shallow enough for steed and hound to pass were raised at the moment, but could be lowered with pullies and rope.

Gilberec said, "Hounds and horses of the elfs! In King Arthur's name I greet you! In my veins is the blood of Adam, first of man, who named you. I speak with his authority. Will you promise not to track me, you hounds, nor follow me, you horses and steeds?"

One voice barked, "You are not including me in that, are you?"

Gil said, "Vertifran? Is that you?"

5. Riddle Me This

Not long after, Gil was seated on his horse beneath the frost-touched black trees. Sunlight shined on each tiny twig, which was coated as if with diamond, and shined shadows of white light on the snow. A dozen red cardinals, red as holly berries, were perched along the swan wings of Gil's helm, or on his shoulders, saddle horn, or horse's head. Rabicane seemed not to mind. Every now and again a cardinal would land on Gil's shoulder and give him a report of where the nearest elf knight hunting for him was, and how their horses and hounds were leading them astray, or into what brakes and briars, thorn bushes, frozen ponds, or other troubles and turmoils.

Ruff said, "I did not figure out your last two riddles. What did they mean? Why did King Brian laugh?"

Gilberec said, "He was laughing at the May Queen because I insulted her."

Ruff cocked his head to one side, one ear up, the other dropping.

Gilberec said, "Do you remember the question?"

Ruff said, "*Four things have eyes but can never see: one in the tailor's hand is found, one in sky and one in ground, the final one in thee.*"

Gil said, "*Four eyes see not and never will: the eye of the needle threaded with thread; the eye of the storm where the air is still; the eye by which potatoes spread; the eye of the fool who will not relent made blind by a heart which will not repent.*"

Ruff said, "So you called Ethne the Fomor a fool? That is kind of harsh, you know."

"Not harsh. Just truth."

"How so?"

Gilberec looked grim. "Ethne offered me gold when my mom is working her last shift at a wine bar out of the mere kindness of her heart for a boss that cheats her. Should I be less than my mother? She offered me glory when I serve King Arthur of Camelot. She offered me women when I have a girl. It was a foolish temptation to offer someone who survived the Green Knight. Practically an insult."

"And why did King Brian turn pale? I thought he was going to puke. Wait! Wait! I remember your line: *Ever more and ever more at end of days you have of me. The more you have, the less you see. What am I?*"

Gilberec said, "That is a child's riddle. I thought everyone knew it."

"What's the answer?"

"Darkness."

Ruff nodded sagely. "So you were saying the Darkness is eating up the elfs in the Night World, right?"

Gilberec nodded, and there was a grim look in his eye that had not been there before. "I wonder if, in years to come, a way can be found not just to overthrow the elves but…"

"But what?"

Gil shook his head. "You'll laugh."

"Maybe. But we're friends, so tell me anyway."

"Can elves be saved?"

Ruff just blinked and scratched himself. "I don't know that riddle. What's the answer?"

Gilberec said nothing.

"Gil? Gil…?"

6. Green Knight's Squire

Vertifran, once again bright green and in his shape as a horse, eventually came trotting through the trees, neighing. On his back, wrapped in a golden lion's pelt and wearing a lion's skull for his helmet, was Sir Bertolac.

He halted. Vertifran stomped his hooves in the snow.

Vertifran said, "Younger brother!"

Ruff said, "Hey. You are bigger and greener than the last time we met. What is the idea of running off with my boy and leaving me alone? Do you know how nerve-racking it is to drive full speed down a human highway in a stolen dogcatcher's truck, with all these Americans on the wrong side of the road? I am law abiding, so I stayed to the left, like in civilized countries."

Vertifran said, "I just got a better disguise kit than yours. Fooled you. So shut your yap!"

"My yap! Your yap!"

"Yap! Yap!"

Bertolac dismounted, and took out an iron nail, and touched it to the green steed. Immediately, the beast shrank and changed into a large white dog with red flanks.

Rabicane said, "That is disturbing."

Bertolac said, "Vertifran! Guard!" And the white dog, with the black form of Ruff following after, still yapping and arguing, loped over the snow, to make wide circles and warn of anyone approaching.

Bertolac said to Gil, "My dog gave me your message, Swan Knight. But what service can I do you?"

Gil said, "Prove to me you are in King Arthur's service so that I will know to trust you."

Bertolac said, "The suspicion is a fair one to have. Will this do?" And out from his pouch he took a diamond shield inscribed with a red cross. Across the top were the initials of the Special Counter-Anarchist Task Force, Heterodoxy Enforcement Division. Along the bottom, it read: THE LAST CRUSADE.

Gil said, "The Faceless Man in the Black Room told me he was recruiting a new member. I assume that is you."

Bertolac shrugged and put the badge away. "If you like. I can think of one task of training you would be wise to ask of me, a man who is twice your height and more, whom wounds do not wound, and mortal wounds do not kill. You wish to learn to fight giants."

Gil said, "The Faceless Man spoke of recovering the Grail."

Bertolac said, "You have much training, training hard enough to break you, if you let it, waiting before you, young knight. I will train you as my squire, but only on your promise to obey me in all particulars, as a squire obeys his knight, until such time as Arthur wakes and commands us to some other war."

Gil said, "Before I promise, answer me this: Will the elfs ever be overthrown?"

Bertolac said, "Christian men never know the outcome of their battles, but in return they never need doubt the rightness of their cause. We know that on Earth, during this life, evil is both more seductive and more powerful than good, strong and cruel and even brave. Devils also have their martyrs."

Gil said, "Your words give me small hope."

Bertolac now touched the iron nail he held in his glove to his nose. Apparently, it had to touch his flesh to work. Tiny lights flickered over his body and vanished as the spell keeping him small began to dissipate. His lion skin and armor, lance and shield and sword grew with him.

He drew in a deep breath, and by the time he was done, he was twice the height of a tall man. In a booming voice now he spoke, "Put no hope in horse, swords, or strength of arms. Put no faith in princes. Even Arthur failed at last, and no kingdom was ever closer to Heaven's good grace than his and David's. The sea will rise, the darkness fall, and the gates of Hell will open. But we Christian knights are assured of final victory, not through our strength, but through our faith in the strength of the Almighty, of whom all kings of Earth are mere shadow and reflections. In Doomsday our victory is certain. Ere then, were are in a fallen world, and all hands are set against us. If you are afraid, flee now. Go live below the sea, and you will escape the worst of what is to come."

Gilberec said, "Whenever you like, you may cease to tempt me, Green Knight. I will work for the downfall of the elfs and the liberty of man until I fall or the quest is achieved. Do I pass this test as well? I tire of them."

The giant nodded. "I have asked Alberec to send me to the Tower Dolorous in Terregaste—ah! Pardon me!—the Tower Joyous, and look for you there. It is a simple enough matter for my art to make the tower seem deserted and empty from without and well adorned and furnished within, and I can return to Alberec and report I saw no sign of you."

Gilberec said, "I don't know the way."

Bertolac said, "I know. I have been the guest of Alain of Corbenec for many a joust and feast. Summon the Swanskiff, and we can pass over the wide waters. In that wasteland, no one will see our drills and exercises and mock battles. You have much to learn, and the lessons will not be easy or pleasant."

Gilberec, without a word, dismounted, and knelt, and put his sword at the feet of the giant. He clasped his hands together, and Bertolac put his huge, warm palms, one to each side, and clasped Gil's clasp within his clasp.

When they were done exchanging oaths, they called the dogs back and went down to the waterside. Gil put one foot in the water. He said, "When I blow the horn, the elfin knights and searching creatures will hear. Elfs, Cobwebs, I do not know how many people are looking for me."

Bertolac said, "I must dwindle to enter your skiff, but when we come to land again, I can call my ax to my very hand even from a distant land. Once it is known that the Green Knight kills any creature of the Night World or Twilight World who meddles with his squire, such spies and huntsmen will find more entertaining prey. Elfs are too long lived to be serious creatures, too craven to take serious risks."

A red cardinal said, "Son of Ygraine, we birds shall speak to the trees. In this season, oaks are weak and pines are paramount. All the paths of those who seek you will be bent away from your true route, and not a single footprint in the snow shall point the way to you."

Gil thanked the red birds, and they flew in each direction.

Ruff said, "I talked with Nerea. Now that you are no longer a secret, she told her dad about you. Glaucon Moth. He can raise a storm on the sea to throw off any pursuit, without the storm touching you or your boat. You have a lot of relatives hidden here and there in the world who can help you in small ways."

Gil rubbed the dog behind the ears. "Good thinking!"

Ruff wagged his tail. "I am a smart dog! A good dog!"

Gil raised the horn. The clear voice of the horn blast rang out and echoed from sea and sky. When the red swan boat arrived, Nerea was holding the silken reins, and the sea-winds were beginning to blow, promising storms to come.

Nerea said, "How'd it go? Are you an elf lord now? Or will you return to the world of men?"

Gilberec said, "I am a Moth, at home in no world. And finally, finally, I know exactly where I fit in."

And he kissed her.

Rabicane, Bertolac, Vertifran, and Ruff embarked. Gilberec put his arm about Nerea, and took the silken reins in his other hand, and called out to the swans.

The hunting horns, soft and silvery, of the pursuing elfs sounded dimly from the slopes of the black mountain behind them. The storm winds and whirling snows gathered to the left and right, but, as promised, the path before was clear.

East they fled and sought the rising sun.

Here ends *The Green Knight's Squire*.

THE TALES OF MOTH & COBWEB continue in

The Dark Avenger's Sidekick

CASTALIA HOUSE

MILITARY SCIENCE FICTION
Starship Liberator by David VanDyke and B. V. Larson
The Eden Plague by David VanDyke
Reaper's Run by David VanDyke
Skull's Shadows by David VanDyke
There Will Be War Volumes I and II ed. Jerry Pournelle
Riding the Red Horse Volume 1 ed. Tom Kratman and Vox Day

SCIENCE FICTION
City Beyond Time by John C. Wright
Somewhither by John C. Wright
The End of the World as We Knew It by Nick Cole
CTRL-ALT REVOLT! by Nick Cole
Back From the Dead by Rolf Nelson
Victoria: A Novel of Fourth Generation War by Thomas Hobbes

NON-FICTION
MAGA Mindset: Making YOU and America Great Again by Mike Cernovich
SJWs Always Lie by Vox Day
Cuckservative by John Red Eagle and Vox Day
Equality: The Impossible Quest by Martin van Creveld
A History of Strategy by Martin van Creveld
4th Generation Warfare Handbook
       by William S. Lind and LtCol Gregory A. Thiele, USMC
Compost Everything by David the Good
Grow or Die by David the Good

FICTION
Brings the Lightning by Peter Grant
Rocky Mountain Retribution by Peter Grant
The Missionaries by Owen Stanley

FANTASY
The Green Knight's Squire by John C. Wright
Iron Chamber of Memory by John C. Wright

AUDIOBOOKS
A History of Strategy narrated by Jon Mollison
Cuckservative narrated by Thomas Landon
Four Generations of Modern War narrated by William S. Lind
Grow or Die narrated by David the Good
Extreme Composting narrated by David the Good
A Magic Broken narrated by Nick Afka Thomas

CPSIA information can be obtained
at www.ICGtesting.com
Printed in the USA
BVOW03*1120131217
501893BV00021B/43/P